The Sharp Teeth of Love

a novel by

DORIS BETTS

SCRIBNER PAPERBACK FICTION
PUBLISHED BY SIMON & SCHUSTER

SCRIBNER PAPERBACK FICTION
Simon & Schuster Inc.
Rockefeller Center
1230 Avenue of the Americas
New York, NY 10020

First Scribner Paperback Fiction edition 1998
Published by arrangement with Alfred A. Knopf, Inc.
SCRIBNER PAPERBACK FICTION and design are trademarks of
Simon & Schuster Inc.

Designed by Robert C. Olsson

Manufactured in the United States of America

1 3 5 7 9 10 8 6 4 2

Library of Congress Cataloging-in-Publication Data
Betts, Doris.
The sharp teeth of love / Doris Betts.
—1st Scribner Paperback Fiction ed.
p. cm.
1. Kidnapping—Fiction. 2. Reno (Nev.)—Fiction.
3. Young women—Nevada—Fiction. I. Title.
[PS3552.E84S53   1998]
813'.54—dc21   98-10985
CIP

ISBN 0-684-84475-3

Grateful acknowledgments is made to Henry Holt & Company, Inc.,
for permission to reprint "Fire and Ice" from *The Poetry of Robert Frost*,
edited by Edward Connery Lathem, copyright © 1923, 1969 by
Henry Holt & Company, Inc., copyright © 1951 by Robert Frost.

With Appreciation to Joseph M. Flora,
Professor of English, University of North Carolina, Chapel Hill

His invitation to speak to the Western Literature
Association in Reno, that Sierra Nevada landscape,
and especially Donner Pass were the inspiration for
this story.

Some say the world will end in fire,
Some say in ice.
From what I've tasted of desire
I hold with those who favor fire,
But if it had to perish twice,
I think I know enough of hate
To say that for destruction ice
Is also great
And would suffice.

"Fire and Ice"
by Robert Frost

Contents

PART I

Food for Thought

~

Chapel Hill to Reno

LUNA HAD BEEN holding her small open diary, indecisive, for too long above the two boxes of last-minute things to keep or throw away, when something in her uncertain swaying made her recall that illustration from an old textbook: an emaciated donkey unable to choose between two equal hay bales, above the caption "Dilemma."

She opened the book to its blank page for today, and wrote the date, April 16, 1993. In fact, since she'd left the hospital, almost all the pages were blank.

The minute Steven came in, she threw it in the Keeper Box. Naturally he picked up that box to load into the van, leaving her to drag the heavier one to their curbside trash. She could feel her face, perhaps even her brain, take on the prune surface of petulance. *What is the matter with me?*

He climbed behind the steering wheel, whistling, while she made one last check of the bare rooms, unplugged the refrigerator, left the door key under the empty flowerpot as promised.

"Did you get film for my camera?" he asked as she got into the van.

For answer, she opened the glove compartment to show him the yellow boxes, thinking, *I used to talk more.*

They drove the loaded van on one last ceremonial sweep

through the green and blooming Carolina campus, up the hill be-hind Kenan Stadium between gaudy azaleas, past the functional ugly new library and the handsome old one, then slowly by the Old Well—university trademark—surrounded now by pink crab apples. The scene filled up her passenger window to its edges like a colored slide, and then clicked out. Luna, who had sketched sev-eral views of this scene for U.N.C. stationery, said, "Did you know they built the Old Well to look like the Temple of Love in the Garden of Versailles?"

"Nope," said Steven. But he was in a good mood and yanked her toward him to demonstrate. "Good-bye South Building," he said with false gaiety as he braked lightly for every stop sign along Cameron Avenue. "Good-bye Memorial Hall and Peabody and Swain." Across the flourishes of his too-white hand he gave Luna a speculative look to see if she was still indulging in advance homesickness.

"Good-bye Franklin Street," he said more softly. "Eastgate. University Mall." He waited. "I'm getting better answers from de-partment stores than from you."

Luna said she was just tired.

On the way to the interstate he announced with a forward snap of his head, "We won't miss this. You're gonna love it in Riverside." His worn golfing cap, surely too hot for this April day but probably left out of a packing box, slid onto his brow along with wisps of blond hair. She wondered if he'd cut it short, now that he was to be an assistant professor. In California, probably not.

He was so good-looking that she had stopped trying to draw him either full-faced or in profile. On paper he was too good to be true: a G.I. Joe doll, a Superman/Batman cartoon. She knew the Carolina coeds in his botany lab thought him a hunk, a beefcake, whatever they said nowadays.

At a red light he asked, "You feel better about leaving Chapel Hill?"

She knew he was tired of hearing how she felt and now only

wanted her to be better. "It's the longest I've ever lived in one place."

"Where you had the hardest time," Steven said. "Where you've been the poorest. The most tired."

"Where I met you," she said, and briefly slid a hand inside his thigh.

Reassured, he got his cap on straight at the next light and began humming "California, Here I Come!" That made her stiffen on the seat. In his family, altos and tenors chimed in. If they didn't sing together on auto trips, they talked, at least Steven and his mother did. Among the Griers, she had concluded, endless talk was needed to fill available space, since silence showed one was antisocial, impolite. The one time they had ridden with Steven's parents through Chapel Hill, Mrs. Grier kept steadily remarking "There's a big grocery store!" and "Look at that yard!" which left Luna with only murmurs in response. She had then understood why Steven would come into their apartment calling, "Home sweet home!" and expect her to say something back. A Southern trait, she supposed, although Steven took the same attitude toward her watercolors. He was always wanting more detail, more objects, a visual clutter that would make everything in the painting equally important but also equally trivial.

But perhaps what he liked in botany were the long lists of parts and categories, the phyla to be memorized, the microscopic structures identified and named.

As if reading her mind, Steven announced, "OK, onto the interstate and here we go!"

"Ummmn," said Luna, knowing she was not being fair. In Steven's childhood, a quiet mother had meant migraine; a quiet father meant booze. Talk was a sign of family health. But how would either of them endure this long drive together from North Carolina to California? And there was no radio; the radio hadn't even been working on the day they bought this van. The day *she* bought it.

When on the used-car lot she'd clicked its button on to static and off to silence and then ran the volume all the way up to SCREAM, Steven had said, "That's probably a symptom of something worse in the whole electrical system."

But she'd been in a good mood that day, and had leaned over to goose him under both arms. Too often the two of them operated on opposite emotional schedules: Steven gloomy, Luna silly; or on today's spring morning, Steven optimistic about their new life in Riverside while in her own electrical system every neuron was taut with pessimism.

She twisted in her seat. "Do you know where the portable radio is?" He didn't. He'd been cleaning out his possessions at the university while leaving the home packing to her. "I want to hear about Waco."

"They'll have to go in after those nuts."

"Maybe it's smart to wait them out. David Koresh says he'll come out when he finishes his manuscript about the seven seals."

"He never will."

"No, he'll have to. The others will force him to come out."

"After killing four agents? He'd be a fool to come out."

The siege in central Texas outside Elk and east of Waco had been under way since February 28, and newsmen now announced their reports as of Day 39, Day 42, Day 48—today.

Though Luna rummaged behind in the nearest boxes, she could not unearth the radio, but the change of subject had healed her mood from the inside out. Halfway to Burlington she asked, "You want to stop at the outlet malls? I'm sure clothes cost more in California."

With even spaces he said slowly, "Clothes do. Not. Cost more. In California."

"I was just thinking we had more cash than in a long time, that's all. As for California, you've been there, I haven't."

"Are you still mad you couldn't go? Is that what this sulk is about?"

"This is not a sulk." She began planning in her mind what a lulu of a sulk she could throw if he insisted. "This is a big change for both of us, honey, no wonder we're edgy." She pictured the word "honey" resting atop her sentence like a red paper rose.

"So make an effort," Steven said. "Not many got jobs this year. Act like you're glad I did."

"I'm glad." She patted his leg. "We'll be able to eat navel oranges all year."

The glance he shot right was checking for sarcasm, but Luna kept her face smooth, quite pleasant, adding, "I hope we can soon get a house instead of an apartment."

"Why not just stop somewhere today and go ahead and get married? We've waited long enough."

"Let's don't act on impulse now. Let's stick to plan."

"It's a dumb plan."

"You thought of it—remember? If we get married in Reno where everybody else gets divorced, it will be more binding."

Steven protested he had never used the word "binding," that he hated bonds of matrimony, marriage ties, even the way a bride called her ring a wedding *band*. He had lived with Luna for two years, and they'd never needed a piece of legal paper. A marriage license now would merely certify the commitment to their relationship that already existed, like a certificate of perfect attendance, an acknowledgment of—

"Time served?" Luna put in, but smiling.

Both of them smiled. Then Steven said, "Besides, I told them in Riverside I was married."

"You what?"

"It's only a question of a glitch in time. To a search committee, married men seem more settled, more mature."

"And married botanists seem less likely to pollinate sorority girls?"

"That too." When a grin lit up Steven's handsome face, Luna wondered once more what he had ever seen in her. She pulled down the visor and squinted in that mirror. Average looking. Face slightly too thin. He said, "Reno then, if you insist. I'm just eager to make an honest woman of you, Mad Lunatic."

Determined not to argue about the term "honest woman," she concentrated on the nickname she should never have told him. Her full name was Madeline Lunatsky Stone, and as an army brat she had carried it around her neck like the boulder it was from primary school to grade school, town to town, one playground bully to the next, until finally she learned to print carefully on her school records: CALL NAME—LUNA. Only her parents still called her Madeline. She always signed her drawings: M. LUNA STONE.

In Greensboro, then later in Winston-Salem, he mentioned again the possibility of stopping right then, finding city hall, speaking their vows in what had become their home state, but Luna held out for the far-off gamble of Reno; and by Hickory she was at the wheel herself and Steven was napping in the backseat.

On the west side of Asheville, after Steven had crawled over the seat and dropped limply into the front, Luna announced her wish to take a side trip to the Indian reservation. "I'm part Cherokee, you know."

He grunted. "You're part Polack," he said with a swipe at his eyes.

"On my daddy's side I am—I've told you that."

"Told me, yes; convinced me, no." The tip of his forefinger on the steering wheel indicated she was not to turn off the interstate.

"Well, I am anyway. It's not much, but you can still tell it. Look at these cheekbones." She lifted her dark glasses and snapped her head to the right. "These black eyes. Deep set."

"Deep shit," Steven said with a yawn. "Looks like we've got plenty of gas still."

"I don't get it. Why would you argue with me about my forebears, something you don't know the first thing about?"

"I know that now since it's fashionable, everybody claims Indian blood. Excuse me—Native American blood. Before that, nobody mixed with them but blacks and Mexicans." He stretched and finally got his body back to the shape he preferred. "Our grandchildren will probably play down every Anglo-Saxon in the family tree. Like the Germans denying anybody was ever Nazi and the Russians saying they never knew anybody in the K.G.B."

Whenever Luna tried to imagine their children she got a picture of tousled, multicolored curls around missing faces. Even farther away, unnamed grandchildren turned into nothing but dollbabies wrapped in thick gray blankets. She could make none of these figures move or cry.

"It's true about the Cherokee, anyway," she insisted. "My grandmother was half."

"Look at these rocks. You want me to drive?"

They swept on past sycamores that would be brilliant yellow in the fall, chunky granite cliffs, evergreens that Steven could have identified if he weren't so sleepy. After a while, eyes closed, he began humming a tune that she finally recognized: "Ninety-nine bottles of beer on the wall / Ninety-nine bottles of beer / If one of the bottles should happen to fall . . ."

But while the day's drive had often seemed tense, that night in Knoxville, after showers and a good dinner, after reports that at Waco loud music had been screamed into the compound of the Branch Davidians, after giggles in a motel bed that would vibrate and groan if fed coins, and midway in a porno film the motel piped onto their TV screen for five dollars, both Luna and Steven found themselves starved for sex, almost violent in their desire. All that week he had been clearing out the desk where he had worked as a teaching assistant, selling science textbooks; all week she had packed clothes, carried scarred thirdhand furniture to the street to sell to strangers. They had left forwarding addresses, reclaimed deposits, canceled deliveries, with no energy left for lovemaking at bedtime and—by Thursday night—no bed but a mattress in an emptied room. Now Steven flung her across the bed as if she were some kidnapped Sabine woman, and in the flickering video light, the noises he made got left behind as her own voice climbed to a high, wild panting sound that started fake but ended real.

Finally his whole weight sagged on top of her body and his breath, slowing, heated up her ear. Luna slid her fingers up his neck and into his hair to press his face harder while she mouthed his shoulder, nibbled, at last had to turn her face aside to catch her own rapid breathing.

Once her lungs had slowed, Steven's body grew heavier, and one of her ankles threatened to cramp. She shifted—his signal to roll off without clash of knee or elbow. They lay side by side on their backs, separate except for skin touching down the long line of their sides and hips and thighs. He caught hold of her hand.

She murmured, "You still want the TV?"

"We paid for it, leave it on."

Hard sex was usually their best, she thought. For some reason, when Steven decided to be slow, Luna turned into one of those plastic dolls whose too-solid arms and legs could be pivoted up and down, even backward, in their hard little sockets.

She felt her hand lifted, the fingers kissed once, laid palm up just by his pelvic bone. She began to drift. With eyes closed, her mind seemed still to be driving the van dead ahead, the dark damp roadway pouring toward her while a mix of greens and grays flowed past on either side. She felt a little dizzy.

After she made herself stare at the knobby ceiling the sensation of motion stopped. "You asleep?"

"Yes."

From his voice, he almost was. Yes, she thought, turning to see, his was a picture-perfect head; in California, some agent would probably discover him for Hollywood.

Forcing her eyes open had made her wakeful again. From the television, faint voices suggested a brief transition of dialogue between couplings. She propped herself up enough to see which peach-colored ass was in motion within which peach-colored legs, but all those naked bouncing people looked artificial, interchangeable. Even their gender seemed a temporary assignment, with extra breasts and cocks waiting offstage until blond players made their next costume change. None of the men was as handsome as Steven; most of the women were prettier than Luna, and one had pert breasts so full she could lift one and suck her own nipple, a contortion far beyond any naked girls she had ever seen.

"Steven?" This time he made no sound. Luna worked her hand free and with the remote control turned off the set.

Once its silvery light had gone she could see only the edge of Steven's profile. He had been gaining weight this spring while she got thinner; from this angle she saw that his cheeks and chin were fuller.

She rolled onto her stomach, her favorite sleeping position, facing off the mattress so no menace could sneak up on her, so she would never fall off the bed onto her vulnerable back. She listened to Steven breathe, listened to his exhalations acquire a slight whistle. Then she slept.

NEXT MORNING she dressed lazily, half listening to a newsman explain that on Day 49 in McLennan County, Texas, former cultists said David Koresh believed the 1990s were the End Times, believed his compound was an island of righteousness surrounded by the forces of Babylon. Luna could not concentrate on the news while her usual postcoital warmth still lingered. *If our days were as good as our nights,* she thought dreamily.

All the small pleasures she ascribed to Steven—the thick bath towels and clean tub and later the huge and fattening breakfast she had not cooked, spare time to linger over a second cup of aromatic coffee.

"You're not eating a thing but fruit," he said on his second trip back from the motel buffet.

She reached across to touch his hand, ended up feeling his pulse. "Very slow and contented," she announced.

"In two years, this is one of the few times we've eaten the same meal at the same time."

True. Usually he came in late from the library and wanted eggs and bacon fixed right then, or a potato run through the microwave and slathered in sour cream.

When he looked up from his food and smiled widely now, there appeared in his left cheek the small dent that shifted his face slightly off-center and made him boyish, endearing. Luna studied it, wondering at its recurrent charm, quickly wondering afterward about herself and whether a dimple on Attila the Hun might have made him attractive. Perhaps cultist David Koresh, behind those grainy newspaper photos, had hair as yellow as Steven's and eyes so blue she'd have needed cobalt on her palette to portray them.

"Did you finally buy a wedding dress?"

"I thought we'd save the money. I can wear that tan linen."

"It's too big," he said. "And you'll need new clothes in Riverside. You can't go around in paint-spattered jeans all the time." The dimple was still there. Maybe Jim Jones had two dimples that showed when he talked out of both sides of his mouth; maybe he had smiled so sweetly in the People's Temple that worshippers had been glad to sign over their money and follow him down to Guyana.

Her thoughts had turned into so deep a betrayal that Luna got an ugly wrench deep inside the body, as if her chest had received some blow that drove her organs downward like toothpaste down a tube. She waited till the nausea passed and then pushed back her pineapple and cantaloupe. For a week she had felt her internal self go to pulp in this manner, but, no, she was not pregnant.

"I'll eat that if you don't want it."

She nodded, swallowing. Then she said, carefully, "I know you think I'm foolish to be so uneasy about starting over in a new place—"

He interrupted. "You're an army brat. You ought to be used to it."

"Or tired of it, Steven. I liked Chapel Hill, it was my first real home. I worry about finding work. New people, weather." By speaking, she tried on anxieties for fit: small, far too small.

"It's not as if you were a big extrovert or something. All you do is hide out with your drawing board or something." At sight of her face he put the dimple into play again. "You know your skills will be in demand in any university town, whether you do medical drawings or botanical illustration or go into other commercial art." Now his voice became impatient. "Children's books. You could draw murderers when the judge won't let a camera into the courtroom." He filled his mouth with only potatoes. "You've always been the portable one."

Looking at his blue, blue eyes she suddenly remembered that in Plato's time the eyes of Greek statues had been painted red. "Lots of routine illustration is done by computers nowadays. I don't know, Steven, it's like that dream when you can't find your final exam, but your graduation depends on it. Or the one where you're registered in a course you thought you'd dropped, and the crucial test is under way in a building that's no longer where it used to be on campus. Or you're calling and calling on the telephone, and there's something wrong with it and the number won't go through, but it's an emergency—"

"Everybody has those dreams," said Steven, eating.

"All week I've felt that way when I'm wide awake." But she ducked her head and gave a sheepish grin to deprecate the seriousness she really felt.

He pointed his fork at her. "So it's plugging into army brat memories—no more, no less."

She hated that phrase. "It's more." But she didn't say: *It's my silence. It's the lack of appetite.*

If he had not kept waving the fork in midair like some lazy bandleader she might not have thought of the claim that savages had first invented forks so they need not touch the flesh of sacred animals, perhaps even the meat of human sacrifice. That kind of selective memory frightened her. She never wanted to go back to the hospital again.

Into her numb mouth she put some grapes and washed them down with orange juice.

After breakfast, while they were settling into the van, locking doors, tightening seat belts, Luna said, "Maybe the West will do for me what it did for Georgia O'Keeffe and I'll start painting giant vaginas."

Steven said he had a better idea. "I'll pose."

His was the only penis she had ever seen. If she flushed, it was from embarrassment at her own sexual inexperience, not from the thought of his nakedness.

Later, at the wheel and speeding along I-40, he showed he had been thinking through her concerns by saying, "Suppose you did want to try your hand at art for art's sake. That's fine with me. As soon as we can afford it."

"Really? I don't think I'm that kind of artist."

"Up to you."

"I'm not obsessed by art. You have to be a convert to art; you have to devote yourself to it the way those Branch Davidians gave up everything to follow Koresh."

"So genius really is next door to crazy."

She said, "Van Gogh only sold one painting in his lifetime."

"Remember, I *said* as soon as we can afford it."

Something about this modern, carefully graded superhighway suggested that the real Smoky Mountains had been moved away, that these neater slopes and vistas still in view were a manageable substitute. Luna thought of plastic Christmas trees, subdivisions landscaped with repeating plots of flat junipers. The identical workmen—*Far more portable than I,* she thought—had laid down this road as well as the California freeways and the Washington Beltway.

Her postcoital mood of contentment, along with her appetite, had worn off, and vague anxiety had floated up again: something undone, something done badly, something missed. Glimpses of the Pigeon River only reminded her that the passenger pigeon was long gone and only garbage-eating city pigeons had survived.

Over the drone of the engine, Steven began telling her one more time about his finalist interview at Riverside, characterizing the search committee members she would soon meet at departmental parties, this time remembering to emphasize how much they'd admired her botanical drawings in his dissertation, saying their partnership might even have secured his job offer at a time when blacks and women usually got favoritism.

She prompted him with occasional neutral questions while Tennessee slid by.

Luna's ability to draw had brought them together in the first place. At twenty-two, just graduated from Carolina's art department, she had intended to go to graduate school in art history; but her parents' prolonged, bitter divorce followed by her father's fast triumphant remarriage had dried up funds for tuition. No. Luna rubbed her own forehead. No, the hospital costs had something to do with that.

Steven was frowning at her movement, probably thinking of his mother's migraine.

How long since she had entered college—ten years? It didn't seem possible. Her Chapel Hill professors, mostly abstractionists, had treated her realistic freshman drawings as a naïveté to be outgrown. "Unless," one said with a lip that rose quivering over a front tooth, "unless you plan to sketch people's children? Advertise in *Southern Living* magazine? Put clothes on the children that match the drapes?"

Then suddenly during her postgrad summer she found herself learning alone how to do illustrations for medical researchers, found a use for her knack at reproduction. At first came the easy diagrams of cells, but soon she had taught herself how to make and fix color charts of a thorax crammed full of abdominal organs, or how to get the green segments exactly placed on a gangrenous appendix as it floated eye level in a jar. She practiced on pathological specimens, whole and dissected; she had to enlarge a sketch of a fetal heart so details could be seen.

In school they had taught her that before Leonardo, all art was outlines; that he blurred the paint to make it more lifelike. Luna went back to outlines.

That summer she divided her time between the art library attached to Ackland Museum and the Health Sciences Library attached to the university's medical school. Sometimes she felt the students she met in each place had been reared on different planets.

Assignments for student work, lab illustrations, stationery with local scenery, came to her first—but her increasing skill brought faculty assignments and greater trust. In one sterile operating room, she chewed hard on her tongue to keep from fainting while she photographed the surgical techniques she would later depict as less bloody and glutinous, more accessible to study. In the beginning, she was not successful at drawing a surgeon's hands with the highlights cast on his latex gloves, for she had taken no life classes at the university; but she mastered it by drawing her own left hand, gloved and ungloved, over and over, and then drawing the same reflected in a mirror until she could sketch the right as easily as the left.

In spite of what she had said to Steven, she did grow obsessive. Because she did not want to think about her stay in this same hospital, she thought only about this new skill. Day and night she drew in charcoal, pencil, pen; she photographed, mastered the airbrush for stippling the retina, worked on scratchboard, studied classic anatomies from the 750 drawings of Leonardo da Vinci, worked on mixing photo print with her own enhancements.

Just as in her freshman art courses the use of invented shape and wiggly colors had seemed to Luna a willful avoidance of the world, that abstraction threw its stormy tantrums against the slightest constraint of reality, she now welcomed the boundaries that being a copyist imposed on her hand and eye. Copyist, she still called herself. A good copyist.

And copying made her *see* more clearly than before, not only the objects, procedures, and organs she reproduced on paper but also the people she passed on downtown Franklin Street, especially the students with their cheeks flushed pink by their healthy hearts. "Beware of coarse outlines," Leonardo had said, adding that the human body was translucent, like air, that flesh was so tender one could confirm it by extending the hand so sunlight would shine through the fingers.

While Luna's student oils had been mediocre and her watercolors muddy, her small metal sculptures neither harsh nor whimsical enough to earn more than a glance, she had discovered late that she had a gift for hanging a scapula or sacrum in midair, catching its shape, finding the highlight, and slowly blending the shadings with finger, brush, and at last just a stump of paper to rub the contours where light did not fall.

Maybe that was all she dreaded to leave—the light she had grown accustomed to. Surely the light would be different in California.

Precise drawings of lab equipment, electrical circuits, chemical charts, were of little interest to her—though for a fee she sometimes did the boring stuff, and even mundane measurement had come alive after she read Dürer on the proportions of the human female body based mathematically on the Venus de Medici.

I am a body, I don't just have a body. I am a soul, I don't just have a soul, she would sometimes repeat before her bathroom mirror. Her skin surfaces now seemed both translucent and penetrable—once she had examined the engravings Jan Kalkar made for the works of Vesalius, Jan Vanderler's illustrations of the bones of the embryo, August Horn on the vermiform appendix, Max Brödel's kidneys, ureters, and bladders. She posed in a mirror and touched herself—but she did not draw her own image. At the time, she was concerned about getting fat.

Because medical schools at Duke and Carolina, as well as

many laboratories in Research Triangle Park, all lay within ten miles of one another, Luna soon had plenty of assignments. And it was true she was no extrovert; she worked alone, read alone, shifted her mind from verbal to pictorial, an intensification of her shift senior year from English to art major. Into this new life she settled like a brush into paint, a pen point wet with its true element.

She told herself that alone was not lonely, though she was surely the oldest living virgin in the southeastern United States, but it seemed to her then that she was content to be so; she envisioned her female organs nestled inviolate above her intact hymen. Untroubled, easy to draw. She got out a hand mirror and held it between her legs.

Instantly, though she could remember only fragments of Catholic liturgy, there flashed into Luna's mind: *Inter faeces et urinem hascinur.* That's what we're born between, all right.

And next came a great longing that someone would love her body someday soon, that very part of her body, love also her soul, that she would be able to act out the first Latin verb she ever conjugated: I love, you love, he loves.

But then she put away the mirror and moved her hands waist high, very carefully. Yes, she was content alone; a virginal future moved toward her, massive and calm as a mountain she was slowly approaching; no, she would never marry; no, she would fuck no strangers, either; soon she would be able to afford the mortgage on a small Chapel Hill house and furnish it only to suit herself, then add one dog and two cats; she would cultivate a circle of good-humored women friends to take trips with, to shop and play bridge among.

After years of watching her mother serve meals and drinks to her father's uniformed friends only to be abandoned in the end for a young girl whose kitchen skills began with thawing and ended in the microwave, Luna vowed to spend her own evenings with pleasant, unmarried women, who would bring their own canapés and, by 10 p.m., help wash the highball glasses.

Yet some nights she *did* masturbate in spite of memories of her brief stay at one Catholic school where all the girls had to sleep with both arms outside the covers, even in winter. In Chapel Hill on those nights Luna would whisper, "Just turn your head, Suster," pronouncing it as children will, while she moved her right hand underneath.

Then Steven Grier had appeared at her door, wearing a dingy white baseball cap with yellow hair escaping below and eyes glinting like sapphires along their facets. He was carrying a box of typed pages from his dissertation manuscript on Cactaceae—a study of the cleft-grafting of many ornamental cactus varieties to produce houseplants that would weep or form crests or grow in contorted, spiny forms. He wanted uniform drawings interspersed in its pages, some of them merely to duplicate older illustrations from botany texts, but others to be made from his own color slides or drawn directly at the plant bench where he would demonstrate steps in the process of grafting on *Periska* or *Cereus* understock, and some that would illustrate specimens resulting if one round cactus, for instance, ended up perched on a vertical one like Simeon the Stylite on a prickly pillar.

He said all this in a rush, but Luna could hardly take her eyes off his mouth and the dimple that came and went as he spoke.

"I don't have much money," he admitted to Luna, but not until after her kitchen table had been covered with pages. He thought his scholarship had sparked her interest. She had been staring at his hands and the pale hairs toward his wrist.

"Neither do I," she managed to say. So recently had she settled into her new role as nature's copyist that she actually disliked his somehow distorted desert plants that meddled with nature, tailor-made for overheated Manhattan apartments and not the Sahara.

"I make good spaghetti," he offered. "I do yard work."

The only yard outside Luna's apartment door was four feet wide—one azalea surrounded by pine needles.

Then he took off the baseball cap so his long blond hair fell evenly to frame a handsome face he had tanned doing yard work. Above those blue eyes were light-colored woolly eyebrows that she wanted to touch.

"Those drawings in the textbooks you could just photocopy and enlarge."

"It's consistency I want, with the style staying the same all the way through in the illustrations and all the way through in the text. Like a book," he said. "A book that's been well designed. Somebody will publish it as a book. In time."

His dimple seemed a bit too high, and she wondered if it might be a scar. She straightened herself and untacked a list of standard prices from the corkboard above the phone.

He dropped his fingers onto her arm so lightly it was as if something the size of a hummingbird had touched down and paused near her elbow. "I hear you're the best," he said, "but I also hear you're out of my price range." Frowning, he read her cost sheet while very slowly withdrawing his fingers, almost stroking them off her skin. Then he sank slow motion into a kitchen chair, filling with despair as a vessel might fill with water and drift to the bottom. He shook his head, then gave her a straight blue look and smiled with that odd notch in one cheek. "What's the exchange rate in spaghetti?"

In the end, there was only so much spaghetti Luna could eat; the rest she took out in trade.

IN MEMPHIS, Luna insisted they stop at Graceland, though Steven stayed across the street in the car museum while she was part of a crowded tour of the mansion. She sat inside the airplane Elvis had named for his daughter Lisa Marie, and saw a chronological film of excerpts from bad movies that showed him in glitter-clothes, moving, singing. Even the bed in the airplane had a safety belt.

Most of the tourists were women, older than she. As they were conducted from room to room, one woman told her, "This trip is my Mother's Day present. In advance. Elvis was devoted to his mother, you know."

"Your children gave you the trip?"

"No, my husband."

Luna caught sight of the speaker and herself in one of the mirrored walls and frowned. Not only younger than the crowd, at twenty-eight, Luna must also be thinner than average. Almost all these faces were a bit pudgy, and white, despite the blend Elvis had made of country and rhythm and blues.

Luna had meant to feel superior and amused among these earnest fans who not only adored Elvis but some of whom, re-entering the mansion after seeing his grave in the Meditation Gardens, insisted that the coffin was empty.

"He just walked away from it," said Mrs. Mother's Day. "He's up in Montana now."

"Detroit," somebody interrupted. "My cousin saw him at a hockey game. He's turned gray."

Women around her drew back like nuns from a heretic.

"Well, it was 1977!" she protested. "Of course he got gray."

After more mirrors, his jungle room, after viewing a sequence of film clips that steadily added years and pounds while wearing away Elvis's pretty milltown-boy face and burning dry that energy, Luna was left with unattached melancholy. It had something to do with what had become of Lisa Marie since her daddy died, and something to do with her own inability to adore King Elvis the way the others did.

In the van, this was one thing Luna did want to talk about. "Didn't it make you sad, Steven?"

"Wish I'd had his money."

After that he kept pointing out this and that roadside object, reading signs or bumper stickers aloud, and complaining that she was too quiet. By dinnertime she didn't even feel like asking to have the pepper passed.

That night they both reacted to an ugly motel room with a carpet stain Steven said was where the corpse had bled. They drooped their separate ways to bed, tired but restless. All night one of them, elbows or knees awry, kept knocking the other awake, so in the morning both bore small grudges. They drank too much coffee and drove on.

Steven asked for more of the cash Luna was carrying from the yard sale. They had already divided it by half—though all the household goods were hers. "You're out already?"

"Don't want to break a big bill just to buy a better map." While she drove he studied his new purchase, complaining that out west the interstates looked too widely spaced, that maybe they shouldn't have gone to Graceland but straight through to St. Louis; now they'd be backtracking and waste time.

"But we've got till the first of July. We were supposed to enjoy seeing the country."

"You should have signed up for enjoyment lessons before we left." He poked her but she moved aside.

"On the other hand," he finally said, folding the map differently, "once we do turn north, the scenery will be more interesting. I mean, what's in Missouri?"

The Compromise, she almost said—but the only books Steven liked were biographies. He preferred scientists and wealthy men like Hearst, Rockefeller, Carnegie—no literature and certainly no history, so he could neither grin nor take the hint. "The Ozarks?"

Soon he complained, "Keep a steady foot on that accelerator, Luna. I can feel the whole car hiccup gas."

Instantly she steadied her shoe sole hard enough so the speedometer climbed. Instead of answering she concentrated on recalling their first kisses, first sex, the first time Steven stayed overnight. The day he moved in to save two rent bills. And never paid any on hers.

From the corner of her eye she saw him raise both arms in a mock gesture of protecting his face from a car crash, so she slowed as the hills sloped down to Little Rock.

With a scornful look at the scenery he said, "I'm glad I voted for Perot."

Luna, who had voted for Bill Clinton, pulled onto the shoulder and suggested it would be suitable, then, for Steven to drive them the hell out of Arkansas. "Besides, the way you snored all night, I need a nap."

"I never got deep enough asleep to snore."

Out loud, very loud, she read the sign, "FORT SMITH 160 MILES." Then she closed her eyes, thinking of Elvis, of how it must feel to be adored by a million strangers. Could he ever have loved Priscilla as much as he loved his mother?

Through the slits below her eyelids she watched Steven's face, a cameo. She had waited for him, saved herself for him, aspired to be what the nuns had carefully explained was "a help *meet* for him," and not "a helpmeet" the way Protestants misread the words.

Now she wondered if Aunt Evelyn's dry pragmatism had not been truer than her true-love dreams. Aunt Evelyn always said, "There's a lid for every pot."

When they had been riding for twenty more minutes, Steven began a tuneless hum, almost a buzz, the sound of some pesky child blowing through a paper-wrapped comb. Luna was determined to ignore it. To keep both eyes sealed shut. But what song was it? How could anyone tell? Tension ran down her limbs and formed knots at her elbows and knees. "The Arkansas Traveler" would be too logical; no, this music she would have to identify by rhythmic pauses alone. Schoolkids used to do that—beat out a rhythm with a stick and make you guess if it was the national anthem or "Yankee Doodle." *First thing I buy in California is a car radio,* she fumed silently, *so I can find out if they're playing Elvis records down in Waco.*

Halfway to Fort Smith she finally recognized the song—with a pang. An Easter hymn? Some praising song that had crept over and under the walls of Steven's agnostic mind because of the Easter season, or because today was Sunday, or maybe because some cross-shaped road sign PREPARE TO MEET GOD had lasted all the way from the Great Smokies until now. She tested the syncopation in her mind. Yes. "Christ the Lord Is Risen Today!" The "alleluias" seemed strung out forever. It was unlikely that Steven, the complete secularist, had any idea that last Sunday's song was in his throat.

Not that she, a lapsed Catholic, was going to tell him. For some reason, that melody fused with Graceland, until the song of joy cast a shadow of dim regret that Luna and Priscilla and Lisa Marie, who had all outlived Elvis, had so much less to give.

But by Fort Smith Luna thought she might scream if one more thump of Resurrection came from the driver's seat, and she popped upright, frowning. "It makes me nuts to try to remember the words to your tune!"

"What tune?" Steven stopped hitting the steering wheel with one rhythmic thumb. "You finally awake?"

"I'll trade when you're ready. Let's drive late so we'll sleep better."

"Aren't you getting hungry?"

"On a car trip every calorie sticks to the butt."

Oklahoma City, 180 miles. Luna sampled the bad taste in the back of her mouth. She was ready to be pulled over for speeding, to come upon a three-car accident or a washed-out bridge. She was bored. The unchanging highway unrolled under their tires like a treadmill.

"If we were in California now, it would be time for our evening swim."

"Or evening hot tub. Or spa. Or surfing experience. Or encounter group."

"Be sarcastic, see if I care."

At a fast-food restaurant they bought hamburgers and fries and milkshakes. Too much food. What she ate hardened into a giant ring of fat under Luna's jeans. She felt very large.

At Amarillo, Steven driving, they turned north, away from a multitude of satisfactory hotels and motels to take a shortcut to Highway 50. For miles before, he had studied the map using her old Bic lighter saved for that sole purpose, since after his many health lectures she had finally given up her occasional cigarette. The smell of on-and-off butane made her long for a smoke in jolts and hungers.

Through the dark he told her to check directions one more time. "And don't set us on fire."

She flicked on the flame. Both lungs leaped. "At Dalhart get on 385 and go straight in." The light circling the cup of her own hand made Luna suddenly wish she could paint the details of modern life with the realistic skill of the masters—could give to lighters and dashboard glows the luminescence others had given candles. She had tried not to think about art since leaving Chapel Hill; now she felt homesick.

Sliding closer so their thighs warmed against each other, she suddenly said, "Last Sunday was Easter."

"I know it."

His answer surprised her. "You were singing about Easter." When he shrugged she asked, "Did you go to church on Easter when you were little?"

"Sunrise services," he said softly, as he drove them deeper into the dark.

"What's that?" Her Catholic faith had been so easily transferable from army post to army post that only in her teens did she discover how minimal it was. But she missed it. Not the stained glass and statues and Madonnas so much as the certainty that those artists had believed their subject matter was holy.

"In Georgia we get up at six a.m. and meet at the biggest cemetery around so we can be singing hymns when the sun finally comes up. Sometimes it gave me the creeps thinking this might be the day one of those graves we were standing on might open up. And a saint come out."

"There aren't any saints in Atlanta," Luna said. "Luke, Christopher, Teresa—those are saints."

"Papist snob."

And April is Bernadette at Lourdes, she suddenly remembered, for as an adolescent trying to cure herself of apostasy she had read the saints' stories, imagined herself someday black-outlined in windows, reproduced in books. Anselm. Saint George.

"Did you look at Elvis's grave?"

"Of course not." His arm went around her shoulders. When he gave a quick squeeze, she felt how hot his armpit was.

We're all right, she thought. *We are. We are.*

THAT NIGHT BOTH SLEPT DEEPLY, near Lamar, uncertain which state they were in, and next morning both were in a better mood, headed west through dry, brown, flat countryside not at all like the wooded Southeast they had shared for two years without noticing much. Now Luna felt the whole back wall of her brain was green with stored memories of vegetation.

Beyond La Junta they could at last see afar the snowcapped Rockies, the sight of which straightened them both in their seats.

"Look at that!"

She *was* looking.

After a few minutes' silence Steven said, as if jealous, "But you've seen them before."

"I was too small to remember."

"All those years I was stuck in Georgia you got to see the whole damn country and then forgot it."

Mostly Luna remembered hot car seats, airports, waiting in empty rooms for the furniture truck to come. Suddenly something shot across the road—a rat? No. The first prairie dog.

After an hour's hard westward driving they skirted Pueblo into the scrubby foothills.

Luna pointed to a road sign for Phantom Canyon. "Isn't that a formal word for the Wild West—'Phantom'? I think there's a Phantom Ranch down in Grand Canyon, too. Wouldn't you think cowboys would have said plain old 'ghost'?"

But Steven's face was pressed to the passenger window as he tried to check the blur of passing plant life. Once they got to Riverside, Luna decided, she would look up all the "phantom" place-names in a western atlas. Such a pretty word. *Phantasm.* And "phantasmagoria" almost made her mouth water.

Once she had to stop so Steven could walk into a field and check some fleshy plant.

They exited Salida between rows of motels and, after a looping ascent through rising rockery scenery that silenced them both, climbed out of the van to stamp their feet at Monarch Pass, where Highway 50 crossed over the Continental Divide at 11,312 feet (said a marker). On all sides great mountains walled them in: Sangre de Cristo, San Juan, Ruby, Collegiate.

The covered-wagon drivers must have stopped at some high point like this to judge what faced them. And the women broke down and cried, Luna thought.

Steven stepped behind her and wrapped her in his arms. Mouth against her ear he asked softly, "Now are you glad you came?" Her nod knocked his chin. She tried not to squirm, although their stance reminded her of many tourist photos in albums back home that showed her parents posed in much this same position before bridges, pagodas, geysers, and monuments.

Steven's voice grew louder, enthusiastic. "Why, this will be wonderful country for any artist!"

"It's hopeless. Too big. Just hopeless." She remembered the misty calendar scenes of Albert Bierstadt, Thomas Moran's attempts to make oil and canvas reproduce light and water in Yellowstone. "What good would it do an astronomer to have a telescope that showed all the stars at once? The sky already does that."

His dimple was lost in a hurtful frown. "Try to take an interest in your work—what does it get me?"

She was still thinking of pioneer women shielding their eyes to stare at those impassable mountains, already in their minds giving up the rosebush, the piano, the box of books. She wondered if danger had proved to be an aphrodisiac. Maybe for the men.

He said, "Before school starts, we'll take a camping trip. You can help me find desert specimens. The saguaro ought to bloom in May. I'm going to need some field equipment."

"Surely the school will lend you some."

His frown meant that he was a free spirit, she a tightwad. They said little more before Montrose, where they stopped for the night. By then Luna was feeling almost physically starved for something to read—an addict in withdrawal—and insisted they stop at a local museum to stock up on pamphlets on the history of the Rockies' western slope. "Cacti—they're bound to have stuff on cacti."

Over their dinner of blue-corn enchiladas, she skimmed paragraphs about Utes in the Uncompahgre Valley. "My goodness!" she suddenly exclaimed. "Listen to this! Alferd Packard—you've heard of him?" Steven nodded over his fajitas, but she had seen that polite, untruthful nod before. "You complain I'm too quiet so listen to this! Packard came out here in 1873 after gold and got snowbound and ate five people."

"Al-FRED," said Steven with a push of his glasses higher.

"No, it says 'ferd' all over the page. The Indians found strips of human flesh and mutilated bodies, but Packard was at large for nine years before they got him. And even then just for manslaughter." She tasted that word for the first time: *man-slaughter.* "They call the place where the bodies were found Cannibal Plateau."

Steven muttered that this was wonderful dinner conversation.

She had to giggle when she read that the student union cafeteria at the University of Colorado is called the Alferd Packard Memorial Grill.

"It's a typo—Al-FRED. Pass the green sauce."

She half read and half listened to Steven talk about his future in Riverside, sounding confident and smooth. Arriving in the spring, he would probably not be paid before the fiscal year began in July—so Luna could take temporary work and not deplete their savings; he'd probably be working late in the lab or the library getting ready for fall semester, but she could use those nights for her drawing, and they'd take some trips into the California parks. One of their first needs would be a home computer, and while he, too, would learn word processing, her skills there were so much greater that he'd have to rely on her at first to prepare his class syllabus, handouts, the drafts of scientific papers he'd need to publish in order to gain tenure; they could move on in the California system, then, to one of the bigger schools—

"You through with the green sauce?" she broke in, and turned a page.

"I'd like to work with *Carnegiea gigantea* now that they're close by," said Steven dreamily, "because there's going to be a water shortage on this whole continent, and we'll need drought-resistant plants in people's yards. In city parks. They can live two or three centuries, you know, and weigh six tons, and who knows with global warming if they might not be the vegetation of the future."

Luna murmured that she couldn't quite see a row of giant cacti in D.C. in place of the Japanese cherry trees.

"They do bloom white."

"What if I wanted to go back to school myself?"

"You got tired of school, you said so."

"Last year I said so."

He looked at her over a forkful of food so heavily sauced that it looked corroded. "Once we can afford it, sure."

"Once you're promoted? You come up for consideration when?"

"Aren't you going to finish that?" He forked over a taste. "Assistant professors usually get renewed for a second contract term at the same rank—I explained that. Six, seven years and a published book and I'll make associate." One of the waitresses was obviously admiring Steven's looks, and he must have known it by the way he straightened in his chair and lifted his chin. When he patted Luna's hand it drew attention to the wristwatch she had given him for Christmas. "With a wife like you, I'll probably go up the ranks faster."

The waitress came over to get him a second beer. Luna had to raise her voice. "Me too."

"Ma'am?"

"Another beer for me, too."

She weighted the next page under the empty bottle. As her father had left her menopausal mother for the young and fertile Corinne, Steven would probably leave quiet Luna for some vivacious ex-cheerleader. She remembered those doctors in U.N.C. Medical School who at twenty-five had married twenty-five-year-old nurses but divorced them before forty to wed country club women who had not hit thirty yet themselves, doctors who went back in time to reconsider first love's precipitate diagnosis.

"Thank you," Steven said with the dimple to the waitress who finally brought *Luna's* beer. When he spread his hand over the page the wristwatch gleamed. "Put up that tourist stuff and discuss our plans."

Our.

Someone switched on the big TV set suspended over the bar, and sound blared out *(Day 51!!!!!!)* before the screen flared orange with flame and black with smoke. ". . . siege ended after an M-60

30

combat engineering vehicle knocked a hole in the compound to blow tear gas inside. You see the results: first white smoke, then yellow, then black, and then the flames and an explosion . . ."

Steven had turned in his chair, but Luna couldn't move.

". . . choppers flew overhead and loudspeakers urged the Branch Davidians to come out . . . not known how many perished in the fire which spread swiftly, fanned by gusting winds. . . . David Koresh has not been seen . . . too hot for searchers to approach. . . . The assault was approved because of concern about child abuse inside the compound. . . . Total destruction took less than an hour. . . ."

There were shots of the burning building from different angles and from helicopters that could not fly too close. Luna expected the microphones to pick up the sound of screaming, but there was only the roar of wind and fire.

"I told you he'd never come out," Steven said. "But maybe there's an escape tunnel."

"There were children in there!"

"They're probably underground."

The newsman went on to say there were no presumed survivors, but the death count would be uncertain until the site was cool enough to examine. The gas inserted had not been flammable, he said; probably Koresh had set the fire himself. Then lawmen and spectators and theologians and Attorney General Janet Reno and Texas Rangers and one astrologer who had predicted the worst came on the screen for interviews. One member of the Branch Davidians who had surrendered earlier said that Koresh had fully expected the raid, that the people who stayed had all been ready to die.

In disbelief Luna said again, "But the children!" Her stomach seemed to fold in on itself. In the restaurant rose the smell of cooked meat. She gagged and ran.

Behind her she could hear part of Steven's answer to the waitress: ". . . takes everything too seriously."

She was lying on the bed with a wet cloth on her face when he came into their room and rummaged through the one suitcase they had carried in. "Luna?"

She said, "There must have been fifteen or twenty children."

"You're making yourself sick over this," he said firmly. "It's done, it's over. They couldn't keep sitting out there all year waiting for him to finish reading the Book of Revelation!" She said nothing. "They've got a pool and I'm going in and get the kinks out. You come on, too. Luna?"

"I don't think so."

"Nobody knew he'd torch his own people! Now get up and come on."

"In a minute." She heard the door close. She lay there thinking that a mind as well as a throat possessed its own gag reflex: the mental gorge she was trying to keep down would, any minute now, erupt and cause her to think fully about Jonathan Swift's *Modest Proposal* for preventing the children of poor people from being a burden to their parents or the country—by using them as food for the rich.

The effort to force back this thought was too much; it spewed full into her mind and Luna leaped up and vomited in the toilet.

When she was empty with every surface quivering, she managed to put on the old black bathing suit left from her undergraduate phys-ed class, then made herself take the elevator down to the indoor pool.

She waded into the water and stood waist-deep, exhausted. Steven swam gracefully past on his back. "I'll never understand why you take on so about something you can't do one thing about."

She walked from him into the deeper end of the pool, her limbs heavy and distorted underwater. She thought about baptism: infusion, aspersion, immersion. It should be done soon after birth. When there is danger of death, even without a priest, anyone may baptize an infant.

She walked deeper and put her head underwater.

When she came up, Steven was treading water nearby. "Maybe I didn't make myself clear. Sure you can go to school if you still want to in a few years."

"I'm not even thinking of that," she said, although immediately she was—a picture of following him down a long and narrow hall while he stepped out ahead and closed all the side doors she might have opened.

"For richer, for poorer. That's what they'll ask us in Reno. Why do I get the feeling you're having second thoughts?"

Why did he zero in on the money part of the wedding ceremony? She said, "I'm thinking of an entirely different sacrament right now."

He got out of the pool and shook water from his hair. A teenage girl sat up in her lounge chair to see his body in more detail. "It's not as if you're giving up some high-powered career," said Steven, toweling his head. The teenager admired every blond hair in his armpits. "You can do your drawing anywhere. You don't need an institution, a faculty, a university library. You don't need grants!"

What did she need? Luna floated, thoughtful, feeling how light her body had become now that it was empty. Overhead was a curving amber glass ceiling above which a few beige stars were starting in their amber sky.

"I guess by not answering you mean you want to wait on this marriage business?"

"Oh, Steven. I don't know. I really don't know." She swam to the cold ladder and climbed it, her suit draining, her torso heavy again. There was something too calculated in the way he came to place both hands on her waist, and his hands were too white and wrinkled. She slipped in a puddle on the tile and fell against him hard, by accident; she thought it was an accident.

Steven must have thought it deliberate. He spun away toward the door. She called, "I'm sorry. I think of those people in Waco. Some of them were married and had children. Some of them loved each other and some of them loved David Koresh and Koresh loved—well, God maybe, or power."

The teenager, who knew from reading *Cosmopolitan* magazine that this was no way to keep a man sexually interested, rose and stretched with her pelvis out. Steven went out the glass door and into the lobby.

Luna swam a long time, not wanting to go upstairs. Finally she dried off and was the only passenger in the small elevator, whose walls were mirrored like Graceland's. She tugged at the nylon crotch of her suit, working wet fabric out of her ass and labia, turning sideways to check her bra size. Still thirty-four? Maybe a thirty-two. She had lost weight again since Steven moved in. Even he complained sometimes that her hipbones made him feel he was lying on coat hangers.

At the fourth floor two laughing men got on. They were carrying whiskey in plastic cups. "Guess who's quit smoking?" one of them asked the other.

"I don't know."

"David Koresh."

She got off and hurried to their room. She was ready to talk, then; she might have asked Steven why he had gained the pounds she had been gradually shedding; she thought of asking why Riverside had sent him no moving expense money; she wanted to know why federal agents couldn't wait longer, why men had so much trouble altogether with the act of waiting.

But Steven was in bed and asleep. He never snored in the usual snoring sense, but during his REM stages would sometimes purse his lips in a ring and forcefully expel air in a thin whistle. *Fat,* she thought. *Whale. Blowhole.*

NEXT MORNING, Tuesday, she woke early, perhaps because this western sunlight seemed to break through the glass and strike hard against her eyelids. Steven must be deeply asleep, since his mouth was closed.

Automatically she clicked the TV remote, saw once more the burning compound in Waco, and clicked it off before the audio began. When she set the control on the bedside table she glimpsed, in the half-open drawer, a Gideon Bible. She carried it to the window's light and turned to the last part, Revelation. The footnote said both Greek and Latin translated the word as "disclosure of what was previously hidden or unknown." She put the Bible back, testing some vague memory that Seventh-Day Adventists thought Jesus, once He went back to Heaven, had opened six of Revelation's seals but saved the last for the time He came again. Maybe Koresh had been so presumptuous that fire had rained down upon them, as on Sodom and Gomorrah.

She dressed, debated waking Steven, decided to read more about the lost prospectors and who had eaten whom.

About 6 a.m. she finally said, "Steven?" with a shake of his foot. "You were half right about the typo. Steven?"

He grunted and drew the foot back under the bedspread.

"The Alferd is correct but the last name is Packer, not Packard."

The grunt was longer this time, maybe half a groan.

"They even got the first name spelled wrong on his tombstone. Some smart aleck like you decided to make a correction."

"Good," muttered Steven, so she knew he was awake.

"Packer. As in *meat* packer. Isn't it fascinating how these things work out? Work out by accident?"

A full groan this time. "Back to sleep." He rolled over.

So Luna carried her booklet about local legend downstairs to the dining room, checked to see that the television set was turned off, and ordered enough breakfast for herself and Alferd Packer, too.

From the next table a man whose brown curls might be the re-

sult of a permanent wave gave her an appraising smile with one
eyebrow up. She stared back, curious about the prickle of interest
she felt.

Then she turned a page and found the face of Packer the
Maneater himself, dressed in a wool tweed coat and boxy hat that
might be prison garb. His long dark hair and mustache were lank,
the eyes deep set, shadowed. He had been thirty-one when he
guided the prospectors through snowstorms so thick they could
make only ten miles a day and were eating horse feed by the time
they came into this valley to be fed by Chief Ouray's Utes.

The stranger said from the next table, "You're too pretty to be
eating breakfast alone."

Any interest in him died. She turned another page, thinking,
*If just once I came into a restaurant and found a halfway decent man sit-
ting there alone and reading a book, I'd jump his bones.*

But the nonreader said, "It's terrible about Waco, isn't it?"

Well, that was *something.* And because Steven was being such a
prick she said, "Yes."

"What are you reading so early in the morning?"

"About Colorado." Luna did not look away from the page,
waiting to see if the man chose invitation or discouragement.

He rose from his empty plate with the coffee mug in one
hand. "May I join you? You can enlighten me about Colorado."

She was almost surprised at her own nod, then *was* surprised
when she gave him a smile. This was all Steven's fault, quizzing
her, asking if she had second thoughts about marriage. Now she
had third, fourth thoughts.

While the man sat across from her Luna sampled the fried
potatoes that were as ubiquitous here as grits in the South. "It's not
appetizing, though, to be reading about cannibalism."

He blinked once but then gave her the confident smile of a
man whose teeth have been straightened and recently cleaned. It
was so studied that she thought of soldiers in armor or monks in

cassocks, men costumed for purpose; but his wedding band had been left on from an earlier performance.

She suddenly moved her own left hand when she noticed him checking it out.

"I'm Kevin Peabody. Coming from Wichita, headed to Salt Lake City."

"Luna Stone. Coming from North Carolina, headed to California. Are you a Mormon?"

He shook his head. "Why cannibalism? I thought at first you said cannabis." He laughed lightly to show sophistication.

She kept chewing, remembering to chew with mouth closed, remembering those movie food scenes where a starlet could make chewing an act of seduction. "There was a famous case here with five men eaten, up at Lake Cristobal. A man called Packer."

"You can read that and still enjoy your sausage?"

"I finished the sausage before I got to that part."

He summoned the waitress to refill their cups. "Are you staying here long?"

"Leaving this morning."

"What's the hurry? I'm not in any hurry to get to Salt Lake, I'll tell you that. The Mormons are almost as fanatic as the Branch Davidians." He waved toward the bar and Luna saw that someone had turned on the big television set but muted the sound. "They don't drink."

"I'm going to Reno," she said, wondering why she had not said "We're going."

"They sure do drink in Reno!" He leaned back in his chair, relaxed now. "You wouldn't want to stay on another day and take a look around that Lake Cristobal? I bet there are picnic spots."

She wondered suddenly what it would have been like to cross the country alone, to pick up men, lay them down, pass them by. *I'm not the type.*

"No thank you," she said politely.

"No *thank* you?"

A waitress had turned up the TV volume. ". . . watched from a field two-and-one-half miles away. Some government snipers say that through their rifle scopes they saw figures inside the compound actually lighting the fatal fire as part of a group suicide pact, while other sources believe that the gas itself may have been ignited by candles or lanterns the Davidians had in use. . . ."

Luna, driven back to reality, said, "My fiancé and I are headed to Reno."

The man nodded without noticeable disappointment, and as he speeded up his coffee drinking they discussed Black Canyon, which neither of them had seen, and the Indian ruins of the Four Corners, which he had visited on an earlier trip. He was a salesman for a company that made construction equipment.

When he had finished the coffee and, with a wave, gone to check out of the hotel, Luna sat thinking that she had probably not flirted with strangers since before her days as a patient in the hospital, that the doctors there had cured her of flirting. Unlike bicycle riding, the skill had not come back to her. Steven had knocked on her door; with his looks, she would never have tried to attract him on her own.

If Steven had come downstairs that very minute, still warm from bed, and fixed those blue eyes on her, she would have reassured him on the spot. *Forsaking all others. Till death us do part.*

But he did not come, and she turned to the next page of her pamphlet and a later photo of Packer, now bald, with no facial hair, and the left eye noticeably larger than the right. And on the facing page were sketches of how the bones of the five eaten miners had been found. To Luna, it seemed almost an omen that their skeletons—with hatchet marks in the skulls—had been found by an artist for *Harper's Weekly* out sketching in the wilderness in the heat of August, that these drawings of their scattered bones (no boots) had actually appeared in that magazine.

She ran her finger down the paragraph to identify the artist.

Randolph was his name. He had been drawing the western version of pastoral scenes when in a grove of spruce he came upon four skeletons lying side by side, and another one nearby.

Like a heavy humidity, the weight of coincidence, or significance, settled over Luna, and she pushed back the book. *Just my luck, I'd be drawing a skeleton and come across a dead artist,* she thought, grinning toward the hotel window and the rising granite slopes beyond. She tried to imagine the weather that early February when Packer had led the others uphill with six days' rations, how in mid-April *(today was almost an anniversary!!)* he had stumbled into the Piños Indian Agency, at first claiming snow blindness and abandonment, finally admitting that in the blizzard he had eaten the flesh of one old man who—he swore—had died from natural causes. He could not explain the bowie knife, the Winchester, he was carrying, both of which had belonged to other men in the party. And then in hot August a man with a sketchbook, perhaps a man who preferred to draw flowers with meticulous anthers and stamens as Luna did—for who could really draw this enormous countryside?—had stumbled on human remains and hurried downhill to lawmen, later to learn that Packer had escaped from the Saguache jail three days before.

She checked her watch to estimate when Steven might come down. He was always the sleeper, she the insomniac. Had kept her radio by the bed, with earplugs, so in the wee hours she could listen to news and music meant for truck drivers. Her mother was the same way, awake and outdoors in the dew with her coffee cup while the bedroom door stayed closed so the weary soldier could sleep on. Even today, living alone, her mother had probably watched this same sun come up over Richmond.

Luna signed for the breakfast and tip, went to the pay phone down the hall, and with her credit card dialed the Richmond number.

"Hello?"

"Mother?" She took a breath. "It's, uh, Madeline."

"Oh good, you caught me before I started weeding the patio. I'm going to put ice-cream salt between those bricks. You're in California already?"

"No, Colorado. I got you that portable phone so you could carry it outdoors." Priscilla Stone was allergic to bee stings. "Are you carrying your epinephrine?"

"All the time. How's the trip?"

"It's fine. What did the doctor say?"

"That it's not an ulcer and to watch my fat intake. I don't see why you wouldn't let me give you a real wedding here. Or Chapel Hill for that matter, where you both had friends."

Steven had the most. Her classmates as well as the students she'd met in the hospital psycho ward had graduated or dropped out and moved away. You couldn't count postmen and store clerks as real friends, despite the warm way they acted in the South. "It's a waste of money. Steven thought Reno was more symbolic."

"And you?" Her mother's voice got a little sharp. "What did you think?"

She couldn't say the truth: that she'd been surprised by his marriage proposal, that all the time she'd assumed Steven would leave her sooner or later. "I thought it would be different and exciting."

"But not even to see you before you moved all the way across the country—it's terrible! I'm flying out for Christmas whether you like it or not."

"I do like it," said Luna, smiling. She could picture her mother leaning against the dark wainscoting in the hall with the phone braced under her sharp jaw, wearing wide-legged shorts and gym shoes with socks, her tool apron tied around the waist and upright handles showing from trowel, weeder, secateurs. She hoped there was also a lump in one pocket with the bee-sting kit. At fifty-five, Priscilla Stone looked younger; her long lean legs and arms were tanned. Her wary face was framed by thick brown hair cut nearly as short as a man's. She used to wear it in curly permanent waves instead. For Priscilla the phrase "forsaking all others" had continued after divorce.

Luna broke into her plans about airlines and jet lag next December. "Tell me this, Mother, do you still miss Dad?"

Silence. Then, "I could kill him."

"I know that, you *said* that; what I'm asking is: Do you miss him?"

She said slowly, "Not anymore."

Through the hotel window Luna could see the equipment salesman loading a bag into his car trunk. He was not smiling now, and had allowed his stomach to protrude.

Luna said, "I remember lots of good times we all had."

"Well, I don't. Is it your wedding day that's bringing all this on?" Luna imagined her mother awake today at dawn, rolling easily across the mattress and over the second empty pillow and up, with no feeling that she had passed through an absence. Now her mother must be frowning at her sneakers, asking, "Or have you heard from your father?"

"I called to say we were leaving and talked to Corinne."

"I doubt he knows a thing about it, then; she has the mind of a mouse."

"He must have been very good-looking when you married him."

"No. He was just very sure of himself." She giggled. "I didn't give him my hand in marriage so much as he took me in hand. And at the time I wanted that. Well, it got old." She paused. "Madeline, is everything all right with you?" A wait. "With you and Steven?"

"Of course. We're already like an old married couple."

Her mother's noise might have been a cough or even a disapproving snort. "And this Reno thing is a big symbol of something?"

"The ultimate gamble," Luna murmured.

"Or just a postponement? On his side or yours or both." There was a sigh. "Your father and I were in Reno once and I never saw a place less likely to make anybody think well of marriage. In the first place, the whole town is a constant reminder that not just marriage but your whole life's a gamble. And in the second place, they say every afternoon the new divorced women head out of the courthouse for the Virginia Street bridge and throw their wedding rings into the Truckee River."

"Well, you're in a terrific mood! Just what I needed." The salesman's car was vanishing up the road. "You ought to get married again yourself."

"Not unless I find a man who wants to wait on *me*. I mean both kinds of wait. Wait-on, wait-for. Listen, do you have enough money?"

"We had that big yard sale, so we've got that with us, and a few traveler's checks and my credit cards. And some still in the Chapel Hill bank."

"And Steven's job is definite?"

"Contract signed and everything. Can you see me as a faculty wife?"

"I doubt it's much different from being an officer's wife—lots of ass kissing. Oh, I forgot! Aunt Evelyn's come through on the European cruise. So—my goodness!—I've just realized we'll be on the high seas by the time you get to Riverside."

Rich Aunt Evelyn got her rear kissed on a regular basis. "I'll let Dad know our new address then. You can call him from London and get the phone number."

"If I have to be polite to Corinne we'll both choke. What time is it there? You sound tired."

Luna said she had just finished breakfast; she was fine; there was no news at all; this was just an impulse call, and a good thing she *had* called now that the ocean voyage was a reality. "You'd have had to call Corinne to leave word for me."

"Anything I leave Corinne will be ticking."

Perhaps Priscilla Stone did still love the major, or else she'd be less bitter. "I guess Aunt Evelyn will have you waiting on her hand and foot." Luna outlasted a silence, not willing to hang up, not willing to say out loud that next time they spoke she would be Mrs. Grier. Who was it that said: *When you come to a fork in the road, take it!* "Don't develop that ulcer on cruise food. Watch out for shipboard romances."

"She's seventy."

"You're not."

"No, I'm wise. I've aged out of wanting a man, the way you aged out of climbing trees. Remember? Barbie dolls. Nancy Drew."

This time Luna waited, sensing her mother was also reluctant to break the connection.

She said, "I hope you're taking all your art supplies. Don't let that talent slide. I've always been sorry I quit practicing the piano."

Luna said she'd packed everything.

"And that's what I want for my birthday—something to hang in the den. Reds and earth colors would be nice."

Luna thought of how her art professors would disapprove. "It's all I can do to draw and play around with watercolors. You know I don't really paint."

"Well, age out of that! Age into acrylics and oils! And Madeline? Madeline? Are you still there?"

Beyond the telephone station, Steven—rested and handsome—had come yawning into view, glanced around the lobby without seeing Luna, strolled to the breakfast buffet.

"I've got to go, Mother. You can always leave word for Steven in the Botany Department if Aunt Evelyn has a stroke or anything."

"You know she'd have gladly paid for a big church wedding. I really ought to be there to see you get married, even in Reno. Your father ought to be there. We always thought we would."

"I've aged out of the white-veil routine. You two have a good trip, Mother. Take care of yourself."

"You too. Madeline? You're eating well?"

43

"I'm fine."

"Don't get depressed."

"Mother, I'm getting *married.*"

"Sometimes they go together." Priscilla Stone gave a nervous laugh. "You know I'm teasing. Just remember your health, that's all. Be happy." They waited. "Be happy," she said again.

"Yes. Have a great trip, Mother."

After hanging up, Luna went on looking through glass walls at Steven, seated now in the restaurant and giving the waitress his juice order and a serving of dimple besides. His own flirting skills were in excellent working order; she knew he had lived with a bank teller briefly before her, and a law student before that. Women had given him cuff links, a pair of skis that were even now awkwardly packed in the van; he also owned a camera and tape player and sleeping bag that represented birthdays spent with previous women. Not pride so much as contrast with her own bland past had kept Luna from asking many questions. The camera and cuff links went all the way back to Atlanta—he'd vaguely said—Kid Stuff. She wondered what stuff he had given back to those hometown kids.

Now she watched the waitress fill his cup, laughing at something witty he'd said. Luna did not even know who had left whom, if the cuff links had been thrown at Steven's head before Miss Georgia Belle slammed the front door, or if, after signing his farewell note, he had carefully balanced his skis upright into the elevator. She could visualize the second action easier than the first.

She thought all this while Steven sipped orange juice. She thought of him while watching him not think of her.

Almost absently she opened her small address book to "Stone" again and dialed her father's number. Their answering machine responded in his very deep voice, so deep he could have done the low rumbles for any barbershop quartet. It almost made Luna's ear hurt halfway through her head. In this very low tone she had for years been urged to shape up, grow up, stand up, perk up.

She told the machine the day, the time, where they were now, when they were due in Riverside, and added that Mother and Aunt Evelyn were sailing to England and had probably been too rushed to let them know. Evelyn was her father's aunt—not Priscilla's—but she had not spoken to Martin since the divorce, and to the new Mrs. Stone? Never.

"You're probably out playing golf. And thanks for the check, Dad. I won't even deposit it till we get to California."

In fact, Luna had not mentioned that check either to Steven or her mother. Steven would have wanted to spend the bonanza on fancier hotels en route; Priscilla to declare at length that money was the very *least* that man should contribute to them both, who had gone all over the world with him, from pillar to post, and kept going all over the world while he stayed busy on the base or in the field or anywhere except where his family needed him. And so on.

It was hard, Luna found, to end conversations with machines which kept winding their tape, wasting power, while you thought up some novel good-bye. She tried to be original because she would be one in a sequence of sound-alike messages, with good wishes or loves weakened by distance and thinned through the wire. "I'll see you, Dad," she said, and added hastily, "Corinne, too." Then she waited too long to hang up and knew they would listen to her breathing and try to draw some conclusion from it, might rewind and replay the tape, testing for whispers. Secrets. For which parent she loved the best. She hung up too hard, and that might be subject to interpretation, too; her father would ask his new wife: *You think she's depressed?*

Luna decided that when Major Martin Stone had come to a fork in the road, he took it.

She went to the restaurant door to wave at Steven and point upstairs, then hurried to their room to gather possessions and see if their bathing suits were dry enough to pack.

. . .

THEY DROVE north on Highway 50. Steven said, "I hope you're a lot clearer in your mind today than yesterday."

"Nothing wrong with my mind," said Luna.

He was at the wheel so did not gauge her expression; come to think of it, he did not often look directly into her face. When he did she sometimes suspected he was checking out his own double reflection in her eyes.

He made several remarks about the heat, the highway, the sound of the engine. Luna kept skimming her tourist pamphlet as they rode toward Delta, an odd name for a town in such dry country. He said his breakfast had been excellent. Finally he asked, "You going to be deaf and dumb all the way to Riverside?"

"No." She waved her booklet toward the windshield. "I'm thinking about what I don't like on this trip."

"Well, sure you are," he said in disgust.

She waved again at ranch land and passing pickup trucks. "Maybe a century ago, I think, travelers left home to see what else was out there in the world and that's what I wanted to see—"

He broke in, "You've seen plenty of it." He drove as if the van were an enemy.

"Children who don't have a home base can't think the same way as people with real roots. People who once took the Grand Tour. Victorian ladies to the Pyramids, that sort of viewing of other civilizations. Young girls would go to Rome to get over broken hearts."

He nodded very slightly. He had left off the cap this time and the chlorine in the pool must have lightened his hair even more.

Luna spread her booklet on the dashboard, slapping pages over one by one. "But now we don't visit what already exists, like the Alps; we're on a trip into somebody's mind, some effect that's been thought up and prepared especially for tourists before they come. Something unnatural. Invented. They've set traps for the eyes of tourists."

"That's capitalism," Steven said with approval.

"I don't just mean Disneyland or outdoor dramas or theme parks. I mean—" Here Luna held up a brochure and gazed through as if it were transparent. "If we'd gone to Black Canyon the visitor center would tell us more than would even interest God about the geology, the history, the plant life. And I bet when we get to Delta—Alferd Packer did—there'll be a museum and probably a nature walk and a historical tour."

"So what? If you had to make a living in Delta, what would you do?"

She didn't know. "But that's all we're seeing while we cross the country. Thomas Wolfe's home place. Elvis Presley's. Wherever you go, somebody sells you a ticket to someplace authentically re-stored or collected or reproduced in papier-mâché or—"

"You think it would have been better with your Cherokees? They get their tepees from Sears Roebuck nowadays. Luna, what is your problem?"

He was right: pick, pick, pick. She kept doing it.

But when they did drive through Delta she pointed silently to the big murals painted on downtown buildings along Main Street—Technicolor elk, stylized horses and Indians. "The one with all the feathers is probably supposed to be Chief Ouray," she said.

"So you can probably buy a Ute tomahawk that's made in Thailand. So what?"

He remembered what she'd said, though, because later when they descended into the valley that held Grand Junction after miles of stark beauty through rugged canyons and mesas, Steven announced triumphantly, "The only mind you're visiting here is God's!" and Luna thought, *Yes, and He's not friendly*.

Maybe she really was depressed. She studied the rock forma-tions sculpted by wind—or by God's persistent thoughts—until the issue of marrying Steven or not, marrying him here or yonder, became no more important than whether some rattlesnake out there found sun or shade. Bridal jitters, she decided. If he asks me again what my problem is, I'll say, "Bridal jitters."

They ate in Green River, Utah. On the road again, Steven talked about how the Mormons had the best genealogy records of anybody; he could probably find his own British and Welsh kin in the libraries. She thought of the Mountain Meadows Massacre and thence about Waco.

"You never did come across my radio, did you?"

He had, in some box, but he'd forgotten which one.

Luna hung over the seat and rummaged through the nearest liquor store carton. "Slow down so I can look." She worked her way onto, then over, a pile of clothes and braced herself, searching, until she found near the door her silent radio as well as her old diary. She came lurching and crawling back with both.

"Got it." She worked through static in search of news about the Branch Davidians, but there was none, just a growing certainty that no one had escaped the inferno alive. Ammunition had exploded everywhere. The temperature had probably exceeded two thousand degrees. Some professor gave a confusing explanation of the difference between Jehovah's Witnesses and William Miller's Adventists.

Luna listened while they passed gray cliffs with talus slopes, the rocks tinged with the red and brown colors her mother wanted to hang in the den. The air felt hot but dry. She snapped off the radio.

Steven sounded almost satisfied, saying, "Koresh got what he asked for—it sure was the end of the world for him."

"I've always thought that's what Jesus meant anyway, that we all have an End Time, that each one of us gets a Judgment Day for all I know, even if it's inside our own minds in the last few minutes before we die. What's the word? I always get it mixed up . . ."

"You and your words," said Steven, possibly bored but at least glad she was talking.

"Eschatology. I sometimes confuse that with scatology." Luna smiled. "Like cavalry and Calvary?"

"This private Judgment Day is what the Pope teaches?"

"I guess not."

When they had swapped places it was as if Steven had been storing up all he wanted to say while being polite to her. He began by patting her knee joint just below the ragged edge of the paint-spattered jeans she had chopped off into shorts.

"This is nice, Luna, just you and me on this long transition. The trip was a good idea. Gives us a chance to talk things over."

He could be winsome, persuasive. Luna's heart rose like a small balloon. "Yes," she said. "I don't mean to be such a problem."

They rode on through grandeur of such a scale it was almost boring. The rock, the blending russets and browns of great stone walls, made Luna long to sit in a small white room and draw fern leaves with nothing but an HB pencil.

"Riding with you like this," said Steven, stretching, "reminds me of long car trips I took with my mother when we were looking at colleges. We knew that once I went off to school, everything would be different, that this was our last time. She hoped for Emory, but I had to see U.V.A. and Rutgers. We spent two days considering Duke, but all those Gothic buildings were too—" He paused.

"Self-conscious," Luna said.

"She was younger then, very pretty. At some hotels people probably thought we were lovers."

"That's because she keeps touching you all the time."

"What? She does not!"

Yes she does. Soon he drifted into a nap with halfhearted whistle snores, so Luna stayed at the wheel for the next 180 miles, wondering if Highway 50 had not backtracked in some inefficient way to accommodate so many cliffs and canyons, especially after they arrived at a second town named Delta—this one in western Utah. Here she woke Steven to drive the next hour through Sacramento Pass, where she would enter Nevada unmarried and leave it on the far side of Reno, married, with her future life as neatly mapped as these states in the travel atlas. Her wife's life. She glanced sidelong at Steven and let her eye paint in gray hair and wrinkles, just for practice.

Small though the town was, Steven got lost in Ely because of so many highway markers and ended up stopped by a roadblock on the wrong road. Deputies told him to turn back; they were waiting there for a group of prisoners being transported to the maximum-security penitentiary straight ahead.

"Might as well stay overnight here, as much time as we've lost," said Steven, following their directions back to town. They drove past a railroad museum ("Another tourist trap?" he asked) and into a parking lot outside the Copper Queen.

Inside, he suggested Luna register them, since the credit cards were all in her name, and while she was signing at the front desk he wandered toward the flashing lights beyond and stood with hands in pockets in front of the first slot machines they had seen.

"Hey, Luna!" he called. "Get some change!"

Her purse was heavy with coins already. She carried it and their basic overnight bag to where he had seated himself and rung up a quarter. In staccato pings the machine spat three other quarters into the steel tray. "Aha!" He laughed aloud. She could have dipped a forefinger into the dimple in his cheek, and she saw why it had been so easy to love him. As he sent one of these coins back into its slot he held out the left palm without looking up at her. "Quarters are what I need."

Luna raked the bottom of her straw pocketbook and picked out the larger coins by feel. The next quarter was eaten without effect, the next came back with a twin; then both of them disappeared while the wrong pictures whirred into view.

She said, "Ready to go upstairs?"

"Let me break even first." He half stood to locate a few more quarters in his pants pocket. The pocket seemed heavy with change, his wallet fat with bills. This time when he released the metal arm money rang down again, and he settled more deeply in the chair.

She said, "What's wrong with the nickel machine? It's got the same bells and fruit."

Steven didn't hear. With a crunching noise the arm came down again and two quarters pinged into the return. This time he left them as if they might magnetize more, and played from his other handful. He stretched out both feet. "You go ahead. I'll just play out what I've got. I want to get some idea of the pattern of payoff."

Not very damn likely, she thought, as she carried the bag to the elevator. He loved money, Steven did. Loved getting it at the bank, loved sorting and handling it. Every bill in his wallet was arranged in sequence, with dollars first, on up to fifties. Now it seemed he loved risking it as well.

Later when he joined Luna for a supper sandwich he was twelve dollars ahead and preoccupied. As he sat at the table, he gave off metallic rattles. While they ate he kept straining to see "his" machine lest some undeserving stranger sit there and cash in on the priming he had already invested.

"Twelve dollars," Luna repeated. "You can buy me dinner."

No, he thought it was luckier to reinvest the same coins, as if compatibly transfusing a circulatory system. It wasn't the first time he had used a scientific analogy that made her blink on second thought.

"You surprise me. I never thought the one-armed bandit would appeal to you."

"It's fun, come try it yourself."

"I don't even remember you playing poker or anything."

He said in a dismissive way, "Oh, cards. I used to play cards with Mother all the time. You outgrow cards."

She was halfway through her chicken fillet sandwich, but he had nearly finished gulping his. "Bear in mind, Steven, that casinos make more money off slot machines than all their other gambling games. So what does that tell you about the pattern of payoff?"

"Nobody's making *you* play." He put down the last crust and swallowed his beer. She watched him head back to the casino room while taking her time. Major Stone used to tell her: *Slow eating nourishes; bolting your food does not.* In her childhood her father had been home so seldom that she took each word for wisdom he had stored up while in faraway places. Had cleaned her plate for him.

After dinner, looking from the tiny balcony off their room, Luna thought that light in the West had different habits. It evaporated more quickly under the rocks and looming mountains, but caught and glittered long on roofs and high windows, buttered the tops of bristlecone pines. If winter's dark was said to make susceptible people depressed, perhaps cowboys on the desert became downright jolly. In California she would be tanned, gleeful.

She got out her diary, turned back the blank pages, and wrote down that part about the light.

It was full dark that Tuesday night when she finally fell asleep alone and did not hear Steven come in, did not hear him stack his seven quarters by the lavatory. The smell of him—several margaritas and an Alka-Seltzer—threatened to wake Luna, but she transported the odors into her dream as bread and seawater. In the dream she stood on shore casting bread on the waters. There was an excess of bread all around her feet; perhaps the stones had been turned into loaves; she was not at all hungry. As the bread drifted out of sight there came in on the tide very large ponderous green bottles, sealed, with papers inside and drawings barely visible on the papers.

While Steven tossed about restlessly, the mattress shifted and shook, and at Luna's feet the soggy loaves and messages floated out and in on the surf.

WEDNESDAY MORNING Steven had a sharp headache, Luna had a bad case of I-told-you-so, and the van had a water-pump problem and maybe worn belts and an oil leak. Steven stayed in the air-conditioning while a mechanic looked at the engine and told her he could fix it.

Luna rode with him in the wrecker, towing it in. The truck radio was on and gave the Waco death count: eighty-one dead, seventeen of them children.

She said involuntarily, "Oh, the children."

The mechanic shrugged. "With that kind of heredity, what future did they have? You on vacation?"

Suddenly Luna realized that he found her attractive, a possibility she often forgot. "Going to Reno."

"I go to Las Vegas myself. Lost Wages, that's the name we call it. Vacation at Lost Wages."

The radio announcer said searchers were just now beginning to work the very edges of the cooling waste in Texas, and for weeks they would be sifting the ashes for, well, for pieces of people. People turned to carbon, people melted to slag.

"Mind if I turn that off?" she said.

While the van was being fixed, she walked to the railway museum, which promised a Ghost Train tour, though it did not leave till afternoon. *We'll be gone, then.* She felt reluctant. She wanted to ride the Ghost Train when it took tourists up and down the levels of the copper mine pit and past a few ghost towns.

In case darker sunglasses would help Steven's headache, Luna bought those at the museum and a postcard on which she wrote to her father, "It seems funny to be the one traveling while you stay in one place and to know that Mother is traveling too." She frowned and blacked out the part about Priscilla Stone. "Everything about the West makes you feel you could strike out and do just anything." She signed it, "Mrs. Steven Grier minus Day One."

She put the card in the museum mail slot, then stood reading footnotes on a wall map that said Frémont and early telegraph lines and the Donner Party had all passed through this area in the middle of the previous century.

Back at the hotel, she woke Steven and checked with the auto place by phone. He was sawing the price tag off his glasses with his pocket knife. "Steven? Do you remember anything about the Donner Party?"

"No. Not ready yet?" He reshaped the earpieces to make the glasses fit securely.

She told him about the map on the museum wall with its dotted trail marked, like tiny footprints. "They were cannibals, too, I think."

"Well, so were some of the Indian tribes, so what?"

That echo of coincidence seemed meaningful to Luna, though she could not have said why Packer and Donner went so neatly together. She looked at her own travel atlas, ran a finger back along the road they had come. Tourist attractions were marked here with black stars, but Alferd Packer and the Donners were not mentioned.

She said, "Have you ever read about synchronicity? No? How about seriality?"

Now that the glasses were settled, Steven put on his golfing cap and checked himself in the mirror. She watched him smile and stop. "Never have," he said absently. "I think it was the Iroquois. They ate Jesuits. You won't study that in any Native American curriculum."

She persisted, stubborn. "Synchronicity. Carl Jung."

"Young or old, no. These will be much better to drive with. Did he say when the van will be ready?"

"Jung thought there was some other law of events beyond cause and effect. He said some events, well, just liked to happen together."

Steven nodded and said breezily, "One appetite, one dead Jesuit. Let's walk over there and make sure we don't get cheated."

"You don't listen," she said. "You want me to talk, but you

don't listen. Are you irritating me on purpose? Or am I just getting irritated on purpose?"

"Some things just like to happen together." He put his hand on her back and directed her to the room door.

When the van was done, the mechanic said he wouldn't take credit cards because "There's too many transients around here. Cash doesn't need a forwarding address."

Luna paid, wondering if she ought to take her father's check to a bank before they left Nevada. As she accepted change, the mechanic said to her, aside, "Las Vegas is better than Reno."

She smiled, turned to Steven. "Sure you don't want to match him double or nothing?"

But the mechanic took her seriously and shook his head.

It was past lunchtime before they could leave Ely, and Steven was hungry but Luna wasn't. While he pumped gas, she got beer and ice for their Styrofoam cooler. He drove, eating; she made a salty half meal off potato chips. After passing mountains of tailings from the copper pits, their east-west road climbed another mountain; she supposed all the north-south roads must follow valleys between these high ranges, while the one they were on kept rising up and dropping down as if to cross great furrows that had been plowed by giants through solid rock. They climbed to cold weather, dropped to warm. There was little traffic.

Steven took his second candy bar. "What casinos need to do," he said thoughtfully, "is to mix the slots with computer games, so you win from skill and not just luck."

"They want people to bet fast and then bet again fast. Not play some long drawn-out game."

"This has got nuts in it. I told you not to get nuts." But he kept chewing. "I'm looking forward to roulette."

Luna warned, "That takes more than quarters."

"I'm told the big Reno hotels start every guest off with a hundred dollars' worth of free chips just for checking in."

"If that's true, they must be pretty sure of getting it back and then some." She changed the subject. "I called both my parents yesterday. How about yours?"

"I put a note in the Easter card."

Luna almost made a face; she disliked ready-made greeting cards with mass-produced sentiments.

He read her grimace the wrong way. "She's glad we're getting married, Luna, really she is."

Luna supplied the censored word. *"Finally* getting married."

"Well, I'm her only son, only child. And you know how Dad is. I guess she's a little possessive."

The Griers had only come once to Chapel Hill, just before Christmas, when Steven received his doctorate at midyear graduation. Luna and he had taken the bus to meet them at the Raleigh-Durham airport, rode in their rented car to the afternoon ceremony, and posed for photographs, then on to the Carolina Inn where they had reservations. Mrs. Grier, blond as her son and stocky but not fat, kept combing his hair with her fingers for the camera. At the inn, she turned from the car trunk Mr. Grier had opened to unload luggage. "And before dinner you'll show us where you live, Steven."

"I live with Luna," he said.

From inside the car trunk, Mr. Grier's laugh sounded hollow and sarcastic. Mrs. Grier somehow managed to condense her face and body; by solidifying she dropped to a lower dress size on the spot. Her lips contracted to a pucker that matched Steven's mouth when he whistled in sleep.

Mr. Grier hauled out the suitcase, red-faced and grinning. His wife turned on him. "I suppose you want a drink?"

They all went into the Pine Room, whose paneling was hung with photographs and clippings of U.N.C. sports events several decades old, and had a drink—even Mrs. Grier finished most of her white wine while all of them watched Mr. Grier's complexion deepen from Rosé to Burgundy.

Luna said to Steven now, "I suppose your mother disapproves of our getting married en route."

"Anything unorthodox she connects with you being Catholic. She foresees all her grandchildren bowing down to Mary."

"But Reno was your idea."

"I didn't tell her that, no need to worry her." Since the highway was empty of other cars, he gave her a wide smile, a pat on the thigh. "Don't mind her, now. She grew up in this little town in Georgia. She's an A.R.P."

Luna said dully that she kept forgetting what those letters stood for.

"Associate Reformed Presbyterian. Pretty conservative."

Luna remembered that part. There'd been no more talk about seeing where Steven lived in Chapel Hill, and the foursome had met in the same hotel for dinner. Luna had dressed herself like a defendant taking her lawyer's advice: white and high-necked and prim. Low shoes with stockings. A short necklace of fake pearls with a small pearl stud in each earlobe. Lipstick: pale pink. She could have taught in any A.R.P. Sunday School.

By the time their salads had been served it was obvious that the Griers had meantime talked over their son's situation, that while the father preferred to accept it with cheerfulness and good table manners, the mother knew a climber, a fortune hunter, even a harlot when she saw one. Mrs. Grier had iced tea instead of the wine that Steven and Luna chose; from time to time she would tap Luna's arm with the hand that was cold from her glass while stroking Steven's with her warmer fingers. Luna couldn't take her eyes off those busy hands.

Mr. Grier chewed his tossed garden salad between swallows of whiskey sour. Every time Luna turned to her right she could not see Steven because his mother was in the way. All she could see of Mrs. Grier was a short green sleeve and a shoulder. And her active hands.

"Of course we expect you Christmas," she overheard Mrs. Grier say. Her napkin in the cold hand rose to touch her probably pursed lips, then she added insincerely past her green collar, "You, too, of course, Luna. If you have no family?"

"I have family."

Mother Grier said to her son, "I suppose Luna's family must celebrate High Holy Mass for Christmas. Our simple caroling and live nativity scenes might be too plain for her." She showed Luna her profile, then flicked a bit of lint off Steven's obviously badly laundered shirt.

Before Luna could say anything, Mr. Grier leaned over his plate and probed the air with a forkful of greenery. He looked nothing like Luna's father; he was soft; there were red squiggles in his complexion; he appeared anxious to please. He asked her, "What do you think about Laurel and Hardy?"

For a minute Luna thought he meant a salad dressing. "In the movies?"

"They're my hobby."

She knew he was largely retired from his Ford dealership—so he would have more time, Mrs. Grier had said; so he could have more alcohol, Steven had corrected later. Steven's voice was like his mother's hands—warm when he spoke of her, cold on the subject of his father.

Luna smiled. "I guess you can see all their old comedies on video now."

"Not the early ones. But I collect still photos and magazine articles. I've got both autographed pictures. You know Laurel used to understudy Charlie Chaplin, back in vaudeville."

Luna shook her head that she hadn't known, half listening to Mrs. Grier extol teaching jobs in Georgia—what about Emory, Augusta College, Georgia Southern? Agnes Scott had a beautiful campus. Mrs. Grier said she had a cousin in communications at Georgia Tech; he'd be more than glad to help.

"I'm working on *desert* plants, Mother."

"Do you think I didn't read your dissertation? Every single word?"

Until then, Luna had not known Steven had mailed a copy to Atlanta.

"I grow sedums and sempervivums myself," she said with a teasing little poke into Steven's shoulder.

". . . and every book about their lives and their movies, too," Mr. Grier went on. He lifted his glass as if in a toast. "Stan Laurel thought up most of the ideas. I try to buy books about other Hollywood stars that even mention them. For instance Oliver Hardy appeared by himself in a John Wayne film."

"I didn't know that."

"The Fighting Kentuckian; it wasn't a big hit."

"And Adelaide Walker asks about you so often." Mrs. Grier twitched her face into Luna's line of vision and said, "Adelaide Walker," and then twitched away. "She's never married and I guess she'll mostly inherit that bank when Chick Walker dies since their boy never did get over his nervous breakdown."

Steven said softly, "It's not a big bank," but whether to Luna or himself was hard to say.

"The boy comes home from the hospital on pills and goes back and then comes home again," said Mrs. Grier, not noticing that Luna's knife and fork had stopped in the air above her plate as if they might cut each other instead of meat. "I told Adelaide we'd all have to call you *Doctor* Steven Grier from now on. We see the Walkers every Sunday. Everybody still eats at the cafeteria out at the mall after church, just like they used to."

"Hardy died first—1957."

Neither Luna nor Steven had been born then. She tried to imagine the Griers as newlyweds, holding hands, holding other body parts. Naked. Not possible. She forked into her salmon. She couldn't see what Steven had ordered. Mrs. Grier had filet mignon that was still bleeding, and Mr. Grier couldn't seem to reach the bottom of his lettuce bowl.

Luna pushed back the bite of fish and tasted the croissant instead. She raised her voice, "Steven has applied for several openings in California."

"Now there's where I'd like to go!" She noticed that Mr. Grier's glass was full again, switched while the rest of his family was too engrossed to notice. He raised his voice, also. "We could tour the old movie lots, Mabel, and see the stars' houses and step in those footprints at Graumann's."

The name Mabel, so unexpected, made Luna lean forward to see if it suited Mrs. Grier's face. She leaned so far forward that a strand of her dark hair trailed into the wine and had to be blotted on her linen napkin without the slightest notice taken by Steven or Mother Mabel, who were catching up on news about people she'd never met. Steven sounded animated. Neither of them had endured a moment's silence since they met in the airport terminal. They were happy, she saw, exchanging the obvious in various tones of voice (. . . so we just rented a car . . . wonderful flowers for December . . . don't want a thing for Christmas but I see what you need—clothes! . . . haven't aged a day, Mother . . . so Adelaide said that Lydia Constance would never marry him . . .).

Luna nibbled the salmon in its too-rich sauce. *When a man marries,* she thought, *he divorces his mother.* Her father had said that once, about somebody else, at their own dinner table. She felt just as excluded from the conversation now as she had when too young to understand, when her chore had been to eat what was put before her.

As she looked across the table, Mr. Grier put down his steak knife and drank deeply from the new whiskey sour, then decided to suck out anything that had been absorbed by the slices of lemon and orange. The process was noisy but went unheard. (. . . told her I knew you remembered those days . . . divorced a year and still asks about you . . . won't cut your allowance yet; you never know . . .)

Allowance? Steven got an allowance?

As Mr. Grier slid one citrus peel under the edge of his plate he said to nobody, "They made over a hundred movies."

A silence occurred while all were eating, though Mrs. Grier did manage to say that the holiday decorations were nice and Steven reminded her of the gumball trees she made and silvered every Christmas. Then, in an effort to include the others, Steven said with a quick gesture at the crowded dining room, "These must all be graduates and family—the inn is filled to capacity."

"So's your father," snapped Mabel Grier.

Now their van was slowing as it ground over gravel at a sign that said Highway 50 would soon ascend Pancake Summit. "Let's switch," Steven said. "I've still got a headache."

While he walked around, Luna crawled into the driver's seat and buckled in. Ahead the road climbed again out of the giant's great garden row, dropped into the furrow, then rose into the Diamond Mountains toward Eureka.

"Ouch! Hell! I've sat on your radio."

"Don't break it." He was opening the small diary. "And put that back," she said.

Not much interested, Steven set both on the floorboards. It was 3 p.m., too early to stop, so they pushed on to Austin in the center of the state, crossed the Reese River—too dry to be called a river—and a hundred more up-and-down miles to Fallon, where there were green irrigated fields and a busy military airport. Downtown there were also flashing lights advertising keno and blackjack and poker, dancing and live music, craps, cocktails. Steven announced that he was feeling better.

"It's an oasis!" He drank in the signs for the Nugget, the Depot, Stockman's.

Luna was sure her memory of the Griers and the black mood it left would have been quickly cured if they could only have made love right away, in daylight, half dressed and noisy, so fast she would end uncertain whether she'd had an orgasm or just an adrenaline rush. Her body was prescribing sex, reminding her how much better accord they had in bed than out; but unfortunately her body had also been notifying her of menstrual cramps for the last hundred miles. This probably explained her moodiness, which had been piped to her brain straight from the ovary.

Steven had always avoided sex during her period, though she'd heard some men liked it then. Perhaps human foremothers had once undergone estrus and menstruation simultaneously; didn't even pedigreed bitches show a discharge the same color during heat? And we got from that to courtly love, gallantry. Juliet and Ophelia.

"Why are you stopping here?"

"I need some Tampax."

As if to escape a low-lying odor, he lifted his nose reflexively.

When Luna came back carrying her small paper bag, Steven had paced up and down the Fallon sidewalk to survey the sights and had decided the nearby Lariat Motel would do. It was on Williams Street, not far from the Depot (NICKEL KENO! POKER SLOTS!). She felt a low ache squeezing her abdomen.

"Why don't I let you take a nap?" he said as if giving gracious permission. He got his cap out of the van and set it on the back of his head. "Think I'll walk around. Now don't you carry any bags. I'll do that later."

"Fine." She got in and turned the key.

He called, "Did they give you any more change?"

"No," she lied.

"OK, I'll get some. See you in an hour or so."

She knew he'd kept currency after buying gas. Also it was still unclear to Luna whether he'd been sent a check to cover moving expenses or only got the promise to be reimbursed. When she had asked, Steven—irritated—answered both times, "I don't have anything yet!" She read in that an agreement to notify her whenever he *did* hear from Riverside. Now she wasn't so sure.

She carried radio and diary with her when she checked into

the Lariat, but only put them inside their room before marching back downstairs to the casino. Sure enough, Steven was there.

"It suddenly dawned on me," she said as she sat by him at the next lighted slot machine, "that we could easily have gone on to Reno today. We can't be more than an hour or so away."

With a heavy crunch, like a predator's teeth, he brought down the lever on his slot. "I was only thinking about you. I know how you get with the cramps." One of the attendants, she saw, had carried him what looked like Scotch-and-soda. She wondered if he would be alcoholic at his father's age. She wondered if she would then turn hungrily to her own children.

After fishing for quarters of her own, Luna levered one in. "Or maybe you're the one in no hurry to get to your own wedding."

"Nobody thinks of the bride having the curse. Luna, what is your problem?" He sounded more weary than concerned.

"Maybe it's you. No, it's me." She fed her machine another quarter and pulled. The wheels spun but the symbols on the payline did not match. It was irritating to hear quarters clang into Steven's metal tray. "I don't see what you get out of this." She leaned forward to read details about winning combinations and their payoffs. "Maybe in Georgia gambling was an interesting sin, but we Catholics have always known even bingo favors the house." He *did* smile; he *did* dimple; maybe she was just tired. He kept pulling his handle more frequently.

While he put in one coin and got back two a waitress came to offer her a drink, but Luna shook her head. Again she pulled her own lever. "This motion reminds me of flushing a toilet."

"That's how you always get with cramps—sarcastic." Steven shrugged. "I guess I'm lucky and you're not."

This time Luna got back two coins. She figured she was down 33 1/3 percent. And Steven's easy comment had reminded her of something his father had said late in that ill-fated dinner in Chapel Hill. By then the other three had finished dessert while Mr. Grier had finished very little meat but topped off his drinks with a brandy. His face had grown soft as a flesh-colored pudding, and he was sleepy. "Stan Laurel married the same woman three times," he had murmured to Luna. "Ruth. Three times. All his wifes, uh, wives made him unhappy."

"Or vice versa," said Mrs. Grier with a sniff, but Luna was thinking about the kind of love that kept on trying.

"See," Mr. Grier confided, "see, Laurel and Hardy are my hobby."

"That's good," said Luna.

"One time somebody asked Stan Laurel what *his* hobby was. He said, 'I married all of mine.'"

His laugh sounded so lonesome in a dining room that by then was nearly empty that Luna laughed also, too hard. Steven was folding his napkin into small fat triangles next to his mother's hand.

"One-sided love," said Mr. Grier, sighing.

At the time she'd thought his parallel was between himself and Stan Laurel, the unknown Ruth with Mabel Grier; now she wondered if he'd actually meant Steven and Luna—one lucky, one not; one giver, one taker. The ones who love versus the ones who let themselves be loved.

She yanked on the slot machine handle. Still no pay. But whom did she have to blame except herself? She'd been the willing sucker, the easy mark. All she knew about love she'd learned off television. She shot a glance at Steven's photogenic face, pushed back her chair, and closed her pocketbook.

"The drinks are free," he said. "Go on, have one. Make you feel better."

"Let me taste yours." It looked pale.

He lofted his glass away in one hand while with the other pulling down his lever. "Order your own. They want you to stick around and gamble. My daddy would love it here."

"Free drinks ought to give you some idea of their profit margin."

He pulled and rang, pulled and clattered, pulled and paid several times before saying, "I've been thinking about what you said about man-made tourist attractions, and you're out of line because everything's man-made now. The highest-paid guys in the country are playing a game with a ball and a hoop that somebody thought up. The rest of us move paper back and forth to earn a living. Nobody's out hunting tigers or anything." He pointed toward her with one of his quarters. "You think this is really silver? And pharaoh thought up his pyramid, too."

She watched him stack coins by his sweaty glass before giving her the smile that turned argument into persuasion. She knew that smile. It had caused her to subsidize her own Christmas present.

"You're probably right," she said. "They'll sell tickets to the site down in Waco, Texas, I suppose. Grill hot dogs." She shivered.

"Premenstrual tension is all it was," said Steven confidently, already returning to his game.

Feeling that all her opinions were probably composed of hormones, Luna nodded, said she would rest before dinner. She wandered down the row of machines with their scattered players, put in a nickel here and there. For a while she stood on the edge of a keno group without figuring out where the men's tickets had come from and how many matching balls and numbers added up to a win. Then she went to their room and flipped through her diary. There was only one entry for all five months of 1993; back in January she had listed the Christmas presents. *Mother: portable telephone. Dad and Corinne: Book on naval battles, WW2; Chanel #5. Mabel Grier: silk blouse. Edward Grier: biography Henry Ford. Steven: watch.* (Expensive; she had saved a long time for that.) *Luna: radio.* It turned out she had been saving for that, too. Steven wanted to replace her ancient clock radio left from her days as a freshman in the dorm with one that would get AM, FM, shortwave, even the audio from area television stations; and when it came by mail order she had to pay for most of it herself. But now when she could not sleep she could tune in the BBC, the Vatican, even the Patriot Network people who thought the Illuminati, TriLateral Commission, and other conspirators were out to destroy America. She could hear about Veronica Luekens, in Bayside, Queens, and her visions of the Virgin Mary from 1940 on. The Virgin, like militia groups, sounded irritable. America had been a great disappointment to them all.

She turned on radio music now while scanning the newspaper that had been left at their room door. It said that burned bodies shrank, contracted into the fetal position. It said that some of the Branch Davidians had died of gunshot wounds—but whose? It said that some of the carbonized children had died in the charred arms of their mothers. It gave different numbers of fatalities.

At dinner what started as disagreement turned into a full-scale quarrel. "You couldn't beat the slot machines with a sledge-hammer!" Luna opened, smiling at first—though the unlikely truths were that (1) Steven had won today and (2) it infuriated her.

"But I did beat them, and you could have done the same if you weren't so stingy with every fucking cent. I might have known you wouldn't lighten up enough to have any fun on this trip."

"Stingy? You call me stingy?" Her voice shifted into acid soprano. "How do I love thee? Let me count the checkbook stubs."

"You know damn well we agreed to take turns on expenses. This year you've had the bread and next year I make it up to you."

"And all year you've been living beyond my means."

"I'm damned if that's so! I've denied myself. You give me one example."

"OK—that party you threw for all the other graduate students."

"We went to theirs when they got their degrees, didn't we? You ever heard of paying back obligations?"

"We drank their beer and they drank our champagne and Jack Daniels'. We ate their potato chips, but I had to roast a ham and a turkey."

"How much does that come to in art supplies?"

"That's my job, that's where I have to spend money to make money. You could have got part-time work!"

"And I'd never have been done with my dissertation if I had. And I'd never have had the time to apply to colleges. You have to write different cover letters every time."

"Oh, I know damn well you do—I typed every one of them!"

"This has been coming on ever since I fucked you the first time and found out you'd been saving it for your old age. That should have told me plenty about stinginess!"

"You bastard."

Luna left her unfinished food without paying the bill or tipping the waiter. Let Steven pay with his goddamned quarters.

She got the heating pad out of the van and put it in the center of the bed, on high, to keep him away. She sank the radio earplug into one ear so she could not hear him either talk or snore. She was awake when the mattress sagged on his side, but she froze herself stiffly into place, an aging marble ex-virgin. And next morning, checking out, she saw he'd signed their room number to the dinner tab, with a generous tip.

When she came into the sunny parking lot Steven was already in the van with both hands locked on the steering wheel. "Good morning." He nodded. They left.

The cloudless sky looked brittle. Robin's-egg blue—if the inside shell looks blue to the unhatched bird. Neither one said anything.

A dry, warm wind kept buffeting the van. The trough through which their highway ran as well as the rounded hills on both sides were the light color of beach sand, with scrubby sage whose green leaves looked sandy, also. A desert seemed an unpromising place to marry. Steven might like it, but Luna thought the arid heat had made her fallopian tubes brittle. Hard-cooked her ova.

As they drove into Sparks he asked (eyes straight ahead), "Cramps better?"

"Never had any."

The lie must have clogged Luna's throat. Instantly came the prick of tears, the ache as her neck and jaw tried to stop them from coming. Because Steven had hurt her feelings about what she now thought of as her *real* wedding night. She was not going to get de-flowered *post facto* way out here in Reno. That first time in Chapel Hill, the weather had been wet, but she, though eager, had been as dry as these desert hills. It had hurt, though she had kept that to herself. The next day she had been too sore to sit down for long. Until last night, she'd thought Steven appreciated the fact that she'd waited for him.

She got the lump in her throat pushed down. It's all hormones. Estrogen is coming out my eyes. Diminished, she turned her face to the side window, determined to control this hard need to cry. It was like teaching bone to swallow. Her father's instruction came surging back: *Babies cry, people act.* But what to do? Get over this self-pity, first. Find a way to make up with Steven.

The Truckee—only half a river this week—cut through Sparks and ran immediately into Reno, the intersecting two towns surrounded by tan-colored hills with higher and higher mountains beyond. Steven must have decided to make up with her, too, for he announced, "Virginia Street! Just like the pictures!"

She made herself answer, "Yes it is."

The slogan on the famous Reno arch, THE BIGGEST LITTLE CITY IN THE WORLD, now set in a beehive of lightbulbs, energized Steven (or maybe he was smiling at the casinos on either side). "Here we are," he said, and suddenly took hold of her hand as if nothing had ever been wrong between them. "What we ought to do," he announced after swinging them down the length of Virginia Street to the concrete bridge and back, "is sleep this afternoon so we can enjoy the nightlife. It'll ease your nerves, too. And who knows when we'll get back this way!"

Bright sunshine bleached out the rows of neon signs for

Harold's and Harrah's and Cal-Neva and others. Luna got out a Kleenex and pretended to pick, not blot, her nose. The lump in her throat got smaller.

"You're feeling better, aren't you?" asked Steven.

She thought, *All right, I can do this,* and slid on the seat and gave him a thin, dry kiss on the cheek, paired with his dimple.

His arm went around her and sort of shook her shoulders. *Perhaps shaking some sense into me.*

"And tomorrow morning," he said, "we can get married." He swung onto Fourth Street and gestured on both sides. "Which one you like best, Mad Lunatic?" His gesture showed her a number of wedding chapels, most with "bells" mentioned in their outdoor signs: Silver Bells, Wedding Bells, Love Bells Chapel. The structures were small. They had been opened up in buildings originally designed for other purposes, like mom-and-pop grocery stores.

Now they drove north on Virginia again and came with some surprise onto the suddenly green University of Nevada campus, where vitex and ivy like Harvard's were growing up the walls. Wild ducks were drifting in a pond. She could have been married in her mother's lush Richmond garden, in the arboretum or outdoor theater at U.N.C.

Steven said, "Even though there's no blood test, we'll need to get a license first thing in the morning, or we could do it today, I guess. Do you need to buy a new dress or anything?"

"I told you I brought the linen."

"You did clean my suit before you packed it?"

She nodded, trying not to stiffen under his arm, not to be as inflexible as the bronze miner who stood with his bronze pick and brass ore in front of the classroom building where Steven made his turn and headed back downtown behind a city bus. By now she had gotten the tears down and digested and had only a slight taste of malice left on her palate. "It's the blue dress you like," she lied, testing.

"The one that's too big for you?" He tapped his horn at some-body who had come out of a casino and stumbled off the curb, blinded by daytime.

It was tan, of course. And he'd never liked one dress a bit bet-ter than another. *Get over it.*

"I don't see the Sands. That's where you made a reservation?"

"Go back to Fourth Street." She had called ahead from Mon-trose and chosen this hotel because some vague connection with Frank Sinatra suggested it might be classy. They found the park-ing lot, much of it full of other vans and RVs and motor homes and even buses that were marked with the names of Retirement Cen-ters and Havens.

Inside, Luna felt for a minute as blinded as the pedestrian Steven had so narrowly missed. She could not even find a regis-tration desk in this crowded, carnival room. Here was a booth, brightly lighted, selling souvenirs, and here two rows of flashing slot machines you had to edge between and there you stepped up into a café/bar and beyond was a short flight of stairs to gaming rooms with more blinking lights and loud music. She turned to go back and start from a main entrance, but found herself facing a hall lined with other machines and a parked car with lottery tick-ets available outside a gift shop selling pink bears and poker chips. She felt as if she had, without drinking, gotten drunk.

When she turned slowly in place again she finally spotted the long, nondescript check-in counter pressed against one wall. It had been blocked from view by a mammoth slot machine—she supposed it was a console like those outdated mahogany radio-TV-phonograph combinations that had once eaten up half a liv-ing room. The box was as tall as Luna, its bandit's arm a formal appendage upholstered in leatherette. She felt uneasy about get-ting too close.

When Steven came into the hotel, she was just getting their key-cards and had to call him before he could locate her among the many-colored optical effects. His smile was wider than ever;

probably he had smiled this way on visits home when his mother rushed forward into his arms. He handed her their basic bag, took his card, and glanced at the room number. "I couldn't find any blue dress or my suit either."

"I'll get them later. Aren't you coming up?"

"I need to work my way through the downstairs one time—it's a maze, isn't it? They give you any kind of floor plan?"

She told him there were maps posted by the elevators. "There seem to be what they call different towers and I'd call annexes. I thought you wanted to sleep by day and play by night."

"Oh I do, I do." In his eyes she could see the tiny reflections of neon going bright-and-dark. "I don't see any elevator."

She had to point beyond the console–slot machine to one, then past the First Prize Luxury Car to another. "That's the one that goes to our tower."

"I'll be up soon. Pretty nice place."

"Nice place! It's a midway. God knows if it gets even brighter at night."

Steven said he thought the atmosphere was exciting, was meant to stimulate like strobe lights at a rock concert. Then he waved to her as he threaded his way between two players who were working slot machines in the middle of what could have been called a lobby. When Steven's head turned gold and scarlet and blue in turns she lost him in the rainbow-colored crowd.

She went the other way, told the attendant she would not right now take a chance on the Mercedes-Benz convertible for fifty cents, and pressed the elevator button to their tower.

It was already riding up, and slow. Luna set down the bag. That's when she spotted the small tour booth to one side, without a clerk, but showing rows of shiny leaflets about bus outings and horseback rides and Lake Tahoe and the auto museum.

Luna had read once that by reflex people use an automatic eye sweep by which the brain processes information, moving from right to upper left, and that well-trained schoolteachers always write important information in the upper-left-hand corner of the blackboard, where it will be seen and remembered. She had tried this when placing messages on the refrigerator door for Steven, but he rarely noticed. Now she took the opportunity to test this theory by scanning the rack to end with a focus on the folder that showed an innocuous log building under the title "Donner Lake State Park."

She shot her gaze at speed over the other folders, but Alferd Packer was not mentioned.

Even while she stared, some of the brash neon lights washed the words in color, tinted the back of her hand as she reached. The elevator came and its doors rolled open, but Luna stood by the cylinder that held sand and bent cigarette butts, reading. She looked at her watch. She carried the bag outdoors to the van.

LATER, Luna was not sure what she had expected at this memorial to members of the Donner Party, perhaps some form of smarmy tabloid history. After all, eighty-one travelers had been trapped in this pass by deep snow in the winter of 1846 and forced to eat their own dead in order to survive.

Eighty-one? Was that not the number burned to ash in Waco?

As she crossed the sand and soft evergreen needles to the low park building, she could still hear the regular cleaving of whispery air on the nearby highway that now carried thousands of vehicles over the once impassable Sierra Nevada. But if this was a tourist trap the bait was fairly mild. Inside was a bookstore and a series of displays: an old pipe, a doll one of the children had owned, maps, and typical artifacts. There were sober portraits of survivors from the Breen and Reed families, quotations from the diary Patrick Breen had kept while his family was scorching the hair off animal hides and boiling them into a glue that could be swallowed.

Luna blended with the busload of tourists who filed into the small auditorium to see a film, not a very good film, but her opinion did not lessen its effect. The pictures it made in her mind were more vivid than those on the screen. Here was a rescue party finding the butchered bodies of a woman and two children next to a pit that their campfire had melted down through twenty-four feet of snow, and below in the freezing water eleven people huddled, their arms nothing but bone under paper-skin, their skeletal fingers scraping out morsels of human heart and brain and liver from a boiling pot. And back at the camps at Donner Lake and Alder Creek waited the mothers whose breasts had dried up, one dead baby, the children crying the whole time when they finally ate the pet dog. There were murdered Indians (stand-ins for livestock) and the moment when one man (who believed his family had safely escaped over the peaks to California) idly tugged at a bit of calico visible through the snow and uncovered his frozen child.

Less than an hour total destruction took in Waco. Here the people were taken slowly, one by one, from October on to April.

Their story grew muddled in Luna's head, the faces interchangeable as the film showed her Mary Graves and homely Margaret Reed, the names confusing until Eddy, McCutcheon, Fallon, made a composite of nobody. Everybody.

More than two-thirds of the men had died. A third of the children. More of the women survived—*Body fat?* Luna wondered—and one of them, Virginia Reed, thirteen, was saved by the Irish-Catholic Breens and later converted to Catholicism.

But it was not Virginia and her faith and frozen feet with whom Luna identified, and not Patty Reed—then nine—who saved her doll and was able later to write almost breezily in a letter to a friend back east to "hurry on and don't take no cutoffs!" since a promised "shortcut" had proved the fatal undoing of the Donner Party. In fact, the film emphasized this perky child's advice, but when the lights came up and other tourists stirred and stretched and murmured, they had to step over Luna's feet where she stayed seated in the back, eyes on the blank screen.

Tamsen Donner. Maybe the last to die. Maybe devoured by Lewis Keseburg, maybe not. Said to have written journals, made drawings and poems, on the long crossing from Springfield, Illinois, to here—all of them lost, left behind, like heavy furniture abandoned along the trail. *Tamsen Donner,* a teacher, planning to open a girls' school once they got to California. A woman who could have escaped with the fourth rescue party, but who sent her three children out with others, while she stayed behind so her second husband, George, would not die of his gangrenous arm alone. Stayed behind for love? Self-sacrifice? Stupidity? Like Luna, Tamsen Donner had come to this place the long way around, had lived in North Carolina, too. Had taught school there at Elizabeth City on the Pasquotank River. From that land of fish and duck hunting and Dismal Swamp she had ended up here in the blizzards, and one man had eaten her time and her strength and her nursing care while another one—though he always denied it—had possibly eaten her flesh.

When Luna made her slow way outside she was shocked by ordinary sunlight. She had been back in a dark and smoky shelter with Tamsen Donner. Now brightness shone off the monument, twenty-two feet high, that gave visitors an idea of how deep the snow had been that winter. As if from just thinking of such snow, Luna went numb.

She got into the van and just sat there. Once she reached behind the front seat and put her hand in the cooler and took hold of a melting piece of ice that felt like a hailstone. Then she drove in a listless, automatic way downhill on Highway 80 toward Reno and easily into Truckee Meadows, which the Donner Party and their starved remaining oxen had reached in late October 1846.

If the Reno streets were shining, she hardly noticed. She was indifferent to garish Reno now.

In the Sands parking lot, with the languor of a sleepwalker, she sorted through luggage in the back of the van, located Steven's skis and his suitcases and garment bags. She called for a bellhop and had these carried to the front desk. She found his cardboard box of tape recordings and CDs and videos, the laundry bag Mabel Grier had monogrammed containing his socks and underwear. One box held his botany texts and computer disks and drafts of his dissertation. She got out his camera and down sleeping bag and scuba gear. Hauling possessions inside, she dropped the briefcase the Griers had given him at Christmas, and when it sprang open so she had to stuff papers and mail back inside, she came across a window envelope from Riverside. It had been opened. Inside was a travel advance, very generous, the check still uncashed. If she had not felt so stupefied—from what? Her period? From Tamsen Donner? (She wondered if starving women could menstruate at all.) No, if Luna had not been so stupefied she might have felt pleased or angry to discover that Steven had more than money enough to get from here to California. She did not really care.

When her last load had been stacked in front of the irritated desk clerk, Luna wrote the following note:

> *Dear Steven,*
> *Let's don't get married after all.*
> *Good luck in California.*

The woman across the counter was frowning. Luna knew Steven would want to know why-why-why, but she had never had the words that satisfied him and did not have her reasons verbalized now. She finally wrote:

> *Some things* don't *like to*
> *happen together.*
> *Luna*

Then she laid down the small plastic rectangle that unlocked their room door. "My husband will be staying on," she said, and decided to call him by the name that matched the credit card she had used. "Steven Stone." She folded the note and wrote that name and the room number on it. "He's probably in the casino now, but if you'll give him this message?" She got out a tip for the angry bellboy. "And put these things in the room, please."

"How long were you staying?" the clerk said with a glare at the heap of possessions.

"I'm not sure. But you have my credit card." Luna came out of her numbness long enough to remind herself to close out that bank account, cancel that card.

She said vaguely to the clerk, "Don't worry."

Then she threaded her way between colorful dazzle and jingling and red glitter and bells out to the van and pointed it west and drove up into mountains alone.

PART 2

A Ghost of Her Former Self

~

Donner Pass

I WROTE IT IN MY DIARY. *Left Chapel Hill, Friday April 16, 1993. Arrived Reno, Wednesday April 22. Came to a fork in the road. Took it.*

That's all the time it took for Steven and me to come from the middle of North Carolina to the edge of California and separation instead of marriage. I don't know how long it took the Donner wagons from Springfield, Illinois, to Sandy Creek in Wyoming, but leaving there July 19 they finally struggled up to Donner Lake the last week in October and by coincidence (?) it was not until the next April 21, 1847, that the last survivor—the man who ate Tamsen Donner—was taken out.

My father would hoot with laughter over my fascination with the close coincidence of these April dates, the number 81. He never heard of synchronicity, either. He yelled over my head to my mother once: "This girl is part pygmy! She's little and dark and by God she's superstitious as a savage!" He predicted I'd end up living my life on advice from crystal gazers and palmists. Often he asked in my presence the rhetorical question: "Are you sure she's mine?" He thought this was funnier than Mother and I did. I can't count the times I watched him roll his eyes almost solid white while he asked her, or sometimes even asked me directly, "Are you sure you're mine?" He'd be smiling. I did not smile while I watched the blue color—less blue than Steven's—slide under his

79

heavy brows and leave the stone eyes that statues had. During my childhood when he came home on leave, he'd at first approve my nature collections, praise my report card, until he dragged out of me that the agate was lucky or that I thought my guardian angel had told me how to spell the hardest word. Major Martin Stone favored dolls for girls until he made me admit the blond one at night protected me from the trapdoor under my bed and the Thing that whispered and knocked on its other side. That doll he confiscated. He wanted me to be a lady but not a scaredy-cat.

If Dad had known what drew me back to Donner Park, Major Stone, U.S.A. Retired, would have stopped payment on his check and rolled his eyes too high for the bank teller to know the color, while exclaiming, "She never got that Zulu brain from me!" If ever I was particularly foolish, he used to send me to bed without supper. He did not consider this serious punishment. "Short as she is," he would say to my mother above my head, "she'll be fat as butter anyway if she's not careful."

Since Mother was aboard ship now, I wondered if Steven might telephone my father to announce that I'd suffered a hormonal storm. Dad would turn at the phone to say to his young wife, "I told you Madeline sounded depressed."

But no, Steven would not call; they had never met. He had disliked "the major" in advance and on principle, being too much a high-minded pacifist himself to bear arms. Or too lazy, I sometimes thought.

Tamsen Donner had been a pygmy, too: five feet tall, less than a hundred wiry pounds even in her well-fed days back in the Midwest. If, after months of later starvation, Keseburg really did butcher her, it must have been like cutting steak off a sparrow.

When I left the Sands Hotel I drove again west of Truckee to the Donner lakefront, now full of motels and cabins for rent, not considered as beautiful as Tahoe because up close these waters are more leaden than blue. I could see that the granite rimrock west would block the sun and bring twilight early. The Donners had not actually camped at the lake named for them but seven miles away across Trout Creek on Alder Creek where Prosser forked into it. The lake froze over.

Now there were cars driving all around its edge, bright lights, the hot smell of food. I wanted soon to walk to the specific place where George Donner, her second husband, had lain emaciated in his tent, ill fed on boiled mice, feeling death burn slowly up his arm and smolder in the shoulder joint. Where on his corpse had they needed to cut in order not to taste blood poisoning?

But Tamsen gave up her life to stay with him, maybe from guilt that she had not been able to save the first family she had loved. Maybe because this second love was greater. It was a puzzle.

On this, my first free day, I only wanted shelter of my own, a headquarters, and because it was early and the weather cool here (in fact, that night at nearly six thousand feet it turned surprisingly cold) I rented a cabin, being told how lucky I was to beat the crowds that would increase during May until Memorial Day made a tourist circus. On my budget, the cabin was not at the water's edge. No matter. I only wanted to sleep, this first night I had slept alone in two years.

I carried in beers from their melted ice as well as the electric heating pad, straight to the bottom of somebody's rickety bunk bed, and mixed the heat and cool until I fell—and I do mean *fell*—asleep without food, plans, dreams, regrets, intentions.

I SLEPT AWAY all the daylight and woke in the dark almost hungry—rare for me. (I'm supposed to eat vitamins and take vigorous walks to maintain appetite, but I forget.) I forgot, too, where this narrow bed was, with its mattress so thin I might have been back in the hospital. "Mama?" Not a creature was stirring, not even a nurse. I was too old for Saint Nicholas, for any of the saints, so naturally I thought of sinners next. "Steven?"

I rolled out of bed smiling, put on a jacket, went to find food in Truckee. The Donner story had evaporated from my mind and from this place that might as well have been Chapel Hill, with street people looking like the same Chapel Hill motley assortment with my age, twenty-eight, as their average. Even in April, they were tan. Those with too much money were moving around fast to scrape it loose, like snakes shedding old skin; some seemed to own nothing but backpacks; a few with prematurely white hair looked like advertisements for Golden Age Resorts or exercise spas; and a handful seemed actively dangerous, salesmen of drugs or sex, with young men as uneasy as Carolina freshmen making their first buys.

I ate an overpriced supper in a nearby motel, while I read that Patty Reed—who lived to be ninety-three—claimed hers was the only family that had not eaten human flesh. The hamburger was too rare; I made my meal off fries. That made me remember how, when my father came home on leave, the menus changed in my house; the pasta and vegetables and casseroles disappeared; the table grew heavy with beef, pork, lamb.

All evening in the cabin I ate Midol and aspirin, slept, listened to low music on the radio, slept again. The cabin had been built for sleeping only, a tourist-monk's cell with minimal furniture, walls of pressed sawdust masquerading as wood paneling, a Permastone fireplace with a gas log that smelled but would not light. The rooms were cold, but I and my heating pad were warm. One time I dimly heard a newsman say that some of the carbonized skulls unearthed at Waco so far showed bullet holes, some children had burned in their burning mothers' arms; and another time I thought a plastic surgeon had recommended Preparation H, but, no, it was Steven who told me once that the hemorrhoid cream could be used to reduce bags underneath the eyes. I went in and out of sleep and time.

When I woke next morning I found one blood drop on my pillow, not menstrual but nasal, a reaction to the altitude that had also made me drowsy, lethargic. I spent this second free day on acclimation, walking here and there on the shores of the glacial lake that was three miles long, just under the granite Sierra wall that rose two thousand more feet above me. How could anyone in his right mind have proposed in any season to cross this rocky range with oxen and wagons? As soon as she saw it, Tamsen Donner should have turned back from California.

On the third morning, my flow was ebbing but I could feel some slight seepage of guilt. My mother had lasted through absence and infidelities. Who did I think I was? What had I thought love was like? I telephoned the Sands. Steven was still in residence. Winning? Had he pawned his skis and cuff links? Cashed his travel allowance? Spoken to one single policeman about his fiancée?

I drove downhill, even rode once around the block so Steven could exit from any of the outside doors of the Sands if we were meant to reconnect, and then I hit the accelerator hard to the post office in adjoining Sparks. Here I sent Dad a card saying I was on vacation and reachable by General Delivery, Sparks, Nevada 89431. No phone. Beautiful Country. Lots of History. Dry.

The PriMerit Bank was glad to deposit his fifteen hundred dollars, put in a transfer for my Chapel Hill funds, and order me checkbooks; that local reference made my credit cards sufficient to buy a small tent, white gas stove, Quallofil sleeping bag, and self-inflating air mattress. I bought boots. In the van were all the jeans and socks and wool shirts I would need on cold mountain nights, and all the shorts and T-shirts for sunny days. I tried to imagine Tamsen Donner crossing the ice on Alder Creek in her cumbersome skirts and petticoats.

Next morning I woke very cold. During the night, snow had fallen on a date I would have expected daffodils. Only a few inches deep, this was a mere "spring snow," said the contemptuous waitress who served me toast and coffee; it would soon melt downhill.

But these contrasts in seasons, these likes and unlikes, the fact that I could ride west seeing desert while Priscilla Stone rode east seeing ocean; the wonder that Tamsen could stay and die while I could leave and live—well, I loved them, that's all. (Across the continent, Father whispered into my ear, "She can't be mine!") I had a superstitious yearning for any kind of pattern. My English faculty adviser had warned me about it while I was trying to comprehend Kafka for my term paper. I would read in God and the Prodigal Son; the professor would read them out. It wasn't a good time, those months before the hospital, for me to picture Kafka's "Country Doctor" racing pointlessly through the snow forever, to read his dreadful love letters to poor Milena, or to sit with the Hunger Artist in his carnival cage. It's always a dangerous time when every little accidental thing in life seems personally significant.

I shook off this mood and decided to find a campsite but first to call the Sands-Regency again. Good; Steven had checked out early this morning. I sent a fax to my MasterCard office, listing that hotel bill as the last legitimate charge before my card had been lost or stolen. (It was the only one with Steven cosigned to use.) Then I cut mine in half and switched to VISA and American Express.

After buying nonperishable groceries, I talked to a ranger about backcountry camping in Tahoe National Forest. His frowning questions made clear he doubted I had enough wilderness wisdom for that, but he did find me a site in the campground at Donner State Park; it was tamer but it fit the gestalt. By the time I'd checked in there, late-morning sunshine that had been gaining strength all the way from Cape Hatteras had hit the desert basin and then struck the foothills to melt snow everywhere but under the conifers.

When I parked at headquarters, the van went on dieseling after I turned the engine off, trembling to go forward, to follow Steven, perhaps. But I jumped out and was almost running to reach the Donner monument before the next group of tourists came out from seeing the film. It's not a monument to the Donners, actually, at least not to Tamsen. The three bronze symbolic figures—doubtless some government committee decision—claim to embody the "Pioneer Spirit," by which no committee member meant cannibalism.

I kept tamping down my excitement. As I rushed down the trail I forced myself to slow down, to breathe deep this thin dry air with its strange, spicy smells. I've learned the hard way about manic symptoms. Alice was hyperactive before she hit that rabbithole.

During the second half of my junior year at U.N.C. I dropped down a hole of my own into the loony bin. Steven doesn't know about this.

I didn't even draw plants or organisms then—that started during my recovery. I read books. Gregor Samsa waking up to find himself changed into a bug, cheerful stories like that. If I'd wanted to read about metamorphosis, somebody should have sent me to Ovid, to love.

If I'd been home in Richmond that summer of 1986, I'd have known my parents were headed for a divorce. I should have known it anyway; they must have waited until I left home for college before they really quarreled openly. Until then they took small revenges on each other. From Mother: errands not run, food badly cooked, a way of looking over his shoulder and past him while he talked. From Father: absences, officers' club, cigars in a closed car, transatlantic phone calls never returned. They gave each other hopelessly wrong Christmas presents, like a swap of weapons.

All that I knew, but the summer I turned twenty-one I was working out an internship with a publishing house in Boston—an English major, only taking studio art for fun, discovering I might be a Sunday painter.

So I didn't see stage 1 and stage 2 of their open quarrels, the dinners he missed while meat grease congealed; the nights he came home late, the nights he didn't come home at all. Priscilla Stone was astonished to get on their wedding anniversary a handsome pair of earrings, so she tracked down the shop's name embossed on the box. There was Corinne, piercing ears with her little silver gun.

When I arrived back on campus in September, I was unprepared to learn of Corinne the Bitch by telephone, of Martin the Bastard by mail. That month there came many separate, highly emotional telephone calls. Even on postcards they accused each other. Both begged me to come home to Richmond, to intercede and translate and help; when I did come they'd plant me in the center of any room and shoot words through me into each other.

The things they said! Priscilla said she would have left years ago if there had been no children. I stood in the middle, an anchor, an impediment. The major said he'd never know, had no way of knowing, who had been in her bed while he was overseas. Were not his own eyes blue? But look at Madeline's—black as a Hindu's! I whirled as they shifted positions, tried to speak, could not be heard. Had she, Priscilla, ever thrown up to him that stewardess whose letters she'd found? No, but she'd never given him one fuck as good as that stewardess, either.

"Stop! Both of you, stop!"

As the two of them circled, backed, reset themselves, yelling, I tried to turn and return in the central medallion of the Oriental rug he had bought for her.

"Maybe if I'd had a son!" he yelled, though we all knew she'd had two miscarriages after me, then disobeyed the Pope with her little orange pills.

My mother screamed, "Maybe you've got a goddamned dozen!"

Such performances went on every weekend I came home, at fall break, at Thanksgiving. I would drag back to campus and a new roommate whom I did not know, who spent most nights with her boyfriend. She had little orange pills herself. I didn't have, or want, a boyfriend. My grades slid down. I liked to read about Kafka's defeat by huge impersonal forces; I was not surprised when tuberculosis of the larynx stopped Kafka from swallowing so that he really starved to death; literature seemed to me justifiably grim.

Between holidays my mother would call me, crying. It would be midnight in Richmond and Chapel Hill, too, and where was Martin Stone? How did I know? Or Dad might call from a bar, from the officers' club, some friend's house, he said, meaning Corinne's; and he'd want to discuss Priscilla's menopause and how much any active healthy man could stand!

At Christmas, naturally, I didn't want to go home. I lied about my late exam schedule. My roommate, then all the others on the hall, left. My only visitor was my roommate's boyfriend, who hit on me with such sudden vigor that it seemed like attempted rape, and I heard myself yelling out to Jesus, Joseph, and Mary. He stopped in a hurry and backed against the wall. I asked him if he knew that when Jesus ascended into Heaven his circumcised foreskin was the only fleshy part of him left on earth, and that a piece of it became a relic in one of the churches where women could kneel before it and pray for pregnancy. He said he didn't want a thing to do with pregnancy and left quickly.

Nobody else came for a long time. Kafka was a vegetarian so I became one, but there weren't many vegetables in the room and the cafeteria was a long way off. The residence adviser, a preoccupied grad student writing her thesis on Emerson, knocked on my door. "I've still got one more exam!" I insisted. "I'm studying!" She said all exams were over. When she came back it was to notify me that only a few U.N.C. dorms were kept heated over Christmas break. We who remained on campus—mostly foreign students— needed a temporary transfer. I felt as foreign as anybody, but I told her there was one exam I had not passed; I still dreamed about it. She argued; the schedule was over; exams were done. I tried to convince her this last was a tutorial, especially designed for me. By a professor who had become like a father and mother to me.

In the end she notified the dean of student affairs, and he summoned the shrinks from U.N.C. Hospitals. Men in suits and ties came beating on my door, not looking at all like doctors. I braced a chair under the knob and hung from the waist over my high window to scare everybody. "Tell my mama!" I shouted. "Tell my daddy!"

The men ran back out the lower main door and waved their suitcoat arms. I had not thought of jumping until they made it interesting. I lifted one leg over the sill. Weighed a ton, it did; I was surprised the heavy thing was mine, since I had been on such a diet. Pinched it. Still wasn't sure.

Below came a red firetruck, people carrying something like a trampoline. Well, I would not play. I stayed in the window frame with my immense cast-iron foot hanging down. My toes filled up with iron blood—I can feel how that weight swelled even now, how every toe turned clay, then stone, then steel. A nice woman leaned out of a nearby window to talk to me earnestly about something that concerned her. I envied her passion. I asked if she knew about Angela of Fogliano, who dined solely on roses and tulips and took her only fluid when nuns would brush water on her lips with a feather. Probably she never decayed, I said, like the rest of us will.

The woman kept changing the subject. I admired that. "Good!" I said. "It's better not to know these things! Good for you! I'm sorry I mentioned it!" Because everyday life will every time blunt that edge of urgency she had.

After she got tired, the suit-men took off my hall door by the hinges. I looked back from my seat in the window and saw it open from the wrong side. That felt funny, like reading a page wrong the way Jews and Chinese do, and it made me dizzy, but one of them ran fast and stopped me from falling. Nobody would discuss the backward door with me, and I tried not to make a fuss as we all marched down many stairs to the concrete and an ambulance—who got hurt? "My God, how much does she weigh?" said the ambulance man. From there we went to South Wing. It isn't "south" of anything in particular, unless maybe "true north" or normalcy.

In North Carolina, the mentally ill can "go to Morganton," or end up at Butner. Carolina students go to South Wing when their compass breaks. There's always a Bedlam, a Bellevue. The man who shot Reagan is at Butner. In North Carolina, South Wing is probably the best. Better academic liberals than those who want to cauterize what's wrong.

Spring semester wasn't bad there, except for the excess food they kept pushing at me, though I lost track of both the academic and seasonal year. We were always at seventy-five degrees with an internal syllabus and daily grades on a chart. Worst of all was the horn blast set off each time the outer door to South Wing opened to those who had ingress and egress. At first I could not even shower without a nurse watching where I put the cake of soap. "Don't look, I'm so fat!" I would call to her. "Poor little thing," she said.

Then I improved and for a long string of days sat alone in a dorm room not unlike the one I'd left. I read poems. Byron ate mostly biscuits and soda water so the process of digestion would not interfere with thinking. But the doctors would not let me follow his example. I did crosswords. I drew flat pictures of the flattened sycamores far below the hospital windows. They had been barbered. I sketched the winter bark and limbs, by spring the blooms and wide, wasteful leaves.

My roommate and her boyfriend came to see me once. He would not look at me. She did not have much to say. Somebody else had been moved into my dormitory bed, and my things were in storage.

I was in storage, too. The season, then spring holiday, passed without my noticing. On one of her steady visits, Mother noticed my halfhearted sketches. Though I had started out majoring in English because she had always told me that, after she left the convent, literature became her second Bible, now she took Byron away and brought art books instead. Art seemed satisfied with the exterior rind of things. Realistic pictures, especially, were comforting. They made nature hold still. Here was a morning-glory trumpet with no bee. Or here a static midair bee, immobilized in oxygen as if it were Jell-O. Painting, like reading, was something a person could do all alone. The only pictures I did not like were still lifes: overripe fruits and gooey wines and fatty cheeses.

Between January and April, I did not feel at all crazy. I felt intense. Everyone else who came and went seemed to me torpid, subnormal.

My father came and went. The door to South Wing squawked loud before it let him in, long-faced, sad about the state of his own life, happy to improve it with explanations. He thought his own good news would cheer me up.

"I have this new chance, Madeline," he began. "Her name is Corinne. She has her own business out at the mall. Ear piercing. Very sanitary. You'll like her."

"Get out of here," I said.

He talked quite a while before he did. He left behind a pair of French-hook earrings, pale as navy beans. I lifted two corners of the carpet and hid one in each place. Nobody noticed the lumps they made except me.

My mother, though, had paid attention to the doctors' instructions long before she passed through that noisy door.

"Nothing is your fault!" she announced early in my hospital stay, though I had not asked. She made a theatrical flourish with one hand. "Your father and me—that's *our* fault. I hope that's clear? Nobody meant to depress you, Madeline. How depressed actually are you? Is it something I said? Your father says too much—we both know that. How are you feeling? Paint me a picture?" She stood there with her wet eyes getting wetter until I got off the bed and hugged her. Her body felt ridged with fat. Both my parents had gotten fat that winter, when it was all I could do to swallow lettuce and slaw.

She had pet things to say on every visit. "We love you just the way you are," was one of them. I wrote what she said in my diary so I could read the same love words when she was gone. I kept no record of what my father said about Corinne.

Of course I recovered. As I improved, the doctors and nurses took note of my meticulous drawings of the gladioli my mother brought, the sycamore tips turning pale green under my window. By the time I got out, I was drawing ganglia for the neurosurgeons, probably to annoy my psychiatrist, who had wanted his daughter's portrait in pastels.

It was April then, too, and the blossoming world seemed orderly, one animal or plant generation like the next, bulbs that came up in the very spot they'd been left last year. I dropped my English major—academic advisers were glad to get me away from suicidal Hemingway and alcoholic Fitzgerald and Gogol turning his face to the wall. They were glad I was drawing flowers; Kafka had not liked nature, had called himself "a stranger among flowers." I was on medication when I moved from English major to art—but found my new professors professionally opposed to order. From Wordsworth to Jasper Johns? It's a good thing I had pills to take. From fall semester there were leftover F grades to pull up. I was allowed to drop without penalty some of the courses that mattered most—William Blake, for instance. I wasn't sure I could make art while holding in my head the knowledge that everything we see and hear is wrong: the bluebird is not blue, since color is only a trick of light and his song is a sound wave; every twinkling star is actually very big and hot.

So I went limping into this belated, second-choice degree in art because I had many credits there, and then dropped that down a notch, also, telling my teachers that I only wanted to be a Sunday painter. I got my degree with Sunday Painter Grades in Studio Art, but that school year and summer I also lurched aside into an unexpected career as medical and botanical illustrator. I could draw a harelip, an enlarged spleen, but my only pictures of anorexia nervosa were in the hospital file—me at 80 pounds, me at 110.

Long after these wounds had healed and I was up to 115, Steven came knocking on my door. I was off therapy. There were pills in the medicine cabinet—still are; I left them when we left Chapel Hill; but I had quit taking anything. I was drawing well, for good fees. My father by then had married Corinne; it was a personal triumph that I could attend that ceremony and be polite, go afterward to the house where Mother had cleared out his half of possessions and be malicious.

I had matured. They both said so.

And look at the chain of events: if I had not had a crack-up, I'd never have started drawing; Steven would never have entered my life; if it were not for Steven, I would not now be standing where the original Murphy-Eddy cabin had been built against a black rock and then turned into an igloo buried by snow. In which they got thin, and thinner.

From a bronze plaque on that rock I read all the Donner Party names. I found Tamsen's. Born November 1, 1801. Died late April, exact date unknown, 1847, her bones long since powdered and absorbed.

Tamsen filled my mind while I drove to the campground where I made several trips carrying gear uphill to my spot. I built a fire but not to cook—peanut butter sandwiches and juice tasted good outdoors; good; I was all right; I was not losing appetite. In fact, I was hungrier than usual.

By sundown after several failures I finally got the tent up and secured. For warmth I crawled inside and then into the sleeping bag and with my portable radio eavesdropped on life in the valley: a woman's body had been found behind the Reno Sak 'n Save food store off—could that be right?—Fantastic Lane; the Sierra Club was objecting to groundwater use at Honey Lake; Washoe County had a new emergency alert system; the Sparks Chamber of Commerce strongly defended the redevelopment plan. In the larger world, Los Angeles residents were remembering the riots of April

'92, when defendants had been acquitted of the Rodney King beating. The Waco Story was—ha ha—cooling down. Commentators were reduced to cheap irony. The Easter Story; the fact that the longstanding local name for where the Branch Davidian compound had stood was Lamb's Hill. It pleased me to be able to catch others in that faulty pattern making to which I was so prone.

To the grumble of voices and the aural blur of music I drifted in and out of sleep. I'm aware that my very drowsiness would cause many (certainly Major Martin Stone) to discount the two events that happened next, to dismiss them as dreams; but I have found that twilight state to be a time for insight, even problem solving.

In the middle of a soft rumbly tune, something outside the tent began to scrabble through my cardboard box of groceries.

I lay very still, thinking of bears.

John Muir had certainly seen bears on his Sierra walks—but now? So close to settlements?

No sounds of tearing or breakage came. In fact, the noise had a surreptitious quality, with periods of silence during which, perhaps, soap and toilet paper were moved aside so food could be located.

I crawled carefully out of my bag into cold and peeped under the tent flap. My fire had burned flat and was only a lumpy red glow to one side, but I could see the thief by starlight.

Short. Thin. Putting jam with a tablespoon on bread. Human. If haircut and pants meant anything, a boy-person.

I yelled "Hey!" and leaped upright, brought down the whole tent in a chilly nylon tangle. While I floundered and fought to free my face from smothering, the thief laughed out of sight. Probably finished his sandwich.

I slapped at the twisted cloth with both hands, rolled with a bruising thump over either a rock or the silent radio, and at last got my head out into the air. He was gone. The lid had been screwed back on both jam and peanut butter jars, the spoon laid on top upside down. Even the wrapping on the bread loaf had been closed.

When I had unwrapped my body from the clinging fabric I ran up and down the path a short way, hoping to frighten him off; I didn't want to catch him. I didn't want to call out to other campers, either; perhaps he was their son. I didn't want to step on a snake.

After that, winded, when it seemed too much trouble in the dark to stake the tent down again, I simply used the nylon for a damp top blanket once I had relocated my sleeping bag nearer the groceries. I scooped out and smoothed new sandy hollows that would fit my body, remembering what one of the pioneer women had said: *I made up my bed with a hoe.*

Just as I began to get warm again, I realized that somehow during all my thrashing struggle the radio had been jarred on. It and its low hum and occasional static were wound deep in tent fabric. I could feel out the overall shape with both hands but not grasp the button that would have turned it off. The hell with it. I curled up to sleep.

(I can just hear my father now. *It was that white noise, Zulu brain. White noise.* Maybe so.)

Whatever provided her entry, my next visitor was Tamsen Donner. Or her apparition.

There were no noises, so I had no reason to think the hungry boy was back. I did not think anything much, not even surprise. One minute I was in that delicious state where you know that if you move one foot it will wake you completely; if you can just keep that foot still, your next moment will be morning.

The next minute my wide-open eyes were fixed on a phosphorescent woman who came down the path that should have led to another campsite. She wore a long gleaming skirt with ragged hem. No visible feet. Though there had been no pictures of her in the film, I recognized Tamsen right away and wanted to tell her so, but felt that locking of the throat that in dreams will prevent you from calling for help.

This first time she didn't say anything, either. I'm not even sure she saw me, although—*you'll hate this, Dad!*—although I believed my thoughts of her had "called her up" in some mysterious chemical way, as developing fluid will call up a photographic image on paper floating in a tray. My fascination was strong enough to develop her image on a layer of molecules. She even looked like a flat print shimmering through gelid air. I guess her dress was linsey-woolsey; that's what they wore. No particular color. She looked down at my dying fire, bent toward the embers, spread her pale hands. I doubt she can ever get warm enough now.

Then she frowned toward the lumpy pile of me and the tent as if trying to recall my name. Her dark hair was parted in the middle and pulled back; the face, half in shadow, seemed small boned, nose and chin sharp. We were about the same size, though I had not been that thin for a long time. Yet, how strange that her phantasm should assume bodily form at all if Lewis Keseburg's body had barely survived by digesting hers!

The resurrection of the body, Christians say. Well, lots of luck.

As if this wry thought had splashed her with acid, Tamsen's gray ghost began to disintegrate. The edges frayed, then a little streak of her torso opened and showed a fir tree behind it; finally the whole image broke up into white tatters.

Perhaps an alert, fully awake person would have felt frightened? But I *was* fully awake, and only curious. I stared down the path, wondering if the last bits of Tamsen might blow downwind upon the boy. Then I saw that the last bits were snowflakes. My face became damp, then wet, then freezing. I burrowed underneath the splayed tent. I slept.

NEXT MORNING I woke cold and found the peanut butter hard in the jar, the milk slushy, the firewood wet. I also woke convinced of the reality of both my night visitations. The boy had come before snow so left no tracks, and in the uneven white inch on the path was no sign that a skirt had swept by; but I knew. I had seen her come and go.

Not that I then thought Tamsen "real" exactly, not objectively real. If fakirs can levitate their own bodies, maybe my own mental energy could transmit one picture five feet tall. Pictures weigh almost nothing. And I made pictures all the time.

Either that, or I had to consider hallucination of the sort that could get me committed again. *Nothing but exhaustion* was always my mother's diagnosis. They wrote on my record: "Severe depression." I much preferred the older term. *Melancholia.* Lincoln had that and could still be president.

I tried to take my mind's temperature; the reading was normal. I had left Steven, and the leaving felt good.

I shook out and spread my tent over bushes to dry, still scanning the landscape for either night figure to return. By this date on the high mountains, I'd been told, winter snow was old and had packed down; at the next-higher level it lay sodden; here it showed patches of bare wet earth, and soon it would melt away with drying rocks and dark ground appearing wherever spring freshets had run down and settled. This little snow would vanish when the sun got high.

In that other April 1847, there had still been six feet of snow left in the pass when Fallon's rescue party took the last Donner Party survivor out, but that was a record year. Keseburg was said to have kettles of human blood on the boil when found. Winters were colder then.

Yet even in the winter of 1952, said the rangers at the park, a whole Southern Pacific train got snowbound for four days near Donner Lake, and men had to bring in food on snowshoes to feed the passengers. If Tamsen Donner was able to materialize herself at will—that is, at *her* will rather than mine—why didn't she ride the blizzard to them?

But as I hung up my sleeping bag, humming, I felt neither haunted nor melancholic but free, almost lighthearted. Smarter people than I had believed in a spirit world. William James read his brother Henry's letter-of-farewell to his father over that father's new grave. And afterward went to séances. And what of those daylight ghosts in *Turn of the Screw?* To make the governess a repressed neurotic was post-Freudian hindsight, like reducing Pentecost to mass hysteria.

I spun in place and chortled aloud in all directions: *Good morning, Sandwich-Eater! Hey Tamsen Donner! Have a good day!*

I knew a Chapel Hill professor who hated that glib admonition; he always snapped back, "No thanks, I have other plans."

Smiling broadly now, I carried my own sandwich downhill and ate it en route to park headquarters, where I sat once more through the film about the Donner Party and bought books there about its history. For a while I drove idly around to get a larger sense of this countryside, so different from the deciduous Southeast: all the way around Lake Tahoe and over to Squaw Valley, where I rode the tram up and drank wine on the mountaintop. *Free*, I thought, looking down on junipers rooted in cracks in the rock that the wind had turned sideways and shoved over, but still they lived. Still I lived, too. There had been a time when I saw myself as a languid Elizabeth Barrett, delicate and abstemious, so naturally Steven had looked to me like Mr. Browning.

There was a restaurant atop the mountain where I ate a big breakfast.

In the van again, humming, I felt as if my pupils had widened and I could see more and more of this tawny countryside, so different from home. The weather was out-of-season, the sparse vegetation strange. Never before had I been cut loose from people, obligations. Nobody could telephone me here. If I drew pictures, they had no deadlines, and no one would own them but myself.

I came singing into camp and surprised a chipmunk nosing in my grocery box. "Get on!" I scolded. "That's for the boy." For already I believed he would come again, if only to repeat some hooky-joke on his tourist parents.

I reset the dry tent, put in new radio batteries and an earplug so I could hear music but toads would not, in midafternoon ate some more. This high, dry air was good for the appetite. I read about the Donners until the light fell over the mountains into California. By dusk I had dragged my sleeping bag behind a granite boulder to lie in wait for Young Peanut Butter. I hid there a long time, bored by station K-PLAY-AM 1270, my open ear listening hard for the hungry boy.

Finally he came so quietly that I almost missed him. At sight of someone bent over the food, I eased around the stone so I could block his escape, and I squatted there, watching him eat. He liked grapes. Was it a "he"? The black hair, I saw now by moonlight, was cut around the head as if guided by the rim of a bowl. With his rounded head and face plus the torn clothes and thong sandals, I wondered: Indian? Mexican? His face he kept turned away, buried now in bread, eating fast. He was too hungry to be any tourist boy. I held very still while he ate and also kept rapidly checking the closed tent for movement. At the slightest noise he turned into a moonlit statue, even stopped chewing; then I could hear a plane pass overhead or catch a grunt through the growing dark that might have come from a porcupine or maybe a lizard's death rattle; how would I know?

He did not drink any juice or beer; maybe he got all his fluids from the park drinking fountain at headquarters. Maybe he lived in Truckee? The only reason I considered the possibility that he might live out in the wild and scavenge was because I had been vaguely considering it all day myself. In cities nowadays, the homeless haunt dumpsters behind restaurants and supermarkets. Up in the mountains, even the animals learn where a food cache is hung.

When Reed's rescue party had come from California after the Donners, they tried to cache food en route, but the animals—starving themselves—devoured it all.

Not until the boy had relaxed, even seated himself by the ashes of my old fire, did I finally stand and say in a fast, soft voice, "Don't be afraid you can eat all you want I don't mind."

He almost bolted. Paused when he saw I blocked the uphill path. Downhill lay the most crowded camps. He took time to identify my voice as female, decide I wasn't tall or armed. After a leap to one side and back he stood still, turned his face left and right, and at last to me again.

Under so small a moon the details did not tell me what kind of face it was. Indian, surely; or at a different angle was it part Asian? Perhaps the nose was Negroid, but the lips narrow. No more than ten years old. As he pivoted so rows of ribs made long lines under the smudged T-shirt he became eight. Surely not nine unless underfed. No one knew better than I about underfed.

I almost whispered, "There's fresh milk in the corner of the box," careful not to move.

He faced my voice and shape while his hand worked behind him into the box, found the carton. He upended it and drank. He gave the same laugh as last night. "Germs now."

"Drink it all, then."

Wary, his feet shifting for purchase in case they must spring, he took more swallows.

"I'm coming out from this rock now." I slid more clearly into his view.

He stood still, drinking.

"I'm harmless," I said.

After a moment: "Come out, Harmless."

Then I stepped out from the shadow of the dark rock with my hands on each side, palm up. He spewed a half laugh. "You're little."

I took very slow steps in silence around the edge of the camp-site, hoping to keep him from feeling cornered. "The candy bars are stuck inside that roll of paper towels."

Matching my movements, he continued to pivot and keep

his eyes on me while he poured one out. "Never thought of that." I heard the paper wrapping tear, then crumple, then the wad thunked neatly into the box.

"I don't mind if you eat here," I said. "You're welcome to it. Can I light the fire? You won't run away if I light the fire?"

He said he didn't know.

Yes, he was thin; malnourishment might permanently stunt his growth. In slow motion I knelt, flicked the lighter, lit the small candle. When the doctors were reprogramming me, they showed me films of survivors from Auschwitz, Belsen. Now I held the candle in place until papers caught under the new firewood and then the damper limbs began to spit. "My name's Luna."

"Moon," he said. Maybe he was older than he looked.

"OK. What's yours?"

"Uncle Sam."

"Whatever. It's warmer by the fire."

"Not in that smoke it ain't." He sat on his haunches where he was and eyed me.

I fed the fire with dry twigs collected downhill. "You need long sleeves after dark. You live here?"

"No. *You* live here."

"Around here?"

"Around."

I turned my head on the neck to show him my average American face with its nose and chin a bit too pointed. "I'm glad to share my food with you."

"That's good since you did." The fire made a louder noise when a cone showered into flame. "You went off and left everything open to the varmints."

"I thought you might get hungry."

He dropped from his squat to sit on the ground, probably wet, and his jeans looked worn and thin. When I added wood so the fire leaped high his gold face showed part Indian, or so I supposed with my Cherokee gene. Paiutes had lived here in Tamsen's day, and when word was brought to them that the whites were eating one another, squaws used the story to frighten Paiute children.

But I could not tell Paiute from Navajo. "Are you Indian?" He did not answer but ate the candy with its nuts that Steven so disliked. It went down too fast; he did not chew enough. "Native American?" Not a word. "Throw me one of those candy bars." It hit the slope of the tent and slid down to my boot. "Thank you."

Motionless, he watched me tear it open and bite into chocolate and peanuts. He shook the milk carton and set it aside.

"Where are your parents?"

The noise in his throat sounded as if he had hawked up phlegm but then decided not to let fly.

"You must have somebody, some family." He shook his head. "Somebody worried about you."

The laugh he gave was sharp, unpleasant.

"Somebody knows you're up here camping, or knows at least that you're gone from where you used to be."

Again he laughed. A mockery.

Then I made a mistake. "Are you a runaway?"

The boy jumped up and backed away. Stood as tall as he could but remained one of the few who, face on and defiant, was still shorter than me. "Don't you tell nobody you've seen me."

"I didn't!" With one hand out, I stepped closer. "I wouldn't."

"You do and I'll burn up your car."

Maybe I smiled at this threat because he added, "The van. Brown. North Carolina plates. Says FIRST IN FLIGHT. I watched you drive off."

"I wouldn't tell anybody. Don't be afraid." But in moving I had unblocked his path, and he suddenly darted past me, yelling back, "You better not!" He was gone.

DURING MY WORST DAYS in the hospital, the ones I barely remember before the medication kicked in, they say that if anybody touched me I would stick out my tongue. This stranger-boy, I thought, must have his own reflex for people who came too near.

Next morning I rummaged through the van, wondering if he might be watching from behind a bush. I found a wool jacket that with sleeves rolled up would suit any age or gender, a pair of stretchy socks, an extra army-surplus blanket. We had used old magazines to cushion stacks of dinner plates; I unleafed a *Sports Illustrated* for him. I gave him a cup and spoon, an extra golfing cap not left with Steven. Among all my worldly goods, there was not much with which to endow a boy. I stuffed what I'd found in a pillowcase, put on a sign with a safety pin FOR UNCLE SAM, and left the sack on top of the grocery box.

Then I went hiking in Donner Park, now that my boots were broken in.

I climbed an easy trail with boring markers, passing other walkers with nods or waves. There was a proportion of Asians or Hispanics, but not many blacks and no adults with worried faces calling a boy's name. As the trail rose I passed more and larger granite ridges and crusty snow that lingered in their shadows but had slid off the sunlit tops of pines. My hand on a sunny slab of rock grew warm.

My father never hiked nor fished; he went to the gym to work out and went to the golf course to play, surrounded by men in both cases. There were no long walks in the woods for Mother and me near Fort Bragg, Fort Hood, Fort Riley, and all the others. I had never tried outdoor sketching, preferring the close-up view, the sharp detail; and I wondered if Cézanne would have been able to say of this world as he did of France: "I wait until the landscape thinks itself in me." Even Paul Bunyan could never have said such a thing here.

When I came back my bag of offerings was gone. The boy had not taken the radio, deliberately left on view in the tent, had eaten a little, left everything neat. Perhaps he was hidden nearby, watching me. Even that possibility kept me from urinating anywhere but in the camp latrine.

In late afternoon, I quit reading about the Donners long enough to build a fire, untwist a coat hanger, and hold two hot dogs over the flames. Perhaps the smell brought him. He was wearing the plaid jacket.

He waited by the granite boulder until I said, "Get us some rolls and mustard out of the box?"

In silence he found them. Spread out a strip of paper toweling within my reach and set them there. Withdrew.

I said, "Since I don't like ketchup I didn't buy you any."

"No onions either."

I could dip the long metal wire toward him without threat. "Here. It's hot."

He slid off the first blackened wiener and put it in a bun. I took the other, used and then passed him the mustard.

"Thank you," he said, and then looked briefly surprised at himself. We ate, he noisily. Lots of saliva.

I said, "I did so much walking uphill today that my knees hurt."

"You get over that."

Seeing how fast he ate, I quickly impaled another wiener and stuck it over the flames. "You could do this one while I eat?" He accepted the cooler end—the closest he had come. I saw what seemed to be marks and then were clearly scars inside his right hand across the pads of his fingers, as if long slashes had been made and then kept open until they healed in ridges. Quickly he edged away.

We could hear late-day birds, then human voices would override and silence them. We ate while people came down from the pass and moved on.

With his mouth full he said, "It's really Sam. Not Uncle."

I doubted even that. I said, "It's really Luna."

"Moon." He smacked his lips, gobbling his third hot dog be-fore I had finished my first. Even with the firelight on it, his face did not tell me his age except that he had no beard yet, and no Adam's apple in view. I had not known many children since I stopped being a child myself. In my apartment complex in Chapel Hill were mostly students, a few with babies, but no boys like this, the size for soccer and video games.

Steven and I had talked about children only in a negative way—how not to have any yet. I had taken the pill since he said with a flourish that he would never "sheathe my sword!" Now that my period was over, I had by habit gone back to taking Enovid just in case Robert Browning should appear in a park ranger suit.

Talking to the boy felt awkward, so in a very casual way be-tween bites I began telling him that rain was predicted tonight; there'd be room in my waterproof tent if he chose, but he could sleep with the ground squirrels and rabbits if they were his pref-erence—

In a hard angry voice he interrupted, "What is it you want?" He bared his teeth the way a dog will, a scared dog, the most likely to bite. There was food caught between incisors, no, a hole of some kind. A cavity with enamel broken out.

His anger had surprised me and made me gouge my bread so the last of my wiener fell out. I kicked it into the fire. "I don't want anything. At least not from you."

Sam put more distance between us, though it meant the smoke and the smell of burning meat would blow his way.

"Suit yourself. If you're through with that coat hanger, give me a turn."

But I did not fix another. There was no more talking. I don't know where Sam had stashed my other gifts, but while I was putting the wieners back on ice and the mustard jar into the box, he unrolled the old magazine and studied its pictures by firelight. Either he read very fast or not at all. Obviously he would never be tall enough to dunk baskets nor wide enough to butt linemen.

"I've come from North Carolina," I said. He nodded and turned a page.

So I got out my own book and read one of Tamsen Donner's early letters sent to her sister, Mrs. Jonathan E. Poor, in Newburyport, Massachusetts, which had been published in the *Sangamo Journal* before anyone could guess how her journey would end. She was writing early in their travel into the territories, then, about finding wild tulips, lupines, primroses, eardrops, larkspurs, creeping hollyhocks. What in the world was a creeping hollyhock? Tamsen had probably pressed one or drawn its picture.

That made me think about drawing hers, and I even got out my old diary and thought about catching her ghostly likeness in the unused pages. I always drew things and not people, but now I considered drawing Sam's face as it had snapped toward me over the fire, so young to show its fangs.

None of Mrs. Poor's letters to Tamsen survived. Kafka said once that letters were sent from the ghost of oneself to the ghost of the recipient, and that the written kisses in love letters "are drunk on the way by the ghosts."

I drew the outline of a woman in a wide skirt. I drew a cartoon face whose bared teeth had a hole in the middle. Before I could check Sam's expression again he suddenly slipped behind the boulder. "Sam?" I could hear the flapping of those hopeless yellow sandals.

That evening the rain was light, almost a mist, but the wind blew it in a wet sting on the skin. Dark came early. I crawled into my tent with the radio and a big battery lantern that would glow through the translucent fabric and make me easy to find.

But not until I had turned off both and was in my bag half asleep did the boy say through the flap, "It's me, don't shoot."

I unzipped so he could back in, sliding off his sandals. He wrapped himself in the army blanket (damp) and rolled as far away from me as he could. That wasn't very far.

"I don't have a gun to shoot anybody," I finally said.

He mumbled, "I'll get you one."

In the morning he slipped out without waking me but left his blanket behind, carefully folded.

Certain that Sam would be back and curious about him, I decided to do exactly as I had told Dad on my card—take a vacation, in some ways my first vacation ever. No business executive kept a tighter schedule than Dad assigned me as a child: day camps and clubs, Scouts, sports, parish volunteers, lessons in dance, art, and embroidery, math tutors, piano practice, field trips, guided tours, teeth straightening. He would read through the yellow pages of each new town, set up these appointments, and go away. Priscilla Stone by herself had to move me from one self-improvement to the next. As soon as it became clear that I did well at the library book club and poorly on the swim team, there would be more new cities, schools, libraries, instructors. I've sometimes thought that when I was at last on my own at college, I chose to "break down" the way an overworked engine would have to. After the hospital I had to prove I was not too sick to live alone or support myself. I worked day and night; even well-adjusted commercial artists have to work day and night just to earn rent and food. Add a doctoral student to the household, and I got capital *E* exhausted.

At this echo of my mother, I had to grin. Her habit was to use capitals or letters that seemed to spell one way and then didn't. A storm had her grumbling that the weather was W-E-T-Rainy; steaming casseroles would be set on the table with the warning that they were Hee-oh-H-T. And until she decided I'd grown up, even her swearing was censored by abbreviation: her G.D. Divorce Lawyer, for instance, and my favorite—the last-minute revision of F-U-C-Kittycat. "I don't give an F-U-C-Kittycat if he *does* marry the little B-I-T-C-Hore."

I hoped she was enjoying Europe with Aunt Evelyn. Not a dull moment with Priscilla Stone, but her husband left her anyway.

Not me. I was the leaver; I was on vacation from love.

Sam did not come to my camp in daytime, so I wandered by car or on foot through the lower hills around Reno. Some of their surfaces were coming to life overnight with a layer of desert flowers and insects. The spring sky got bluer. In fast-food joints I read about Tamsen and felt guilty that in every season calories now came so easily to all of us.

The next few evenings Sam appeared at my campsite for a fast supper but not conversation. Whether he ate anything else all day I wasn't sure. Since it didn't rain, he did not stay the night.

I began to press him. "Where have you been?"

"On the move," he'd answer.

I asked what had made the scars in his right hand. The first time he pretended not to hear. On another night he said, "A man did it," and thrust the fingers into his jacket pocket.

He had to be much older than I'd first thought or he looked, maybe as old as thirteen, but stunted. I brought him from Sparks a bottle of vitamin pills, but he recoiled as if I might poison him for fun, although this time he did elect to sleep behind the boulder.

I thought darkness and the nylon barrier might be easier to talk through. "Now Sam. Sam? If you're hiding out or something, Sam, I'm not going to tell. I could have reported you already when I went into Truckee today."

From a distance his preadolescent voice said, "I was in the van. If you went to the wrong place I could have got out there. Hitched a truck."

"You were in my van? All the time?"

"Who did you call?"

"My, ah, stepmother, Corinne." From a pay phone. "I was calling my father, really, but he was working out at the spa." Getting younger for her. And, obviously, neither one worried about me.

"I nearly got out and run then. What'd you call him for?"

"I think I got tired of how quiet everything is on the mountain."

He said he liked it.

"Sam, don't you have any family? Don't you have a home someplace?"

After a long wait he said, "I got sold out of it."

"What!"

"I'm going to sleep."

"Sam? Sam! Sold by who? Sold by your family? Sold for money, you mean? Sold to who? Whom, I guess."

Nothing but an owl noise came back.

"Sam, that's terrible. Don't joke about such a thing. Are you serious?"

Not even the owl this time.

I lay in the dark, thinking: *Sold for what?* What would you sell boys for? Maybe in trade for your own cocaine. Maybe for migrant labor. Maybe to furnish another man sex. Sam was too small to be good for much heavy work. Males forced into prostitution would once have seemed unthinkable to me, but last year I'd seen a black teenage boy brought into emergency after a stabbing, who when his mama died had been rented out by her boyfriend. That slickly dressed boy with the watch and gold chains seemed satisfied with street life, arrogant; he could still strut with one arm in a sling and, no, he had no idea whose knife had cut him. Called it an accident. "It was a walk-by cutting. You've heard of drive-by shootings? This was a walk-by cuttin'." I, who had been down the hall delivering medical sketches and overheard, ended up quizzing the unfazed cop who had brought the boy in for treatment.

"It happens," he answered me with a shrug. "Maybe five to seven percent of everybody that disappears every year will never be found. Some die, of course. Some end up in big cities. But, lady, if you ever have a boy or girl kidnapped and used for shoplifting and porno movies and sex and as much as a year goes by—listen, you don't want that kid back. He's ruint. This boy here probably never had much in him to ruin."

Remembering, I put my mouth close to the tent flap. "How old are you, Sam?" Nothing. How old had they made him? "Sam, you could report to the police anybody that sold you. Anybody that bought you, too. They need to be stopped." Of course Sam might be ruint in other ways, for other reasons, and just lying for sympathy.

"You let it alone," he said, and then added, "Luna," the first time in days he'd said my name.

"Was this in Reno?"

After another pause he said, "San Francisco."

"I don't see how you got all the way up here by yourself from San Francisco."

"I wasn't by myself. I'm going to sleep."

"Well, now I can't sleep for worrying. You must be headed to someplace or somebody. A sister, maybe. A brother?" I waited. "They've got offices now that will find you nice foster parents. Or could put you in a boys' school where you'd be safe. There must be residential schools on the reservation." Not a word. I said desperately, "There are nuns!"

When nothing was said I lay down again and was almost asleep when a harsh voice, so changed that a third person seemed to have arrived, said, "A rough set of fingers gives a different hand job."

I put my own hand over my mouth. Now that I'd quit babbling a few distant frogs thawed out their voices. Mine did not work as well. "Sam. I'm so sorry, Sam."

"You? What's it got to do with you? I'm going to sleep."

A rising wind suddenly slapped the tent so hard I begged him to come inside. He wouldn't. I said I was moving outdoors myself, then, and would also sleep by the boulder. Angrily he told me to stay where I was. A splatter of small rocks then struck the tent slope.

"You've no call to throw stuff at me, Sam-Somebody, me who's never done a thing to you!" A larger one hit broadside. I was afraid the tent would tear. "All right, all right!" I shouted. "I'm going to sleep."

"About time."

THE SHARP TEETH OF LOVE

That night when Tamsen Donner came it was not as a phantom—see? I know where the edge of reality lies!—she just appeared in a perfectly normal dream, and we were nowhere near the Sierra Nevada but in adjoining seats in the Varsity movie theater in downtown Chapel Hill. I kept thinking I'd never dreamed of being at the movies before, and with a film running it was like double value. (When the dreamer knows she's dreaming, that's called lucid dreaming: my favorite.) Naturally Tamsen knew nothing about movies and didn't even watch the screen; she paid attention only to me instead of the colored images. In Chapel Hill, nobody would look twice at her hairstyle or clothes. She might have been a fan of the Grateful Dead, a hippie-holdout, a guide at a nearby historical museum, or just in costume for the Carolina Playmakers. She kept standing in front of me so I could not see clearly the film about Catholics, with its priest on-screen intoning, "There are seven capital sins, three theological virtues," while he heaped up counters, or perhaps they were poker chips. "Four moral virtues." He fixed me head-on via the camera with eyes so blue I thought Paul Newman must be playing the part. He said very carefully, "There are seven candlesticks, churches, trumpets, thunders, vials, spirits, and stars." He held high something I did not recognize except it was not the Host. "There are seven seals."

He was in color, of course; Steven's dreams never were.

Again Tamsen blocked my view. In the dark she still kept the drabness of a sepia print, but she was shading her eyes against Technicolor. "You can go snowblind," she said to me while one of the moviegoers made shushing sounds.

I knew that; some of the Donner Party who tried to hike over the winter mountains did; Stanton, for example, and then he died. I could not see the priest, who added, as if in triumph, that there were seven sacraments, seven gifts of the Holy Spirit.

In dreams I rarely speak—the other characters intuit my thoughts. I thought about Stanton feeling ahead with his bare hands, snow upon snow. She read my mind easily. "The Forlorn Hope," she said with a nod, giving the traditional name for the group of eighteen who had set off on crude snowshoes and (starving, freezing) finally on the day after Christmas ate both the arms and legs of Patrick Dolan from Iowa.

The priest's face was blotched by the words THE END, followed by rolling names and credits. On all sides people stood up and pushed to the aisle as they do when the bus stops, the plane lands. By mental telepathy I reminded Tamsen that those athletes whose plane had crashed in the Andes had also eaten human flesh to survive, and had compared that horrible necessity to the sacrificial body and blood of the Mass.

She waved a hand—perhaps because she did not know what an airplane was?—and would clearly have none of it, since as far as I know she never ate human flesh herself. On the marriage-finger of her thin white hand I saw a wide gold band. I wondered whose surname was engraved with hers inside: Tamsen Dozier / Tamsen Donner? Tully, her first husband, dead of the cholera back in North Carolina, Tamsen Eustis / Tully Dozier. Two dead children back there, too, Dozier children.

Theatergoers were clearing out. The lights came up and faded Tamsen somewhat. I wanted badly to know what unfinished business had brought Tamsen back, and why to me—for if she could come in a dream-place of Chapel Hill, mine was the mind she wanted. There was one lucid-dreaming moment when the Dreamer-me said to the Waker-me, *Tomorrow, call your doctor;* but I could not hear that voice for the rising symphonic music that makes such a special pleading on film, such angst, such glee, in the ear. And besides, Tamsen was there, leaning over my seat halfway down the middle section of the movie house.

I have no theories about the dead, not even whether souls live on or not, much less whether any ongoing spirits do (or can) keep up on subsequent earthly events or must stay locked into their own mortal time spans. Did Tamsen's ghost "remember" Tully

Dozier and those dead children at all; had she "met" them over yonder? And did she know that her late-born daughters made it through the snow without her, that Frances and Eliza Donner along with Patty Reed (then nearly eighty) had come to dedicate the Donner monument in 1918? Had her specter been watching then? Was it required of me to bring a ghost up to date, to tell her that Donner Lake was now a reservoir, that a children's hospital had been built off Donner Pass Road? If she could see me, she could see water, the hospital?

My thoughts were a turmoil, then, not merely questions, so Tamsen could not absorb what must have hit her like a dust storm. She reached for my hand and turned it in hers. In thirty seconds the ring had disappeared from its white circle on her skin; my doubts had erased it. Nor did I wear an engagement ring; Steven had considered it sexist for men to mark women with possessive symbols. (Or maybe he was just stingy.)

Her cold fingertips made me shiver. Actually her hand felt more like an icy mitten without distinctive fingers. Did she still have a fingerprint? A chill ran up my arm and froze the elbow. I woke to find my arm half out the tent opening into the cold night air.

"Sam? Are you still there?"

This time he came and squatted by the tent flap. "You had a bad dream."

"I'm not sure it was bad."

"Noises like that—it's bad." He almost touched me; I could feel the moment when he chose not to do so. "Go back to sleep," he said, and I did.

Thereafter Sam was willing to ride up front beside me in the van. His profile was worth drawing, to explore whether the round cheeks could be shown as not cherubic at all, or how to convey flat black eyes that were far too old for a face that had never been shaved.

I decided to think about Sam and not Tamsen. When Edison

made his talking machine, everybody thought it was magic. Tamsen's apparent ghost was not magic, not supernatural, though I did not understand the principle. Sam was real. Together we drove mornings downhill into warmer weather and normal America, to eat at the Dairy Queen and read posters for rock musicians performing in Sparks or Reno (Papa Clutch and the Shifters). He went with me to bookstores, where the titles of poetry books also sounded like MTV and rock groups. I bought sketch pads and tried to make of Sam what I called "a faithful copy." He would not pose, so I had to do it by memory, or when he had dozed off by the campfire.

Once when he saw my awkward drawing he said, "Do yourself first."

"I'm not distinctive," I said. "And look how fat I'm getting!"

He turned around, showed me his buttocks, pinched with one hand. "Fat is OK," he said, as if showing merchandise. "You're still a chicken butt."

I was shocked and tore up my rough sketch of his face.

Sometimes at night when he slept in the tent and I sat up and tried to reconstruct in the dark his face, his hair, those awful scars in one hand, I would lecture myself. *Listen Luna Stone, you're nobody's fool; you know love doesn't cure everything, even tough love, whatever that is. Sam is much tougher than you'll ever be and he's not your vacation; you're not his. OK, so today you heard him laugh happily; it was the first time; it was the only time; so what? It was a rubber-hammer-to-the-kneecap laugh. Any stranger could bang him there. Well, that's terrific, that's just great, BANG him, oh that's wonderful. You're just a bundle of charity.*

One time I got, by general delivery, a postcard from Major Martin Stone. "Priscilla and Aunt Evelyn are doing London. I'll let you know if the bridge falls down."

I put that in the glove compartment and for no special reason asked Sam suddenly, "Tell me what he looks like."

Caught off-guard, from the way he frowned and mumbled, twitched his mouth, I think he did try. Then he shrugged. From this I decided that the man who had slashed his hand was some-body nondescript. It did something to me, thinking that evil could not be recognized for itself but stood next to you, buying stamps at the post office.

On the Reno streets, Sam became especially uneasy, then grew proportionally more relaxed the farther we drove into the countryside. So I widened our scope. To Virginia City, the top of Mount Rose. I filled Sam's lap with tourist junk and thus con-firmed that he could read but in a monotonous, mechanical voice. He had learned slow reading to please others, not himself. I thought of the last century's music boxes with automatons, human figures that played their robot music; we were uneasy that Caruso's voice came disembodied off a celluloid cylinder when we needed stand-ins, human counterparts. Sam read like a coun-terpart, a teacher's mannequin sent to the front of the class to pre-tend he was a regular boy.

But I wanted his regular self to learn to love Blake and puzzle over Kafka, so I forced him to read aloud while I drove or in camp, where I claimed my eyes were smarting, had him make long and laborious recitations about the Comstock Lode, Mark Twain, the Ponderosa Ranch from the *Bonanza* TV series, and those thirty thousand gold seekers who came over what's now I-80 only a year or so after Tamsen Donner died.

He grumbled, "This is more reading than I've done in twelve years," which I took to be his age.

When we drove the streets of Reno he read even worse than usual, breaking off in midsentence and mispronouncing even the shortest words. I thought the nondescript man or his nondescript friends might be living there. As we drove out of the city and out of danger, Sam would even read about the Donners in his slow, hesitant voice.

"Had you heard about the Donner Party before?"

"Naw. I saw *The Blob* on TV and it ate people. You like vam-pires?"

We were not far then from the Ponderosa Ranch, which had been built, of course, *after* the TV series to duplicate the Hollywood set. I asked if he wanted to go and, for a flash, saw the Child in Sam want it, then the Cynic change his mind.

"Stupid Cartwrights."

It was easy to mock the virtuous cowboy myth now that he had seen for himself that the Sierra Nevada was dog-eat-dog terrain where the Brass Rule—*Do or be done to*—prevailed. Sam was too young to hold this view. Hell, I was too young myself.

"What are you, Sam, about twelve?"

He said yes so firmly that he wasn't sure that I believed him. "When are you leaving?"

"Leaving? I hadn't thought about it. Leaving the camp, you mean?"

He had turned to look out the window.

"Leaving you?"

He gave several reflexive jerks of the shoulders, shaking off my distasteful question. But I saw it was the accurate one. "I've already left somebody back in Reno, a man I almost married, and it took me forever to do that."

"I don't care if you leave."

"I said I'm not leaving."

"Makes no difference to me!"

We both sounded furious. I decided to offer him a gift, to treat him like a grownup. "When I was in college," I began, getting nervous, "I had a, well, sort of a breakdown. I was in a hospital." He turned toward me frowning or sympathizing, it was hard to tell. "It was like stepping out of a life that went right on without me like a train or something while I didn't move at all. When I stepped back on, it was a different train going someplace else. Someplace better, I hope."

"You got well."

Statement or question? "I got different. And now, well it was April 22 exactly, I stepped out of my life again to see what it looked like. And the train went on with Steven Grier to California without me."

"He'll be back for you."

"No. He won't."

We rode on. "OK," he said.

I wanted him to ask me what my new life looked like under this scrutiny, but he was only twelve. I told him anyway. "And it's not what I meant it to be." My voice was half a whine. Tamsen Donner had earned the right to complain, two thousand miles out of Springfield, where the worst winter snows had never risen above her yardstick.

"What you want me to read next?" He sounded embarrassed, shifting colored folders in his lap. My confidences had embarrassed rather than reassured him. But if he was "ruint" the way that cop had meant, Sam was way beyond embarrassing.

"I want you to tell me something about yourself and your own life."

Instead, painstakingly, he read: "After her family died of fever at Christmas, 1831, Tamsen Donner went home to . . . to . . ."

"Newburyport."

". . . in Massachusetts. Her brother wrote her in 1836 and asked her to come to his farm in Illinois to teach his children. There she became a schoolteacher and had taken her pupils on a field trip where she met George Donner, who had already buried two wives and fathered ten children. They were married in 1839."

I said, "Go back just a little way in history, Sam, and people just died like flies. When I see the TV news I try to remember that today at least children don't die all the time."

"I wish you did have a TV instead of that old radio."

"Oh, all right, don't talk, don't tell me anything, don't bother," I said, wondering if my impatience sounded like Steven Grier's.

We drove into the High Sierra and were peppered briefly by a rattle of hail, then dropped out of it. I thought that, by contrast with whoever had injured Sam, implacable nature was almost clean in its disregard for individuals. On other days, of course, I thought the opposite.

As we rose and fell on these journeys, except when I made him read, Sam was mostly silent. But Fool Luna; I poured out my heart so like would call to like. I confided to him about all those spankings Dad had given me, how hard and abrupt they had been, for unclear offenses. The shift in Sam's face told me that he dismissed such punishment as a luxury domestic problem, something restricted to the upper classes. I told him more about Steven, that I had felt used and drained, had left him before he could leave me. I added that marriage had always meant to me: *For Better, for Worse, for Good.* Sam didn't care much, did volunteer that he didn't know who his own daddy was. I told him that for the first week in the loony bin my nervous system lost track of automatic responses so I did not know when laughing or crying would be appropriate. He measured me then with his opaque black eyes. He said, as if to convince me, "You got well." I asked if he had ever seen a ghost. No, but his sister once saw the Virgin's statue blink her eyes. "Not just once, either. Over and over."

So finally I told him Tamsen Donner was not just back in time, that Tamsen's spook had begun to visit me. In camp.

He stacked up all the tourist folders, set them on the van's floor mat, and pinned them there with his sandal. "What's she look like?"

"Light brown like an old photograph."

"Does she moan or something? Does it scare you?" To my headshakes he added, "What's she want?"

"I can't figure it out. It's like the Ancient Mariner stopping the wedding guest—why me? She doesn't seem to want anything except to go over what happened."

"Next time you call me. I'll run her off."

"Thank you, Sam."

With his scarred hand he rubbed above both eyebrows, a gesture he often made when thinking hard. "We could get us a cross. It scares off vampires."

"I don't think she means any harm."

"OK I lied about going into park headquarters. I been inside a lot where the windows don't lock good. I've seen that movie a hundred times almost. She's not in it."

"Not her picture, no."

"Does she say whether that last guy killed her?"

"Not so far. Keseburg always claimed she had fallen into the creek and then froze overnight."

"But he did eat her, though."

"I guess so. Tamsen hasn't said." It was a relief to talk so matter-of-factly.

"She must still be mad about that."

"If so, why wouldn't she haunt her cannibal?" I'd given this some thought. "In New Guinea and places like that, people thought they'd turn into whatever they ate, so you'd get strong as a lion or fast as an antelope. And then there's the Mass, where the bread and wine really turn into Jesus after you swallow." (Sam was nodding; ah, he as well as his sister was Catholic.) "Wouldn't you think that anybody who ate a woman would feel her inside you? Kind of?"

Sam made a disgusted vomit-face, but he was as fascinated, I saw, by the lurid part of the Donner story as he had been by horror movies. "I wouldn't eat any dead body no matter what."

"Don't be so sure. We none of us know what we'd do to stay alive."

We drove a lot farther before he finally said that he could maybe eat part of a foot if it was cut up into little unrecognizable pieces. A foot stew, I said. We were laughing.

·   ·   ·

NOW THAT I'D SEEN SAM laugh enough to know how the muscles moved the planes of his face, I made him pose. He had trouble sitting still.

Faces were harder than flowers. First I tried capturing the profile he'd shown me in the van, the egg-shaped head at an angle, the eye halfway down, the base of the nose half between eyebrow and chin. Those were the proportions, but, no, his head was rounder than an egg, the nose less cubical, the eye less spherical, and the bony eyebrow ridges sharper than I had noticed. I did not like to watch him swipe across that brow with the scars inside his fingers.

When finally I began to catch his likeness and handed him the pad, he sucked a surprised breath through the hole in his front teeth.

"Can I have it?"

"Of course, but I'm getting better with practice; you'll like the next ones better." I felt flattered, but after he'd carried away the second drawing, the third, even every one of my rough geometric false starts, I decided he was simply afraid that some pursuer would recognize him on paper.

"Are you tearing these up?" I finally demanded. He said no. I did not know where he hid out in the state park when he was not with me. When I rented my space for another week, I tried to get Sam to come into headquarters with me; I could claim he was a friend or my adopted son, and thus he could move around more openly, but he said no.

"The ranger's seen me. He's caught me inside before."

I reached out and, before he could flinch away, touched my finger to the cleft in his upper lip. "There's a story that when the angels put a soul into a baby that's getting ready to be born, they lay a finger here, like shush, so it won't be able to talk for a year, and by then it won't remember Heaven."

"Shit," he said, jerking back before I finished talking.

"OK, so I got a little cute."

"You and Tamsen Donner talk about stuff like that?"

"She hasn't been back."

I made a full-length drawing of how Sam had looked when a cold wind whipped his coarse black hair—a baby Geronimo or Sitting Bull with a touch of Frederick Douglass. I knew no fierce Orientals to name, though Chinese laborers had worked surrounding mines, had laid the railroad track; and surely some must have left a gene or two in the population. I liked this new sketch and hid it from him.

"Sam, are you Indian? I'm part Cherokee myself."

"I'm mostly Mex and Cuban. I think my daddy was Cuban. I think Castro's got him in jail."

On some of the warming spring days when I did not draw and Sam did not ride the roads with me, I read books from the Sparks library with an avidity lost since my English-major days. I read for the first time since childhood H. G. Wells's *Time Traveler,* where the traveler, like Tamsen, took his machine into the future, took himself all the way to the very end of time. It made me wonder if Tamsen had been chatting with Sierra Nevada visitors every year, if maybe she'd met the first Hearst who came hiking through toward riches. When we went to town for groceries, Sam would not go in the library, but I checked out books for him, too. He liked pictures of the place we were in, a kind of double-viewing like that I had experienced in my dream. He studied the differences in bark between Jeffrey and Ponderosa pines, a mountainside marked in belts to define plant-life zones from the chaparral on up. He would thrust a page under my eye and point so I could pronounce for him "Sonoran," "Hudsonian," the "Mariposa lily." Especially he liked bringing a flower to have me draw it, so the real thing and its copy were there alongside. If we hiked together now, he drew my attention to the hawks and buzzards and jays, since he was always scanning at large, while I made him notice the first green breaking the soil as spring advanced slowly to us from the foothills. He was talking; I was talking. *What do you make of that, Steven Grier?*

But what would become of Sam when I finally did drive away? How would he even eat?

Gradually the rains felt warmer. Mosquitoes hatched out in the puddles. Sam was willing now to sleep every night inside the tent. We talked in the dark to each other, and while we were talking, Tamsen stayed away.

"You haven't been in school all year, have you?"

"They threw me out of school. I was selling bennies."

"What about juvenile court?"

"What about it?"

"You and your sister, Evangela, were Catholic. Didn't a priest help you?"

"Hitler was Catholic."

Mornings when we looked up, the snowcaps were more ragged. A garter snake came into camp; nothing poisonous; I thought of the Reno waitress I'd overheard saying: *All I want is to find a man who'd pick up a snake for me.* I guess she meant a rattler. Love.

"What you doing?"

When I drew, not only Sam but all the Griers, my doctors, Mother, and Aunt Evelyn, Sam would catch me mixing words with the sketch, copying from books on the edges of what I had drawn. I read him the latest sentence I'd wanted to save: " 'Colors are the deeds and sufferings of light.' Goethe."

"Gertie who?"

"Dirty Gertie who wants to take you to the dentist. Get that front tooth filled."

"No way."

"When it breaks off you'll be snaggletoothed all your life and it'll rot and stink."

"Doesn't matter to me."

"No girl will kiss you."

"No girl better try."

"I'd call it a distinctive identifying mark."

He frowned. "So I'll grow a mustache."

Until now, I'd always assumed people became friends to the very degree they were able to lay open for each other their separate lives for comparison, that the mix-and-match process was essential. Lovers, too. That was really what bothered Steven when I did not talk, did not "share," as he so often said. Yet Sam told me almost nothing about himself, even when asked. He had lived in San Francisco, had seen Las Vegas, had one sister grownup to whom the Mother of God had squinted, and one brother in jail.

"Where?" I meant the sister, the brother, anybody. "Where?"

He said he did not know.

Like booty, like trade beads, I piled up before him my own parents, their divorce, my scientific artwork (he wanted me to draw his appendix but claimed he did not remember where or when it had been surgically removed). I even struggled to recall the fool girl I had been at his age, but I had been caught up then in melodramatic stories. I thought I might become a nun and finish what my mother had started; she discouraged my vocation. I loved the saints' stories, the literalness of relics, the legends about Padre Pio having stigmata for fifty years.

But if Sam had ever been caught up in that dreamy devotion which expected, any minute, that God would intervene on any boring army post and *do* something, I could not find a counterpart. Listening, he gave me no clue to what had fascinated him beyond movies and TV and the taller boys in his neighborhood who were running coke.

Nonetheless, day by day, inch by inch, the boy sat closer to me, looked more directly into my face, dredged up that rare smile that changed him into a poster boy for southwestern travel. The brown hole eroding between two front teeth made me ache, but I was faithful to reproduce it in every sketch. I could touch Sam now while passing food or books, but never unexpectedly.

I had bought him a sleeping bag, which he used in the tent, so

I became privy to his sighs and nightmares and he to mine. Worse were the groans. That talkative cop back in Chapel Hill told me they have to dope up girls and boys for the porno flicks, the disproportionate size and all, and that each confiscated reel shows their Technicolor sedation, and still in the sound track you hear them groan.

Yes, there's a circle of Hell for those moviemakers. Listening to Sam as he grunted and shifted, I knew I would dig it myself.

He woke me some nights, too. "Luna Moon? You're talking. You're talking out loud. Is she there?"

"I think it was my father."

Some days I decided I had stitched Sam's abusive biography out of whole cloth and coincidence, the same way I'd summoned Tamsen Donner from sleep, who was now only dust on a mountain range. The summer before, I'd heard, the U.S. Forest Service with twenty-six metal detectors swept Prosser Reservoir and the area around Prosser Dam, but found nothing clearly related to the Donner Party. They clicked up oxen shoes, parts of a plow, a draft-horse shoe, some possible buttons. I had some nerve to reach beyond all their scientific batteries to Tamsen, beyond Social Service and welfare workers to Sam.

In the increasing warm sunlight, I made Sam pose with his shirt off. He was still far too thin, but we had both gained weight.

Then the ranger notified me that a new wave of campers would be moving in. No one could squat on a campsite for too long. Turnabout.

Sam hid while the ranger and I had our polite discussion. Afterward I had to call him from behind the boulder. "So where shall we go?"

The stare he gave me! The mix of its doubt, accusation, surprise, all over nothing but the one pronoun: *we.*

"Sam. I told you I wouldn't leave you."

"I can look after myself."

"So can I, but we get along OK, don't we? So let's don't leave each other yet. I do hate to leave Tamsen, though." *Could* I leave her?

Seated in pine needles, Sam picked at his new sneakers.

"So it's settled. You've got all the tourist stuff—so where should we go next?"

He untied and retied the blue shoelaces, then wiped his forehead with that damaged hand. I waited. "Desolation Wilderness," he finally said.

"You like the name," I guessed.

"Don't you?"

"Yes, I like it. Let's pack up in the morning. Have you got other stuff"—I waved an arm—"uphill?"

"Not much," was all he said.

PART 3

The Carnivores

~

Desolation Wilderness

SINCE WE LIKED THE NAME, Sam and I kept waiting for the park to become desolate. The main trail from Echo Lake into the wilderness climbs a set of steps held in place by used railroad ties and has been worn into a neat, broad path for city dwellers. The whole area is only fifteen miles long (so Sam read to me off a forest service sheet), and maybe eight miles wide; and in this sudden warm weather we were finding the trail crowded.

They were vacating the desolate parts for us, I decided, so I smiled and spoke pleasantly to the day hikers who passed, mostly young and healthy with faces I took to be wholesome; but each backpacker who came in sight ahead of us made Sam tense until the stranger grew close enough to be dismissed. It was even worse with men who unexpectedly caught up from behind. A twig snapped at his back made Sam jump and even take one or two running steps.

I finally said, "If all these people are making you jumpy we could go someplace else."

His neck got ramrod stiff to keep him from twanging another look over one shoulder. "They're OK."

"You're not."

"Don't be a mama."

It was as if my chest blushed from the ribs out with the surprising warmth that brought, so I made my voice gruffer than I felt. "Jumpy *and* touchy."

In the next narrow section he moved in front, his bowl of black hair maybe as high as my shoulder, his torso still boy-soft, the buttocks slightly too high above legs that were growing at a faster rate.

Since his face was hidden, perhaps it would be safe to ask: "What's your real mama like?"

We walked. He spoke one word I could not make out.

"What?"

"Dead."

I didn't believe him.

"She'd have made three or four of you," he said.

"You don't know how thin I *used* to be."

A line of Boy Scouts leaving the wilderness came toward us and wound past, some of them saying "Hey!" to Sam. When the last uniform had edged by, Sam stopped so abruptly I almost ran into him, drew alongside, saw how he was watching them move downhill with what I read as contempt and envy scrambled in his face.

We came to a meadow slope beside a much smaller Alpine lake and rested and ate nuts and raisins and admired the granite mountains all around, their tops still white. Sam washed his feet in the icy water; he didn't want his new sneakers to smell. From his pack he took Steven's old golf cap and put it on, tucking his black hair out of sight. Under the pines we passed back and forth the trail mix I had brought so we could feel authentic. Rat food, he called it. "Not that you've ever seen a rat up close," he said. "You hit one with a board and it screams, did you know that? Screams like a baby."

He spread out in a sunny spot softened by forest duff and fell asleep. The search for an enemy face had tired him, I decided. He had thicker eyelashes than I'd been putting in his portraits.

I was restless but also reluctant to leave the camp. He would wake up and have his worst expectations of abandonment confirmed. Finally I set my pack near his head so it would be the first thing he saw when he woke, and pinned there a note that said I was walking in the area just off-trail. I drew Uncle Sam for the greeting, a crescent moon for the signature.

Then I climbed through trees up a long granite bluff with some vague idea of keeping the lake in view to guide me back. In sunny patches black butterflies with orange-tipped wings were working; I followed them toward water noises and found a small but churning creek that must feed into the lake below, where Sam lay sleeping. Another excellent landmark. Mosquitoes were biting, too. As I walked I sometimes would see in soft wet sand tiny paw prints, maybe of ground squirrels or chickarees. I was not drawing animals these days, having skipped straight from plants to people. Birds? The trouble with living now is that every Audubon in the world has been there before you. I moved on across loose scree and a slope with stony outcrops among scattered trees.

I rested on a fallen pine trunk with most of the bark gone and was inspecting the shallow grooves where borers had cut their delicate canals into wood when there came a sharp whistle—human, not bird. Downstream the water kept rushing by, and all I could see that way was a faint gleam where the lake must be. Uphill the whistle seemed to call *Cuckoo, cuckoo.*

To locate the sound, I climbed on the log and shaded my eyes. Not far up the mountain on the highest of a pile of gray boulders stood a naked man, legs spread, his back to me. I could not tell much at this distance—a lean shape, hair that was brown or reddish, depending on how the sun and shade fell. When he turned his head slightly there might have been either a beard or a dirty face.

Since for all I knew he might be Sam's enemy and undressed for action, I hoped I wouldn't fall off the tree trunk and draw attention to myself.

The man turned to look into the frothy stream that was rushing by him and coming toward me, put one hand to his ear. Then both hands? Scratching?

Now he was stretching, then he climbed down one layer of rock and pulled on shorts. He slapped his leg after a mosquito. He must be chilly in the darker shade where he now stood. He took a green shirt off a nearby limb, put that on, and hopped barefoot from the wide stone to a smaller, then a smaller one still, until he was on the ground and hidden by trees.

It scared me to lose sight of him so suddenly. Sam's fear was contagious. I ducked low, slipped off the dead tree, and tried to move quietly downhill beside the stream, since I was no longer sure how far off the trail I had wandered. Was the man camping up there alone? Had he climbed on the rocks to look for someone?

Sliding down a long slab of stone I scraped a thigh and an elbow. The illusory shine of lake water between the trees had disappeared, but I kept following the noisy stream down a hillside steeper and rougher than the way I'd ascended; in fact, nothing looked familiar. That is, it all looked too familiar, too much the same, with more paw prints but not a single mark my boots had left. When again I heard the distant two-note whistle I began scrambling on loose rocks and then slid over fresh pine needles. He was much closer.

At last the water glimmered ahead. I ran toward it, but this was a different part of the lake with no grassy beach, only pines and huge rocks all the way to the edge. A fish broke the surface. Which way to go?

Away from those starved mosquitoes, first of all. I hurried right across a hoof-pocked deer trail, clambering over stones shaped like hippos or elephants, then having to detour inland around some that were too sheer. Ahead of me rose smoke, light and pale and drifting over the lake. Since Sam would not have lit a fire without me, I slowed down and picked my way carefully over rock and between twisted trees that had rooted in its cracks.

The naked man, now in his green shorts and unbuttoned shirt, was lying on a foam pad near his campfire, reading a book. His was a young fire, smoky and threatening to go out. He was still bare-foot so would not be able to chase me far. I did not know whether Sam was beyond him or somewhere on the lakeshore behind, though a trail seemed to lead from his camp downhill. In the cold shadow of a boulder I sank down to puzzle it out. Something was cooking on his fire, a meaty soup.

Its odor seemed to steam unpleasantly around me while I squatted there, wondering if Sam was worried. I peeked at this stranger with his wispy red-brown hair (fine in texture; he'd be bald before forty) and a matching beard that curled but seemed to need vitamins. A long string was hanging from the ear I could see—no, an electrical wire. A hearing aid! This discovery re-moved all threat, although there must be deaf rapists in the world.

I rose and moved noisily toward his campfire, but he turned a page without noticing. My boot rolled a stone, snapped a stick; the bearded man never looked up. His absorption was a mark in his favor.

At last I called, "Hello?"

He jerked once at the unexpected sight of me, then nicked his finger into the book. "Hello." His voice was just slightly too loud, the inflection on the first syllable.

I came forward, letting his face assemble itself for evaluation. This could not be Sam's enemy. His eyes were brown, and every-thing around them bore the risk of curling: his scanty beard, fine-textured hair, even his eyebrows. Yes, and the chest hair, too.

He set his book down on gravel and when I saw it was Kafka's stories, my stomach lurched. I had daydreamed of finding a man with his book, but Kafka? Too much. Almost alarming.

"Are you lost?"

"Maybe so." I hung back on the edge of his clearing. "I left my, my son at a campsite by the lake and thought this was it. Were you whistling?"

"What?"

"Whistling."

"Trying out the sound, yes." He did not stand, as if he feared frightening me. "I've got a topo map if that will help."

"The shoreline I left was grass and sand, almost a beach."

He pointed. "Then you're headed in the right direction."

I frowned at his lean-to of branches, the stones set neatly around his campfire with its cooking pot. "You seem to have settled in. I didn't think you were allowed to stay long here."

He shrugged, got slowly to his feet, and moved to stir the soup. Maybe he had killed some small local animal to give it that dense, hot smell. With back turned, his shape recalled the nakedness I'd seen posed on the rock. I was not sure whether I'd actually seen or only imagined the shadow of testicle between those long spread legs. Besides, men think they look sexy when naked in front because of the venerable penis—the vulnerable ass does more for me. Frontal nudity by emphasizing difference seems to require surrender; the backside suggests that we're-all-in-this-together. I tried to explain this to Steven once, and it hurt his feelings.

Some tenderness, a prelude to sex, did stir in me now as the firelight shone on his curly-haired thighs. He was less handsome than Steven, a supporting actor and not the star, but I liked his Achilles tendons, the backs of his knees.

He stirred the pot and replaced the lid. He squatted to poke the fire.

I was free to inspect how the wire hung from a lump like pink chewing gum inside one ear. I cannot imagine anything less sexy than a hearing aid. Deflated, I leaned on a block of granite and read the cover of his book: *Collected Stories* by Franz Kafka. The memory of reading them all at the worst possible time made me swimmy-headed, the coincidence of finding this stranger with the book made it worse. Kafka's thin face was on the cover, emphasizing the big pointed ears at the age when he went to the mountains himself, carried his tuberculosis into the high wintry air of Poland, and beat back his own nervous breakdown by writing four stories, including "The Hunger Artist."

"Sit down, you've gone pale," the man said. "Have you been lost for long?"

"An hour or two. I need to be going."

"Sure you're not hungry?"

I was the polar opposite of hungry. "I just follow this trail by the shore?"

"I'll come with you." He set the cooking pot on a flat rock and tucked his topo map into a pocket. "Just let me fix the fire."

Despite my objections and headshakes he doused his coals and reswept the clear area round them. When he put the Kafka book in the lean-to, I saw he had other paperback books there in clear plastic bags.

"What do you think of Kafka?" I asked him, trying not to hold my breath.

"Neurotic as hell but fascinating. What do you think?"

I said I didn't read him anymore, though once I had hung on every word. "I hung over his pages as if it was all a giant Ouija board. 'The Hunter Gracchus'—remember that? Where the dead man travels after his death and speaks from his bier?"

"It's all like that. Dead men and victims, bugs and apes and dogs under some awful power that can't ever be satisfied. I don't know what those stories mean."

"They don't exactly *mean.*" *Any more,* I thought, *than this tree and mountain mean.* But he was ready to leave by then and moved behind me as I hurried along the lake's edge. Having him at my back made me stumble ahead too rapidly, the way a tailgating automobile makes you drive too fast.

Even at speed, the walk took longer than seemed reasonable. I must have unwittingly circled half the lake. The slope to its edge grew more gentle with smaller rocks and tough grass. Ahead rose thinning smoke, so maybe Sam had fooled me and thrown in the shreds of freeze-dried bark and fragments to boil.

"I think that's it."

"What?"

I'd forgotten you don't talk to a deaf person who's directly behind you, so stopped to turn and point. "I think that's our camp!" I shouted.

"Easy," the man said with a tap on the small box inside his shirt pocket. "I can hear you."

He followed me toward an even louder shout: "Luna? Luna, is that you?" Sam's voice was high as a girl's. "Luna!" He came into sight topped by that ugly golf cap, half running toward us and carrying a twisted club of old juniper. "Who's that?" He whipped the club broadside in front of him.

I didn't know until behind me the stranger said, "Paul Cowan. I was just seeing your mother safely back to camp."

Sam's eyes locked with mine before he said, "OK."

"This is Sam." Mr. Cowan put out his hand and Sam had to do some clumsy juggling of his weapon in order to shake it. The three of us separated ourselves, awkward, in the clearing where I could smell supper—wet cardboard with salt and pepper; what a rat would like for his occasional hot meal.

"Now that you're in good hands Mrs. uh—"

"Luna Stone." He frowned until I faced him directly and said my name only a little louder. Now I had to shake hands, too—Cowan's fingers oddly smooth after Sam's, but the grip strong. He had long fingers and toes, but I had too little experience with genitalia to know if the myths were true. "Thank you again."

Sam was edging around to trace where the wire went from shirt to ear. I did feel like his mother, then, trying to teach him not to stare. "Have a beer before you go," I said.

Cowan smiled. "Yes, good. Where are you people from?"

Sam and I looked at each other like conspirators. "All over," I finally said, and sent him to fetch the six-pack where it drifted in the lake on a string. I unsnapped two from the plastic, and Sam reached out, too, but I said, "Certainly not." With a shrug he went to realign wood on the fire and add his club to the fuel.

Paul Cowan and I sat across from each other on folded towels and popped the beers. I was not sure how severe his hearing problem was nor whether the coming twilight would be enough for lip-reading.

He said, "You've come up here early—most of the campgrounds don't open till later in May."

"But everybody says this is an early spring. When did you come?"

"When there was still snow. I wanted things to be quiet themselves, for everybody, and not just quiet to me." His voice had a certain flatness to it, as if he were reading unfamiliar prose.

The sharp smell of Sam's burning club came from the fire where it was sparking. He planted himself foursquare and with no manners at all asked flatly: "You a deef man?"

Paul Cowan answered calmly, "Halfway. I was working road construction and too close to a dynamite blast. The left ear has improved some, the right ear not as much." When he turned his head I saw that a second hearing aid, presumably on battery, was in his left ear while the weaker one needed the box and wire. When he smiled his beard rose lightly and three thin wrinkles flared beside each eye. A nice smile—I hoped Sam was noticing those perfect front teeth.

Instead he whispered, "Can you hear me now? Can you hear this?"

Paul nodded. "But I'm helped by the questioning look on your face and the way your breath pushes out on a hard C and also the tip of your tongue shows when you say a word like 'this.' "

"When was your accident?" I wondered how much he'd practiced before he could link mouth movements to sounds.

"January." He pinched the right earlobe. "This one had more internal bleeding, so if after six months it still doesn't improve, well." He spread his empty fingers.

I said with fake optimism, "Then you'll go back to work?"

"That was a temporary job. I was saving to go back to school."

Sam blew a nostril to show what he thought of school.

"You can still go," I said. "In literature, I guess."

"Maybe not. I had planned on seminary. Preachers listen a lot." He took a long drink of beer. "They listen to people like Kakfa who think it was Daddy alone with Original Sin, or God alone, never themselves. Sam, what are you cooking?"

"Trail mix soup," Sam complained, waving its bland steam away. "Luna bought it."

I saw Paul Cowan register that: Luna, not Mother. "Want to pour your pot into mine? I bought real beef at Echo Lake."

I didn't want one single mouthful of real beef, but Sam was enthusiastic, so the two of them set off up the lake to check that Paul's fire was out and fetch that stew, leaving me in a jangle of nerves. Some of this sense of short breath and itchy skin might come from the surprise of finding a man so unlike Steven attractive—it was just the nakedness, I decided, that skip of preliminaries all the way down to bare body. But most was the eerie link to Franz Kafka, whom I wanted to defend. My term paper that fall semester before the hospital had been on Kafka's "Hunger Artist," about a man starving himself as a public carnival spectacle; and it had its eerie links as well, such as the fact that Kafka's tubercular larynx made swallowing difficult, and his final illness had reduced him nearly to starvation, too, by the time he was rereading that very story in proof. I had set my paper in the nineteenth-century context of real-life examples of young girls too pure to eat. P. T. Barnum actually tried to get one of them, Mollie Fancher, to join his traveling show, exhibiting her skeletal frame and parchment skin while she read printed pages solely through the tips of her bone fingers. Only one of her hands was clairvoyant; her catatonic and illiterate right arm stuck high above the bedclothes, in midair. Maybe Paul was right to ascribe Kafka's themes to morbidity (and he *was* a vegetarian), but we Catholics were taught as children about the fasting of Catherine of Siena, who yearned to live off the Host alone and would thrust twigs down her throat to make herself vomit. I had thought of her often in Chapel Hill, where they were building then the Siena Hotel, but in honor of horse racing, not of her.

Weekdays back then I kept filling note cards with this starvation stuff; weekends I was sickened by my parents' quarrels; so that December when they led me out of the dormitory people groaned at how thin I was—though I only felt unencumbered and a little cold.

To remember those bad days made me shiver even now, but I opened a second icy beer and sat closer to the fire Sam had made. As soon as the sun fell over the peaks into California, this side of the mountain grew dark and the wind blew. It played through the evergreen needles with such a mournful noise, and I had gotten myself into such a nervous state, that while I stared into the hot coals I even considered going ahead to Riverside and begging Steven's forgiveness. For a few minutes, staring into the wavering fire, I could even glimpse the blond stair-step sons we would have made together—beautiful cherub-children—could imagine myself carpooling them everywhere and sending them to bed without supper if ever they misbehaved.

But then Sam and Paul Cowan came laughing around the curve of the lake, and the mere sight of them—of the three of us, really; damaged goods—cheered me up completely.

I TOLD PAUL I had heard his whistle, not that I'd seen him with no clothes. In fact, I wished the ghost of Tamsen Donner would reappear so I could tell her I had seen him "in the flesh," but perhaps ghosts have no sense of humor?

She did not return, but Paul did—early the next morning with fish (caught from the icy lake) that we ate for breakfast, and in the afternoon on a trail Sam and I were exploring. He was easy to talk to, much different from Steven, but sometimes I would be in midparagraph when in my mind's eye all his clothing fell away and he turned into one of those muscular young men who might have stepped straight off a fitness machine and into a Blake engraving, wearing no more than a strategic drapery. Then my tongue would tangle, and I would say something garbled; but it was all right, because Paul assumed that for that moment his hearing had failed, and with an apology would ask me to say it again.

The next night he brought fruit and stayed for supper. Something had won Sam's trust; I overheard him describing a man who'd had "a poison body," and another time Sam talked about a bad time in the winter when during nights he could hear his finger and toe nails growing in the dark, and woke up every morning afraid he would have claws.

It made Paul take from his hip pocket the small volume of Kafka and point to the cover photograph. "Don't tell Luna," he said with a grin toward me, "but I bought this book because of his ears—see? They look like the ear-trumpets old ladies used to carry. I thought his stories would be full of exquisite hearing—the kind wolves have, but he never mentions it."

Gradually, without planning, our campsites adjoined and then combined. We three went hiking, ate meals, sat dreamily staring into campfires. Most of the talking took place before sunset, when there was still light enough to give Paul visual clues.

He told us he had come into the Sierra Nevada before snowmelt because of his deafness; he'd wondered if silence itself might help. When first they had fitted his hearing aid, not the cosmetic and unobtrusive kind, but with batteries so strong they required an extra pack and wire like earlier models, he'd been told to practice its use against distractions and background noise. By then he had lived some weeks with no sound at all, with the result that he felt less that his hearing had died than that the outside world had perished. Other people had come to seem like numb robots; whatever they mouthed silently to one another made him suspicious, even paranoid. Accustomed noises of his own rustling clothes (did I blush here?) and his own footsteps had gone away, and from his window he could watch dreamlike traffic flow by without a sound.

So at first this new hearing aid made a ringing telephone rattle his whole skull; the faucet drip banged onto tympana; and the gargle of car engines below his apartment sounded obscene. He'd been warned of this reaction, of course, and instructed to keep wearing the aid despite it, to turn the volume high, to retrain himself—because hearing, the doctors said, was in the brain and not the ear.

But his brain hated screeching, banging, roaring San Francisco. Remembering that African tribesmen, even when old, were said to retain their hearing, Paul decided to disobey the audiologists and start with the fewest decibels, then gradually work up. Perhaps the stillness of the winter woods would so sharpen his attention that a mouse stepping over snow would come to sound like castanets.

"And is it working?" Walking behind him on the trail, I got rid of the mental overlay of those rear-nude males from Blake's *Milton* and *Jerusalem*. "Can you hear better?"

"What?" Paul had to turn and face me while I asked again. "Oh. Some days I've thought so, but other days I know my mind's playing tricks. It *imagines* that it hears. The audiologists aren't interested in what the mind imagines."

Sam said impatiently, "But you hear Luna and me OK. You can still go preach if you want to."

"You'd never want to though, would you, Sam?"

I said that Sam and I were both cradle Catholics, and we didn't put a premium on preaching. Sam nodded. I wondered if the family who sold him had lit candles, worn rosaries.

Paul threw up his hands, saying that in California preaching was a constant. Converts could marinate themselves in one baptism after another. There were preachers for gay rights and Marxism and massage, he said. Hypnosis, Esalen, Satanism, and astrology. You could have faith in Zen, acupuncture, meditation through chemistry, deconstruction. There were congregations for Perls's Gestalt, Hare Krishna, Rolfing, Dianetics, Crystals, New Age, Jogging, and Frisbee.

At "Frisbee" Sam snatched up a flat stone and sailed it out into space, so like a normal show-off boy that my throat hurt.

"It's because California residents have been sentenced to sunshine and happiness," Paul added. "Nobody can live in a resort all year long."

"You've got earthquakes," I offered, but he shrugged. "You've had race riots."

"Californians recover very quickly," he said, adding, "Myself, I'm a Lutheran."

The Catholic "susters" never taught much about denominations, but I knew Martin Luther. *"Sola scriptura,"* I said, but could not reproduce the tone that conveyed Luther's sinful dismissal of the Mother Church from Saint Peter on down.

He said more about religion during one of our long predinner conversations, and when Paul got up to pace the campsite he probably intended to look away from my face and gesture and avoid interruption. What I intended was to watch his back and buttocks. Construction work had sculpted his surfaces, indented the spinal column. Maybe Steven's suggestion that I could draw nudes was a good one.

He began making a speech. "If Scripture alone was all there was to Luther, he could have been right at home in California, making bumper stickers." He waved off my frown. "What the cults and sects love in California is initiation. People want to be initiated into an elite group. To be Illuminati or Rosicrucians or alchemists or anything else. Initiation evens them all out at a high level, so you can be a fry cook and still rub elbows with some TV star who's seeking enlightenment. Californians are suckers for hand signals and secret languages, whether they go back to Atlantis with Shirley MacLaine or tell the future with this week's Delphic Oracle."

Was that what I was doing? Channeling? Getting ready to table-tap code from the spirit world?

"It's idolatry!" Paul said. Sam yawned.

"You Protestants think everything's idolatry." But when he turned in his pacing something happened to my stomach lining— that moment when appetite disappears and you doubt you will ever eat again. Was this a new anorexia, or was I getting lovesick just because of how his backside looked from a distance?

"The climate's too good here," said Paul, "and the cost of living too high, so it seems anybody who's sensitive ought to reject these worldly pleasures and rise to some higher spiritual plane. One of my neighbors built her own prayer wheel and slept under it on the bare wood floor with a big fan blowing all night long! Soon she'll be giving lessons in how you do that. They love Buddhism out here. You could make a fortune selling potted bo trees somebody had blessed. But Luther—no—Luther thought God started us off with a good world and a good body to move around in it. You know where he was when he got this big revelation about God? He was in the privy in a tower at Wittenberg monastery, so high that gravity took everything down and out better than any flush toilet. Sure, he was a raunchy, crude man, but he was healthier than one of your monk nuts that would scald himself for God."

"That's not *my* monk nut!" I was indignant even though there was once an adolescent time when I yearned after saints like Teresa of Avila, whose heart was pierced by an angel and the hole verified after her death and autopsy.

Paul sat on a rock and checked to see if my mouth was open and indignant. More slowly he said, "If it hadn't been for the accident, I might have gone back to Wisconsin to school anyway. It's a cold climate. People make cheese. These California seminaries offer two kinds of degrees: a doctorate in gnosticism or one in redneck fundamentalism. Of the two heresies, I prefer the second, but not by much."

Sam said, "Did you ski in Wisconsin?"

"Cross-country." They talked about skis and sleds and ice skates for a while. When Paul looked back I had my head down and turned away like some of the paintings of Catherine of Siena: no chin, eyes downcast, her whole self withdrawn. I was averting my eyes from this much gratuitous religion as if from a public nosepicker.

He handed me the Kafka book and tapped its cover. "Here's poor little Franz, his psyche twisted up because once he kept whining for a drink of water and his father shut him out on a balcony all night. Child abuse, right? And here's Martin Luther whose parents beat the blood out of him. He grew up to be a depressive, too, but he got more out of it."

"He broke up the Church instead of reforming it," I argued—I, who hadn't been to Mass for ten years.

Sam entered the conversation the way girls used to leap into a turning jump rope. "My sister saw the Holy Mother move!" but Paul was facing only me at the time.

"I thought if I stayed in California I could join the redneck types and, you know, not get sucked too far *into* all that literalism? So I signed up to take one basic course on the Gospels—they tell a story, after all; I thought I could get straight in my head the different ways the synoptics told the same story, but the first night I walked into the classroom there was this big bulletin board full of clippings about AIDS. Lots of obituaries. And the teacher—I guess it must have been the teacher—had pinned them up under a sign that said: GOD HATES FAGGOTS, ROMANS 9:13, so that was my first and last class in that place."

Suddenly Sam said with venom, "I hate faggots, too."

We stared. Finally I struggled to say, "No, Sam, people who

use children for sex can be men or women, and they can hurt boys or girls."

"Not where I come from," he growled. Both hands were hard fists now; Paul had not seen those scars.

"She's right," Paul put in. "Her Church and mine would say that gays and straights can all be sinners."

I began waving a hand to get him to change the subject.

Paul was saying to Sam that "faggot" was an insulting word. I thought the risk of insulting someone must seem minor to Sam. "Not that gays are any better," Paul added. "In San Francisco they call us heterosexuals 'breeders,' and they say it with a sneer."

I picked out the word "us" and smiled. There was one question answered.

As the days passed, I watched Sam thaw, refreeze, and thaw. Doubtless he had not known many men he would dare to like, certainly none who would buy a washbasin and try panning gold with him, or give lessons in finding fingerholds up sheer granite cliffs, or share his fishing license so Sam could catch rainbow and brook trout.

When Sam refroze, it seemed the result of two-fold jealousy. He seemed to want me to prefer him at all times to Paul Cowan, and also Paul to prefer him at all times to me; so he had sullen spells I had not seen before.

Sometimes his temper flared toward a substitute—the way he swore at the park ranger who told us campfires were forbidden, not enough firewood available; gas stoves required. Sam cursed in some mixture of language—Spanish? Paiute? Washoe? Shoshone?—only his furious tone was easy to translate. I had to apologize for him.

"That's no way to act, Sam," I scolded later. "They have to have rules."

He reacted to my "rules" as to Paul's "insulting word"—such minor matters were far below his scale of real offenses. We had a long argument that ended with his going off in the woods and missing a meal. Paul finally whistled him up, but by some male partnership sided with Sam's refusal to discuss it further. In tandem they changed the subject and tried to tease me out of my anger. That was a day when Sam was warm to Paul, cool to me.

"Don't be a mama," he said, but I noticed who kept bringing the matter up.

We hiked on from Azure Lake and along volatile Cascade Creek on well-maintained trails, then south in the rain into Dick's Pass. Wet, smelly, and cross, we put up both tents and huddled inside. Sam, in my tent, was irritable at being shut out of Paul's, and I wanted to be with Paul myself, for I felt starved for the tidbits of his childhood, life in Wisconsin, even his Lutheranism—whatever crumb might fall. I wanted to stand the Cowans up beside the Griers.

But later I sent Sam next door to sleep, perhaps because I had some forewarning that Tamsen Donner might show up, even this far south of her territory, and she did.

Misty nights apparently suited her. She sat down at my open tent flap, where surely Sam and Paul could see her if they only looked out. I told her mentally: *You've got on a different dress.* She shook her head. She did, though, a dark navy-blue hard to outline against the cloudy night sky. In my head I asked her how she'd found us this far away.

"That damned Hastings killed us all, him and his damned cutoff," she said. "What happened to him? What price did he pay?"

Nothing like that paid by eaters and eaten in the Donner Party. *I knew you'd ask, so I looked him up at the Truckee-Donner Museum.* Tamsen didn't blink at this name, nor did she want to know about lipstick or nuclear power. I decided the second tent was invisible to her, that she could not hear Sam's groans any more than Paul could. *Hastings took a bunch of Confederate sympathizers to South America, that's all I know.*

Tamsen struck her little fist into her little palm. Quite solidly it thudded there like a mallet in a wet sandbag.

You should have gone over the pass with your daughters.

She said impatiently, "Till death us do part."

I couldn't see what difference twenty-four hours would have made. In one more day George Donner was dead, would never have missed the shroud she stitched in place around him. And in the warm California valley with its woman shortage she could have married a third time, had grandchildren, gone into a peaceful grave with no unfinished business; but no, for the sake of intangible promises she stayed and died in the snow. No wonder she was both intangible and restless herself.

I don't know much about the kind of love that requires such sacrifice.

She cocked her head at some animal noise, and it confused me to see that sometimes her senses functioned, sometimes not.

"As soon as we crossed the Humboldt River," she said, "the geese flew over us going south. We should have known. We should have known."

I was sitting up, now, in my sleeping bag. I told her, earnestly, *I'm developing this theory that the human psyche is evolutionary, so it's natural that in every generation a few personalities may be far enough advanced to survive after death, but most are not complex enough for immortality. Houdini must not have been, see? So it's no wonder you never meet Hastings or Keseburg or Patrick Breen on the other side. Or George Donner for that matter. Their souls were more primitive than yours—*

Under my words Tamsen shook herself as if plagued by flies. Of course. She had died before Darwin's *Origin of Species.* I doubt if evolution was ever much discussed in the Comstock Lode. *Are your girls over there? They were older than you when they died so I doubt you could—*

Without any noise, Tamsen glided back and forth. I had to move to the tent opening to watch her silent pace. *This is how deafness sounds,* I thought.

"Mrs. Murphy," she said, more to herself than to me. "When her driver died. Milt Elliott. She ate all of Milt Elliott except the face."

Naturally.

"I want to know everything about Lansford Hastings."

What difference can it make now?

She slid away so gracefully that I could see a metal peg on Paul's tent snag her dress tail and then pass through it as if through smoke. At our old fire—the one the ranger had made us extinguish—she bent and picked up a coal that might still have warmth in it, placed it lightly between her lips, like Isaiah. She turned to stare at me, with the dark cinder making a skull-hole in her thin face.

Is it Hastings that brings you back? And why to me, Tamsen Donner? The woods are full of people. Your girls lived on; you loved them as well as your husband. Even now I see names like Breen and Fallon in the Sparks newspaper. There was a play about you on Broadway. There have been novels. They made a television show! Her silence, her stare, the round black mouth, made me increasingly nervous. *I hope you don't think there's something accessible about my mind like a crack or a hole or a weakness!*

All this passed over her head the way my lectures about Sam's cursing had passed over his.

She spat, with contempt, "Hastings wanted to be governor of California," and the bit of blackened wood rolled down her front where the starved breasts were almost flat and into the folds of her dark skirt as she disappeared.

In the cold dawn afterward, I decided that my mental weakness, which first showed up in college, had now, sure enough, swollen into schizophrenia, that something about leaving Steven Grier had also left me with every mind-door open to hallucination, that eventually I would fall deeper and deeper into myself the way sailors move to the core of their sinking submarine, bulkhead by bulkhead, until I'd be altogether sunk. Then out of the mountains they would carry the hull and outer shell of me wrapped as tight in a straitjacket as George Donner had been in his wife's improvised shroud.

During such terrifying predictions, my tongue clumped deep in my mouth, and I thought about waking the others. I even knelt at Paul's tent and unzipped an inch or so and set my eye there and listened to their two breaths come and go.

Yet daylight rose without my foaming at the mouth, and in the next tent they woke up and muttered, and in silence I helped with the packing and walked behind them both, high into winter or low into spring, over wet meadows or onto slick rock. I decided that if Tamsen ever appeared in daylight I would head for the nearest emergency room. Once Paul turned back to say, "You're so quiet; anything wrong?"

"Don't I seem all right to you?"

Before he could answer a blacktail deer ran by ahead of us, and farther along Paul saw a coyote with xylophone ribs, but all Sam and I saw was the quiver of leaves where it had disappeared. I heard myself accuse him, "Maybe you imagined it!"

We came out again at Echo Lake, where the van had been stored for safety inside a chain-link fence, and stood looking at it, feeling awkward. Paul said he had sold his old VW as part of self-discipline—burning his bridges, he meant. Now he shrugged the tall orange backpack that rested weight on his hips, the weight of all he owned.

By sticking his sneaker toes into the wire Sam climbed up and down the fence, restless as a monkey.

"So where do you go next, Paul Cowan?"

"Another park. It's easy to hitch a ride around here."

Sam leaned out of the fence, wire squawking, and poked my back.

I said, "You want to hitch with us?" I thought if Paul left these woods he would be run over the first time his bad ear mislocated a car horn.

"Hitch it where?"

"Sam and I" (I watched Sam balance in the fence, no hands), "Sam and I are just rambling around."

Paul only smiled with half his mouth, more like the Mona Lisa than Steven Grier, but its very restraint reduced me to lique-faction. Yet he never flirted. I was beginning to think his problem was not same-sex but no-sex altogether, maybe a vow serious Lutherans took?

He reached for Sam's arm and, though by reflex it jerked away, held on. "You ever seen the car museum?"

So to give ourselves the bends we came out of the wilderness straight into Reno's Harrah museum, where they had eight hun-dred classic automobiles from the A-Model on, celebrities' cars, limousines of every vintage, vehicles that ranged from the '59 Edsel to steam-powered experiments. These were arranged in one huge warehouse room after another against period backdrops, and if you stepped off the gravel path tempted to sit in one and twist its wheel, an ugly alarm would blow that even Paul could hear.

After we had walked for what seemed like hours up and down these identical paths among cars that began to look the same to me, Paul and I sat in a car-theme restaurant while Sam went back to see the old fire engines one more time, or maybe the Maserati and Hupmobile. In the well-lighted café Paul could see my mouth and movements; in fact, he considered me a big talker. "I love to hear you go on," he said with that half smile.

"It's you," I said. "I say things several times because I'm not sure you can hear me."

He shook his head no.

"OK, I talk more to you because you listen so well."

He said he had to.

"How much difference do you see between people who are born deaf and those who become deaf, like you? I don't mean very old people, either. For instance, do you feel any connection to Gallaudet?" In recent years, undergraduates there had rebelled against having any president less deaf than they.

"Oh, that whole deafness community thing—no," said Paul with a heavy expelled breath. "Civil rights applied to the sign language crowd, no, I hope not. But they're well organized, and I think for the congenitally deaf they do a lot of good. People came when I was in the hospital to be my support group, and I was so scared then that I did learn A.S.L.—American Sign Language." He lifted both hands above the table and made several intricate movements. "And I can finger-spell fast. But the leaders of those who are born deaf find this their separate language. They want to be separated from hearing people, but I was so recently one of them. One of you. They consider themselves separated already."

"Do that again."

He made the movements, but when I pressed for translation said it was just about the weather, nothing important; but he got slightly flushed and cleared out his throat hard as if gravel had fallen there. "When we were children we just absorbed vocabulary and syntax and tone, but deaf babies have to learn by will what's automatic for everybody else. Suppose you had to learn to lip-read Chinese? It's like that."

"So you wouldn't preach to the deaf in sign language?"

"Nor by closed caption TV, either. If this had happened to me in the Middle Ages, I would never have been able to take communion because I couldn't confess aloud to your priest. Most deaf people then were mute as well. Nobody taught them to speak."

"In the Middle Ages there wouldn't have been dynamite."

He told me that Lutherans had special missions to the deaf, even a magazine, "And maybe I could work on that? I'm interested in acquired deafness—teenagers who overload their ears with electronic sound or workers in loud factories. There's a whole new breed of deaf rabbits living around the runways at Dulles Airport, for instance, and there've been hundreds of generations in the thirty years since it was built. Deafness is natural to them. I wonder if they sign?" He asked abruptly, "Why did you say Sam was your son?"

"It seemed simpler."

"Safer?"

"I didn't know anything about you."

"I don't know much about Sam, but I gather he's been abused by strangers, maybe for a pimp, is that right?" To my nod he added, "Then he certainly needs to be somebody's son."

"I don't have any home to give him." There was no sight of Sam in the small café, and an occasional distant squawk suggested he was still approaching the Rolls-Royce or trying to get away with lifting a bat-wing door. I told Paul what little I had learned about Sam. He listened; oh, how I liked the attentive way Paul would listen as if every pore of his skin had an eardrum in it. Some men's faces are so chiseled that women should admire and move on, Apollo faces, while others—like Paul's—simply lack guile. He had a trustable face; I've never been able to draw that quality on paper. In fact, after Lombroso, after attempts to read character into features or skull bumps, we shouldn't trust trustable faces.

He broke into my details about Evangela and the jailed brother or father or both with a quick anger, reflexive and strong, altogether dependable. "You have to go to the authorities, Luna, police or somebody, get him protection. Get him some therapy. Somebody that's got an investment in Sam might be looking for his property, somebody dangerous. Was it Reno where he escaped?"

"I can't see Sam in the court or the welfare system, can you? He'd run from them the way he ran from the others. He'd end up on the streets. He came up here to postpone that kind of life, I know he did."

"Does that mean you're taking him on for life?"

I'd never put that blunt question to myself. I slurped on my fattening milkshake and stared at the Henry Ford place mat.

"Or will you leave him, too, the way you left what's-his-name?" He saw my surprise. "Sam."

I said Sam was mighty cagey about himself and mighty talkative about me.

But Paul was persistent. "Have you asked Sam anything about

the future? Do you know what he expects?" I didn't. "And once you get out of national parks and forests, where will you go in real life?" I hated that: *real life.* "Have you even got a job, Luna?"

Have you? I could still hear an occasional squawking horn from one of the many sections in this vast complex of automobile warehouses, so I took a deep breath and—starting with Chapel Hill in mid-April—went back and filled in any of the blanks Sam might have missed and came all the way up to this very table and my melted milkshake. I even told him about the hospital, something I'd hidden from Steven.

During all this Paul watched me in that urgent way that seemed to pull his whole personality into both eyes and forward. His intensity put to shame the casual way I'd been drifting through my life. As I talked, it sounded as if any Steven would have sufficed, any reason to leave him, also.

"So maybe Sam's not the only one being pursued. Maybe Steven is pursuing you?"

"You don't know him. He's in Riverside hooking up with a new illustrator that likes spaghetti."

"Then he's a fool not to come after you."

It was my turn to heat up my face and hack out my throat. People pushing by said, "Excuse me," and some who were waiting for tables stood near us and directed hypnotic stares. The increasing crowd was a sign that another tourist bus had arrived from some Reno hotel.

Paul said firmly, "We've got to ask, excuse me, *you've* got to ask Sam, Luna, what he wants next, what he expects. And no matter what he answers, you've got to know your own mind."

I didn't know it, did not even trust its stability. The one thing I had not told Paul concerned the phantom of Tamsen Donner.

A wave of visitors moved out of the café, snacks in hand, to visit presidents' cars and mobsters' cars; almost immediately a departing wave rolled through to stock up on food before riding the tour bus back to gamble.

During my silence, Paul gazed so steadily at my mouth that it felt unclean. I glanced at his, thought of kissing, and quickly checked my watch. "I ought to find Sam and we ought to pick a new campsite."

"If you're not going to talk to him now, when are you?" Paul frowned; I stood up. Shaking his head, he carried his milkshake behind me down the path past Al Jolson's 1931 Cadillac and into the fire-engine section, now crowded with the latest busload of tourists. Each time the alarm blew I turned toward that warehouse room, expecting to see Sam make one of his nimble monkey leaps back onto the walkway.

We hurried down more paths that crisscrossed, calling. Automobiles began to look like carriages whose horses had just been unhitched from their radiators. "This place goes on forever; weren't we just through this section?"

Paul, nodding, pointed to an exit by the 1899 Locomobile and into another gym-sized room that contained Roaring Twenties cars. I thought I glimpsed Sam hiding in a rumble seat, but it was a stylized flapper doll. "He's probably gone back to the café some other way," I grumbled, but then called, "Sam? Sam!" When my father was angry, he would call every syllable—*Madeline Lunatsky Stone?*—in a bellow that would have snapped whole battalions to attention, but I did not know Sam's full name. There were too many noisy people on all sides. I began to move faster and push through the crowd past the collection of roadsters from thirties films. *"Sam!"*

In the next huge room we separated, and since I was so short I ignored the horn blasts and climbed onto a running board to see above the crowd. A security guard came hurrying toward my calls for Sam. I ran straight into him. "Oh good, yes, there's a boy missing, shorter than me, black hair, maybe looks Indian or part Mexican, has on jeans—"

"Come back from the edge, ma'am, and stay on the path." He

waved a long black flashlight that could double as a billy club. We stepped over the low ribbon into the crowd again and the alarm stopped.

"Named Sam, a little stocky, jeans and a white T-shirt, he went to the fire engines but now we can't find him—"

"Happens all the time, ma'am. It's a big place. If you'll wait at the main entrance, he'll turn up and we'll put it on the loud-speaker."

Paul came trotting toward us from one of the broad doorways, shaking his head. Now the alarm was blowing again, though most of the visitors had stopped in the walkways to stare at the three of us.

"Please help us find him, we just left the café and he wasn't there, and he could have been kidnapped or—"

"Oh, no ma'am," he interrupted as he put hard pressure to hoist me by the elbow while sweeping Paul in with his other long arm. "Not a bit, no, if you'll wait at the main entrance I'll run a quick check. This way, here." He propelled us on either side. "What's his name? Sam, all right." When people fell back against the ribbon barriers to let us pass, more hoots sounded, and for the first time I could see alarm lights flashing over the doorways to pinpoint the room where the offense occurred. The guard spoke into his belt radio to the main office as we walked.

Paul told him, "Sam may be in danger," and said it again, louder.

The guard nodded but kept talking. He herded us out of the automobile maze sooner than expected and back to the café and entry where we had bought our tickets. "Wait here." The guard walked off much too slowly while continuing to speak into his walkie-talkie with no urgency at all. When he had passed into the first doorway a speaker system began to repeat: "Sam, meet your parents at the main entry. Sam, meet your parents at the main entry."

We waited. I said, "This is crazy. Here's a boy who's been look-ing after himself I don't know how long in the wild and as soon as he's out of sight I think the worst."

"He's not crazy," said Paul, catching only half my words.

They kept broadcasting the page for Sam. I don't know what made me think of stepping outdoors into that white glare, but after two steps onto cement I squinted against the sun, unwilling to believe that was really Sam being hauled between two men to the open back door of a silver-gray car. I screamed his name and he flailed around between them, yelling, *"Luna!"*

I flung myself between two Citifare buses into the parking lot while behind me the museum door slammed against the wall as Paul came after. Running, I saw Sam brace outspread arms and legs on the door frame—a parody of how he had hung on that fence—but now one man used his shoulder like a football guard's to drive him into the car's backseat. This second man was half into the front when the car took off so abruptly the passenger door must have slammed against his lower leg. He jerked it inside—brown trousers—while I ran hard over the parking lot hoping to read the mud-smeared license plate, and Paul pounded past me on his longer legs.

They were gone.

I drooped over somebody's hood and panted. Way down the concrete field Paul was still running, though the chase was hope-less unless he might be able to tell which way they had turned into the street. I rolled off the car to dash aside to my parked van while groping blindly in one pocket for keys, fell gasping behind the wheel, revved it up, and ground gears. Paul waited by the curb, swooping his arm to the left. As the van careened between rows of cars I threw open the passenger door, which clanked in and out until Paul grabbed hold at the exit and slung himself into the seat during my squealing left turn.

I could see no gray car. "Where?" Paul's chest was heaving and he could not speak. We raced down Mill Street, whipping past the Reno Hilton; they could have turned in anywhere.

At top volume I screamed, "License plate?" and Paul croaked back NO.

When we came to signs for the Reno-Cannon airport, that seemed as good to try as anything, and on Terminal Way none of the other overdue drivers paid much attention as I wove in and out at speed. Now we began seeing plenty of cars with that silver-gray color in that general Toyota-Honda-Mazda shape. Paul got on his knees in the front seat to scrutinize the interiors of cars beside, behind, in long- and short-term parking lots, at curbside check-in, seeking any sight of Sam, looking for any suspicion of a backseat struggle.

He finally said, "Go back to town," and braced for my dangerous U-turn, adding, "Find the police station."

I was crying by now. "It's hopeless. Hopeless."

"Police," he said firmly. "Now."

We drove back from the airport more deliberately, with one side trip into the lot at Bally's that had room for thousands of kidnapper cars, even its own RV park. Paul shook his head so often and so hard as he directed me up one row and down the other toward the right-colored car that his hearing aid fell from his ear, and he left it. "Police station, we're losing time," he said with one more headshake. On the street he shouted out the window for directions, had to shove the pink mold back in the ear, relayed instructions to me.

It's a wonder we didn't get arrested between there and police headquarters. And at first the policeman who tried to calm us down, slow us down *(Speak one at a time, be specific)*, seemed ready to put out a quick all-points bulletin on Sam. But gradually our answers made him write more slowly, look into our faces more appraisingly. No license number? Make of car? Description of kidnappers? (It took him forever to write down "Brown trousers.")

Sam who? Sure even about the name Sam? Age? Next of kin? Reported missing where and when? Used for what? Used by whom? And you've known the boy how long?

He spread his hands and the sight of the wedding band made me hope he had sons, but he said, "We can be on the lookout for a Chicano boy behaving like a hostage, but there's not much else to go on, is there?"

Paul took hold of my hand and went over the whole thing again with the policeman, very slowly and distinctly, as if the wrong one of them were deaf.

Slowly we realized that not only did he mistrust Sam's story to us, but ours to him. He asked for Paul's and my IDs. He looked doubtful when neither of us could give a permanent address. Paul's frustrated need to have mumbled questions repeated also made the policeman frown. I paced and fidgeted while this interrogation slowed and at last creaked down to silence, so he probably saw one of us as retarded and one as manic, or one on sedatives and one on speed. He walked with us to the curb to record the van's license plate and check the N.C. registration card, but all he said about that was that Dean Smith coached some good basketball teams in Chapel Hill. "Where can I telephone you if the boy turns up?"

Paul and I stared at each other. I hadn't counted up how much money I had left, couldn't remember when the bank closed; but Paul said quickly, "The Sundowner," naming a hotel we must have whizzed by at breakneck speed. The policeman wrote that down.

We climbed in and sank onto the hot front seat, speechless. Then Paul called after the policeman's back, "What about Mustang Ranch? Would they take him to a place like that?"

"No way. That's women," said the cop, with a nod that seemed approving. I leaned around Paul to show my puzzlement, so he explained, "It's a whorehouse, ma'am, over the county line in Storey. They're not legal here, or Vegas either, but lots of the tourists think so." He stretched. "I hear it all the time: 'What's the differ-

ence between a parrot and a Nevada woman? You can teach a parrot to say no.' It isn't funny."

Paul said there were plenty of prostitutes turning tricks in
Reno.

"Never said there weren't. There's free enterprise on the
streets and in some hotels, sure, but we hold it down. I don't know
if this boy you took in was a hustler or not, and whether he worked
here or in California, or if one day he just got sick of junior high
school and took off."

Paul said firmly, "We *do* know."

"His hand! His hand!" I stretched out my own to illustrate, but
the officer shrugged.

"Could be it's a street-gang initiation sign, could be he got it
caught in machinery." He turned away but after a few steps came
back to spread his own outstretched hand. "You could hit it on an
electric heater. You could fall on one of them floor furnace
grilles." We just stared. At the station door he spun toward us one
more time. "Catch it in a metal door that had grooves in the edge?"

Paul couldn't hear this last and frowned toward me, but I told
him it didn't matter. The door to the police station closed, and we
went on sitting there.

Paul suddenly gave me a pat on the arm. "We might as well
cruise around and look. It won't cost anything but gas and time."

The hours between afternoon and twilight drew a graph of
jagged peak hopes and despairs; one minute I'd hit the brakes to
check out a boy the right shape and haircut but wearing a
stranger's face; the next minute a passing silver car showed hands
flapping at the back window—but when chased turned out to be
full of boisterous children.

"If they're not gone already, they will be after dark," Paul said
as we worked our way up and down streets parallel to Virginia.
"Big cities are where the boy-porno business would thrive. San
Francisco, L.A."

"He'll try to get away, I know that. But even if he does, he'll never find you and me again. I guess he knows where his sister is and which jail his brother's in."

"If they're real. If they're not the ones who sold him the way Jacob's boys sold Joseph."

I took my frustration out on him. "Don't patronize me—we Catholics read the Bible, too."

"And you lit majors read Thomas Mann," he said agreeably.

I swung by the El Dorado, swallowing down both tears and smartass answers. They balled up in my throat the way they used to when my father drove away another time for an overseas assignment. I felt then left behind, resentful, sad, but free of him.

"You're right, I should have talked with Sam about his future," I almost wailed, driving along the crisscrossing Third and Fourth and Fifth Streets. He and his kidnappers were probably far away on I-80 by now, Sam shrunken and apathetic as an animal returned to its cage.

"If you're going to feel guilty about that, remember I'm the one who suggested the car museum."

The longer we drove around, the faster, the angrier I got. "Paul, you better tell me now how you feel about turning the other cheek because to get Sam back we might have to kill somebody."

He shook his head, but I said, louder, "Oh, I could kill the sons of bitches, all right, for what they've already done to him and what they plan to do and—"

"Beat 'em to death with a rolled-up T-shirt," Paul said, still agreeable. "Let's find them first."

Under the darkening sky the city streets began to glow, then increasingly to shine and glitter. Pedestrians now were adult party types. Under colored lights it grew harder, then impossible, to see inside these faster, passing cars.

Paul said that if I was ready, we could check in at the Sundowner. I saw he had been humoring my rage to act. "Maybe the police are trying to call us."

"Trying to call us fools and idiots."

He unfolded one hand in midair toward the glare and bustle. "Luna, what else can we do tonight?"

"He's gone, isn't he? And we'll never know."

Tired, discouraged, I let him register and check for messages at the desk while laughing couples in sequins and bright colors swept by me into the flashing casino. I felt like a lump of lead in a sparkling stream. Still, it was impossible to quit scanning these gamblers for Sam, and inside every pair of brown pants I thought a sadist might be walking.

Paul's arm went gently around my shoulders. "Come on. You're worn out."

We took a high elevator ride and then a long walk (Paul said there were six hundred rooms) to blue beds on blue carpet. "I didn't mean for you to spend your VW money; this is my problem, really—," but he said, "Hush. Take a hot bath. I'll call the police."

In the bathroom I slouched against a wall. Nature doesn't make marble that dark blue color, but every surface had a convincing marble appearance. After two weeks as a camper, tubs with instant hot water had almost left my memory. In a jar were little gelatin eggs of bubble bath (blue, of course) that topped the hot blue water with a white froth into which I sank and soaked, drowsy. Blue and Bluebeard. Blues. What was that Billie Holiday song? The meat is sweeter closer to the bone. Its sexual message hit me.

In the outer room the door opened and closed. Paul called, "I've left you a drink and an ice bucket on the table. I'm going down for my backpack—which bag do you need?"

I told him and rolled over in the steaming water. The kidnappers would make Sam wash off his woods dirt, too. I did not know how boy prostitutes readied themselves. Deodorant and clean fingernails, of course. White teeth, shampoos. They would need to take steel wool to Sam's heels and elbows. Dental floss on the front teeth.

Close to crying, I pulled myself out and dripped onto my clothes where they'd dropped by the tub. The huge blue towel wrapped around me with terry cloth left over. My skin felt hot and tender as if it were turning cerulean, indigo, but my nose and red eyes were running like a child's. Just seeing myself in the mirror, sniffling, was a surefire way to undermine sincerity and dry my tears. I used to be spanked for crying—it wasn't brave—spanked until I had swallowed every hurt and made it forever indigestible. When was the last time Sam had been allowed to cry?

In the bedroom Paul had left malt Scotch and ice and soda, not what I like and far too expensive for our budget, but without the soda it would do. Pacing, I drank it straight while my neck cooled off but my throat lining heated up. The wide fixed window overlooked a broad parking lot in which at least ten tiny cars resembled the one that had taken Sam. All around the hotel were too many buildings and garish lights for me to see the tawny surrounding bowl of hillsides.

I turned on the TV—a talk show about incest. In one corner, victims; in the other, fathers and stepfathers with denials. The host said there had been child abuse in Ranch Apocalypse, that girls who were barely teenagers had borne David Koresh's children. Somebody brought up Mormons and polygamy. I turned it off.

Despite the Scotch, I felt chilly in the air-conditioning. I set my glass by one of the beds, took off the damp towel, and crawled between the sheets naked, hurrying in case Paul should come in, half hoping that Paul would come in—his turn. As I covered myself I remembered my father's old admonition before every date: *If you keep your skirt down, he'll keep his pants up.* Under the blue bedspread I was shivering. I slid both hands between my legs to warm them, thinking of the mouth above, the mouth below. The pursed mouth. *Oh Sam.*

Later, in my warming drowse, I could feel Tamsen Donner pushing to come through, but it would be ridiculous to imagine her skinny image in homespun materializing in this lighted blue plastic room, and that reaction—like watching my tears in the mirror go dry—stopped her apparition before it could form. *If you want to be useful go find Sam for me.*

Then I was dreaming and then I disappeared also.

PART 4

Wild Game

~

Reno

WHEN I GOT BACK UPSTAIRS Luna was muttering into her pillow—"Out of the blue," I thought she said, meaning Sam or me or something worse—and I told her to go back to sleep. Her lips kept moving, but I heard no more.

It was a temptation to touch her, at least to stroke her bare shoulder, claim only therapy was meant. Bereft of Sam, she might even turn to me with both her arms wide open. That's how Steve what's-his-name had gotten her, taken advantage, gotten in her bed first and mind last and life not at all, but I, a slow learner, have finally learned this much the hard way: that most of us men start with passion and expect it to turn into intimacy, while most women expect the opposite.

I set her bag and mine on the second bed, finished the Scotch she'd left on the table, turned off the lights, stood watching her sleep. Some dim night-light from the bathroom had a blue bulb, and the light made her face look cold, almost frozen, as if her skin were fed only by veins and not arteries. I wanted to wake her just to make sure she was still alive, but instead I pulled the sheet up to her chin and set off on foot into the Reno streets.

The hotel telephone book had given me listings for escort services, hostesses, convention entertainers, masseurs, mostly with numbers only, but some located on specific streets I planned to walk, just in case. I hoped some pimp would make me an offer and then modify it when I stated my preference for dark-complected boys. I'm not sure how much my motive was to rescue Sam and how much to show Luna that I could.

It was a help that my deafness muted the horns, the blaring music that changed its throbbing rhythms from one front door to the next, since I could concentrate on faces and their invitations. First I tried the Amtrak station, then the gambling district between Fifth and the Truckee River, but finally decided that most sexual deals must be made one-to-one nowadays inside the bars and casinos, or else I didn't look horny.

Eventually in the cooler night I just walked for the sake of movement, trying to figure out what I'd gotten myself into. Luna herself was big enough risk, but how about her decisive "we might have to kill somebody"?

The Church has always asked its followers what they would *die*, not *kill*, for, unless you go back to the Crusades and Inquisition; and all the Christians I know get slain by nothing worse than embarrassment, including me, who'd never thought much about dying or killing, either one. What I'd really been doing in California was trying to decide my vocation by working through the verses of Scripture the way you'd pluck daisy petals: *I-believe-this. I-believe-this-not.* Now Luna had me plucking at the Fifth Commandment.

Reno was not the right setting for theology. I passed the blinding pink and red and orange Reno arch (graven images) and stopped by the police station to talk with a new man on a new shift, so bored he was glad to clarify the difference between a pedophile and a pederast, but not very hopeful about finding Sam.

"They get into that life and—well? How to get out? Doing what? He'll never go back and take algebra, much less shop or computers."

Mary Magdalene without job training or a support group. The Prodigal Son—no Social Services.

Back in the Sundowner people were finishing dinner, and the hotel was coming to life at an hour when every Wisconsin farmer had gone to bed with nothing to hear but snores and whippoor-wills.

By the time I unlocked our hotel room, I was feeling lonely—not all that unusual. Once I thought farm life itself had left me disaffected in crowded cities where I never met another soul who knew you had to mow alfalfa before it bloomed. But no; it's my temperament; I'm not sociable. Luna calls herself shy, but to me she seems a thorough extrovert.

California taught me the patter that passes for conversation in singles bars. After the accident I seemed always to be leaning toward a heavily lipsticked mouth that was shouting over the music: *"Gemini, what's yours?"* I could talk about TV shows, since I owned an amplified set. And movies. *Films.*

Some women found my handicap intriguing—those who believed that one damaged sense intensified all the others. In the crowds, under the blasts of stereo rock, they could not hear much themselves, but somehow in bed they expected every word would count.

But in the mornings their faces looked lonely as my own.

The Sierra Nevada wilderness seemed to enlarge this everyday loneliness to a profundity, to give me a vacation from lip-reading empty words. I liked camping where a fish would make no sound when it cut through the surface water, then air, then sliced down into the lake again. Thoreau was right that nature neither asks nor answers questions. So when the tallest pines there would dip to a soundless wind, I began to accept deafness as the ailment best suited to my natural temperament, a withdrawal that might even lead to wisdom.

I intended to sit on the mountain and read. And think. I thought I could still hear God if He had any news for me. From time to time, like Merton, I might issue guidebooks about my specific pilgrimage.

And from time to time, too, like a bracing tonic, I would ingest other guidebooks that scared me the most. Nietzsche. Kafka.

Then Sam and Luna came and made me long to hear every rise and fall of their voices, even whispers. Especially whispers. What I miss most is not hearing but overhearing.

I sat on the blue rug to unlace boots so I could walk through this hotel room in socks and not wake Luna, though she was beyond dreams now and had her mouth slightly open. Corpses relax that way; the neck lets go of the head it is so weary of upholding, then the jaw declines. A month after my accident a man in the next apartment shot himself in the heart and, of course, I didn't hear a sound, but was the only tenant home to go with the complex manager to check on his absence and silence. He lay like that, with his mouth cavity dried out, his whole body with its juices gone. Most suicides aim for the temple and straight into the brain. Heart shots miss. Nothing is instantaneous. Probably he lay without moving for far too long while his life leaked out on the sheet, through the tirelessly absorbent mattress, in winding-down circles along the steel springs, in a drip to the floor, where a pool congealed.

I could not stand seeing Luna so frosty and gray; I said, *"Luna!"*

Her body leaped stiffly on the bed as if from electroshock, and I was ashamed and caught hold of her rigid shoulders. "Sleep, nothing new, go to sleep, I am here, go to sleep," I kept chanting until she subsided without reaching consciousness.

I was reluctant to let go her shoulders, especially after they softened and warmed. I had not often seen Luna off-guard and still.

Especially since Sam disappeared she has been a whir of activity, like a bantam hen bespangled and fervent, even to the point of wasted energy. Somehow she even flares her face the way a chicken puffs out its feathers.

"Good. Sleep, Luna. Sleep," I said like the sandman, thinking that she was much too thin. From what she tells me there have been spells of anorexia since she was fifteen or so, perhaps the result of a father she could never satisfy? As Kafka could never please his. No wonder Luna left a church headed by a pontiff, with fathers in every parish, and Our Fathers to recite all the time. Before Sam's disappearance, she told me in the café that her father made her take off her pants for spankings and lie in her parents' bed, facedown, where she smelled their sheets with every blow. I hope I never meet Major Martin Stone; I'll turn *his* other cheek.

Now Luna slept again, not talking, and her jaw that had closed began slowly to let the teeth separate.

She has sharp brows in an intense and pointed face, deep-set eyes almost as dark as the lumps of coal we stuck in our snowman heads, and wiry dark hair she sometimes gets too busy to comb all the way through. There's a matted place in back of her scalp like the one on a baby's head that she overlooks because it's out of sight and she's often in a hurry. Sometimes she grabs all that's out of her view into a rubber band, where it sticks out like the tail of a terrier.

I had a baby brother with hair like that. Crib death. I was ten. Why did I ever think my parents had only heifers to talk about?

The drift of my thoughts sent me straight to the toilet to pee and to turn off that stupid blue-bulb night-light that tried to make this stupid place celestial. On the way to the second bed, I fell over my backpack and swore, but Luna slept on.

Compared to her I feel not only tall and thin but clumsy, with gross reflexes and joints that stick out. I'm unable to hear nuances in her voice, either because they fly by so fast or else disappear when she's forced to speak louder and slower for my benefit. She'll start off walking beside me but soon be two feet ahead despite my longer stride, and her words inaudible. Yet in the wilderness, through the walls of both our tents, I sometimes heard her talking fast in her sleep.

THE SHARP TEETH OF LOVE

I sat on the second bed now, watching her occasional chthonic movements. *A great blue room for blue balls,* I thought, half afraid she might wake and find me jacking off.

I gritted my teeth and rolled under the covers. As if this breaking of my attention had cut her lifeline, Luna suddenly sat up to stare where I was halfway down to my pillow. She snatched at the sheet that had dropped to her waist, but not before I had seen the small breasts with their tips raked to points by the slide of that fabric. I kept staring. Not since the accident had the hot surge of sex caught me unaware, moved me from shall-I to how-can-I-stop? *Sweet Jesus.* The fullness of the reaction made me grin, proud of myself, even of the one-way trip from passion to what-ever; also tickled at the link between sex and religion because both carry us outside ourselves, which Luther knew.

"You're awake," I said stupidly, but couldn't make my mouth quit smiling. I still had on my underwear and regretted every thread.

But she had skipped beyond mere waking and was already mentally busy. "Of course, Paul, I should have given the cop one of my drawings of Sam; I've still got a few he didn't take and they're a good likeness. I don't know why neither one of us thought of that." She frowned an accusation at me and then said, "You're not dressed?"

"I'm going to sleep. We can take them his picture in the morning."

"Isn't it morning now?"

"Two a.m." I knew that disorientation. Clocks are for night, not day. With the blue bedspread I covered my erection and spoke rather formally about my walk and second visit to the police station. "There's a whole pederast subculture that buys these kiddie-porn magazines and videos, men that set up homeboys in apartments like full-time mistresses. These guys deny being pe-dophiles or homosexuals; and in fact the cop says they're mostly middle-aged and married with children and high incomes, and they defend themselves with high-flown talk about ancient Greece and man-boy love. They want the age of consent dropped younger and younger, call it children's liberation." This account was certainly dampening my own desire. Luna shook her head, looking sick, and I stayed still and wilted in silence, adding, "This cop says boys get kidnapped off the streets of Guadalajara and Acapulco to meet that trade. The men they go to can get pretty self-righteous about how much better a life they provide than the boys would have had in poverty across the border. Same thing the slave traders said."

She lay down, covered herself to the nostrils, said two words I did not catch. "What, Luna?" She said them again, "Sex. Love." Then she hacked out the phlegm in her throat. I waited. She turned her face away. "Sam told me once that right after he was sold his sister tried to get him back. Evangela? But she told him somebody mailed her dogshit in a shoebox so she'd have to quit. He never called her up after that."

"We haven't quit," I said. Then my body settled into one bed while my mind got into the other one, with her. Reaching to snap off the light, I found her watching my face; for one minute too long this extended look stretched and even vibrated between us. Or I imagined so. I clicked off the lamp though no Reno hotel room goes entirely dark, not with an aurora borealis flickering beyond every window, so the covered shape of her was touched by wandering color. Not all blue, I was glad to see.

Not sleepy, I lay there remembering that mornings back home the stars would still be shining when we (we, the women and children) went out to milk. I rolled over away from the shape of Luna and bent the pillow several new ways.

In the blue-dark she suddenly said (and I could hear her easily with no visual clues), "You don't think we'll ever see Sam again, do you?"

I was surprised at my own truthful answer, "Actually I do."

"Why? How? One shot in a million, right?"

It's hard to shrug lying down, so I kept still. I could see her sheets thrashing around like a sea tide but I had cut down my battery and laid the box on the table. I eased toward the volume switch.

"Oh, I get it, Mr. Seminary Student. *Sola fide.* Well, if God's ever going to fix things, God should have stepped in however long ago they bought Sam and cut him and used him." More visual clues to her restlessness. Pillows lifted and thumped downward. "But no, God's too busy wasting His time working on the Pope's side. God's busy cursing the condoms husbands use. God's demonstrating at abortion clinics. God can't be bothered—"

"For me you'll have to skip the Pope."

"I don't see why, it's perfectly clear when Jesus says 'On this rock' and the word means 'Peter'; don't you guys get it yet?"

I watched her roll like a whale with a harpoon in it before I said, "Later you'll feel bad about saying these things." I lightened my tone, remembering to touch my Adam's apple to test my own volume. "Don't you have to tell these things at confession?"

"Shit," she said, and then, "Job." (I finally figured out the word—it sounded like "show-bee.") She slapped her pillow a few hard blows (yes, I heard each one). "Let God do miracles now and not two thousand years ago, let him heal a boy that already has the taste of leprosy inside his throat."

Without conviction I said, "Maybe He hears that prayer, Luna." In the silence I thought of what the Reno cop had said, that hand jobs and blow jobs for hire were nowadays preferred to anal intercourse, solely to protect the merchandise. Less risk of disease. But I, who had not yet studied the first course in theodicy and no longer believed its syllabus would be any help, had no answer to Luna's rage or petition. Did I dare say that for all I knew one deaf vagrant and one furious runaway bride might be God's only healers conveniently nearby? Even my fellow dweebs and dorks and twerps and nerds in the boys' choir back in Stockholm, Wisconsin, must have learned more convincing answers by now.

She was insistent, harsh. "Well, why doesn't He?"

I hid in a question. "Was that a prayer?"

"What?" she snapped, and so novel was it that *I* had spoken and *she* not heard that I repeated the question, and she rolled over with as much noisy thrashing as a beached Leviathan and lay with her back to me and the sheets rising and settling over the entire bed in her tumult.

But under all that racket and floundering (was it possible I could hear her bedsprings squeak?) I knew how small Luna really was, how undernourished after all, how well I could fit my body along the back of hers like a hand that loosely cups but does not trap a bird.

Not now. "Good night, Luna."

"It's morning," she grumbled with a shift and flap of covers as if even the late hours were my fault. I thought she must have been more falsely polite with Steven what's-his-name and gave myself points on the intimacy scale. Propped on one elbow I outwaited her; at last she said in a small voice, "Good night, Paul." She was still turned away. "I never liked the New Testament Paul," she said irritably. I said I never asked her to. My good ear decided that although her voice was soft I could hear the pout running through it and also its dislike of pouting; yes, I had started to hear Luna very well.

Next morning even my teeth had a bad taste, and Luna's shoulders and neck drooped from lack of sleep. Like an old married couple we were seeing each other at our worst, jockeying for position at the blue marble basins to wash our faces. She looked so cross that I decided the intimacy part wasn't working yet.

We found the hotel's copying service and reproduced for the police her best full-face drawing of Sam, then ran off others that said MISSING! CALL POLICE! 334-2121; and then we separated to show and post these anywhere in Reno we could.

She called after me "Be careful of the traffic!" and when I turned as we simultaneously read on each other's faces the echo of Sam *(Don't be a mama)* she lifted the photocopies and covered her mouth.

Afterward, when I talked with clerks and cashiers and dealers and even a priest at St. Thomas Aquinas Cathedral, most of them jerked a thumb toward wicked Las Vegas as the likely headquarters for boy hustlers. Not only on Vegas news racks, they said with pious indignation, but even in many yellow pages of that phone book, all kinds of sex services were offered with home or hotel delivery. They were very superior, Judea over Samaria. And especially when we had fanned out from the casino district to gas stations and Laundromats and hairdressers, those who glanced at Sam's picture kept insisting that Reno was really a *family* resort; in winter tourists came here to ski and only gambled on the side. I did not mind Reno's moral superiority to wide-open and more profitable Vegas except as it might prevent their memorizing Sam's face and looking for it everywhere, but when Luna heard it she got angry.

During the afternoon, we worked adjoining Sparks. A fireman told me that some Mexican boy had tried to jump a train in the yards behind Ascauga's Nugget where bums and dopeheads often hung out, had slipped and cut off two fingers. So, full of hope, I ran to a pay phone and called the Washoe Hospital, but the "boy" was in his thirties and with his uninjured hand answered his own phone by his own bed. He had not seen anybody who matched Sam's description.

At 4 p.m. I met Luna at the Sparks police station, where they already knew about Sam but could not promise much.

Back in the van we both stared at the dusty windshield. She finally started the car as I said, "Maybe we really ought to try Vegas?"

She shook her head. "I feel like the drunk who lost money on one block but keeps looking for it in another because the light's better. That we know Reno better than Vegas. That he's therefore nearby. I must be crazy." She pulled into the street and drove slowly with constant searching looks out every window.

I had to touch her wrist to divert her attention, something she had often done to me. "Fine."

"I do believe he's still here."

We put announcements on the radio stations where she paid in advance. Seeing her count money with a frown, I said hastily, "I can get a local job," to which she said, "Doing what?" I told her I could wash dishes, cook hamburgers, lift and carry, and I still had some money left from selling my car.

"Nobody'll buy this one," she grumbled.

Deciding that even donations could help, I went to three Lutheran churches: Faith, Holy Cross, Good Shepherd, where I found sympathy and an offer to buy me a meal. I put Sam's picture on each bulletin board beside their Fellowship Meetings and accepted twenty dollars from each pastor.

Luna, worried and irritable, asked me if I really thought that belief in Jesus was the only path to God. Were all the Muslims and Buddhists not merely mistaken but doomed?

"I doubt it. We all practice the religion that's available to us in our place and our lifetime."

"So for all you know the lady with the prayer wheel is just fine," she said triumphantly and was thus able to accept twenty more dollars from St. Therese, "The Little Flower," Church in southeastern Reno. She handed the bill to me when she got back into the van and said defensively, "So I don't go to Mass, but didn't David eat the shewbread out of the temple?"

We had not discussed details of our dwindling finances—the *real* intimacy between American men and women—and I suggested now that it was time we pooled resources and counted up what we had.

"You're right, Paul." The neon had begun to glow, although it was barely twilight. "We need to spend more on gas than a hotel room. Let's go back to camping."

I nodded. My ears were tired from the all-day strain of sorting sense from noise.

Telephones are hard for me, especially here where Nevada and California come together so some calls are long distance and some not and campsites are under various jurisdictions, so at the Sundowner I did the packing for us both while Luna called Tahoe National Forest Headquarters. It's funny the way you have to fold brassieres, one empty cup inside another. I was smiling while Luna wrote down directions to three no-fee, no-reservation campgrounds northeast of Truckee near the Boca Reservoir and one four-dollar camp at Prosser.

She wore bikini underpants. Except for a little lace, a pair almost disappeared in my closed fist.

"Stop that," she said, her face flushed.

After more calls, she finally reserved a tent site at Prosser with a fireplace and picnic table.

"As if we need a picnic table," she muttered. "Who can eat?"

"You can. I'll even cook it, but it won't be spaghetti."

She gave that slow smile that made me want to lip-read her mouth with mine. "No, you're nothing like Steven Grier," she said.

But she tensed up again on the drive from Reno and, while backing the van into place, ran it hard into a pine trunk and broke off a rear-door handle so only one side would open. I walked back to check how the dented right door was jammed in place. Luna stayed where she was and bent to rest her forehead on the steering wheel.

"It's not too bad," I called, though it was. "We can still unload, and I might be able to hammer it loose from inside." She didn't move. Last straw. "Don't take it so hard. One lousy door." I came to her window, and she rolled her face with its wet eyes into view. "If anybody can find him, we will," I told her. "Want your stuff out or shall I build a fire first?" At six thousand feet, the air was rapidly cooling, the first stars coming through. She said it didn't matter, so I built the fire while she climbed out with no energy and tried a halfhearted yank of the back-door handle.

"Insurance?"

"It's not worth filing a claim. Way back in Chapel Hill and all." She broke off a chunk of bark that had been dislodged. "I'm losing it. I can't even drive."

"You're not losing it." There was piped water. "You want coffee? Or would you rather have some more Scotch?"

"It wouldn't be the first time I lost it."

At that I crawled over the seat of the van and was able to brace myself and pop out the worst dent with my boot heels. There was no fixing the door latch.

She was walking around the clearing. "You think Sam's kidnappers might be camping out themselves? Just to lie low for a few days?"

"I doubt they're camper types." I threw her a blanket. "Stretch out awhile; you're just tired."

But she held it folded to her chest and watched me test which ground was both level and soft enough for tent stakes. The pine needles seemed dry and fluffy, but on this slight slope we would want to lie with our heads uphill.

My intentions were far from pure when I said, "One tent should be enough?"

She held up two fingers without smiling, and again started walking the edge of the campsite while she hugged the blanket. She mumbled something about "coincidence" that I couldn't make out. "What?"

In a tone so flat it was almost numb she asked, "Don't you think it a little strange that the only space we could find was here, at Prosser, instead of Boca or Boyenton or Boca Rest?"

"Strange? No. The others are all free so they were all full."

"A strange coincidence." She stared uphill, then down, as if she'd heard someone coming. Then, since I hadn't unloaded it, she crawled into the van and brought out the second tent. She busied herself locating instant coffee, instant cream, instant sweetener.

By habit, my tent went up easily, but hers had too many stakes, and one of its poles had rolled loose in the van. I spread my hands to show that the job was not going well, that one tent would have been plenty, so she found me the missing pole. We poured coffee and stood apart, drinking, watching shadows grow darker as the wind blew off the lake. From close by, a spillway waterfall sang in my bad ear like a poultice.

Using the folded blanket as a cushion, Luna sat at the picnic table. "I want to tell you something, Paul."

With my back turned, I knew I shouldn't have tried the tent business as I waited for her speech that would begin: *I will always think of you as a friend but . . .*

"Can't you come over here?" she said. "I don't want to shout."

"Sorry."

"I don't think it's just a strange coincidence that we're here at Prosser instead of those other camps," she announced as she set her tin cup next to mine. "We were drawn here."

I didn't get it.

"This place" (she waved at surrounding trees) "is close to where Tamsen and George Donner camped."

"Who?" Then I remembered the names, though it took another minute to recall that the whole wagon party had not spent that awful winter at Donner Lake. "Surely it's underwater now."

The firelight was making her dark eyes glittery. "I think Alder Creek flows into this reservoir. George and Tamsen made their camp close to where Prosser and Alder joined. It can't be far. That's why we're here. We were brought here."

"Brought here?" She was making me uneasy. This was intimacy? "Brought by what?"

"By who. Whom," she said, looking mysterious and a bit uneasy herself. She wandered to the van while I took several careful sips of coffee, came back carrying a candle that she lit from the cook-fire, then slowly let it drip wax onto the redwood table, her movements rhythmic and ceremonial. After one false try she was able to affix it upright in the warm puddle.

"All right, who? Or whom? I'm asking."

A bloom of light that spread over her lowered face made Luna seem a stranger. Only a few feet away in the dark, I wondered if we really knew each other at all, just from walking the same paths in the same forest, just because of Sam.

Luna gazed into the flame without speaking. Shut away from her like that, I half sympathized with churlish Steve what's-his-name who had called her Mad Lunatic without ever being told she'd been on a psychiatric ward and, worse, without ever getting a clue from any reflexive twitch on her part. If there were clues here now, I could not read them. On a wild guess I said, "In the Catholic Church today, you lit a candle for Sam."

Her nod made light wash up and down her face, but she seemed to be thinking of something else.

I tried to be cheerful. "Well, unlike the Donner Party, we can eat!" and I made noise finding a cooking pot, rolled her a few potatoes to peel, and started browning hamburger. At its smell Luna wrinkled her nose.

"I'm turning into a vegetarian."

"Not till you get more meat on your bones." It was my turn to read a clue from the quick jerk of her head. Asshole. Her anorexia. She was sorry she'd told me.

To keep the food from burning, I carried the whole pan to the table to apologize. "Luna, that's not what I meant. I only meant—"

She said with a small laugh, "You were being a mama." When I squeezed her shoulder she added, "Watch that hot grease!" so I went back to cooking but kept an eye on how the candlelight changed her face.

She rinsed the white chunks of potato, dropped them in the pot, and chopped in a little onion. I stood enjoying the fragrant cloud that now drifted from the stew, but she drew back.

While I stirred in the canned tomatoes, Luna crawled deep in the van to rummage among boxes. I called, "See if there's bread or crackers left," so she brought half a loaf and set it near the candle along with a library book entitled *Ordeal by Hunger* by George Stewart, the basic but fifty-year-old report on the history of the Donner Party. I remembered reading it when I first rode the train through these same mountains, over a railroad that had been laid through the very pass that in 1846 had been snowed shut for them.

She lifted her eyebrows and the book and I said yes, I'd already read it.

"He tells what happened to Hastings, at least part of what happened," Luna said, thumbing the last pages. Hastings who? I raised the volume on my hearing aid until the thing whistled. "Paul? If I really was losing it? If you saw I was going off the deep end—you know, cracking up—you'd tell me, wouldn't you?" She waited till I tuned the whistle out and then repeated herself. "If I"—tapped her curly hair—"was getting sick again?"

"Just because you don't want any hamburger doesn't mean you're getting sick."

"But you'd tell me."

"Yes, of course." I stirred the pot and then put on the lid. "I'll pick out the potatoes for you." Trying to make her smile. "I'll rinse off the gravy."

But her face stayed serious, and she motioned me to sit by her at the table. While the food simmered, she began slowly to tell me about the visitations ("I don't know what else to call them") that she'd had from Tamsen Donner.

And I did wonder, at first, if Luna was all right. Mended objects and people often do break in the same old places.

But her voice was calm, the words examined before she said them. Sometimes she turned pages of Stewart's book, though she did not read from it. Staring into the candle flame, she spoke with deliberation and a child's earnest determination to stick to the trivial details that must add up to evidence of truth.

She said that Tamsen and George and their children and the Jacob Donners had come to Alder Creek on November 3; snow was already falling; they'd set up their lean-to in haste against a broad tree that would serve as the north wall. They faced it east.

(When Luna herself faced north, then east while talking, it gave me the creeps, to tell the truth. I could hear every word just fine, but she was working too hard to be objective. She sounded almost mechanical.)

"And made pole beds because the ground was already muddy, and took some of the oak bows off the wagon to shape the walls and tacked the white canvas around. She'd waxed it with beeswax back in Springfield, but from the desert hot sun the wax was long gone. The snow must have wet right through."

Luna kept talking, and I would keep listening until I got jittery, then might find myself walking out of earshot to poke a fire that didn't need poking, to relocate the pan, to gnaw on a dried-out heel from the bread loaf. Perhaps she had lit the candle so she would seem like a fortune-teller.

I broke into her flat recital: "Dreams. Of course. Everybody dreams, and you've been in a susceptible frame of mind in an unusual place. Perfectly understandable." I gave a dismissive wave of the bread slice but, when she looked hurt, added, "I've dreamed about my baby brother and he's grownup in those dreams, though he never lived but a few weeks."

"I'll tell you why it's more than dreaming."

Luna began counting on her fingers the specifics she couldn't remember from any book, things only Tamsen herself could know, had told, things Luna had jotted in her diary. She went through a string of these in a drone: how the men pissed yellow holes in the snow; how the Breens insisted God was punishing them all for leaving Hardcoop behind and also traveling on Sundays; that while crossing the plains they'd churned butter by tying the milk jars under the vibrating wagon bed, back when there was milk to churn; how horsemen heading east on the emigrant trail would carry back mail postage-due from the territories and into the first post office in Missouri; that consumptive Luke Halloran had drowned on the red sea in his lungs and been laid in a grave of pure salt and might be preserved there still like a cured ham; that the Donner cattle would walk around and around a pine tree until they wore a sleeping trench in the deep snow and how had they learned that back in Springfield?

"And me too, how did I learn that?" Luna asked me.

I told her a lie, that I thought I'd read some of these facts myself, that she must have read them, too.

Tamsen had explained (said Luna) that people slept outside the wagons anytime the weather was warm enough because a diet of beans made everybody fart; that Lewis Keseburg's face bones made him look like a squirrel carrying acorns too high in its cheeks; that you measured the day's miles by the Mormon odometer which involved the turning of three nested wheels that kept knocking a pin over, notch after notch, the notches to be counted at sundown in camp—

I stopped her. "Well then, it doesn't matter if you've had a dream or a real ghost. Put it in perspective. What matters is Sam."

"To let a wagon down a cliff," Luna recited, "what you do is stake down one wagon with its back wheels high and you wind a rope around a wheel—it acts like a windlass, you see—but you'll need oxen to hold up the tongue, and then the men grab the spokes of the wheel and gradually lower the second wagon—"

"Luna? Luna. Enough." Seated by her at the picnic table, I caught her unsteady hand and then took her own fingers and turned them into bars across her mouth that no ventriloquist could get through. Her eyes looked frightened. "I believe you."

Her fear may have lessened. I kept her mouth caged.

Finally I said, "This Tamsen never threatens you, this dream-woman or phantasm, whatever she is?" I didn't say *hallucination* as she expected.

When Luna shook her head I could feel her slow smile spreading under our fingertips and I took back my hand. She said, "You do believe me?"

"I believe you've been having this experience."

"You believe it's all in my head."

"Well, what isn't?"

She jerked back from me as if struck and then blew out the candle with a great explosion of air. "What a thing for you to say! And you were going to be a preacher someday!" She almost leaped away from the table. "You say there's Scotch in the van?"

While she marched toward it, I called, "Listen Luna, anything that's back in the past seems symbolic once it's finally holding still to be examined. This Donner story has plugged into some memory or some predisposition—"

"Like," she shouted, "the New Testament plugged into yours!" She came back swinging the bottle, angry. "Where's my cup? And what does that say about the present? That every day would be symbolic, too, if we could see the forest instead of the trees? That Jacob was wrestling with his impulses and not an angel?" When she slung coffee away the droplets spattered my shirt. "If you don't believe in ghosts, just say so. If you don't believe in me . . ."

It seemed better to say nothing at all just then. We poured drinks in our Sierra cups, and I followed her to where water, silver now, spilled over the causeway.

Above the rim of her cup Luna said in a voice louder than the splashing, "Funny that you don't believe in my ghost but you believe in the one that showed up on the road to Emmaus."

"One. That's the key word. One."

"And didn't Luther throw his ink pot at the devil?"

I offered to throw something at Tamsen tonight if she came, tried a laugh, heard it fail. "Or you could stay in my tent. I guess that's one reason you wanted your own—you think you're on her home ground and you think she'll haunt you here."

"It's not exactly a haunt."

We left things unsettled. In camp again Luna did not eat much stew but kept on steadily with the Scotch, a bad combination with how tired and grim she felt. Maybe it would be therapeutic to get her drunk and take advantage; sex might have kept some of those Catholic women from being such ecstatic brides of Christ.

But this was Intimacy Night, not Passion. Talk? Luna almost babbled. She would leave her bowl of stew on the table while she paced before our tents, using her spoon like a bandleader in charge of syncopating words. By rational talk she was determined to prove to me how rational she was. At one point we had to pour all our money on a blanket so she could count it and draw up a tentative budget in her diary—demonstrating logic, math, planning. She told me a number of normal (and boring) dreams to illustrate the difference. If Tamsen was a figment of her imagination, why wouldn't Tamsen talk about what Luna wanted? Luna wanted to ask about love; was it different then? Had she kept nursing George out of love or duty? After his arm began to swell, did they have sex?

On and on she talked, moving so rapidly that, if her back was turned or when a wind passed by, only snatches were audible.

She had theories. "It could be," she began firmly, "that all bodies emit this electric force field that the dead sometimes leave behind, the way you'll forget an overcoat. Or it might just be a strong waking-dream, not the kind you mean but the kind people get in trances and when they're hypnotized—maybe I project into the air some thought my own mind is interested in, but so strongly that it now gets to exist on its own because the nervous system is electrical, you know, and they say some people have burned themselves up by spontaneous combustion when they just shorted out—oh, that reminds me of Waco!"

"Luna, your stew's getting cold." *And you're getting drunk.*

". . . some people might be good receivers and some not. Or some might be plugged in and some not. If you're a good receiver, it's as though a switch clicks on and some image might get transmitted across time and space; isn't time a dimension now? That would be electrical, too, because how else do you explain these mass sightings of the Virgin? Does she just *come* like good

Catholics believe or is there by coincidence some general shared electrical brain pattern, like the same one that produces popular fads, and the Virgin Mary's picture rides in on that current and—bingo!—Fatima! She showed up in Yugoslavia in the 1980s and spoke Croatian to three children, and for all I know if I were a Japanese tourist Tamsen would speak Japanese to me! Now I don't know why she doesn't come to you or Sam; in fact, I wouldn't really *want* you to see Tamsen now; I'd feel almost jealous, but I just want to talk about love and she wants to talk about anger and revenge . . ."

While Luna was turned away I set the Scotch bottle under the picnic table. I said if there were real ghosts seeking revenge every attic in Germany would have a Holocaust Jew shaking chains, but this time she didn't hear *me*.

". . . the idea of ghosts got started." Pacing my way again she wrinkled her brow and made a floating gesture with her cup. "Say you're watching an old man die and it's wintertime in a cold room and his breath and yours make a vapor and then his makes its very last vapor and expires—so what would anybody think?" The cup rose overhead. "If God breathed into Adam, souls breathe back out, yes? You can see it in paintings—souls being dragged out of the mouths of corpses by angels or devils. Depending. There's a big fresco in, in Pisa, I think? Why is it that the Mediterranean countries outperform all the rest when it comes to tacky miracles? If any saint's blood is going to liquefy, if any Madonna figurine is going to cry, it'll be there; have you noticed that? Must be something in the water." She giggled, then quit.

I said perhaps the Pope was contagious.

"Oh you—you Protestant!" she said with a waggle of her empty cup. "There it is." She bent and poured more liquor from the bottle; either she'd vomit soon or go to sleep. "What I like about Catholicism is that it's so *literary*. That's what I kept even in the hospital, the silly symbolism of the saints. I'd tell the doctor that when Saint Veronica fasted she would stop on Fridays and eat five orange seeds for the five wounds of Jesus. Don't you love it?" I said no. "They even thought the gallstones of Saint Clare were the symbols of the Trinity. How can you not love a thing like that? A construction. An edifice." Liking that word, she rolled it through her mouth several times *(Edifice. Ed-EE-FISS)* and then washed the syllables down with Scotch.

"What's literature"—she paused—"what's literary is better than what's truthful. Padre Pio had the stigmata for fifty years— was that Naples or Sicily?—but they said he kept the wounds open with carbolic acid. Probably you Lutherans said it."

I tried to bring the subject back to its start. "But Tamsen Donner's no saint, so she got no special privilege."

"Oh Tamsen? Tamsen. Well, there's Purgatory, of course. Maybe dying's a long process and she's finished letting everything else die except the anger. Maybe they sent her back from Purgatory. Catholics thought that's why a ghost sometimes would shine—it had just come straight from Purgatory." Looking around she spotted a shine herself—the reflection of light on the Glenlivet bottle—and asked if I didn't want some before she drank it all. "Or maybe astrologers would say the birth date is decisive. Tamsen was born November first, All Saints', might have made a difference?"

"Eat something now, Luna. Here." I got the cup loose from her fingers and put a bowl there and filled it.

". . . replace every cell in the body every seven years, so what if the process of molecular turnover once in a while keeps on going?" She took a spoonful of hot stew without thinking, and her throat forgot temporarily to talk while she touched her windpipe in surprise.

I put my arm around her. She seemed to be humming with energy. I wanted to make love to her and thought it possible, now, but not like this. "Eat some more stew before you sleep, Luna."

"Sleep," she murmured, thinking it over. She took a few more cautious swallows, but said it was cold and when she hit a chunk of meat she spat it back into the spoon. "I hope Sam's asleep." Then she got down on all fours at her tent opening. "By himself."

I held back the tent flap, wondering whether more ghosts than Tamsen could haunt Luna at a time when she was so vulnerable, whether only one ordinary dream of Sam might convince her that he, too, was dead but his spirit earthbound. Slowly she crawled inside and struggled into her sleeping bag with shoes still on. Maybe Tamsen Donner was her second personality, split off from her Luna-psyche and only able to surface here because of the sheer accidents of geography and history. Bridey Murphy turned out to be no reincarnation, just a little glitch in a woman's memory and mind.

I reached in to pat her padded hip. "Sleep, Luna." After all, I was no perfect specimen myself.

"I don't feel good."

"No wonder. We need some sleep." I waited until it seemed safe for this Lutheran to say, "I'm glad you lit the candle."

She was rolled away from me but still speaking distinctly. "Tamsen was *literary*. Tamsen read *Pilgrim's Progress* to the children before George had to throw her books off the wagon, but in the end they couldn't concentrate on any stories she told them. In the end the children had only one game left to play, they fed their dolls snow over and over all day long."

Some other sounds followed—a growl? A snore? I zipped her tent closed and waited outside. Up the pass I could hear the westbound train coming. It leaves Reno about 8:30 p.m., so it was earlier than I'd thought. Luna began talking again, but the tent muffled her exact words. I slid my better ear against the nylon but could not make out her blurred sighs and noises. Blurring is really the point in everything called "occult." The decisive edges disappear, so a ghost isn't either quite dead or quite alive, and a werewolf isn't exactly human or animal either, and a vampire—

I shook Luna's fancies out of my head, lit her candle again, and got from the van the newspapers I'd collected from coin boxes during the day: *Sierra Sun, North Lake Tahoe Bonanza, Tahoe World, Tahoe Daily Tribune, Sparks Tribune, Reno Gazette-Journal,* and started a list of their locations. Tomorrow we'd take Sam's picture to each one. And we hadn't circled Lake Tahoe yet; we could try that, putting up posters, still looking for the kidnap car, stopping at pay phones to check in with police. And then what? Would we give up? Go our separate ways? Luna back to Steve what's-his-name? Or maybe she'd want to hang around Donner Pass and keep listening to spirits. Try to contact Sam in crystal balls and on Ouija boards. No, I would take her with me to—well, to someplace. She'd be my ear; I'd be her appetite.

But I, who was deaf to Tamsen Donner and so much more besides, would I ever really make sense now of a Book in which a great Voice kept yelling, "HEAR, O ISRAEL! HEAR! *Let there be light! In the beginning was the Word."*

There's not as much seeing as hearing in the Bible. Yahweh would shout out of Heaven, but for generations His visual self burned in a bush or mooned His backside for Moses.

I went back to listing newspapers. Just as I copied an address from the masthead, some adjoining story would catch my eye. At Donner Lake this August they expected 250 swimmers to make the annual east-to-west swim across. In Sparks, a teacher had stuck duct tape over the mouth of a rowdy student. The town government was debating whether or not to permit sex films to be shown in entertainment booths; how far pairs of consenting adult viewers would be allowed to go themselves while watching inside such private booths; and if legislation for the handicapped might require that each of these booths provide equal wheelchair access. The library summer film program was showing Charlie Chaplin's *Gold Rush,* which had been filmed in this area; there was a still photo showing a starving prospector who suddenly visualized his partner as a very large, edible chicken. And near Truckee a tree trimmer had committed suicide by taking a chain saw to his own neck.

I blew out the candle. In a world so full of the unbelievable every day, what kind of sense did it make to believe in the bread and the wine but not in Luna's ghost?

I WOKE NEXT MORNING to the unmistakable harshness of near-by retching. Luna had not been able to stagger very far from either tent before vomiting a little stew and a lot of Scotch. I peered between my flaps and figured out that she'd gone to the van for the spade to cover what I could now smell. When she came by, her face looked gray and puffy. Perhaps she would sleep some more. No, once sand had blotted the odor, she stood with one hand pressing what must be a painful throb in the fontanel center of her skull. She gagged a time or two and spat phlegm. She sat at the table, silently reading my newspaper list weighted under a rock, still bearing down on her own scalp. Then she stared at my tent. I watched her swallow the ball of nausea in her throat. "Paul? Is that you?"

"Who else?" I came out in a squat and felt for my nearby shoes. "Good morning." Luna made a nasty face and gave a final rub to her uncombed dark hair. "You look awful," I said. "I'll make the coffee."

She spasmed and stopped. "Please don't." But I needed some and fired up the camp stove to boil water. While it slowly warmed she said, "There was always a bar at my house and there was always a cocktail hour, but after I left home I never had money enough to learn to drink." She lowered her head between her knees until her skull had filled up with nausea, then leaned back with eyes closed and let it crash into her abdomen again.

"Got any Alka-Seltzer?" I suggested. She didn't know and didn't care. In the van I dug out her box marked MEDICINE CABI-NET and brought back a bottle of Emetrol. "Big swallow." She took one. "Wait about ten minutes and take some more. You should have put food in first to cushion the Scotch. And a lot less Scotch."

Eyes closed, she said, "My father taught my mother how to smoke so she'd look sophisticated. Inhale and cough, I can hear her yet. Now she can't quit."

I fixed the coffee, but instead of tasting hers she took up my list and squinted at it. "We need to get to the dailies early. Let's not strike the tents."

"Coffee," I insisted, and made my cup last until she had taken her second dose of medicine and looked a little better.

"But you drive," she said plaintively. She lifted one boot. "I think my feet swelled. I think I'll never get these off."

She didn't comb her hair until we were driving down the mountain. Each tug woke up her headache. On our first calls, she waited outside while I talked to reporters. A few took notes and quotations for a news story; most of the time a bored clerk accepted our poster about Sam; and in one place I had to pay for a display ad.

Gradually Luna's color improved, though she would not eat. We were driving around the north rim of Lake Tahoe before I asked, "Did Mrs. Donner come?"

"If she had, it would have been *her* turn to wake the dead."

We swooped in and out a jungle of subdivisions with cute realtors' adjectives attached to cute realtors' nouns: Heights, Estates, Meadows, Shores, Palisades, Vistas, Marinas, and Ridges—the natural habitat of *Homo consumens.* By noon she took ginger ale, and I restricted myself to cheese crackers and Coca-Cola, something whose smell would not rush straight to her stomach lining. In the afternoon we grew silent, discouraged. Sometimes I reached across the seat just to squeeze her hand, and by then she managed to squeeze back without a reflexive touch to her forehead.

Most of the seventy-six road miles around Tahoe, certainly the glitzier parts, are in California; the eastern Nevada side has more unspoiled public land and beaches until you cross the border again at Stateline with its high-rise casinos. Our sweep came down the crowded California side on 89, then crossed to ride Highway 28 up through Tahoe Nevada State Park and back to Incline Village. Between heavy traffic and Luna's frequent commands to slow down so she could more closely check out this silver car and that, the drive took over four hours. We had more time to talk on the lake's eastern side, where boulders had rolled down to the blue shore so the water sprang into view and out again.

"I talked a lot of silly religious stuff last night; it's because of you, that's why, because nobody else I know even mentions God. I kid you not. He's deader than Tamsen Donner to the people I know."

"Their loss." But I'd had enough of her masochistic saints. "I've been thinking that maybe the police put us on the wrong track with this pederast/pedophile business. I've been thinking about regular street prostitution. In San Francisco, for instance. You certainly get call boys in Polk Gulch and the Castro District."

"A needle in a haystack. Even if that's where they plan to take him, we've got to find him before they leave." She opened a tin of aspirin from her pocketbook and ate two. "Why should they be in a hurry? He was by himself when he left them. They think he's still by himself."

"He might talk about us."

"Sam's no big talker. Usually I'm not either."

"Deaf people need to be talked to. They need to feel worth the effort."

Occasionally I turned off the highway to see where tourists were going and parking, some to ride a paddle wheeler on the lake, others into Cave Rock, a tunnel said to have been struck through the stone by the Great Spirit of the Washoe Indians. Maybe He'd lifted his loin cloth to some shaman or showed off by flaming up in a cactus.

"How can you smile at a time like this!"

Yes, feeling better. A side trip to the big lots at Sand Harbor gave Luna a surfeit of cars to examine all at once; she liked that efficiency, though there was no reason Sam's captors would lead him down any nature trails.

On one quiet stretch of road she asked why I'd come to California in the first place. I told her, knowing already how much she'd make of pattern and symbol. My father's family, Cowans, were Scotch; my mother's Norwegian. About the time the Donners were dying on this part of the continent, the Cowans came from Vermont on the Erie Canal to Buffalo, then on by steamer to Milwaukee—not two thousand population then—and past it into tough rural Wisconsin where farms and new settlements were springing up atop Indian mounds, just the way English villages thrived on top of artifacts left by the Romans and Druids. But the link between Wisconsin and California, the merest spider-silk thread that (sure enough) made Luna's dark eyes light up, was naturalist John Muir, another Scot, whose immigrant forebears had settled in the rocky hills of southern Wisconsin and whose original farm became the state's first nature sanctuary. So back in the days when I was surviving perhaps my fifth or sixth faith crisis, made doubly guilty by the fact that I'd taken some formal vow to serve the Lutheran Church, I took time off after college to seek—not my Fortune, but my Fate. And where would I go but to the Sierra Nevada John Muir had loved, where—indeed, Luna!—he had tended two thousand or so sheep, more than the herdsman Moses on Hebron or the boy-harpist David; and had decided on those heights that his own messianic vocation was to serve the Range of Light and not the Father of Lights. So I came west, riding a train through the same notch that the Emigrant Trail had cut between Muir's granite mountains, and worked at this and that on the California side while waiting for nature to enlighten me on weekend backpack trips.

"And don't tell me you love it because it's *literary.*"

"Worked at this-what and that-which?" asked Luna. "But first, get closer to that car—no, never mind. It's not them."

I sped up and slowed down. "I bused tables in San Francisco. I learned to make dim sum—that's a dumpling with different fillings. After the '89 earthquake they were hiring anybody for cleanup and that's where I learned to operate heavy equipment and moved through *de*struction to *con*struction. I was on a road crew near Santa Cruz when the dynamite went off too soon. I'd been in Berkeley for a while—there are about five seminaries there—but I chose Santa Cruz, where I thought I could take some religion courses at U-Cal. But in that part of California, religion is just a—well, a mood, an attitude."

"I think Chapel Hill must be like Rome was. People who go to church don't mention it during the week. I *think* that, but I didn't really go myself. So after you got the hearing aids, you came back to John Muir's mountains."

"It's a cliché, all this going to the wilderness. Moses, Paul, Jesus, they all did it. You could walk out the gates of Jerusalem and be in the desert within two miles."

Suddenly her breath hissed in between her teeth with a snake sound. "Sssstop!"

Surprised, I hit the brake. A horn screamed behind me and then all the way past on the left side.

"Don't just stop!" Luna yelled. "Two cars ahead now! That silver one. See?"

The reason I couldn't see was that the angry Buick driver in front was giving me vigorous jabbing finger motions out his window while weaving back and forth in the lane to teach me a lesson.

We were coming into Incline Village, where condos the colors of pine trunk and pine needles blended into the woods. Ahead, the Buick deliberately made a left turn with no signal, but I—straining past toward the second car in front—said with disappointment, "Surely we've seen that exact same car a dozen times."

"No." Luna bounced on the seat. "Look, look what's drawn in the dust! Look, Paul!"

Driving closer, I saw then the large crescent shape more shiny than its background scrawled on the car's roof where only the driver of a higher vehicle, van or truck, would notice; and then spotted other crescents made the way a child would outline a crude boat or watermelon slice or smiley-mouth, drawn with spit on a fingertip here and there on the trunk lid.

Beside me she whispered something. I said, "What?"

"Luna. Moon."

I closed the distance toward that bumper and told her to write down the California license plate, but it was obscured by mud, deliberately obscured; there was no mud around here. She wrote the likeliest numbers with ballpoint in the palm of one hand.

Now what to do? The silver-gray car sped along, oblivious: Mazda, one driver, two heads in the back. Mazda 626. "I should let you out to call police with the description while I keep following."

"Let me out where? Tahoe police or what?" Ahead the car swung onto a secondary road. I, too, swung right sharply by a sign to Folsom Camp. "Stay close," she said.

"Not too close. Can you see Sam? That back window's so dusty I doubt the driver can see much of us, either."

"They maybe never saw us driving anything, you know. They may have just spotted Sam alone, by luck—"

"Luck?"

"Luck or pattern, the same way we've found them, but they went to the car museum because they thought a boy might go there. They just think two nosy strangers ran after them in the parking lot."

"Strangers aren't nosy these days. Strangers don't want to get involved."

She fell silent while I tried to decide if we were following too close to look accidental. "Nobody was following us that day, I'm sure, so we're nobody to them." Suddenly she pointed. "Look there!"

On the inside back window glass, as if by magic, there appeared part of the slow upright outline of a crescent moon, broken off halfway. She cried, "Sam's seen us!"

"Maybe not, maybe not. He's probably been drawing moons one at a time every chance he gets."

"He knows this van." Her voice got choked in her throat. "Sam knew we'd come. He knew it."

"He hoped it."

We were barreling along this unfamiliar secondary road that seemed to run beside—or in?—the Tahoe National Forest. Suddenly the silver car ahead made a quick left turn onto dirt. IN-CLINE LAKE, a sign said; but Luna put her face against the windshield and said tensely, "Go on by and then turn back just in case." She repeated it, louder.

I couldn't believe we amateurs could fool Brown Trousers and his partner, but it was worth a try to let their dusty trail move down that road before following. This seemed a private road with occasional drives leading off to houses or mobile homes or places far out of sight. Ahead, like a pillar of cloud, there hovered the evidence that the kidnappers had turned off one of these and begun moving more slowly down a narrow track between pines and scrubby underbrush. I, too, drove more slowly, holding back.

"Are we making a lot of noise?"

"What? Oh. We rattle, I guess."

Beside an abrupt slab of granite the twin wheel marks ran straight into a creek whose waters were still swishing and proved to be less than hubcap deep.

I muttered, "What in the hell are we doing?" when to my relief we made it through. "We're getting a long way from help, Luna."

"What we're doing is going after Sam," she said, still pressed to the glass. "I didn't know the shocks were this bad. Slow down so we'll be quieter." (I couldn't hear anything but my heart, her voice.) "Let's pull off a minute."

Soon I found a flat place just behind a pile of boulders and cut off the engine. Luna said she could still hear theirs, in low gear; I could not. She sat with her finger up, then lowered it when the rumble stopped. "They're waiting for us?" she said, as we stared at each other. "Coming back?" I pointed out that if they did come back they might pass these rocks and miss seeing the van, now as tawny gray as the stone barrier it hid behind. What I hoped was that we wouldn't get stuck in sand.

We waited, breathing with so much depth and care that it recalled that California woman meditating under her prayer wheel with both lungs synchronized. I reminded myself to tell Luna, later, that in California they do yoga to the Hail Mary prayer, half of it breathing in, half out, till they slide toward trance.

With a puff I let go the breath I'd been holding and whispered, "Hear anything?"

She shook her head. Her hair, still only half combed, wanted my hand to be laid on the tangles, but I didn't.

"It must be a hideout," said Luna so dramatically that I thought her words had been preserved intact from comic books or kids' TV, or maybe she chose to use standard phrases I could read on her lips no matter how softly she spoke.

I did stroke her hair, only once. "Or it could be a dead end where they're waiting now to see what assholes were following in a brown van."

We gazed at each other while cocking our heads this way and that in search of noise. Her copy of my own struggles to hear made me, for some reason, recall how little she had eaten all day. "Are you all right?" She nodded. In the silence I put forth a tentative hand so she thought I was going to touch her lips for certitude, but I touched the curve of her small face.

"I'll take a look," I whispered. "You drive back to the first telephone."

Luna shook her head. I clutched her whole shoulder and pointed to the ignition keys.

"No," she said stubbornly, so loud I was afraid she'd be heard.

Her expression had solidified almost as firm as the rock we hid behind, and I could see for the first time the vestige of Cherokee fatalism she'd earlier claimed.

So we both got out and eased shut the doors. I caught her hand. There was still an edging of charcoal around her cuticles from when she'd tried to improve her rendering of Sam's face. We began moving quietly forward about one hundred feet off the narrow road but keeping parallel. There wasn't much cover. The tall pines let the last of late-day sunshine through, but few bushes thrived between their trunks that, as second growth, weren't broad enough yet to conceal two people. Once much larger trees grew on these slopes, but most had been cut and sluiced down to build mining camps and establish ghost towns.

Ghost, I thought, easing forward with Luna alongside, wondering if Tamsen Donner's ghost might have been a harbinger of death. The possibility made me grab Luna's arms and with a fierce expression yank her behind me. Her fingers hooked onto the back of my belt as tree to tree, yellow pine to white fir, we padded on a slight downslope still too high to grow chaparral or manzanita, sometimes rustling past a dwarfed cedar or between poison oak and buckbrush.

On the road behind us, the last dust had settled now. I could hear nearby bird noises, black-billed magpies, perhaps; they liked running water. But I could no longer hear the shallow creek or Luna's footsteps or mine on the soft forest duff. In fact, it was good to be deaf. I began stepping forward with bold strides while she jerked on my belt.

When we had walked, by my watch, five minutes or so, Luna's hand ran up between my shoulder blades. I turned to see her finger fly to her lips. She had caught some sound I could not hear. Then she motioned us forward again. From here on I placed my boots more carefully and lightly on the forest floor.

Finally I heard their voices ahead of us, voices on the same pitch level, probably the two adult males, since Sam's was still boyish in tone. I nodded to let her know they were audible. The road turned. As we made a wider curve a new silver gleam appeared through the trees, too high to be the car. Roof. Metal. By instinct we both bent to half height and stopped moving in a straight line but took a more wandering random track, like two chimpanzees posing as harmless light and shadow, toward the cabin at dead end in the Sierra Nevada woods. There was a second shine when the car came into sight.

I pointed. Ahead the two voices dropped in volume. Must have gone inside the car or under that roof.

Toward them we made our circuitous, almost ceremonial, way. An odd thing: in that moment my skin tingled with what had to be adrenaline but felt like happiness. From a clearing to our right rose a sudden clapping as a covey of quail flashed up and flew away from us. We froze into tree trunks ourselves. I looked closely at Luna, pressed against that tree like Joan to the stake. Yes, happiness.

Now I could hear no more voices ahead, and Luna answered my raised eyebrows with a headshake that said she could not hear them either. Silence and stillness. In front of us, gradually, ordinary natural noises resumed, though I could make out no details since the wind was slight. We came to a clearing, edged it, and reached a spot between trees where a brown cottage was visible. Against one wall a third block of silver turned out to be a cylinder of bottled gas. This close, we could see all over the parked car a dozen or so dust-free crescents as vivid as if they had been embroidered in metallic thread on Merlin's robe. How could the kidnappers have missed them?

When I pointed Luna nodded. Her eyes were wet.

The men had taken their voices indoors, along with Sam, we supposed. I looked for something to duck behind, but there was no woodshed or toolhouse or pumphouse. The dry side of the Sierra Nevada is no place to dig a well. Nor could I see any place for a generator unless it was inside. To this cabin, hunters and fishermen would pack in all supplies and, after dark, might rely on fire, lanterns, flashlights.

Well, we were the hunters now.

With eyebrows high, Luna was pointing and making odd motions with both hands. I figured out she was asking me to dismantle the kidnappers' car. But how? If I raised that hood, someone would surely spot it through a window. I shrugged and she poked. Perhaps if from this side I crawled in and stayed low on the front seat I could yank out wires. I gave her a doubtful nod. There was occasional movement indoors beyond the dusty windows, but by crawling on all fours I kept the car well between the house and me. Squatting, I reached overhead for the door handle: unlocked, thank God. Slowly I eased open the passenger door. The interior stank of old meat sandwiches with onions, and as the smell rolled past me I wondered if it would make Luna gag. Feeling upward past the glove compartment, underneath the dash, my fingers met only a smooth hard plastic slope. I pulled my weight by the steering column and slid prone along the front seat with one boot easing the door almost shut. The dome light had gone on but in sunlight it wouldn't show.

I could feel Luna's warm hand around one leg, a rope that would warn and pull me back. As I wormed past the gear shift (left in reverse) and the hand brake (set) it suddenly seemed more useful to roll the whole car downhill where I had glimpsed the edge of a small canyon. I shook my leg, but Luna would not let me go.

After some acrobatics I finally got it in gear and released the hand brake, then whacked my head in surprise at its instant downhill lurch. I'd be trapped! She was yanking on both legs now. Forgetting to be quiet, I went scrambling backward out of the car that by then had stopped a front tire briefly against a rock.

Now there was no time to see if Brown Trousers was gaping out the window. I motioned Luna for help (had I kicked her?), grabbed the door frame, and shoved hard. She leaped to the back and pushed. Slowly, then faster, the wheel climbed over the rock;

then the car moved in one direction while we flipped aside in another and rolled into the trees and scrub. I pressed myself flat beside Luna who unintelligibly tried to scream in a whisper in my bad ear. I said, "Did I kick you?" and she flapped one hand to dismiss that and pointed.

Inch by inch but with gathering speed, the car drove itself forward as if feeling its way down the uneven hillside, its back window ornamented with a dozen narrow moons. If it made any noise crossing pine needles, I could not hear. Then a muffled shout rose from indoors, but they had seen it too late. The cleared backyard eventually dropped off into a gully ten feet deep and steadily deepening even more the farther it had cut, and the car's front wheels had found it. The Mazda nosed over the edge and then slewed itself until it tipped over and with a great crash dropped in upside down. I could not have placed it more perfectly with a crane.

Two men were pounding out of the house and racing behind it while—slowly—Sam, staring, edged out the door they had slammed shut. Luna caught my hand. He looked wary but uninjured. Brown Trousers shouted and waved both arms to slap through the dust cloud, then got outshouted by the second man in khaki shorts who yelled that he goddamned sure had put on the fucking brake and the goddamn car had not been left in gear; he never left a car in gear; at which Brown Trousers hit at him wildly with a fist but skidded the blow by mistake under his ear.

Neither man had any reason to look for Luna and me, nor—at that moment—did they notice Sam easing shut the front cabin door, backing away under the eave. Luna shook my sleeve. We did not dare wave to him or call out. From the front corner of the house Sam trotted into the far woods beyond us all, down the wild mountain and directly away from the road that had carried us here. The house blocked my view; then I caught sight of him thrashing beyond it and downhill. As the crow flew, his path might have been vaguely pointed toward Washoe Lake and Virginia

City, but he was no crow, and I did not know what lay ahead of him. Luna stood up to follow, but I jerked her down.

The two men had run to the canyon's rim to stare down at the upturned wheels and axles. For one moment nothing moved but the last dust settling; nothing sounded, changed. Then, with a single movement, both men spun and ran full speed for the cottage door that Sam had wisely closed behind him, so at first they crashed inside, bellowing, to search the rooms, perhaps closets and hiding places.

Luna said softly, "I can't see him anymore."

"Shhh."

The men ran out and circled the house. Though we tried to lie flat as lizards, they could have seen us easily had not their gaze rapidly swept the woods waist high for the shape of a running boy. I thought: *I must remember to tell Luna that if we get out of here—how people see what they look for.*

I could make out none of the angry words the men shouted before they started at a jog side by side and down the road they had driven in on.

As soon as they had gone a ways, Luna plucked at me and took a step. She was anxious for us to run on after Sam, but I pressed her down until the two had moved farther away and taken a turn.

In my ear she said, "They'll find the van."

"If they go that far before they turn back," I said in hers. We had kept our hands joined, so as soon as the men grew indistinct beyond the trees we sprinted around their house and into that part of the rocky pine forest where Sam had disappeared.

But soon the terrain made us drop hands. Not since boyhood had I run so fast in that wholehearted headlong way, back when it was routine to believe on the school ground what was now true— that my life depended on it. Mine and Luna's. Sam's.

Since at speed we could not be quiet, we no longer bothered but fled blindly, gasping and thudding, with breath making a long roar inside our heads. On my chest, the aid unit banged like a fist.

We dodged around trees, gray stone, a thornbush. There was a gentle slope at first, then more edges of more canyons and gulches, some of them blocked by boulders. There was no sign of Sam, still no way to call. Once we stopped to listen for the thrashing of some other runner, but I could hear nothing but my own body. Once, too, Luna stumbled and slammed into my lifted leg, so we both rolled grunting downhill and got scraped and cut, but were up and running again before the first blood had reached the scratches.

I touched my ear, made my gasping mouth say: *Hear the men coming?*

With a headshake Luna drew even and passed me, leaping onto, then over, a fallen pine trunk. She seemed to hit the ground as hard as the car had hit bottom in the gully, but then I could *hear* Luna no matter how muted the rest of the world.

We needed a hiding place, a rest, but now the steeper mountain had hold of us both and was forcing us to race even faster, half falling along whatever temporary openings could be glimpsed and shot through between brown trunks and gray rocks with stunted bushes stuck in their cracks.

At last behind one of the tallest granite boulders she collapsed to catch breath, and I slumped beside her, facing the way we'd come, for now my hearing aid gave me nothing but amplified booms in every artery. I pushed the molds deeper in my ears. Neither of us could talk. I didn't know where we were, where Sam was. I could see no roof, no sign of life, and from Luna's face she could hear nothing, either. I couldn't find any nearby stone the right weapon size to break a skull. Panting, feeling my sweat bloom and go quickly dry, I took out and opened my pocket knife. *Lex talionis.* No time to tell her. Genesis 9:6. Didn't quite fit. Have to do. What history needed in Berlin back in 1939 was one handful of decent murderers. Guess John Wilkes Booth and Lee Harvey Oswald thought they qualified.

I saw rather than heard her hard suck of breath. Two dark

bearlike shapes came distantly into sight, not moving downhill toward us but farther uphill and parallel, as if they expected Sam to double back to the road. They were wrong. He'd take the wild way down.

Luna, blowing out hard, had pressed her fingertips between her breasts. You'd think they could hear our lungs, feel the pull and puff of the wind we were making!

Now sounds floated to us downhill. First I watched Luna's listening face, then finally caught the wail of voices myself. The men were calling him. I could not decipher the name they knew Sam by, nor make out any words, but caught the tone shift from threat to cajoling and back again.

Except for these calls that in regular waves ascended to lure, then dropped to menace, I could hear nothing but my own body getting calmer. Luna firmly encircled my hand with the open knife in it, so we waited as if prepared to share any stabbing that might be required.

Still calling, the two men moved on. Were they following Sam's trail or ours? Surely we two had cut a wide swath for any tracker, but these city men in city shoes were not likely to clamber through rocks and underbrush for very long.

Except for the noise, I would have sharpened my knife on the rock we stood behind, listening. Rather, Luna was listening; I watched her red face cooling. There were twigs in her hair, a spot of blood on her chin. Brier.

She spread her empty hands. Out of earshot? I know all about that. Up to twenty feet, the ear works well, and two people can communicate; up to one hundred feet, one person can be heard by another; more than that and the Indians privileged the eye with the smoke signal.

So the men couldn't hear us, either. We took a few cautious steps but I stopped, told Luna it was surely more practical to head for the van, bring help, cops, search parties. She argued that Brown Trousers and Khaki Shorts were still in motion between us and the road by which we'd parked, but even while she talked she was moving on, downhill, hell-bent to chase Sam down the steep passes.

More slowly I came behind her, glancing back, trying to see how high the sun was. We were somewhere east of Tahoe and, from the pines and cedars and white fir, still in the montane zone; but I could see nothing that would have oriented me—not a toy ski slope that would have signified distant Incline Village, nor the recognizable Slide Mountain, not Tahoe behind nor Washoe Lake below. Just countryside getting steeper.

I said softly, "We'll never find Sam by ourselves." Then we both became statues when one more call sounded from behind us and uphill, far away.

Its echo was still returning past us when Luna dislodged her stiff body and hurried on. I knew her, knew she had this unexamined conviction that anything meant to be would devise its own means to be, by magnetism, like a homing pigeon, through the *I Ching*, whatever. The world was Swiss cheese through which some magical power leaked.

"Slow down," I grumbled behind her, for really we were now climbing downhill, with handholds onto limbs and ledges.

She grunted. "I want to get far enough away from them to call Sam myself." Even as she clambered ahead, her eyes were scanning the hillside for signs of him. "Surely he knows we're coming."

I used to have more optimism myself, I thought, coming clumsily behind her; I was optimistic like Leibniz—another Lutheran—who said God only allowed evil without endorsing it, set limits to it, would overcome it in the end. Then came the Lisbon earthquake. Then came the Holocaust, or Hiroshima, or even one little dynamite blast on a road construction site. One boy toppling off a cliff like a single sparrow falling.

She snapped an accusing finger back at me; I must be crunching pinecones underfoot with more noise than she liked. We stood still to be certain other shoes were not making those noises, too. Nothing. I decided to put up my knife before I fell on it.

Soon we were at risk of sliding. It became necessary to stop more often, to choose a route down that we could retrace up if necessary. Her hair was sprinkled with sand in which mica sometimes shone.

At one rest stop, now that I'd stopped panting, I managed to ask, "What name did they call him?"

Ahead of me she was edging carefully along a switchback ragged path that wild animals must have scraped down this precipice, and I could see blood on the palm of her right hand, a cut on her wrist. She turned up a disgusted face. "They kept changing. Pedro. Manuel. Injun Joe. To them he doesn't really have a name."

"Is it really Sam?"

"It is to me." For her small feet, this ridge was wide enough, but I had to set my boots heel to toe and lean twisted into the rock face. There was no sign that anything fatter than mice had come along this way, and Sam could be pressed like a tree frog against some other vertical block of granite, within earshot or not.

At a wider spot in the trail I caught myself from sliding. "Soon we'll have to call out. Before we're too far apart."

"So what if they do hear? The name Sam means nothing to those men. They'll think Sam's a rock climber or a hiker. Besides, they've probably given up. They've got to figure out a way to town."

Her long speech had used up all her breath, and she waited, forehead on the rock.

"Me in front now," I wheezed, and for one moment, edging behind her, had her whole body underneath mine—seed and husk. "They'll walk out."

"Find the van?"

"Maybe not. Big rock."

"Keys." She pushed off to follow. "Identification."

"Everything you own."

"Your backpack. Money?"

"Got that."

"Me too," though I knew her purse, driver's license, check-book, and so on were still in the van. I jumped a crevice where the rock wall had simply cracked open when the mountain was heaved up from earth's core and into place. She leaped to my out-stretched hand. "Left," she added with a gasp, "receipt. Campsite."

"But." I waited for breath. "No. Connection. Sam to us."

We waited against the rock, Luna nodding. "Stranger's van," she concluded on behalf of the two men we could visualize searching its contents.

"Ready now?" We moved on, dropping slowly down the wall of a rugged canyon that had a few pools of shining water trapped behind stone. I could already taste it.

At the next wide spot Luna, always impatient, got in front again. I thought how much she must need that water, dehydrated still from booze and hangover. Suddenly she recoiled, then hunkered down with what seemed a shudder. Over her dark head I could see that the trail was broken. Rockfall or flash flood had barreled through. The gap was six, eight, ten feet wide, and the drop one hundred feet or more. I looked uptrail. It would be a hard climb back.

We stayed where we were, immobile and silent. I got this picture of God looking down on us the way I might look down on two stymied beetles.

It was terrible.

Luna said something, then louder to bestir me. "I can't jump that."

"Me neither. Stay still. Let me look." On the edge I worked my way precariously past her. Below, the rainwater ponds were glittering, but so was the waning sunlight on shafts of stone that stood upright below us, well placed to fracture skulls or snap spines. I won't pretend; the risk of falling scared me. Not until now had I mentally allowed that we amateurs could actually die on this Sierra Nevada descent, which I had mistaken for an inconvenient walk home. Nobody was searching for Luna or Sam or me in these granite mountains. We could drop here, break bones, and decay just as unnoticed as sick old eagles or lost Pomeranian dogs.

At the end of the trail I paused to study the space in front and the back side of this great gouge. I'm no real rock climber. What little I know I taught myself out of books, then by falling (not very far) and scrambling up again. Luna and I are alike in that way; we've lived too long in books alone.

I tracked a possible route across on the granite face. My boots were too stiff for certain shallow footholds and, for someone as short as Luna, my handholds might be out of reach, though her thinner fingers could find narrower grips than mine. I wiped both palms on my clothes, then the fingertips against springy lichen thriving in the stone.

"I can work my way across," I said more cheerfully than I felt, "and help you."

I paid no attention to something she said about being too tired but stepped onto a spot that the side of my foot could support. I slid my hand left on the rough surface, not overhead but staying below the shoulder, keeping my heels down and striving for equilibrium. There! "See where my foot is?" I called, hoping these were not to be my last words. Then came the spider, the insect, the frog movement, when the left foot flies onto the next crack of wall while the right shoe leaps home into the former place, balancing. A wonderful feeling! As if you were only lying full length on the welcome home-base of flat rock and could rest horizontally as long as you chose—which is how such scenes are faked for the movies.

Luna groaned from behind, "I'll never do that!"

THE SHARP TEETH OF LOVE

"Don't think about it—you will." And I edged on across and emptied that long-held breath. "Here. Catch my hand right where you change feet."

She froze on the far side, afraid.

"You're lighter than I am, it'll be easier. And I won't let you fall."

She was shaking her head. I said, "If you don't, then what?" She felt the rock but did not launch herself onto it. I said lightly, "If you turn back and I die over on this side, Tamsen Donner ain't going to be nothing!"

As if this might be her last chance, Luna suddenly howled down the canyon as a she-wolf might, *"Sam? Sam! It's Luna! Sam?"*

The echoes went tumbling; maybe I heard half their diminishing roll downhill. I kept my hand out toward her, over the breach. With too much care, too much body stiffness, she stepped onto the first easy place but hugged the rock too close, off-balance. Her boots were still pretty stiff; she must be blistered by now. "Good, fine," I said. "Ready to shift feet?" She plastered herself to the rock with a noise that was almost like a squeak. I stretched while her flung hand glanced off mine, flew back. "Dance on over," I said. "I won't let you fall. Take a long breath." We both took it; then she came to me.

Without giving any thought, I just wrapped Luna as close as bodies can get. The hand I had almost pulled loose kept trembling against my back, but the rest of her held on tight. We slow-waltzed away from the chasm to where the ledge widened and had collected sand and stunted plants. Her hair tickled underneath my chin. Once we were safe on this flat interval, Luna tipped her head and fixed her mouth there, her sharp front teeth. I thought she might vampire the life out of my neck, but I was willing, very willing.

She shuddered once. From here the path led on, wide enough for two deer or for us two humans who hung on to each other while our reflexes still hung on to the granite cliff. I heard myself

208

murmuring things like *Great, Good work, Attagirl,* and occasionally she gave one of those squeaks.

Though we were walking in lockstep now, turned to face so her mouth was still wetting my neck, I sensed that part of Luna remained alert in case Sam's voice should call back to her; and for all I know that's the difference between women's love and men's love. They subdivide for other people; we for work or things. Fathers resent new babies, and I saw why. Was I jealous of Sam? Not yet; in domestic routine, I might be. I kissed Luna's salty hairline, but we were not yet firmly rooted enough on this ledge, so we stumbled awkwardly on. When it became too narrow, we had to let go of each other in favor of the mountainside we kept easing down, step by step. From behind I sometimes stroked her back or shoulder—intimacy, passion, fuck it; and when I touched her she would nod without turning.

At last in the bottom of the rocky canyon I dropped alongside a seep and scooped her a handful of water. Then one for me. Afterward each of us dipped for ourselves, not needing to look down, eyes locked. It made a funny contrast—this romantic fixed gaze contrasted by noisy slurping, the water made pink in our hands from all our injuries. We couldn't help our smiles. Hers was very tired.

"I thought we were going to die."

I said, "We might yet." But danger is an aphrodisiac, and while she kept gazing I slid my wet fingers gently up her jaw, tested her cheek, raked them tight into her hair, and then very slowly bent forward with care to let my open mouth lightly sample the soft places all around hers before it went lightly, then hungrily, home. Maybe that roundabout lingering was the best part, that and our silence. Her mouth felt soft as a child's, then gradually wide as a woman's. In it my tongue and then all of me disappeared. She made a humming noise high in the sinuses; I broke off to kiss those spots over and under her eyes, but then back to her tongue where she tasted of ocean water and something more weary and acid.

I breathed into her ear, "This wasn't the way I'd planned it."

"You've been planning?" She put her index finger on my neck. "Did I bite you?"

"And we're worn out. And you must be starved."

"That's right" (I think she said) as she nodded but slid one hand inside my leg and onto the ache I was feeling.

"Jesus." I believe it was a reverent word; it was certainly awed. I got my pants off in some contest for speed. She didn't; in fact she feigned helplessness. I considered and chose to believe she had left to me this button, this odd undersnap, this zipper, then underneath those tiny, frivolous underpants before I could touch wet curly hair, had left her clothes on for reasons of her own, maybe to feel like Rapunzel in her tower; who knows what goes through other people's heads, even lovers'?

But at last even lace was an impediment; I grew impatient and too fast; my hearing aid flew out and the battery box left my shirt and probably broke—but who cared?

"Not so fast," Luna said. "I'm tired of fast." Maybe she was only whispering; I had to hear her with the whole surface of my skin so had no trouble at all.

I agreed, and with a jerk rolled her on top of my body so the gravel would stick to my back and not hers. Two of my miniature faces were mirrored in her eyes. "Not so fast," but first I needed her to let me inside before I'd be able to muster any delay. An easy fit; right away: deep. And hot; we must both be feverish. I took a long, controlled breath and made myself hold still, far in. Dissolving. If I moved it would all be over.

"Luna?" Not a word. She moved her hips in some way that caused a clutch. We rolled over; I had been unable to feel the stones anyway. Her strong legs flew up to embrace me, scratch upon bruise upon scratch. With one hand I tried to press her in front while we moved, but she was still new to me, her parts mysterious under my awkward fingers, and maybe this first time finesse would matter less than it later would. During all this clumsy

groping her wide eyes gazed into mine and showed me my miniature faces. She said three syllables—I think they made up my first
and last name. Suddenly she shifted her body in some minor way
that pleased her more and quit looking and that inner grabbing
forced me to thrust. Her face became closed to me, then, eyes
shut, the twist of her mouth almost pained, and her teeth showing.
I could not keep still, could not even slow down, while her breathing sang higher and faster.

Then I was gone, much too fast and too far, but I managed to
get my hand onto her, working, with thoughts of hot custard, and
take her along (or I hoped so) and then we were both abruptly
used up and drooping loose from each other's heat. The sensation
of melting spread all the way up my body. When I looked down at
hers, the late sunlight slanting into the canyon warmed and made
bright maybe half her bare skin.

"Whoo."

Luna turned her head, gnawed at my shoulder, slid aside.
Slowly, hard lumps of stone became real under my back and hers.
I reached to stroke a breast that had been neglected in the rush.
"I've bruised you."

"No" (I could read on her lips) "I was already bruised."

It was a small shallow breast, the tip pink and faintly chilly in
the fading light; I had been wanting to touch it ever since that
glimpse in the Sundowner. With a little lazy squirming, I got my
face against it, prepared to rest there till morning. Her fingers
wandered pleasurably in my hair, along the beard that always felt
thin, even borrowed. She pulled me close against her. We were
melted together like all those buttery tigers that spun around Little Black Sambo.

She turned up my face so after two tries I could read the
words on her mouth: "You know what I'm thinking of?"

I wound a leg between hers and murmured "Sambo" around
her nipple.

"Binoculars."

I got that word because it vibrated through her chest. "What?"

When she sat up my head rolled loose down her torso until, mood broken, I had to sit up, too, and pick tiny pebbles off the new dimples in my back.

"People with binoculars." She reached for her bikini pants—they were flowered—and slid them on smoothly after one swish at loose sand on her backside. "There's probably condos and ski lodges downhill."

"Not for miles." I was discovering that both my elbows were raw.

She snapped on her shorts. "That T-shirt?" I found and handed it to her, managed one quick kiss to her shoulder. "Oh!" In a crouch she scuttled down the canyon and fetched my battery box with the attached pink amoeba that had been shaped to my ear canal. "It landed on sand. Does it still work?"

I cleaned the mold and, still naked, fitted it into place and fiddled with the volume. "Hard to believe, but it still works." I didn't want to dress yet; I was still, in a way, wearing her body. I wanted to see on her flesh some mark I had made, but the only signs had been left by the mountain. When I touched her chin, the blood drop that had dried to a brown beauty mark came off and stuck to my fingertip. I tried to affix it to my own chin.

She was laughing when there came the distant thump of helicopter blades—or to me they were so distant I did not even identify the throbbing sound until Luna pointed. The pilot far north in the darkening sky was not seeking us, though, and as he faded away I caught and directed her hand toward me.

"Later," she said, "but we need to find Sam before full dark."

I shook my head. "It's a needle in a haystack, well, three needles in a very big haystack. We need to get ourselves out of the mountains first and bring help" (I waved toward the helicopter's speck) "to find Sam. Professionals."

"All right." She did not look at me below the neck. Embarrassed? Another man-woman difference? They're all out of fashion nowadays. Then Luna was on her feet, pulling her hand out of mine, ready to move; no postcoital lingering for Luna; no easy stereotypes for me.

She started yelling, *"Sam!"*

Half irritated but half amused, I dressed more slowly. I thought she might even like to look at me; construction work had built my muscles and focused my strength. But Luna could not stand mere waiting and kept yelling his name up and down this steep ravine.

I sucked back a yawn as we descended more deeply by jumping from one heaped rock slide to another. "Aren't you tired?" Miss Gazelle leaped on. On either side of this great cleft grew tall pines that shadowed the depth, so we still had many hard miles climbing way down toward the arid belt. I hoped we would come out near a road.

Scrambling behind I called, "Slow down, Luna. If either one of us breaks a bone, we'll never make it out!" Such fatalism seemed crazy when I could visualize a map of this area with the two of us as pinpoints inside a swatch of land that had to be outlined by highways, yet there was plenty of wild, steep country between us and the sagebrush plains. You didn't have to be a Donner to die in this terrain. Luna kept moving too fast until I yelled, "Good place for rattlesnakes!" and her pause helped me catch up.

Sadly she said, "Maybe Sam has already broken a bone."

I just pointed to the last place we had seen the helicopter as a sign that we needed outside help, regardless. I wanted to say, *I love you,* but that's hard to yell at somebody's back, and did I? Really? If you ask a couple on their golden wedding anniversary if they really love each other, do they still have to think it over?

My parents loved each other—I'm sure of that—but to me it seemed all affection, their passion spent, the intimacy taken for granted.

I clambered along behind Luna, tracing with my eyes the out-line of her skimpy underwear. *Maybe she wants me to say it. She hasn't said so herself.*

Jumping and sliding and feeling our way, we finally reached a point where a second canyon had cut its way into this one with a drop over what in wet weather must be a long waterfall. Then the canyon angled off. A thin stream ran in its bottom, disappeared into scattered stones at the waterfall's lip, with its shine emerging down the scarp where an unexpected cottonwood had seeded it-self and clung.

I tried not to brood on Fast Steven.

Picking our way toward this irrigated pocket over accumu-lated and unreliable stones, we both took our first hard fall and al-most made the broken bones come true. I managed to roll like a shield over Luna, but our double rain of rocks could not be stopped. We hung on while they rattled by, pelting us both, then gave each other a grim nod and worked more carefully down the rubble slope.

With all that lovely shifting of the backside, how can elastic hold?

I watched her moving hips, thinking of California girls I had screwed, some wanting love words whispered, some thinking actions spoke louder than words. Some were holding out for a man with a house and car. One was more avid for birth con-trol than Margaret Sanger—she planned on someday being the fortyish mother of a genius conceived at a sperm donor center. One claimed to be bisexual, but she thought that was politically correct.

I watched top and bottom of Luna's spine while thinking this, the stubby wings of her shoulders sliding in and out as she walked. I mouthed with no sound the words *Maybe I love you,* but she couldn't know without lip-reading.

In a bowl beyond the cottonwood a very small meadow had formed with pale grasses and tiny purplish blooms. Here at last we were able to straighten, stand erect. When Luna stretched, her wings became internal. I glimpsed a swelling knot in my left temple that obstructed my sideways view, but could not remember being hit there. Luna was also scraped and scratched, her face dry but fiery, with one deep and gritty dent in her kneecap that ought to be cleaned and stitched. After she had bared her teeth and stuck the knee into a small cataract, I tore a strip off my shirttail to wind around and tie.

I asked her, "Now? Will you give in now?"

Against a boulder she worked herself into standing position and then seemed to wilt down again. "Oh, all right. We'll rest. And we'll stiffen up." Though she snatched a hard breath deep enough for opera, she could not shrill as strongly as before, "*Sam! Sam, it's Luna Moon. Sam!*" and remained taut and alert while an echo of *Am-Moo* rolled down the canyon and out of my range. "We don't even know his other name."

I decided to say it aloud now. "Luna, I—"

But she broke in, "Likely he's fractured his skull by now."

"Sam's a lot more nimble than we are." I got beside her, and we sat enwrapped under a sky with its first faint stars, untrustworthy, as if forming themselves behind gauze. West of us I could imagine but not see the last hot streaks of sunset. She asked what time it was, and I showed her my smashed watch.

"Throw it away?"

"Souvenir."

I didn't have the energy to lead up to loving, to ask about speedy Steve what's-his-name, to ask her if maybe passion could come before intimacy after all. She certainly hadn't come west in search of a bulldozer driver who read books on lunch hour, much less a man so ill adjusted to his handicap that he'd considered joining the silent Cistercians and using hand alphabets for the rest of his life.

Clearly she loved Sam, at least loved him the most, could get up from sex with me and holler for him. But what was I—

some emotional accountant? This was not the time or place to tally up love.

My muscles were stiffening, the calves quivering, and rust was beginning to grate in knee joints and ankles. Every drink of the chilly mountain water began freezing in our bendable places. Without speaking a word of love or of anything else, Mr. and Mrs. Tin Woodsman kept congealing there while the last daylight withdrew backstage of the sharpening stars.

She said sleepily, "Now you call him." There was no point. I yelled to the granite as loud as I could: *"Sam! Luna! Paul!"* We waited in the silence. The rock wall shadowed us so Luna's face was reduced to contours the color of steel. From time to time she relocated the injured knee.

I yelled for Sam one more time. Then I tried saying more softly, "Luna, when this is over," but her whole body made an impatient vibration in my arms. *Intimacy,* I promised her silently. *Maybe love.*

It got darker. I could smell my own dried jism; then our bodies cooled so I could only smell something pungent blowing up from the basin, perhaps the sagebrush we and Sam would be walking through tomorrow. Gingerly, Luna and I began to extend our limbs, half expecting elbows to creak, shoulders to groan. Finally we managed to lie down on the mixed sand and scree and talus, and our skin got cool and then cooler and at last cold, but we slept anyway.

During the night, grunting noises woke me. Luna was talking some foreign language against my ear. I jerked up painfully fast, thinking stupidly I would intercept Tamsen Donner myself, order her away, throw a rock if necessary. Deep in her dream, Luna went right on talking gibberish. Until then I had almost forgotten how my mother, in her sleep, would call out "Bruce!" after Dad had died. I thought then she was *remembering* him, not *seeing* him.

With one careful hand I tested which part of my legs hurt

most. I was hungry, too. The moonlight had turned us into pewter figurines.

From far away I could hear one long undulating sound—maybe a faulty siren? Coyote? More likely a rancher's dog with muzzle uplifted to the moon, but in which direction lay the god-damn ranch? The howl waned and did not come again.

Not until then, in the safe dark and silence, did I say silently the prayer for Sam's welfare I'd have been embarrassed for Luna even to know about. A candle is one thing; we smile at it; coins in a wishing well. But admit it: prayer is a secret vice. I'm not even sure the old Jews were right claiming God intervened in national history, much less in a personal one. Prayers notwithstanding, my father's sixty-year-old heart attacked him and won, and he never came back when Mother called. I don't like other grownups knowing that now, at half Dad's age, I still throw out prayers on the ether, and that it comforts me to know that in Wisconsin so does my mother. Hers are for me. Sometimes she prays for the soul of the baby whose still wispy spirit did not breathe out of those lungs but breathed in and got stuck there, got smothered. I used to ask how she would know him in Heaven, since all babies look alike. *I leave that to God,* was all she said.

Her prayers and mine and a sense that they intersect not far aloft, these have a California counterpart, a category suited to such shit—harmonic convergence—the moment when a crowd of outdated hippie types hold hands at some prearranged time, while standing on agreed longitudes, and exude positive spiritual energy toward peace.

Some preacher I'd make! Some theologian! I neither had nor understood what David Koresh meant to the Branch Davidians. One escapee from Ranch Apocalypse, though still ashamed that he had outrun the fire, had told a reporter Koresh would be back. His love for and faith in a madman like Koresh were strong as ever; why couldn't I be half as committed to Jesus of Nazareth?

Committed or not, I invoked Him in my prayer for Sam.

While I was choosing my petitions, Luna slept on and extended her long private argument with the cosmos and its spokeswoman.

I faced the stars, whether there's anything up there besides satellites and transcontinental planes or not. *Take care of Sam. Bring us all safely through. Cancel that stuff about curing deafness—a trade-off, OK? Help Luna most of all. Oh, show yourself to me, show yourself, show yourself!*

But what short of a burning bush would have satisfied me, Paul Cowan, who by a long shot is nobody's Moses? Instead of *Amen* I tried a more democratic and plain *Good night* before lying down again beside Luna, who was herself burning with warmth.

COME MORNING we loosed and separated, then straightened our soreness with care, got cautiously to our swollen feet, paused to see if anything essential might give way. After she took one step, Luna sucked air between her teeth.

"The knee?"

"And my feet. They're stuck to my boots with . . . with fluids I don't want to name." She reached up. "That lump on your head is blue and, ugh, it's oozing."

Then, with stubborn weariness, she drew in a chestful of air and blew out several shouts of Sam's name. Her face was puffy, sunburned.

"Don't look at me," she said, as she limped back from the stream and turned away to pee. Why do we hide from sight those parts of our bodies that have been locked in delight? I, too, turned aside toward the water, so narrow here that I could piss a liquid bridge across, while remembering that Tamsen had told Luna how when the Donner wagons crossed the Continental Divide, Will Eddy had pissed both east and west, thus into both oceans. When Luna had told me this, I'd doubted any nineteenth-century schoolteacher would use the word "piss," and insisted that vocabulary alone proved her just a figment of Luna's contemporary mind. "Hah *hah!*" she'd said. "You keep on and I'll get into Scripture and Greek and Latin and Aramaic and culture and whether Saint Paul had epilepsy!"

Without turning now, I called, "Anything new from Mrs. Donner's spook last night?"

Taking no offense, Luna pulled up her clothes and answered in a dreamy voice, "Tamsen says George and Jacob Donner spent their childhoods in Salisbury, North Carolina; I could hardly believe that. We passed those road signs on the way from Chapel Hill! But she says her first husband, Tully, was better looking, and I can understand that because of Steven." (That made me shoot her a look.) "But was that a love match or was it better the second time? After Tully got the cholera and then he and their children died so close together like that and all at Christmas, too? Tamsen just lost heart. They hadn't been married but two years. Two years and mostly pregnant."

I squatted down to drink as she added, "I always thought George Donner was mostly for security, like Ruth with Boaz, but she says they met in a meadow when she was taking children out to press flowers, that he met her among flowers, that they sat down in the daisies and asters." Talking, Luna suppressed a groan as she knelt beside me to drink water. The wrapping on her knee was bloody.

"Drink a lot; I wish we had a canteen." It was obvious we could not keep hiking alongside this stream since its canyon visibly became impassable. "Wet your shirt." We both did; I tried to touch her breast without grabbing. "Are you OK? Are we OK?" Her talk of Tamsen made me think for the first time of pregnancy. Well, so what? She could ascribe it to synchronicity and I to God's will, but I'd marry this girl; I would, and we'd have Sam and a baby, too, and my mother would think her prayer had come back home like some sweet boomerang.

I pointed downstream to where the canyon was blocked and animals had cut an exit trail, making myself look confident, smiling. "We're bound to be in the middle of some kind of parkland—could be state, county, forest service. Anyway, we'll come to people and trails pretty soon."

"Good," she said with a nod, but not sincerely. We drank as much water as we could hold, though one ranger had earlier warned us campers of cystic *Giardia* in some of the mountain streams. We concealed that knowledge by avoiding eye contact and climbing. I faced into nearby tree crowns, promising Luna that as soon as we got out of these forests to a vantage point where we had a real view of Nevada, we'd be able to chart a direct course toward houses and highway.

Looking discouraged, she said, "When Sam and I were riding around, we saw an awful lot of empty country. They didn't pick this state for atomic tests for nothing." Suddenly she wrapped both arms around me and pressed her face into my sore ribs. I stopped moving to hold her. After a silence she added wistfully, not *I love you,* but "Bacon would be good."

"If we keep heading toward it, we'll work out this stiffness."

She said, "I saw my face in the water. I look like a witch."

"It'll all be over soon and there'll be food and sleep and Sam." Watching the ground, I led us out of the canyon, but few tracks showed in this path, none made by shoes.

At the top she stood beside me to look over the wild countryside—steep, unchanged. "I used to dress up like a witch for Halloween," she said. She seemed to lack the strength to call Sam's name, so I did. This time her face did not seem alert enough to show concentration on even the farthest, faintest responses.

"Nothing?" I probed. Luna shook her head.

As we climbed down, each bend of that knee made her wince. A long boring time passed, though our muscles did loosen and the sunlight did warm our aches. Sometimes I reached back to tug her onto a boulder pile and down. When she got a questioning look on her face I would bellow Sam's name, wait, then keep moving. We made slow but steady time.

On one of the easier descents I thought of something I could talk about besides love or prayer and keep our minds occupied. "You know quantum physics? Chaos?"

She grunted. "Lord, no."

Sorry, I thought reflexively overhead, then became as brisk as a cruise director, a camp counselor. "They say now that subatomic particles might just be vibrations of little invisible loops of string; but the point is that nobody knows if that's real string or not, if it's really *there* in the same way these rocks are really here!" Like a fool, certain this line of thought would please her, I held up a stone for her inspection. "They're just making up a mathematical model for what we guess about."

"No shit."

"Here's what I'm getting at," I said with a toss of the rock, "just reverse that idea; try deciding the ghost of Tamsen Donner is really *there*, real as that rock"—somewhere far below it hit with a thud—"but we don't have a mathematical model for thinking about her!"

A slow smile grew in Luna's dirty face. "It's nice of you to say that, Paul," and she patted my arm. "You're a good person."

I didn't want to be good; I wanted to be passionately desired. "After the Civil War," I said, flustered, "there were dozens, maybe hundreds, of sightings of Lincoln by ex-slaves! All over the South!"

"Sure. And just as many of Elvis Presley by his fans. Then there are the people who are taken up in space ships and get biopsied in the worst possible places!"

"Whose side are you on?"

But Luna was smiling, walking a little faster, and it seemed important for us both to keep talking while we toiled downhill. At last our muscles were more flexible, but a long streak of blood had found its way down Luna's leg and inside her boot. She said, "And there's Lazarus. Didn't have a single piece of news to tell, either." I decided not to mention the Witch of Endor, whose "familiar spirit" had laid the groundwork for all those Victorian mediums spitting out gauze and calling it ectoplasm.

Downhill we worked our way for what seemed a long time before Luna delivered up what she'd been thinking. "People say when somebody dies, 'he gave up the ghost.' But it might well be possible to die, for all we know, and not give it up. Maybe a few people like Tamsen can fight like hell not to give up the ghost."

I wasn't about to argue, tired as I was on this steeper slope, so I switched sides. "Houdini died on Halloween while you were playing witch on the army post, right? And Tamsen's birthday is All Saints' Day? Houdini swore he'd come back but he hasn't been heard from since."

"Not that you *know* of."

We passed the next few minutes trying to avoid bone fracture. After she had straightened up on a patch of level ground she announced, "When we get out of here, I want a dog. I couldn't have one when we moved around so much. In Chapel Hill, the landlord wouldn't allow it."

"Fine, fine," I puffed.

"I brought home this stray dog once and my father was angry and took it away. It looked like his eyes were smoking. The dog was scared of him."

"One dog for you, one for Sam." We came out into a surprisingly easy, well-watered ravine, not a stone's throw across, fed by springs and with old conifer parts packed into sponge underfoot. Here we sank onto a dried-up trunk to drink while a little wind of cooler air moved past us and fell below. "What kind of dog?"

Unprepared, she said, "Big."

"Big retriever? Rottweiler? Great Dane? Newfoundland?"

She named a new breed, "Smartass," dismissed me, and wandered on downhill. Her limp had gotten very bad.

I called, "It's so cold in Wisconsin we'll have to bring the dogs indoors in the wintertime," and waited to see if she objected. She hobbled on.

Though we seemed to be inching a slow descent on some vast granite slope, it was still a shock when we emerged—quite suddenly—onto a stone prospect and could see out of this steep sierra onto mesa and then desert foothill below.

I came first upon the scene I'd predicted, and spread my fingers in the air to stop Luna so her senses could slowly filter forward into the view and all it promised.

She did gasp. Yes, the panorama was beautiful and unreal all at once. *Thank you,* I thought overhead by reflex. Far below the line was uneven where green merged into tan, tree dropped into scrub, woods flattened as desert. On our left rose ragged mesas, but to the right a gentler slope matted with something gray or olive stretched for many miles, some steel-wool vegetation; and farther away ran a stream with rows of clumped aspens, their small trunks bent downhill the way winter snows had weighted them.

Without that vista, we never would have hoped. In cars, on horseback, you gain a sense of changing scale, but only on foot does this terrible climb whether uphill or down reveal landscape too much the same, too impervious, too disinterested. You're embedded and cannot draw back, whether here or on Horeb. No wonder the Indians needed their elders to testify to far longer cycles of season, height, moons. Otherwise the winter would catch them in the same place in this changeless land.

I caught her hand as we looked upon irregular greens where they blotched into the golden curving hills of sand. But the basin had opened below us so suddenly that I dizzied, as if this were not Nevada but some spiritual abyss for which I needed Luna's hand. With the other one she pointed to some faraway settlement the size of an anthill, the way Yahweh must have seen Sodom. Still holding her hand, I sank onto a rock. Unless I was nuts there was even one line scraped black at a distance on the landscape, so ruler-straight it had to be laid in asphalt, somewhere between the mesas and the anthill. How far away?

"Paul? You OK?"

I nodded while she asked how long it would take. In the West, distance is so deceptive. Maybe as tricky as in the Sinai wilderness. I thought my head was buzzing but then identified bee sounds; we had climbed down low enough for pollen, bees.

"We're fine," I said with a squeeze of her fingers. "We're nearly out of it, Luna."

"*Sam?*" she bawled suddenly. "*Sam?*"

PART 5

Love Feast

~

Sparks, Nevada

THE BOY KNEW he had ridden many miles into the desert foothills beyond the limit promised his father when he was given his ATV—all-terrain vehicle—for Christmas. Both parents worked; neither one knew his promise had been dead since New Year's Day. They had assigned him a patch of the flattest, most boring dry landscape from whose arbitrary border he would still be able to see home base, his small concrete-block house sunk in the tawny sand like a bunker. They'd also said if he hoisted and flew the red scarf on a bamboo pole braced on the seat upright, the first adult home would be able to spot his location, too, and know he was in trouble. Though the boy still carried the scarf and often tied it outlaw style over his lower face, he had carefully lost the too-long bamboo and replaced it with two canteens, a row of Smurf-elves tied by their colorful hair to the handlebars, and a radio with earphones.

Clearly, his parents did not know what Trouble was. Trouble was not an empty gas tank, not an overturned machine. Trouble lived full time at school, grade 6, where the boy was neither popular nor smart. Trouble kept turning off lights in the boys' toilet and then shoving him around, bending his glasses. Their earpieces got bent because the tallest of a whole gang of Troubles liked to wet the crotch of the boys' jeans and then laugh. He would be crammed painfully between sink and wall while these stronger boys splashed handfuls of water from faucet to zipper, and once even peed on him there so he could not go back to the classroom but had to run out of the building, where he hid in a parked school bus until he could ride home, dry, and be punished there for truancy.

Now the boy lived only for afternoons after school when he could ride too far, too fast, turning himself into a jet that threw back contrails of dusty rings and dusty angles.

Today's bright sun had heated a metal button in the crown of his cap: enemy shrapnel. His was the last fighter heading home with one wingtip ragged.

When the boy spotted two tiny figures far ahead, sliding downhill onto flatter ground, he mistook them at first for his angry parents appearing at the wrong place to intercept. Quickly he swung back wheeling into his own dust and coughed into the red cloth protecting his mouth. But surely they would not both take off from work; both would not walk so far in the heat just to surprise him along his forbidden path? The boy turned back with a delicious skid and kept the brake on. One of the distant people waved. If angry, his father would never wave. The boy took a slow drink of water, watching. Where had they come from? Most of the houses and trailers stood in a row just parallel to the highway, in reach of water and sewer lines. Ahead lay the rolling tan hills, empty except for the track pattern he had left yesterday, then a rising hillside of juniper and sagebrush before the sharp rocky slope.

He checked his gas, then drove to meet them.

A GROANING ENGINE soon made it clear that the boy's junior vehicle could not for long bear him and Luna and Paul all three across the heated sand. He handed over both his canteens, with instructions. They were to follow his track, his main track now, not those detour places where yesterday he had fashioned swirls and crosses. After quite a while they would reach one barb-wire fence with a gate. By then the boy would have used the phone in the white-block house that would come into sight ahead, and he would have ridden back out to meet them. Probably he would meet them long before they had even glimpsed the gate, he said. It was aluminum. At some sunlight angles, it would shine a long way.

The man and the woman nodded. They kept holding hands, walking crooked, but like a pair of dancers they tended to stumble simultaneously in the same directions.

He could see that both of them were hurt, and the woman unsteady on her feet. In weary but fast voices they told him a boy about his size was also coming down the mountain, might even be down by now, and he must tell the dispatcher that when he called 911. Immediately the boy gaped in all directions. Not even a speck on the far horizon. He lifted one spread hand, helpless. In his whole life, until then, it had not really come home to the boy that someone no taller than he could actually die, die of exposure or injury or plain bad luck, and die in his own extended backyard. He carried this new definition of Trouble while he sped toward home to summon help. Racing and rocking and scattering sand, the boy thought that this, his only experience of rescue, was bound to change his life, perhaps even at school. He flung his mind onto that certain future change as if it were solid as an altar; he could see the years ahead of him uplifted into the life of a heroic man. His swollen chest ached from the great heart so recently acquired.

IN ANSWER to the boy's emergency call, at first only a sheriff's department car was sent in case this should be a prank, but then the deputy radioed for an ambulance and ran out between the tire tracks to help the man and woman reach the air-conditioned house. Indoors, he could not make either one sit down with feet up, could not keep wet cloths on their foreheads. They interrupted each other and babbled on about a formerly kidnapped and now-lost boy. The deputy checked by radio with Reno police. They set in motion the helicopter sweeps above the standard search parties made up of forest rangers and law enforcement people and volunteers, since in this rough terrain, tourists were always wandering off.

The man and the woman—Cowan, Stone—wanted to join the search themselves instead of seeing doctors, but they were bruised and dehydrated, hence overruled. Perhaps even delusional: when lifted onto the hospital loading dock, Paul's gurney rolled by a young girl in a T-shirt that pictured a garish Christhead under dripping red thorns with a red-letter message—WON BY ONE. Paul sat up to stare. Luna, who had a slight concussion, did not notice, or else he dreamed it.

In Reno they were admitted to St. Mary's Hospital, located near Circus Circus casino, and there were separated for treatment. Paul, rolled into one examining room, was given an instant I.V. and asked to respond to questions about the two of them and their medical histories while blood pressure, pulse, and heart sounds were taken. Down the hall, as soon as Luna found herself surrounded by four safe white walls, she faded into a blur of sleep and faint, so fearing concussion, nurses kept jarring her awake by snapping their fingers and calling "Ma'am? Ma'am?" After someone brought information back from Paul's room they began touching her scraped chin instead to urge, "Miss Stone? Luna Stone?" Each time she could barely get her iron eyelids cranked up halfway, and when she whispered "Sam?" that confused everybody.

Both were treated, palpated, and swabbed. Pinpoints of light tested their pupil reflexes. Paul's two broken fingers were set and taped together as, after X rays, Luna's knee would be cleaned and stitched. Paul then wanted to go straight to join the search parties, but everyone insisted on twenty-four hours' observation at the very least.

On another floor, in X ray, Luna roused enough to mistake the machine for some slowly descending dead tree. The technician stopped between exposures to soothe her. "You're fine now. You're both here at St. Mary's."

It was very confusing. *Both?* Luna went swirling back to the half-forgotten moment when she'd finally learned that her mother, Priscilla, had once as a teenage girl intended to become a nun, had even lived as a postulant in something called Holy Mary Hall. Luna thought they had both been somehow captured now by those Catholics, Priscilla to fill out her old term and Luna to make up for the long defection. And back in the early sixties the novitiate had actually been a term; a sentence, Priscilla said; it functioned just like any other religious cult. Separation from family. Brainwashing. No worldly clothes. No decorations allowed even on underwear. No scented soap. No uncensored mail in or out. No tampons allowed. ("Did they think they were dildos?" Priscilla had demanded, still angry, and Luna, who at that age did not know what a dildo was, had nodded dumbly.)

Priscilla Lunatsky had not made it into the last, even more enclosed, canonical year, during which even family letters could only be received at Christmas. Before that decisive ceremony for which she would have been dressed in white bridal garb to marry Christ, received the heavy, many-layered habit of her order, then had her hair cut off and head covered, never to be uncovered again—before that moment, Priscilla had simply walked away in the night, crying at every step that carried her both toward home and Hell. Six months later she met Luna's father. The Robber Bridegroom.

Now, when the nurse whispered, "You're at St. Mary's," Luna recoiled against the cold table. Obviously they were treating her head, her brain, with electricity. They were burning away doubt. With seven laser probes they would sear into scars the seven organic and deadly sins until Luna was transformed into some virtuous stranger who would be able to call her own mother "Sister."

She might have kept whimpering had it not been for her sudden glimpse of Tamsen Donner, her homespun skirt drooping through the bendable black arms and brackets overhead, where she was perched above the main camera like a small bird that had lit on a huge nest.

The nurse stopped patting to ask, "What are you laughing at?"

Luna managed to answer, "The ghost in the machine."

While Luna and Paul were being examined and tested, two crews of rescuers were working their way toward each other on foot, uphill and down. The downhill group by following Paul's directions had found Luna's van, still undisturbed, and from papers and possessions inside had tried without success to notify her mother, then had telephoned Major Martin Stone, U.S.A. Retired, who was catching a plane the next day. Of the two kidnappers there was no sign, either on the ground or from the air by volunteers from the Tahoe-Truckee Civil Air Patrol chapter. Lawmen did find and search the cabin where the men and Sam had been, but its indoor surfaces showed hundreds and hundreds of visitor fingerprints, too many to help. They were hoping the rented car would provide more useful prints once they could hoist it into reach.

They did take prints inside the van, though, especially the small ones under the passenger window that might belong to Sam, in case he was somewhere on a missing child roster. All this took time, and it was past dark before they turned up Paul's backpack with its ID cards inside, and even later before they reached Mrs. Erika Cowan in Wisconsin. She had gone to bed. "Who?" she kept asking at first. "No, he's in California. What? Oh mercy. Are you sure? Is he hurt?" Talking, she fell back onto the edge of her bed, absently unwinding the plait of her graying hair in case it should need to be fixed anew for the public. She wound a long tail of hair around the telephone to choke off what she was hearing. "Wait, I need a pencil," she said, untangling herself. On the other end, a California man spelled everything for her. From time to time,

Erika spat on the pencil lead for no better reason than it was her dead husband's habit. *Bruce ought to be here now,* she thought, resentful. Then on a deep breath, she said, "Fine, I'm coming, just how do I do that?" She had never been on an airplane in her life. In the next silence the stranger thought of travel agencies while she thought of Lutheran pastors. She said, "Never mind, I can find out. I'm coming, you tell Paul that. No. I'll surprise him." They were about to hang up when she snatched back the phone to say rapidly, "You tell those doctors he's got a hearing loss; make them speak up; he's smart as anybody and smarter than most," and to hear, "Yes ma'am."

The "ma'am" comforted her. Some mother like herself had instilled those good manners. Erika Cowan got up and tried to dress in the dark; no need to burn electricity until crisis actually came into the room. But she could not pack without light and, in the end, needed its aid to find a clean slip and stockings.

Her Lutheran pastor—German in temperament and heritage—was a member of the Wisconsin Synod that dates back to 1850. Erika hated to telephone him so late, having never done so except when Bruce Cowan died at another postmidnight hour; but ministry was his vocation, after all.

Erika caught back and swallowed a sob, thinking of Paul out on the desert, and deaf, suffering thirst like Ishmael.

They had never wanted him to go to California. Bruce said there were spiritual dangers in a climate with no real winter; it would be like having seven weekdays with no real Sabbath to slow you down.

She put on the last of her clothes, angry at someone yet unnamed, and telephoned and woke the pastor of her church who said he would telephone airlines and call her back. Interpreting his pause correctly, she said into the mouthpiece, "Yes, I have money." Quite a lot of cash, in fact, secreted here and there throughout the house since Bruce had thought banks were risky.

After hanging up she moved quickly to collect greenbacks

from jars and vases and fruitcake tins, and wrap these neatly around her yellow pencil, largest denominations inside; then she snapped on a rubber band and buried the fat green lump under the last-minute items she kept stuffing into her Sunday purse. She turned on the porch light five minutes before the pastor might arrive. When he rang her doorbell she snapped open her suitcase and, on impulse, added a scrapbook of family photographs. Then she turned off all the lights and made her way smoothly through the dark to the waiting car, though the minister stumbled once. Three hours later Erika was strapped into a seat overlooking a silver wing wider than her own hallway, and seeing for the first time how treetops must look to wild geese and eagles.

Still, trees were less remarkable than the glitter struck off tall buildings stuck upright in Nevada sand like chunks of firewood. By dawn Erika had grown tired of America spread out before her like quilts with toys and birthday candles showing, and had realized besides that Paul would probably not appreciate her rushing across the country to his hospital bed. Just after his eardrums burst, he had called her directly and (unable to hear a single one of her worries or plans) had overridden her desire to come with shouts about his well-being.

She followed her pastor's instructions about collecting baggage in the Reno airport and asking the curbside taxi driver to state in advance what he would charge to deliver her to—Erika read off a church notepad—"Sierra and Fourth."

"Circus Circus," he said and whisked her suitcase onto the backseat.

At sunrise the Reno lights must be blinking half strength, but they blinked on all sides, a waste of electrical power sufficient to prove what Erika had always suspected: that gambling cleaned out a lot of gamblers' pockets. In disbelief she finally stared at the tall pink towers below which the cabdriver parked. She paid him not a dime more than she had contracted for, thanked Mr. Fernando Cabanillo (as his posted taxi license said), and carried her own suitcase past the giant clown and lollipop sign and several pushy young men in plush uniforms. Inside, a thin and weary young woman in a tinsel swimsuit stopped juggling fake barbells to show her the check-in desk. Erika came back afterward to stop her movements again and ask where the elevator was.

But when Erika had sponged off and ridden downstairs again, that girl was gone, so she had to ask a clown with rouge patties on his face how to get to St. Mary's Hospital and if it was safe to walk.

Visiting hours there had not yet begun. In the waiting room, several men were sound asleep in the softer chairs, so Erika chose a straight wooden one. It was too low. Both knees stuck up and slanted her lap with the photo album downhill toward her stomach. She saw herself reflected in the wide window glass as a tall, flat-featured outdoorsman ill suited to women's clothes. Never pretty, she had always been comforted by a God who looked straight through countenance to soul. Besides, there had been Bruce—just as tall, just as gangly—who liked the way she was put together.

She must have dozed off with the scrapbook propped at the wrong angle in her lap. Bright sunlight through that window was the next thing she knew, a light that did not seem to match the time shown on Bruce's old pocketwatch, which she wore on a ribbon around her neck. She rushed to the visitors' desk to learn Paul's room number, then fell back when the woman said Paul Cowan had already been discharged.

Discharged to where? His former California apartment? Or Truckee, from which he had called her before setting off into the woods? (That time she'd done the shouting, though he had his hearing aid by then.)

The woman volunteer said soothingly, "I imagine he's gone to help search for the boy."

While Erika was asking what boy, the woman said, "But his girlfriend is still here—306. She's doing well, but they want to run some more tests."

So it was a girl who had caused all this! Erika shoved the photo album hard into one armpit and hung her shoulder bag on top, repeating, "Three-o-six?" She chose to climb the stairs so she'd have time to think. In Stockholm, there had not been many girls, not enough, perhaps, but at Paul's age and in California and if he was anything like Bruce, well—

On the third floor she stood outside the room with its name posted inside a brass slot: Madeline Lunatsky Stone. Polish mixed with English? That would do. During Paul's early adolescence she and Bruce had shared an unspoken uneasiness about how slow he seemed to ask girls out. Bruce must have feared too much farmwork had worn Paul's libido down to a nub; he began taking him to see the Green Bay Packers and telling mild girlie jokes during the half. But Erika suspected her own too-serious Christianity might have overheated and then sanctified Paul from the waist down. Either that or—well? She could never bring herself to raise with her husband even the dimmest possibility that some older man might have inserted his finger and worse into young Paul and thus blighted his destiny. After all, he read a lot of books. He went perhaps too willingly to church. He'd never had a teacher who didn't rave about his manners.

But in time there were girls, dates, betrayals, and griefs. Paul's first broken heart caused more celebration for Erika than first tooth, first word, first step. She would have liked to bronze that cracked valentine alongside his baby shoe.

And first sex, too, she supposed. One of those wide-faced Nordic girls with watery blue eyes? She didn't want to know. Once in Paul's underwear drawer she found—not just a condom—but condoms in several colors with odd projections on one end. She never said a word.

Into Miss Stone's hospital room she now tiptoed, but the high bed was empty. A big man with hard facial bones and a bristly haircut rose from a metal chair.

"I'm Erika Cowan," she said. "Paul's mother."

His flat mouth seemed to turn down. "I haven't met Paul yet."

"I haven't met Madeline."

Each level gaze measured the other's until finally she pushed her stare against his as if it had been a wall of thorny shrubbery, pressed through, and came to sit on the other chair with both ankles crossed. "How *is* Madeline?"

His face solidified even more. "I haven't seen her yet myself, my plane just got in. But the nurses say there's a skull fracture, not bad from what I'm told. Posterior fossa." Erika nodded as if she knew what that was. "At first they thought just a concussion, but her headaches kept on, and the spinal tap wasn't good. She's having a CAT scan now."

"I'm not clear what happened. They were in the mountains and she took a fall?"

"A lot of falls—your boy, too. He must not know Madeline very well, she's always been clumsy. He should have had better judgment."

Erika measured this man, shined shoe to haircut and back again. "His judgment is fine."

"I see he was able to leave the hospital and she's not. And I don't know where Steven is, do you?"

"No. Is that the boy?"

"Oh no, the boy is some juvenile delinquent they took up with, a Mexican kid, a street boy they thought to rehabilitate. That's just like Madeline. Here she's about to marry a man with a future—too easy for her—but give her a bird with a broken wing? She's hooked." After a pause and more of Erika's stare, Mr. Stone cleared his throat. "I don't mean your son is the rescue case; I mean this boy that doesn't even have a name."

Erika nodded, still waiting, still letting this jigsaw of information assemble in midair, wondering where Madeline's mother was.

"But let me just ask you one thing—is his deafness permanent? Naturally I talked to the doctor about Paul as well. I'm sorry to press when you've just arrived, but my own experience with heavy artillery is that most of those gunners got better, most of the near misses in the field even got some of their hearing back."

She said firmly, "I'm sure my son will be just fine whether his hearing comes back or not."

Just then something quite strange happened; she was sorry no Bruce would lie in her bed tonight to hear it told. The man called Stone quite suddenly, quite obviously, ran Erika's plain and motionless face through his computer and then regrouped; he changed tactics because of some flicker she had not been able to control; he summoned forth from some attic or closet of himself the devil-with-women he used to be. His flat smile got rapidly resculpted, softened. It sent, like a jack-o'-lantern flame lit at last in the mouth, a late rush of warmth behind both eyes. Even his long, large body resettled itself; broader shoulders arose and girth that withdrew from the waistline climbed to expand the chest. Oh, he was not to be trusted, this man!

He stood and stepped toward her. "Forgive me," said this new man rather gently. "Let's have some coffee and catch each other up." Like a British member of the House of Lords, he thrust out an elbow.

Bruce, have you ever seen the like? Lightly Erika slipped her fingertips through the crook in his arm, but not very far; and she stayed very much on guard while they walked to the hospital cafeteria to talk about what had happened to their children.

IN RADIOLOGY they made Luna remove her watch and asked if she was pregnant. "Not that I know of," she said, considering it. "If so, not but a little bit." They positioned her on a table connected to a large scanner with a doughnut ring into which they slid and braced her aching head. She had to lie completely still while this doughnut moved around with clicks and buzzes, and the table also edged forward every few seconds.

Even Paul could hear every one of these noises, she thought; lately she had begun to measure all aural experience on that scale. She slid one hand over her belly button, the spot she had once thought would flare out from a bud and into a giant dahlia bloom to let women's babies arrive. It was still a nice thought, that image of a tiny but quite mature homunculus lifting his head among petals, and then climbing out of a torso as if it were a canoe.

After thirty boring minutes or so she was rolled back to her room, surprisingly tired from the full-body effort of immobility. It was a shock to see her father and some woman she did not know— surely not Wife #3?—standing some distance apart.

Luna blurted, "I didn't send for you!"

He said stiffly, "Of course officials notified next of kin. I'd have sued them if they hadn't. And of course your mother is out of the country touring cathedrals!" (He reset his irritable face in the way Erika had noticed before—*His civilian face,* she thought now.) "Madeline, are you all right? Does Steven know, where is he? Why would he go on to California and leave you behind?" he asked rapidly. "Oh. This is Mrs. Cowan from—?

"Wisconsin. Stockholm, Wisconsin."

During all this the orderly had been smoothly unloading Luna onto the bed. She reached past him to the woman with Paul's eyes, who shook her hand while Luna first explained where Paul was and why, and where he was hurt and how much, and then to her father who Sam was and why he mattered.

He rolled his eyes in the way she knew so well. She could still hear him saying: *If you don't quit sucking that thumb I'll cut it off and flush it down the toilet.*

From time to time the woman nodded. Luna said then to her father, "There was no need for you to come. You could have telephoned." Her voice sounded weak as a child's. "I appreciate your check, but we're just fine."

"I don't anymore know exactly who *we* is. You and Steven? You and Mrs. Cowan's boy?" With more eye rolling he paced beside the bed. "And when did you acquire hospital insurance? Did they tell you what a CAT scan costs? Are *we* paying?"

When Luna shook her head, pain ran along the back of her skull, ear to ear. Through it she saw by changes in Mrs. Cowan's face that she was anything but passive.

"I'm certain," said Erika Cowan almost through her teeth, "that nobody has come across the country to discuss *money.*"

Martin Stone said too softly, "Of course not." He waited. "I ought to call Corinne. Oh. She sent you these." He took a tiny, clear plastic envelope out of his pocket; inside were gold hoop earrings with gold hearts hanging down. "For your wedding. Something new."

The next silence went on too long. Luna took out one gold circle and held it to an earlobe, but the silence was still vibrating in the room when a nurse came to take routinely her pulse, pressure, temperature. All three waited without speaking.

Martin demanded of the nurse, "Is she OK?" and got back a nod and smile.

"A wedding," said Erika in a neutral voice. She drew closer to the bed and took a hard look at Luna's left hand, bare except for some small bandages. When Luna asked what the book was, she smiled. "Perhaps you'd like to see these photographs of Paul's family?"

Luna closed her eyes briefly: *Thank you.* "Yes, I would. We haven't talked much about our"—she waved toward her father—"families."

But he just kept moving through the room, too agitated to sit or be polite, while Erika opened the album and began putting lives behind the flat black-and-white faces laid across Luna's lap, grandparents and uncles and aunts as a solid phalanx lined up behind Paul. Luna especially lingered over shots of him with Bruce Cowan at various ages, posing with caught fish, new cars, assorted dogs, straddling a bike with a clicker-card in the front wheel. In one he wore a sling on one arm. His wide but slightly anxious smile, made in one picture even more vulnerable by missing baby teeth, made Luna smile herself, though in her throat there swelled a hot ball of loss and regret.

She showed Erika a drawing of Sam and his dental gap. "Your son is out looking for a boy who never had a life like this. Sam would think it was Heaven to live like this."

By the window her father lit a cigarette.

"Paul wanted brothers and sisters," Erika offered as a corrective. "He got lonely out on the farm."

"I wanted them, too." She turned to a page of color photographs of Bruce Cowan's grave with a mound of flowers in blotched pink and white and green. There was a much smaller grave nearby, and some of the wreaths had slid onto its marker.

"That's where I'll lie"—Mrs. Cowan pointed matter-of-factly—"with the baby in the middle." She turned to another page: flowers gone, the gravestone that said COWAN and snow on all sides. "When Bruce went so sudden, Paul had to come home from San Francisco. He seemed to think if he'd stayed home to help that would have kept his dad alive, but of course that was wrong. Bad hearts run in Bruce's family; I hope Paul takes after me."

Blowing smoke, Martin Stone looked toward them and away.

"Paul wouldn't go back for a month afterwards, but by then the insurance had come and I'd rented out part of the fields and hired help for the stock. And I'm in a strong church," Erika added.

"I've heard about that church, and how the bell was tolled Saturday nights at sundown, and about Luther League. You have dairy cows, Paul said."

"And goats now, too, because they're easier to handle. Mr. Stone, if you don't put that thing out the smoke alarm will go." They watched him wet the cigarette in the lavatory. Then Erika flipped to late pages with head-on goat stares from pedigreed Toggenburgs. "The nannies and babies are just fine, but this billy is mean and he smells just awful because" (she hesitated, moved her hands parallel and added softly) "his parts are so arranged that he wets on his own stomach and chest." Luna laughed; Erika, too. The major came to look down on the photographs, briefly. Erika said, "I guess all billy goats are like that. I didn't want to go asking the farm agent if maybe mine was deformed."

A nurse stuck her head in, smelled the air, and said there was no smoking allowed in this whole building. Major Stone lifted and spread his empty hands. "Well, ladies, I'm not doing any good just waiting around here. I'll see what I can find out about the search parties."

"Call me if they've found Sam," Luna said before he closed the door, and Erika asked what kind of Southern accent his was. "Virginian," Luna said, loud enough so her father could hear. "It's fairly new."

Martin Stone shook his head and moved at a good clip down the hall. He took the stairs with a series of bounces (elevators made people flabby) and marched to the rental car at the far edge of the hospital lot, where he always preferred to park. It seemed to him that he had arrived just in the nick of time to save Madeline from going sentimental over a street-walking Chicano boy as well as these milk-and-cheese Cowans. Already he wondered if she was on one of those killer diets by which she somehow offered up her own calories into midair to nourish others. His early willingness to convert had been a serious mistake, since Priscilla's neurotic Catholicism had poisoned the whole family; and then to withdraw so he could marry Corinne among the tolerant Methodists had stirred up the whole thing again.

He blew his horn at a too-slow driver. Organization and self-discipline were what Madeline had always needed, still needed now. She'd always been poor at cleaning her plate, finishing what she started.

Martin Stone stopped at the first public telephone he saw,

slapped loose a long packet of credit cards, and started the process of locating Steven Grier by calling the Botany Department of U-Cal at Riverside.

THOUGH HE SHOULD have known that a saddle was no place to locate a full-body set of sore muscles, Paul Cowan ended up—ended all too literally, he groaned to himself—going with a party on horseback into the mountains to look for Sam. Those experienced in such searches had already found the start of Sam's flight and the end of Paul's and Luna's on contour maps, made calculations, and divided the terrain among several groups. They mounted Paul on a leopard Appaloosa that had fleshy pink rings like fungus around both eyes and a bumpy gait. Paul had not ridden for several years, and then not in western gear with high horn and pommel, but as he got the hang of the longer leg and looser rein and trusted the horse to choose its uphill footing, the generalized pain in his joints settled down to a roving ache, so he only had to think about specific physical miseries one at a time.

Every few minutes the leader would shout through a battery megaphone *"Sam!"*—the one name those two chicken hawks (as police called them) had never used.

Paul leaned forward into his bruised ribs to climb the rocky slope and tried to keep the reins from snagging on his bandaged fingers. He could hear the occasional megaphone shout but not much else, and none of the comments or warnings that the horseman in front made over his shoulder.

He had last ridden a horse back home just after his father's death, when he was longing to escape the house that had soaked up and now gave back memories like dew on the walls. (That made him think of Luna's ghost, which might be, she said, an emotional recording like a spiritual film or a videotape of the personality.) Erika Cowan had urged Paul to go into town, look up his high school friends; and he interpreted that as her wish that he find an old girlfriend, marry, and stay.

So he had borrowed a neighbor's quarterhorse instead, trailered it to those lakes in southern Wisconsin that lie at the edge of the deep-snow line. People said ancient Indian pyramids were submerged in Rock Lake, that before Columbus these tribes had maintained crematoria, perhaps had sacrificed to sun and moon or even eaten girl children when they became too numerous. All Paul wanted was to submerge the new death of Bruce Cowan below this old story of so much anonymous death, to make his own grief abstract. He had ridden the bored gelding most of a day, with the result that his sore and spraddled legs would hardly straighten at all that night, and he did come to understand why nobody with toothache gives a thought to metaphysics.

After he'd delivered the horse back to its stall, he still had to hobble across the porch by the post he and his father had painted, to limp past the boots with that smell inside, to search for more aspirin behind the brown bottles of Mevacor pills that now had no cholesterol left to fight. He saw these concrete objects, but through the self-centered blur of pain.

For two days after her husband's funeral his mother had cried hard and then reached the dry bottom of everything and stopped. Paul's physical misery was a relief to her as well; she prescribed hot baths and Ben-Gay. The daughters of several rural neighbors dropped in with more gifts of food or flowers, but—seeing Paul was not interested—Erika had almost ordered him back to California "or someplace else where you'll find a wife and give me grandchildren."

Instead he had met his fate on a highway job with a deafness that did for him what Paul Tillich had said about sin: it increased his separation from other people.

In the saddle, Paul Cowan shifted his weight so his other side could hurt for a while. When the riders came to the next divided path and split into separate parties, Paul found himself smiling at something Erika had once declared to him, exasperated: "Paul, if you came to two road signs and one said TO HEAVEN and one said TO A DISCUSSION *ABOUT* HEAVEN, I know which way you'd go."

Because the megaphone had moved on with the other horsemen and because they were out of the brushy slope and into a rocky climb, Paul felt obligated to yell periodically for Sam himself. At each unexpected shout, the man riding just ahead jerked up his shoulders and bobbed his cowboy hat.

Later that morning the rider reined his sorrel horse off the trail and motioned Paul in front with inaudible but not very puzzling words.

They were into the sameness, now. The rocks and gravel, patches of sand, the taller trees, dry washes between gray rock: Paul had seen them all before. Perhaps he had held Luna's hand in this small meadow, under this tree, or maybe miles away. He wanted to ride into the very canyon where they had made love for the first time, thinking their act had sanctified it, but saw that unless he could smell like a deer or a bear, he would never find the exact place again.

The sun had climbed high when a helicopter came to waggle at them overhead, then drew back, returned, moved at a rising angle along the face of the mountain and hovered there. Paul could hear shouting. A hand gripped his shoulder, pointed to a scramble that would carry them to a better view. The two horses blew irritably as they were kicked ahead on the rolling pebbles.

But from the rock shelf Paul could see a human shape, half blue denim, part white shirt, some flesh showing but no red blood—thank God!—on a slope of stone. Yelling, he slapped the horse's speckled rump and dug in his heels.

"Watch it!" shouted the second rider from behind, loud enough this time as the talus hillside threatened to give way under their skidding hooves.

Somebody else from the group of horsemen was already running to the boy, then he threw his hat away to press his head onto Sam's chest.

Not dead! Not dead, God! Paul rode upright in the stirrups and bounced so the sight of the kneeling man also bounced to his eye.

Thumbs up! the man motioned. *Thankyouthankyouthankyou.* He wished he could notify Luna right away, could send Tamsen Donner straight down the wind with the news.

Beating up dust, the chopper came back but could find no place to land. Hand signals were given. By the time Paul had leaped off his horse and felt his numb knees fold under him, a stretcher was dropping its jerky way out the helicopter's door, at each descent swinging more and more like a dangerous pendulum.

He lurched over rubble and heated slabs to throw himself down by Sam's head. Even the eyelids were sunburned in the boy's swollen face. The blood Paul had missed had all run underneath and dried into his clothes from the break in a lower leg with bone showing, insects above it, dirt inside. "Sam! It's Paul. Sam?"

"Shock," said the first man, waving overhead.

Paul talked to the boy, any words at all, thinking how odd it was for him to be talking so fast and loud to one who could not hear, while the stretcher leaped and twanged downward and swayed with its black shadow passing back and forth across them. He jabbered to Sam about Luna and himself, about those kidnappers gone forever, about what good things they would do when Sam was well. When the eyes did not open, when no sound was made, Paul faltered into the Twenty-third Psalm, headlong into green pastures and then, remembering Sam was a cradle-Catholic, switched into a half-accurate Hail Mary. The swinging shadow crossed and recrossed them while he talked. More men and horses arrived. He was dimly aware they were all standing around, silent except for a horse snort or the bang of a metal shoe on stone.

After what seemed a long time, men began taking Sam from

him, moving Paul gently aside, covering Sam's face against the spatter of grit before they strapped him down papoose fashion and hooked the stretcher onto ropes that looked no more substantial than spiderweb, testing connections, making Paul back even farther off—no, farther still. For the first time in months, his whole head filled up with a clattering noise.

Then Sam was rising. Paul thought too fast at first, and on too wide an arc! He would slam upward into the stone face or down into pine!

Yet gradually someone unseen withdrew Sam overhead toward the dark door of safety while the noisy helicopter fought air currents as it also rose slowly, so slowly Paul feared its engines must stall until the whole thing would come down upon them like the fakir's rope trick. He pressed his forearm over his stinging eyes and allowed his broken fingers to take their turn at hurting. While he watched, the stretcher may have actually banged the undercarriage once near a wheel, or maybe Paul had begun to hear noises that didn't exist. In the shape of a bier, Sam dangled in the sunlight for much too long while disembodied hands tried to maneuver all the corners inside.

Below, the men cheered louder than the sound of the clacking propeller blades. Sam went out of sight; the overhead door slid shut, and the helicopter, in a motion almost insolent, flicked itself into a high sharp turn and flew toward Reno.

DURING THE TIME it took Paul to urge his horse downhill with the rest of the search posse and then, one handed, drive Luna's van back to St. Mary's, a swarm of Social Service bureaucrats had clustered around its admissions office on behalf of the rescued boy. Sam was an orphan, a kidnappee, a juvenile, an indigent, a victim of child abuse, a potential prosecution witness, a member of an ethnic minority. He had been lost and then injured in different park jurisdictions, kidnapped within the city limits, and perhaps had residency in two states. So the hospital's hall filled up with staffers from competing agencies, carrying clipboards and snapping their ballpoint pens, in a crowd that included news reporters and one gray-haired priest.

Erika Cowan zigzagged through this crowd and upstairs to Luna's room. "I only got to see him from the doorway," she reported. "His leg's broken and infected and he's out of his head with a fever and maybe heatstroke, but they think they found him in time."

"Out of his head," echoed Luna, who felt imprisoned inside hers with its eggshell crack.

"He told the nurses he'd seen the King of Death in a black suit. Blackbirds. Things like that."

Luna sat up and swung her feet off the high bed. "I want to go see him."

"The doctors say no, on his end and on yours." She took Luna's soft hand. Her own palm was rough from tool handles and hot water. "Your father says you're an artist."

Luna blew out a sigh. "Aren't Paul and I a pair, though? Art and God?"

"Probably so," said Erika.

She let herself be pressed back on the pillow. "So you and my father got along all right?"

"We managed."

Paul limped into the room, trying not to tug at the seat of his jeans, which felt glued to his buttocks with lymph. "It's crazy down in emergency, but I did get to talk to Sam; he'll be all right. And you're feeling better?"

"Did he know you?"

"He's not conscious. My God! Mother? Are you here?"

Erika admitted dryly that she was. After looking back and forth between the two women, Paul hugged her so tight it made her ribs spring in and back out. He looked, Erika decided, both terrible and happy. *I guess this is the one, Bruce,* she thought, and turned back to assess the genes that had formed Luna's pale face with the bruised rings around both eyes. *Maybe she takes after her mother.*

"They called me so I flew right out," said Erika. "I've been getting acquainted with Madeline and her father."

"Luna," Paul corrected her, and then, "Her father?"

Luna said the hospital had called him, too, while Paul took hold of both her hands. "But you're all right?" He rubbed her index finger where ink had made a permanent blot in the skin. "You draw Major Stone's picture and I'll burn it. Make up a G.I. Joe doll that's like him while I find a pin." She smiled. "What about food? Are you eating anything?" He located a glass of juice on her bedside table and made her take some through a straw.

"Actually when I woke up I was starved," Luna said.

"Another swallow." She took it. The telephone rang on the other bedside table, and Luna said it was probably her father. While she rolled to reach it, Paul set himself—Erika noticed—in the braced stance she remembered from days when their bull had broken through the fence.

Luna slid the phone onto her raised pillow. "Yes Dad," she said. "Yes they have and Paul's here. He's still unconscious. All right. Did what? Oh no. He won't. Well if he does I don't want him to. I will not. Did you hear me? Dad?" With closed eyes she felt for the table and replaced the phone. They remained closed as she said softly, "The closest I ever felt to my father was by telephone when he was overseas. He was great long-distance. He told me long travelogues and told me his voice was coming by Atlantic cable, and I would think about how all his words were crawling along under the ocean through this gigantic worm of a tube, oh me."

"You want me to send him home?"

She shook her head and waved away the glass of juice he offered again. "Once he sent me to fat girls' camp in Vermont," she said in monotone. "If I didn't quit eating ice cream, he said, I'd soon weigh as much as he did. I was eleven. After a while I got so thin I didn't have enough body to cover my mind decently."

Erika didn't know whether to smile at this or not. Paul didn't. She moved quietly to a far chair.

He asked if her head still hurt, and she said yes, but they were giving her pills, and added rapidly, "Dad sent for Steven Grier."

"What the hell for?"

"For control, I guess. He always said that he'd learned in the army that all men are animals, and yet he reserved the right to choose the best animal for me. He thinks I've gone off the deep end." In frustration she slapped the mattress. "Oh, Paul, I'm not being fair. After all, I *have* been off that deep end before. And he also taught me how to change the oil in a car and how to do calculations in my head. If it hadn't been for dinner table arguments I wouldn't have tried debating club. I made straight As for him."

"You also got sick for him," Paul said.

Across the room, to keep from feeling so much like an eavesdropper, Erika Cowan began a busy cleaning of her purse into a waste can; she discarded old Kleenex, a voided check, and cough-drop wrappers. As she fingered the wad of bills, she thought briefly of Bruce and *his* father, old Mr. Cowan had only one arm and maybe half a heart, she'd always thought; mean S.O.B. wore his wife to an early grave, used to beat all his boys with pieces of mule harness until finally every one ran away from home. If there was any justice at all the old man was in Hell deep-fried by now, and none of his sons would lean out of Abraham's bosom to lay one drop of water on his tongue.

She saw that Paul could not keep his hands off this girl. If it wasn't her hand, an elbow, a shoulder, he was touching her hair, her chin, the spot in the center of her brow where, he said, "you see spirits with the third eye." Erika wasn't quite sure whether to worry about that or not.

"That must be why they put the ashes there on Ash Wednesday," Luna said. "They used to smell of kerosene." She added that her father planned to be at the Reno airport at 10 p.m. when Steven's plane arrived and, no, she didn't want Paul to go. "They've never met. Maybe they'll miss each other."

"But I bet your father *looks* like retired military."

"True."

Seated on her bed as lightly as possible, he leaned forward to still her entire head between his fingertips as if the brains might overflow. "Now before old Steven what's-his-name gets here, Luna, we need a chance to talk. I'm not sure how you feel about what happened up in the mountains and you can't possibly know how I—

She interrupted. "In radiology they asked if I was pregnant."

Erika coughed. She upended her purse so crumbs and dirt and a few coins—let 'em go—fell into the wastebasket. She heard herself humming "Blest Be the Tie," and made herself stop. Not that Paul could hear. She stood up with a number of loud snaps and zips of leather compartments. "I'm going back to my hotel," she almost shouted, for it was not clear to her yet how well Paul's hearing aids worked, and even though "hotel" seemed an understatement for a place with clowns and jugglers in the lobby. Who was that juggler who claimed to perform for the Christ Child in Bethlehem? She could never remember these modern innovations.

Neither Paul nor Luna had looked away from each other's face. Toward her, they were both deaf. "I might even gamble!" she announced recklessly, "because you ought to know what everything is like, at least a taste." Part of that remark got through and made Paul stare. She yelled, "I do drink, for instance, though Paul may not know that. I got very drunk on my honeymoon, and ever since I've been competent to advise against gin."

She marched out, stopped in the hall a nurse who was carrying Madeline Stone's chart, and said, "Don't go in yet. He might be proposing."

"No kidding!" The nurse backed off. "Well, that would cure me!"

They walked together to the station where the nurse told others on duty that maybe Miss Stone was getting herself engaged so her blood pressure reading would be unreliable anyway. As long as they had Erika captured, they showed her a copy of the *Sierrandipity Cookbook,* and although Erika never expected to cook at any altitude where coffee brewed at the wrong temperature, she bought one, thinking it would do her good in her Circus Circus room to read about Sinful Pasta (blue cheese and sour cream with fettuccine) and 459 other recipes that allowed her to cling to the hope that women were basically the same at any longitude, notwithstanding Gloria Steinem. She could read herself to sleep on cookery because—in spite of all she had heard about hotels—there was no Gideon Bible in her room.

One of the nurses walked with her to the elevator and made them tiptoe with conspiratorial giggles as they passed room 306.

Afterward, nobody entered the room until the orderly delivered Miss Stone's supper tray. He came out saying that the young man was feeding her green peas with a spoon, and both were moon-eyed. That report made everybody's day, which had heretofore been hard. That afternoon the rescue squad had brought in a young girl who'd been found taped inside a wooden box and left at Martis Lake, nearly starved. Somebody had also tried to burn the box with her inside, but the fire went out, so only the girl's toes would have to be amputated. The event distracted those social workers and rival charities already on hand for Sam. Then an eastbound semitrailer with a sleepy driver, striking the divider on I-80, had crashed and spilled hundreds of empty Hidden Valley salad-dressing containers across the freeway, and the scattered chunks of cement flung in the westbound lane had caused an old lady, Rosita Sue Taglivia, to run off the road and overturn. She died in Truckee; her husband, in cardiac arrest from the news, died at St. Mary's. The U.S. Immigration and Naturalization agents, arresting thirty illegal Mexican aliens, had to send some in for TB testing. They were all positive. The night before, a woman had been raped near the post office on Vassar Street; she said rape; police said the unknown man had only failed to pay for services rendered, and at that insult she had struck out at a doctor with a bedpan. A man who'd stolen a Bobcat drove it so fast he turned it over on himself. A girl on a bicycle got hit by a truck that granulated her collarbones. And one of the nurses on Luna's floor knew personally a woman accused of killing her husband and dumping his body in the Ninth Street pits in Sun Valley: "I can't believe it! She doesn't weigh but a hundred and ten pounds!"

Everybody was tired. The smallest glimmer would suffice.

NEXT MORNING Paul came early to St. Mary's—he wanted to be standing by the hospital bed with Luna's hand in his when her father and Steven what's-his-name walked in; but just as he touched the handle of the main outer door, somebody behind called a few unclear words. He turned in the flow of air-conditioning to blink through the glare at an older man who looked as if his uniform was temporarily at the cleaner's and a younger man who—oh shit!—would have made Narcissus seem homely.

Paul let the door drift shut. "You call me?"

"See there?" said Major Stone aside. "Deaf people always talk loud like that."

The handsome one shouted, "I'm Steven Grier!" but did not put out his hand.

"Madeline's father." The muscular one did extend his, noted the bandages on the left hand, said "This one's OK?" Paul let him crush fingers to prove something.

He could not take his eyes off Steven what's-his-name, the hair that might be bleached to achieve such gold, a dimple that leaped into view now that he was showing fangs in a false smile, eyes so deep a blue they seemed more ornamental than functional. Perhaps they were contact lenses, dyed. He lowered his voice to say, "Paul Cowan," but offered no handshake, either.

"Thought you must be," said Major Stone, "since your mama mentioned the beard. She's quite a lady, your mama. Cold climates make for strong people."

Paul studied his face now, nodding. He was remembering a thin, wry Luna on the hospital scales, giving a shrug that shook the reading of her dehydrated weight. She'd said, "I'm always a good loser," and Paul had said back, "Don't joke."

He said now, "Mother would have been strong in Tahiti."

But he turned to check his first impression of Steven—yes, far too handsome for his own good, for anybody's good, must have been spoiled from birth, always got to play leads in the school play, only sport was swimming, best-looking in the senior superlatives. He said, "You're the botanist." Mind of a potted plant.

"And you're?"

I'm the one who knows you had her; you're the one wondering if I did. "Just a laborer." They went on staring at each other.

The eye-messages got deflected by the major's saying, "Let's us three men get some breakfast and talk. We need to understand one another before we see Madeline."

Steven said fine, but Paul knew it wasn't fine; Luna wouldn't like this; by then Major Stone had dropped on both their shoulders his heavy arms in their long tan sleeves and yanked their bodies toward himself and each other. It was as if a python had thudded down from a low overhanging branch. Both men stumbled and shrank away, but not before Major Stone said to Paul, "Work out, do you?"

"Just on the job."

"One thing about Reno and Vegas, breakfast is always being served, and it's always big and it's always cheap. My car's over there; let's go to the El Dorado." He whacked their shoulder blades, testing Paul's solidity, then moved ahead as they fell in behind him. Though he knew the major *did* work out and lift weights, Paul decided it was almost abnormal that a man old enough to be Luna's father had a sculpted ass that looked hard as marble, and could move across the parking lot at a parade march that made his own muscles remember their soreness.

He told Steven that the major worked out in the gym daily, and Steven said, as if to top him, "Luna told me."

After that Paul said nothing, not while they quick-stepped to the far corner of the lot, not inside the rented Audi. He noticed that Steven carried a glasses case in his shirt pocket and was glad for any minor defect.

"I didn't get to try the games at the El Dorado," said Steven, making conversation. "Have you enjoyed gambling here?"

"No."

The major was more talkative than both of them. "I've been in Reno before, of course. Came one September for the air races. With the army you go almost everyplace that counts. I got to feed potato chips to the kangaroos in Australia. They're bound to be open at eight, I think." He checked his watch. As he talked he kept taking his eyes off the road too much, half turning in his seat to speak far too loudly to Paul or to give out his salesman's laugh. "Reno is over four thousand feet and dry all the time, but I don't need to tell you that, do I, Paul? They tell me you and Madeline have been out *in* it. They get maybe half a foot of rain all year, Steve." Pointing out places where he'd won this and lost that and overriding Steven's roulette reports, he drove them along Virginia Street, then past El Dorado's twenty-five-story tower to a parking space an acre away. While they were getting out the major made several remarks to Steven that Paul couldn't hear; that made him suspicious, maybe paranoid. "Lock that door, will you?" yelled Major Stone. "Though the big-fish Mafia keep out the little fish."

They hiked in silence across asphalt *(Dry asphalt, no dew,* Paul thought, *no condensation here; I miss Wisconsin)* to what the major promised were six or seven restaurants with breakfast on buffet.

Inside, waiting for a table, Stone seemed to grow uncomfortable at their silence and finally said, "You know the difference between a parrot and a Nevada woman?"

"You can teach a parrot," said Paul, "to say no."

"Well that's it, yes."

The waitress took a serious interest in seeing that Steven what's-his-name got just the table by the window that he liked.

Silent, tense, Paul filled his plate from the heaped food on a long table: citrus fruit, halved grapes, melon balls, tiny muffins, sausage patties, scrambled eggs, small berry waffles, bacon, shredded potatoes, mini-omelettes, toast, assorted jellies and jams. He was trying to remember how much money he had put in his pocket this morning and how much he had left with Luna. They carried mounds of food to the table where the waitress filled Steven's cup first and then got around to theirs. She asked Steven through perfect teeth, "One ticket?" The major said yes.

At nearby tables, others were talking, giggling, retelling jokes from last night's floor show, blaming the dealer, or simply showing grim determination to make food overtake their booze and crowd out the hangover. Paul fell to eating, depressed. Background noise was always a problem.

"So Riverside's OK so far?" Steven said things were off to a good start. "How did you explain your missing wife?" He said he hadn't. The school year hadn't started. There weren't many people in the department offices except secretaries.

In the next silence Paul was not certain if the sloshing sounds under his eardrums were his own or came from group masticating that his batteries had amplified. He thought: *If this was a book or film and Stone looked this short haired, thick necked, and bullet headed, he'd turn out to beat the stereotype and have a sensibility like Thomas Merton's.* From time to time he glanced from one pair of blue eyes to the other; Steven's now looked weaker to him, in need of optometry, and the major's paler ones—deep set behind knobby cheeks—were not unlike those of Lewis Keseburg in Luna's book. "Pass the salt, please."

The major took a small ivory pillbox from his pocket and swallowed a fat capsule with his red, too-thick tomato juice. "Multivitamin," he said. "I sent some to Madeline before she left Chapel Hill. I hope she's taking them." Paul hadn't seen any.

As he ate he watched Steven Grier fork up his food too carefully. Yes, handsome enough for grade-B movies, tall enough to be MTV accompanist to the solo singer, with a newly tanned clear skin suitable for some vice presidency. And Steven was long accustomed to the handsome part, Paul knew, but not yet the vice/sub/assistant/second/runner-up shadow Paul hoped he saw. He was glad Luna had no idea of the playground crap that filled his mind. The others, though, were also studying him surreptitiously, and he doubted their thoughts were any better.

Part of Paul's beard had been shaved where a laceration needed to be stitched, so his jaw looked paler and thus weaker than Major Stone preferred, and half his head was still bruised and bluish—or dingy? For a bookish type, a churchy type, he did look strong and fit, though.

To Steven Grier, Paul looked Jewish; he had seen those Jews with wispy hair and sharp features all up and down the college library, knew their type: listened to classical music and read—not saw, but *read*—plays. Liked logic. Wrote the longest term papers in the class.

Both men thought Paul looked intelligent, though he kept too quiet for them to test him. Each man believed he knew the true definition of Paul's kind of intelligence. The major meant bookish, withdrawn—Steven might be intelligent, too, but at least he drew a monthly check for it, whereas Paul probably had an unprofitable free-floating intelligence like uncontrolled munitions, electricity with the wires down, what his navy friends called "all sail and no anchor." And although Steven Grier had begun with the assumption that he and Luna's army-nut father would have nothing in common, he, too, found Cowan well-read but impractical; he considered him a hippie sans portfolio or diploma, a possible impostor. Paul probably read only parts of books and underlined nothing, trusting to memory and unlikely free associations. He probably read entire books of poems, all by the same author. It would be easy for Paul's thoughts to fly free of gravity and circle the real world aimlessly in an accidental orbit of no use to anyone. Surely Luna had been able to see through the kind of thinking that lacked product?

When Steven's eye caught that of the major, their pragmatisms almost nodded to each other.

Actually Paul had stopped thinking of them; he was enjoying the eggs and bacon and wondering if Luna had eaten a good breakfast. He liked the new concreteness that had grown in him ever since Desolation Wilderness, an inner pressure to make plans and choices. The very fact of Luna's existence, the sight of Sam's sunburned, stoic face, the unexpected arrival of his mother, had pulled him out of what he now considered a phase of New Age California Drift, where he'd tried to fit himself into religions that professed at most two Commandments plus maybe eight Suggestions. He was busy thinking about the difference between the verbs "to hear" and "to listen" when Major Stone said, "I'm going back for more of those potatoes—get you anything?"

He had eaten, Paul saw, a huge amount already. At fat camp, Luna said, they had lived off boiled shrimp and carrot juice with celery sticks for snacks. He shook his head, but Steven went back to the buffet table, too, and the two seemed to be whispering.

They both brought back heaped plates. Did Steven think it more manly if he matched the major's appetite? Paul tapered off to coffee, having remembered with some distaste Martin Luther's belief that in Heaven the saved would eat eels and liver.

"Now when she just up and left," said Major Stone, "what day was that?" He added, "Professor Grier."

"April twenty-second, I'm not apt to forget. And I hadn't a clue that it was coming, not a clue."

Turning to Paul, the major said, "I doubt you know that Madeline has a medical history of—"

Paul broke in, "I do know." That made Steven angry, he could tell.

"It's hard to judge her mental state right now, but the doctors see no problem. Of course they didn't know what stress might have done to Madeline till I got here. I know you haven't seen her yet, Steven, but I did tell her you were coming. I didn't think she was up to surprises right now."

"She's doing well," Paul said. "I called St. Mary's this morning and they might release her today. The dizziness is gone, her headache's not as bad, and they now think the small amount of blood in her spinal fluid was caused by the tap itself."

"Not everything's physical," said Major Stone with a frown.

Steven assumed a friendly, confiding tone. "At first I thought, *Well, let her go if that's what she wants;* but now that her father has told me she's had certain episodes before?" He said that only this new information had persuaded him to come back to Reno and hold nothing against her. "If Luna's not herself, then that's different, then I have some obligation—"

"She's very much herself."

"I believe a psychologist at least ought to have a little talk with Madeline."

Paul insisted that all Luna needed now was plenty of rest. "And fluids. And food. She's staying with my mother and me while she regains her strength and we wait to see how Sam is."

"But Sam's not a personal problem, he's a social problem," said Steven patiently. "His case is being handled."

"Case?" said Paul.

Major Stone wiped the last bacon grease with a toast crust. "Now I admire your mother a lot—you know what Mrs. Cowan told me, Steven? She told me all these gamblers are just modern-day alchemists that want to change wishful thinking into gold when not a one of them can tell how cows change grass into milk. I told her I was going to write that down. But smart as she is, she's

no mental health professional. And Luna's no adoption agency."
Perhaps Paul's face was showing anger. "These two have been engaged for months, you know. They've made plans. Steven's willing
to overlook this little wilderness interval so they can move on."

The smile he gave Steve what's-his-name made Paul even angrier. "You let her old man buy your plane ticket, didn't you?"

"My salary doesn't start till the fiscal year, July the first, and
yours doesn't start at all anytime, isn't that so?" Steven sat up
straight and kept eating, the way Stonewall Jackson was said to believe a vertical body line meant better digestion.

"And before that, Luna paid."

"Wait." Major Stone held up a forefinger. "Mr. Cowan, do you
consider yourself in the running? Do you want to become my son-
in-law?"

"Not really," Paul said, "but if I marry Luna I can't get out
of it."

In their next silence, Martin Stone slid back his chair and
threw his napkin so a corner fell into his glass and began wicking
up red tomato juice. Otherwise, nobody moved. While the reddish
stain climbed higher in the white linen, they watched the major
make a conscious effort for self-control. Jaw rigid, he said, "You're
nearly deaf, I believe."

Paul bore down on enunciation when he answered. "To
higher frequencies and in crowds. Both eardrums and the organ of
Corti were ruptured. Most music sounds flat to me now because
I've lost range, but there's some new equipment with computer
chips that will help with that. My mother also notices that my
voice has changed since the accident, that some of my syllables
are muffled and some seem to sing through my nose." He touched
the right side of his head. "Since one ear is so much worse, I can't
always locate sounds or estimate their distance."

"And the professor is right—you don't have a job."

"No."

Steven got his attention by touching Paul's arm. "Has Luna agreed to marry you?"

"Not exactly."

Steven allowed himself his first genuine smile, and Paul saw by the dimple in that charmed left cheek that Grier was going to get tenure after all, would probably become a dean.

"Well, then," said Major Stone. "It's Luna we need to talk to. And perhaps a psychologist." He slid his chair farther back and, rising, began "Paul," but because a loud burst of laughter came from the next table and because the letters *p, b,* and *m* all look alike when the mouth makes full lip closure, Paul thought he had said "Balls!" and he leaped to his feet.

"You leave her alone. Leave us alone. It's between Luna and me!"

"And possibly me," Steven said.

The major said more, a lot more, but Paul was already hurrying to the cashier's counter demanding a separate check. When they appeared behind him, he threw down a ten-dollar bill and left it—*Stupid, needed the money*—and strode rapidly outside onto hot Fourth Street, pretending to be fully deaf to his shouted name, turning fast up West toward the hospital. On foot he could be there before them, considering how far away the Audi was parked. When he jogged into the sunlight, pain crashed from his knee to his ankle.

They're bad for Luna, just alike, two of a kind, we can get Sam away from the bureaucrats and go, we'll just go, we'll go home if she'll come, goat's milk is very nutritious, they give it to invalids, build his own body and let hers alone, he's such a pimp, he's a pimping professor, the type grants were made for, I'll take her away and Sam too, not about Tamsen, good they don't know about Tamsen, she mustn't tell them, tell nobody, not a soul, soul— that's a laugh, that's a spirit—

Thus, trotting and muttering, he rushed down the street and in fact at the hospital's entrance met Luna in a wheelchair, wearing a foam-rubber neck brace that kept her head erect, being rolled to a taxicab door that Erika Cowan was holding open.

"Don't run in this heat!" Luna called. "They let me out early. Your face is on fire!"

He nodded, panting. As he bent to kiss the unpeeled side of her nose, she put her cool hand on the skin where his beard had been shaved. "How patchy you look! What's the matter?" Erika was already peering beyond to see who pursued.

"Let's hurry," Paul said, and would have lifted her into the rear seat but for the nurse's snapped headshake.

"She's still my responsibility, curb to curb," the nurse said as she knelt to turn each foot plate aside so Luna could stand. "Don't you dare bump that head!" Luna ducked inside. "Now if you get married in Reno, remember the whole floor wants to come!"

"They've leaped to conclusions," Luna told Paul, and before he could actually press the subject of marriage she nodded as much as her brace would permit. "Thank you. Paul? What's the rush?"

Erika Cowan climbed in front, and Paul got in the cab beside Luna, deciding he would nail down the proposal as soon as he stopped panting. He thought he could see the Audi a block away. The sight made him say uneasily, "I hope you haven't been telling the nurses all about Tamsen Donner. Let's go!"

The taxi driver, Jesus Calico, bit his unlit cigar but started the car. "She can't hit her head," he said, easing into gear, inching in to the street, turning the wheel slow motion. "You want to get me sued?"

Luna said of course she hadn't mentioned Tamsen. She said her doctor had sent some counselor in to consult, and they'd talked about David Koresh and how some kinds of love are sick.

His mother, who could always tell when Paul was angry, turned from the front seat to eye him and reached back to pat his knee with one of her wide hands, big joints and knuckles, then settled back.

She used to have smaller hands before work expanded them, he thought. One profitable year, Bruce Cowan had bought her a piano on which she played "Largo" over and over while Paul flunked basic sight-reading. *I'll buy Luna a drafting table, he decided. Maybe one of the outbuildings could be a studio.*

That Audi was definitely pulling into the space they had just left. Beautiful Steven got out alone.

Quickly Paul said, "Could you bear living in Wisconsin?"

"Bear?" his mother exclaimed, apparently to the driver.

Luna said, "Have you decided because of Tamsen that I really am a chronic wacko?"

Controlling her frown, Erika said, "Bear Wisconsin? Imagine! The winters are beautiful, not like here! Let me tell you, Mr. Calico, that when the snow comes it makes along my fences this long string of big oval shapes, just as if there were giant beads outlined from underneath. I guess the wind makes them. We never have summers this hot where I live!"

The driver checked his air-conditioning.

"Hell, you can bring Tamsen with you," Paul said.

"And Sam?"

"I took Sam for granted."

The taxi crept along, its driver scowling.

"What would we do in Wisconsin?"

"I'm still working on that. You'd draw and paint and read books. We'd get you and Sam a dog, maybe one dog apiece." When Luna moved her head too fast toward him, it seemed to twang on its stem above the thick tan collar. That hurt, he saw. "I haven't asked Mother, but I'm sure she'll take us in."

Erika said of course it didn't snow in Stockholm all the time; Luna wouldn't be stuck with all-white paintings or anything like that. "We have lots of flowers." The driver said something to her about the desert and spring.

Paul touched Luna's hair very lightly. It needed combing. "I'm thinking I might go back to school. It's clear I'm nobody's preacher now, if I ever was, but maybe I could teach theology somewhere. If I ever learned it, that is. If I ever learned enough to write about it."

In the front seat, Erika smiled.

"Two book readers, one painter, one boy, two dogs. We'll starve," Luna said.

But he heard "we'll" with its tinge of intent and went on winding a curl around his finger.

"Not at first you won't starve," Erika Cowan put in smoothly, "because of course Bruce never wrote any will, so half of everything is Paul's—I told you that, Paul, but you were preoccupied. Certainly there's enough collateral to borrow tuition money and expenses."

The driver must not be going over ten m.p.h. so he could steer and still disagree with Erika about the benefits of Nevada, which she seemed to have insulted. He was saying that this was a dry heat, beneficial, not like the Southeast, where you got humidity and fungus.

"What if we ask Sam and he won't go? Or they won't let him?"

"You know he'll come. And if they don't let him? Then we'll have to kidnap him ourselves. Not quite as radical as killing somebody, which you once suggested."

"If my neck would bend, I'd put my head on your shoulder," Luna said. "But he's going to be in the hospital a week at least."

"So we'll wait."

Luna sat up straighter. "Maybe this is all happening too fast."

Like sex, Paul thought. *Luna needs coaxing.*

The driver edged them into a line of cars waiting with motors running to reach the main drop-off at Circus Circus, which was spread pinkly over several blocks. As the line shortened, Jesus ordered them all to sit still. "And you let a bellboy get that door and take the lady's arm." He nodded briskly to Erika Cowan, having proved that Nevadans were just as compassionate as anybody.

The cab kept moving forward, stopping, moving ahead. Although an Audi did pull into place far behind, Paul decided it was probably not Major Stone; he'd have parked on the outskirts of Sparks by now and hiked in.

But it seemed prudent to say, "One reason I seem to be hurrying you, Luna, is . . . well, I've just come from breakfast with your father and Steven what's-his-name." Luna groaned. "It could have been worse." At her louder noise the driver asked if she was feeling OK and blew his horn at the slow car in front. Paul said rapidly, "This is the worst time and place, but I do want it to be absolutely clear that we're getting married."

"That's *it?*" Luna said. "The official proposal? And what does my father have to do with it anyway?"

"That's what I told him. I told him I loved you." *At least,* he thought, *I implied it.*

"Tell me," she said.

He did, but now the words seemed a postscript. Her sunburn grew redder. "Say something, Luna."

"This is definitely too fast. You and my father. You and Steven Grier. You *men*. And stop fooling around with my hair!" When he pulled back his hand she said, facing the window, "We hardly know each other."

That comes much later, thought Erika Cowan, *and then the time flies by.* Something was wrong inside her throat, and both eyelids felt wet and sore. At Bruce's funeral, the choir of unmarried women plus one male tenor, one overweight bass, two pimply boys, had sung "Just as the Flower Withers." That tune had pestered Erika for months afterward. Just as she would be almost asleep in her half of the cold bed, that melody would torment her awake and rush through her head just a little too fast, over and over. She had even asked her doctor if persistent mental music was a symptom of dawning mental illness. "Not unless I've got it, too," he said, naming some TV commercials he could not get out of his head. Erika could still, if she let herself, hear the tune on the organ now, with every quickened wheeze in place. She wondered if the deaf, in dreams or memory, could hear the past perfectly. Bruce's voice. Could Paul remember?

In silence, Luna was helped out of the cab while Paul paid.

"What did you think I meant? Just live together?"

"Some people do."

"I don't want to hear about Steven."

They led Luna, one on each side, Erika deciding not to butt in.

"That's right, call it adultery, let your Bible call it adultery."

"The Bible calls it fornication, but I've been there myself, so that isn't the point."

"Oh you have, have you? Mr. Self-Righteous has been there himself!" Even Erika could feel how every muscle in Luna went stiff.

Paul, who had never been inside this hotel before, was at first alarmed by a distant glimpse of flying flesh-colored birds above the next-door casino; these turned out to be trapeze artists performing above the gaming tables to no applause and not much interest.

"That's what you told my father? That you'd been there yourself? You men talked me over, did you? Shared your sexual experiences?"

"Certainly not."

Erika handed him her key, dropped Luna's arm, and said she needed to buy some cough drops because of this dry air. When the elevator door closed, Paul was saying "... old Hebrews took adultery seriously because it's a betrayal of trust," and Luna broke in: "It's just that no patriarch wants a bastard cuckoo bird to show up in his nest!"

Ah me, thought Erika below, watching the numbers light up till they got to her floor—seventeen—wondering how long it would take them to learn to quarrel usefully. Now she had time to kill. When she turned aimlessly toward the casino her big purse seemed to tremble on its shoulder strap. *All my money is scared to death*, she thought.

Wandering between players she shied away from the table for craps (which didn't sound nice) but lingered near the roulette wheel; that game seemed prettier. Smiling toward her, the dealer raised and clacked in one hand a cylinder of chips, but she pretended not to see, watching instead the few early morning players. Maybe they had been here all night? She could not figure out whether it was better to play a single number or divide the chips among two or three; neither method seemed to be winning.

But since she had sometimes played twenty-one for tooth-picks, Erika next pulled a tall stool to the blackjack table, murmured, "Just looking, thank you," and waited while the lone bettor risked $5.00 and got back $7.50, risked $5.00 more and lost it. When she leaned toward the cards the dealer became alert, but she only told him, "You must find this a very boring job."

"No ma'am. Give it a try? A free one on me?"

She pointed to the overhead swings. "I'm glad to see that girl has a safety net."

"Doesn't need it."

Fifteen minutes passed while a few stragglers came and went. Yawning, she wondered if Paul and Luna had worked through their argument or if she'd be here till lunch. Then from the doorway came Major Stone, leaving behind that boy who must be Luna's ex-fiancé. He looked effeminate. His wide cheeks provided him now an appealing dimple, but by middle age he would be fat-faced with broken capillaries.

She nodded when the major said—as if it were her fault—"Your room telephone doesn't answer." She wasn't surprised. "You have to be put through by the switchboard; they won't just tell you the room location!" Erika said in these high-crime days that seemed sensible. He waited for her to say more.

"Is that the cactus student?"

"Professor!" he emphasized. *"Professor* Steven Grier. He's here to see Madeline. We both want to see Madeline."

"I'd keep telephoning, then."

"He's come a long way."

"Haven't we all?"

"I've not had a minute alone with Madeline since I got here, and I'm her father; we've got things to talk about. I'm not even sure about her health, about her state of mind."

"You had some minutes alone with Paul, though."

After a pause, the major said, "He's not as coolheaded as you are, Mrs. Cowan."

"Give him ten more years." She got off the stool, standing almost as tall as he was, and made a sudden decision. "Sorry to rush off, but I'm due at the hospital to see Sam; he's much better today."

"Well, Steven and I didn't come to Reno to spend our time with Sam." He stopped her by putting out a hand. "I know you don't like me much, Mrs. Cowan, but I am Madeline's father and I do love her."

"You must," she acknowledged, "having come all this way."

But she was thinking how hard love was, how some people were better at piano playing and baseball and love than others, the mess Paul and Luna were making of it right now, how love wouldn't hold still but kept running out ahead of you, changing. Even lying sometimes.

"I've made some mistakes," said Major Stone. "I don't want Madeline to make worse mistakes."

"How old did you say she was?" Erika left him with his head held sideways, whether to squint after her or attempt to read the dealer's hole card was hard to tell.

As soon as she drew near enough young Grier gave her the dimple. "I've been telling Major Stone that I can get Luna some counseling at Riverside; I think it's covered by my health insurance."

Erika raised both eyebrows as high as they would go.

"I thought you might mention that to her if you see her first."

She moved her head in what could have been either a nod or a shake and went rapidly past.

At St. Mary's Hospital, when she stepped into Sam's room and the boy cringed into his pillow, Erika said quickly, "I'm nobody official, just Paul's mother. Mrs. Cowan," she added, since she thought the young needed to have honorifics clarified.

The face that had at first looked pudgy and sullen gradually flowered into a slow smile until one by one his features were alight, the same glow Robert Redford could summon to illuminate a movie screen. Sam's face "lit up"; she understood that description now. His smile was not even marred by the cavity she at first mistook for a thumbtack stuck between his upper teeth.

That unexpected force field of his radiant smile had almost stopped her in midstride. Steven Grier's dimple didn't hold a candle to it—literally.

Erika stretched out her big hand, came forward, and took his stubby fingers. Immediately she felt the raised scar tissue Luna had described, and it almost burned her hand and sent heat all the way into her heart.

"But Paul and Luna are OK? The nurses said they're OK."

Erika said yes and let go the scarred hand with some reluctance. Perhaps the feel of it suggested stigmata; it might be sacrilegious to leap from that scalding touch to the anguish in Jesus' words to Jerusalem: "How often would I have gathered thy children together, even as a hen gathereth her chickens under her wings. . . ."

Erika sank into a chair. Sam's family sold him, like Joseph's brothers had sold him.

She managed to say, "Not long ago Paul was a boy your age," though she knew her words sounded predictable and stupid. Sure enough, the boy Sam said nothing but turned off his smile and through a plastic straw filled his mouth with ice water. Compared to *his* mother, she must seem a sentimental curiosity.

"I never lived on no farm," he said.

"Never even saw snow, Paul says." She watched the boy slide his damaged hand out of sight under the sheet.

"They say Luna Moon's been in, but I was asleep."

"They've both been in. A lot. They were both hurt, but they're out of the hospital now." She was thinking: *If Jamie had lived, he'd have been twenty by now.*

"You taking Paul home?"

"He's too old for me to take anywhere, even to the woodshed." She saw that woodsheds meant nothing to Sam. "They're waiting for you to get better and get out."

That smile of his erupted. "The cops haven't caught anybody?"

"No, and they say it's not likely unless you give them names and places."

"Names change. Nobody stays in one place."

"Well, some of us have. Luna wonders if you want to get in touch with your sister. Evangela?"

"She don't stay in one place either."

"But the brother in jail? Surely that's a fixed location?"

Sam said, "I hope they fix him good."

On the table by his bed were numerous forms that were waiting for information, X marks where Sam or his guardian must sign. "Is that you?" She pointed to what must have been a Polaroid snapshot of an unconscious Sam, stapled onto a file folder.

He did not answer. She asked if his leg was hurting. "They're giving you something, though. Good." When he turned up the volume on the TV mounted overhead, Erika did not think it rude so much as socially inept; that could be repaired; Paul had been polite from grade 1.

And after the dentist, yes, maybe a size 28, 30 waist with a medium shirt but probably no haircut—this style suits him—and the dog could be spaniel or beagle so they can ramble in the woods together but a sheepdog

*would try to herd the goats . . . young bones grow back fast . . . I haven't baked
cake or pie in six months but for a good appetite . . .*

"What's your last name, Sam? There's none on your doorplate.
Oh. Names change, I see."

He lowered the TV sound. "Where's Luna now? Is she sleeping OK?"

"I guess so," replied Erika, puzzled. "You know how they
found you and everything?"

"People have been in here all day. Questions, questions, questions. Nobody's answered nothing." Abruptly he rolled up his hospital sleeve. "That's smallpox, ain't it?"

She felt the rough oval on his skin. "Sure is."

"I thought so, I told them that; Mama did that much at least."

It must constitute his entire medical history. She sat still,
thinking that Jamie had only begun his first infant shots when he
died. The death was her fault for letting a baby sleep on its stomach. She had always known that.

Then she took a deep breath and began telling Sam about the
boy on the ATV, the horsemen, the helicopter.

"I knew Paul and Luna would come for me." He broke in so
urgently that it was obvious he had been in great doubt anyone
would come.

Leaving out nothing but this morning's cab ride and Paul's
proposal, she finished, "So Major Stone is here and Steven Grier
is here and Mrs. Stone is in Europe. Nobody's been able to find
your family."

"They forgot me, I forgot them." He snapped off the TV remote control and laid it on the pile of nearby papers. "I wrote
down stuff about them wrong. Nobody wanted to know, anyhow.
Everybody just wanted to keep busy."

When he opened that fist, Erika could see where the hand had
been slashed so scars crawled across all four inner fingers like rows
of earthworms. She thought you would have to do something to

the original cuts to make them heal that way, keep them open, slow the process. Maybe pour in a corrosive fluid. On animals, that kind of scar was called "proud flesh"—she felt her face twitch. She wondered if tendons had been cut, if Sam had lost precision or grip. Probably not grip. When the leg was better and that front tooth filled, there would be time to consider something, plastic surgery perhaps?

"Well, television does get boring, doesn't it?" she said brightly. "I should have brought my picture album since you've never lived on a farm. Let me tell you about mine." And she went on and on, watching his face as she made her home bucolic and pastoral, telling him squirrels in winter would wear their tails slung over their backs for warmth and—uh, yes—she supposed they did fall in the rodent family, but no, they weren't rats exactly. Sam knew about rats. She described the birds for which she made suet cake, the calf she could lead around by letting it suck her milky finger. Ice-skating. Paul's homing pigeon that didn't fly home. One hired man she'd had to fire because he brewed beer in the barn from potato peelings and chicken feed.

Even though he kept his hand hidden, she could see how Sam's body slowly relaxed while she talked. "I have, too, seen snow! Up in these very mountains!" he broke in, and in turn began to tell her about being lost there. About falling. After his leg broke, he said, he had dreamed worse than Luna ever did. He dreamed that the King of Death had come to dance around him. There was a blackbird on his shoulder, and while the King danced it flew over his head around and around and sometimes would swoop down toward Sam's face as if it might feed on him. The crow could talk because the King had split its tongue, but it talked a crazy language. "I think it talked Cuban."

Afterward they were both silent for a while. A nurse came in and went back. Sam raised the head of his bed higher, and they could now see each other's face more clearly.

Erika dug into her purse. "Can I sign your cast?"

"Sure, good!"

While she was scrawling her name in blue letters she glimpsed under the hem of his hospital gown, on skin inside his pale thigh, what looked like other dark writing. She pointed. "Somebody's pen slipped?"

Sam lifted the gown to show her: s.c. in a black triangle. The blurry capital letters both did and did not look tattooed. Sam said he had done this himself last year using a regular sewing needle. "You burn a plastic spoon and when that's melted add ground-up pencil lead and some soap and stir till it's black and thick. Then you just stick it in. It'll stay."

Lead poisoning. Erika controlled her face. "Where do you learn such things? What's the *C* for?"

"Friends. OK, so that's my real name—Cristo."

Although at this confidence a similar warm smile unfolded on Sam's face again, her still-functional mother's instinct knew he had made up the name, had chosen it. But he was a far better liar than Paul had been, far better trained at lying. Maybe Sam's mother had been far better trained in the higher reaches of deceit.

Lying's a hard habit to break, she thought, frowning. Paul had been unable to lie with much success. She'd seen him involuntarily block his own winning grin from reaching his eyes whenever he used to claim that of course he hadn't been smoking, despite the haze billowing out his window blown by the electric fan. His open window. In winter weather. Nor had Paul ever seemed to recognize when a particular lie was innately doomed to fail. Probably the Cowan ethic or Lutheran sermons had crippled him young and held him back in this dishonest world, the way Orientals bind women's feet. Maybe today a conscience was like that— beautiful and uncommon as a lotus blossom, but certain to make anyone limp and fall behind the crowd.

Erika tried to imagine what the "crowd" in Stockholm public schools would make of Sam.

"All right," she said agreeably. "Sam Cristo. That's pretty."

He showed her the signatures of doctors and nurses and so-cial workers up and down his plastered leg and had a comment on each one. "And this nurse wasn't satisfied with me having nothing but smallpox, not her, she said what other shots had I had so I showed her, here," he said, exhibiting a black freckle sunk in his bicep, "here was a BB shot. And this other woman came in, she didn't care about shots; all she asks is where I went to school and if I failed any grades."

"Did you fail any grades?"

"Not the ones I went to."

When a nurse sent Erika into the hall so Sam could relieve himself, she paced a straight line on the green stripe in the tile. So she and Bruce had led a life protected from reality? People shot each other in yards and down dirt roads just as much as on city streets, and yet? The year she'd been pregnant with Paul had been one long conflagration of civil rights marches, police dogs, cattle prods, and between news reports of beatings and murders, noth-ing but silly giggles appeared on TV—*My Favorite Martian, Petti-coat Junction,* mindless sitcoms. She'd thought then: *What a world in which to bring up children!*

And didn't get to bring up Jamie.

She paced faster, thinking about Sam who didn't know squir-rel from rat. Cristo. The Count of Monte? But Luna had said he was Catholic. Ave Maria, some equivalent of Christ? He might be-long to the Cristo Gang in some California slum.

As for Stockholm, Wisconsin—there wasn't a therapist within fifty miles; she didn't know a single Lutheran pastor up to speed on Sam's experiences.

She had prided herself on being the kind of woman who could *do* things. But to *un*do?

Erika got out her pen again, tore off paper from her used air-plane boarding pass, wrote and posted the name SAM CRISTO on his door in case it was really his name, in case they could find his real mother. . . .

She took the name down again and put it in her purse.

Major Stone had said his daughter was a sucker for a bird with a broken wing. He had called her a Zulu brain, as if the term were affectionate; Erika thought not. Two suckers: Luna and Paul. Three Zulu brains.

She went into the ladies' toilet and asked herself in the mirror how a hot-country Catholic boy would react to a population of Scandinavian types whose metabolism seldom shifted out of low gear? For that matter, could Luna Stone paint depths of character into those phlegmatic faces? Would she want to?

When she came out, the doctor had gone in on rounds, so she walked the length of the hall twice more, then was surprised to see Steven Grier—no dimple this time—marching out of the elevator. He said angrily, "I just want one look at this little Mex."

"They're busy, we have to wait."

"All I've done is wait."

Once Erika stopped pacing, Steven began, so she had to turn her head back and forth to pick up his irritable voice as he passed. "She's turned us all down for this runaway kid, her daddy and me and your holdout hippie son—excuse me, but he is; California is full of 'em—and she plans to get legal custody of this boy, says she'll stay right here in Reno by herself and fight the system for him. Raise him by herself. I asked her: And make a living how? I told her: They won't be buying charcoal portraits at any slot machines! But no, Luna says she'll go to the University of Nevada and take courses. She says you can major in hotel gaming; some nurse told her. I bust my ass getting a Ph.D. and it turns out you can major in gambling! She'll end up a goddamn croupier! Her daddy is fit to be tied! And I see things a lot clearer now that I've met him, now that I know!"

Erika tried not to let her sigh turn into a groan. "She turned down Paul, too?"

"Not that my mama didn't warn me Luna was the doubtful type, the type that would keep things to herself and then blow. So why does she blow here and not back in Chapel Hill before I made plans?" Up and down the hall he continued to march. "Once Luna heard that we three—well, we three smartass *men* is how she put it—well, once her daddy made clear that we'd put our heads together to discuss her future, especially in view of her past and all in her best interests, she just blew all the way up at everybody. I could've warned Cowan what a temper Luna's got! I've seen her throw a storm nearly that bad just over the monthly bills!"

Thrifty, thought Erika with satisfaction. "Where's Paul now?"

"Damned if I know. She got us all out of that hotel room so fast it was like—" He threw both hands high.

Like driving billy goats, Erika thought.

"I'm asking you, what is this kid in there—some genius? Some future rock star? The next president?" He stopped to glare into her face, so close she could smell mouthwash. "This is a slum kid that does porno, right? Luna's lost her mind, that's what Major Stone thinks, and I'm inclined to agree. He thinks she'll have to be committed. A Ph.D.? In gambling?"

Erika said nothing.

"Not that they'll let her keep this boy, not with her history."

Erika sank into a straight chair so she could get both hands deep into her purse and estimate how much money was left.

PAUL WAS SITTING on the hall carpet with his back against the outside door of room 1710. He had been there for two hours, missing lunch, occasionally reaching overhead to rap on the wood. One maid had vacuumed around him; another carrying clean sheets and towels had been refused entry.

Paul asked this one, "How did she sound? Would you say she's been crying?" Through the door barrier, neither of them could tell.

His legs were still sore from that horse, from his run through the Reno streets this morning. He took rigid turns sitting with legs extended, knees up and open, knees together, out in front again, but nothing was comfortable for long. On a regular schedule he bent forward in order to unkink his back, then rapped once more on Luna's door. There was nothing to look at but the relentless symmetry of numbered doors and black carpet stripes converging at the end of the hall, all of it monochromatic—white, black, shades of gray. He thought of old photographs that had sucked the blood from living faces.

In the first hour he had gone downstairs and telephoned her. "Hello?"

"Daddy?"

"It's Paul and—"

Luna hung up.

Late in the second hour he began calling her name through the locked door. He hoped that when he changed cramped positions the door bulged slightly in its frame, that she was watching the inside knob jerk. It was some comfort to picture an alert Luna inside the room, transfixed by these clues to his constancy.

No matter how he sat, his ass grew numb, stayed numb. Bored, Paul shifted to a leaning squat. "I'm not going away!" he shouted, but nothing happened. He stared down the regular lines and angles of the Circus Circus hallway, letting his eye rove and trace, then refocusing so he could see the whole thing at once. That was the big difference between sight and hearing. You could only listen to words in sequence, words arranged in time. The ear could never match this easy shift from close-up to vista.

Suddenly he fell backward when Luna jerked open the door, and he found himself looking up her skirt.

From far overhead, at an awkward angle beyond the neck brace, she said, "Are you going to make me call hotel security?" He noticed she was taking enough pains to bend from the waist so he could see and read her mouth.

It felt good—his back resting flat at last, her smooth legs stretching up. She was barefoot. He felt for her toes. "No."

THE SHARP TEETH OF LOVE

"No yourself." She shook that foot loose and backed away. "I am fed up with you. I am fed up with men in general."

"Not this one, not yet. Please." This time he grabbed her other ankle. "So I talked with your father and what's-his-name. So they tried to boss you around, and you thought I was in on it. We're going to talk this out."

"We're not."

He rolled into the room and managed to get his mouth onto the calf of her leg. When she slammed the door, that took long enough to give him access to the tender bend behind her knee. Then she kicked loose. She said, "I'm going to be the world's best single mother."

He lay sprawled with his shoes propped high on the door. "Sam and I both might have something to say here. Talk to me. Let me talk to you."

"That's what *he* always said."

"Leave Steven out of it. Nobody here now but us. And I didn't betray you."

She repeated the formal, old-fashioned word with scorn. "Betray!"

"Absolutely not." Now he rolled farther into the room, got up, slid the chain on the door. Luna looked as if she might go into the bathroom, the closet. "I'm not Steven and I'm never going to be your father. We didn't have a thing in common except breakfast."

"Breakfast and me." Anger made her eyes blacker, more opaque. "I'm not chattel! There's no dowry! If anybody asks my father for my hand in marriage I'll . . . I'll . . ."

"Put salt and pepper on it? Sorry. I didn't mean to laugh."

"You did, too. And that's another thing. You can laugh about Tamsen Donner because she's not real to you. She's just my figment. You keep humoring my figment." Though she continued to back away, arms thrashing, past the chairs and a small table, and by the foot of the first bed, she also kept granting the courtesy of letting her lips be read.

"They caught me just at the hospital entrance. And I was try-ing to tell you in the taxicab—"

"I thought you were proposing. Not very well, I might add."

"You're the one answered the telephone and told them to come on up."

"He's my *father!* He flew all the way across the country!"

"To give you to Herr Professor."

"And you kept hurrying me to get married and rush off to Wisconsin like it was some male competition where you had to get to me before they did!"

"Well, maybe so." He sat on the bed, speaking more slowly. "They were going to say you didn't know me very well and I had no job and in time I'd probably go stone deaf and never be able to sup-port you and it was too cold in Wisconsin and you'd have to leave the Catholics and God knows what all. They made a strong case."

She watched him. "I heard what they said."

Heard it, and then made them all leave. Flew, almost literally seemed to levitate, into high rage. Screamed at them—so close to Paul's amplifier that he had clapped his hands over both ears. Grabbed up a bed pillow and pummeled Steven on first one side and then the other of his excessively handsome face.

"What a temper!" he said now. "We ran out in the hall and you know what the major said? He said: 'Now she's manic!' "

"Good, he'll wash his hands of me then. It scared him when I got sick before. He thought I might be genetically contagious and he could inherit it uphill." Now she dropped on the bed beside Paul and gave a sarcastic imitation. "You know you can't think straight, Madeline, once your metabolism drops. How often do I have to tell you: you are what you eat!"

"Well, you put a slightly different spin on that than he did."

"And he called Sam a leech. You and Sam both."

Paul nodded.

"And Steven—the granddaddy of all leeches—Steven said he'd be willing to take me back and start over."

"Fuck Steven. Not you, I mean. In general."

"I don't want to start over. I want to start new."

He said, "That's three of us. Counting Sam."

"I don't want ever to see my father again."

"Yes you will, Luna. When he gets his heart attack and your mother gets her cancer, all this will look a lot less important."

"You think I couldn't manage to raise Sam all by myself?"

"Is that the best for Sam? To say nothing of you and me?"

It went on like that for a while, her statements, his questions. Luna said if she stayed in Reno she could consult Tamsen all the time, like an oracle. That would be weekdays. On Sundays she and Sam would go to Mass.

But she wound down by stages, spoke slower, spoke softer. She sat less tensely on the bed and looked at him. He slid a little nearer. Put his arm on her shoulders so his taped fingers could come into view on the far side of her neck brace and look, he hoped, pitiful.

"Careful," she whispered. "I'm sore all over."

"As a boil," he said. "Me too."

There was no way to kiss her throat through the bulky collar, so his mouth slid down to knobs of bone and then fell upon cloth that was in his way.

In a lazy voice Luna said, as if to herself, "I'm not even sure you're all that different from Steven *or* my father. It might be the Y chromosome."

He found his way past a few buttons.

"*Y* stands for 'yes,' yes you do it my way, yes men are still in charge," she murmured. "That Y chromosome."

She was relaxing against his arm. They eased backward to lie on the bed, but Paul's first groan was not from desire but because she had lain on his bandaged fingers. By inches they gingerly resettled their bruised limbs. It was awkward to undress her or himself, one handed.

He said, fumbling, "This is how we'll make love when we're old, this carefully."

He stroked her body with his good hand. "Ouch," Luna said.

Her response seemed to be cooling. Now Paul could not tell if she was still angry or if she had grown shy in this half-light as she had not seemed shy in the sunny canyon. They were at cross-purposes: she lifting his face so their eyes could meet while he strove to lower his head and press his mouth against her body, to wander and smell and graze and linger. He managed to get her underpants down but not off; then, just when he expected her to yield and open, she puckered instead and withdrew her womb all the way into the back of her throat and held it there.

Paul found himself looking straight ahead at the closed V of her thighs. He tried to wedge his uninjured hand in between. "No?" he finally whispered.

"You think this solves everything, I suppose," she said in a voice that reached him with no lip-reading.

"I think it's a start." He could feel her skin change, as though a thin top layer had melted. Then Luna's fingers slid into his hair. She lifted him by the scalp until he thought his whole head might peel if he stayed where he was.

Her voice was so throaty he would not have understood had he not been looking at her mouth muttering the words. "I don't, that is, I haven't. Like that. Done it."

Joy popped out of every pore on his body. Old Speedy Steven, Hasty Steven, at-full-blast Steven! He said, "You don't have to do much but lie still."

"I just can't turn off an argument one minute and go right into that."

Into? The way she had grasped his head was giving him a crick in the neck. He managed to nibble one breast mixed with nylon and wait, breathing hard. She seemed to be breathing hard, too; a good sign.

Between puffs she said, "Steven never—"

"Last time," he said. "I ever want. To hear his. Name." He was glad to lay his head against her diaphragm, but the sound of digesting food was not romantic. After a rest he said, "It's just my Y chromosome wanting to control you. Suggesting a little variety."

In a pouting voice Luna said they didn't have enough routine yet to need to get varied *from*.

"All right, all right." He rolled away from her.

There was no sound in the room except his breath and hers, which did not seem to be synchronized.

Then, as if she had made some sober and rational decision, Luna suddenly said, "OK, I'll try it!" and flung her whole self downward, neck brace and all, and tumbled past his belly button, striking her chin against his hipbone and poking something else—elbow?—into his throat, all of this human avalanche so fast and hard that his recoil to the edge of the mattress turned into physical withering, and suddenly he thudded limp onto the hotel carpet and landed on buttocks and balls, already vibrating down into a dull ache.

"Aiiiiii!" he managed to breathe. By reflex he ran his fingertips through pubic hair for an equipment check.

"Paul? You OK? Paul?" Her face was hanging off the bed. "I didn't mean to scare you." Her eyes were wide, one with a yellowish bruise around it.

He knew, quite sharply, that this was what marriage would be like and one-night stands were not—these ups and downs and pleasures and farces. Sex you had paid good money for was not allowed to turn inept. He murmured, "Jesus."

Her face moved from his line of sight. After a silence from the bed above, Luna's crisp and easily audible voice said, "That's not a cheap trick? Calling on Jesus in the middle of *this?* I don't know what kind of theology you've got, Paul Cowan, but it's not what the priest told me."

They were already rehearsing the future, he thought. The

Catholic thing. The Wisconsin thing. The art thing. Already they had both invested in accounts that would draw long marital payoffs.

He stayed hunched on the rug, though he gradually smiled as his whole system slowed and ticked down, and even while that smile seemed to be dislodging one of the stitches on his face, it continued to spread. In another moment he felt her hand drift onto his neck, over the smooth jaw where his beard had been recently forfeited. "Paul?"

"You might as well marry me, Luna Stone. We're going to need years." Time passed while he straightened one aching leg, then the other, and rebent them to preferred angles.

Her hand kept playing up his cheeks, over his brow. Then her head popped into view, and she lowered her face against his and whispered in his ear, "OK." The word hit his eardrum with a papery rush. *Olé*, it seemed to say over some general acoustical roar, perhaps from spectators in the stands.

"OK yourself," he said back.

They rested awhile, he on the rug—unzipped but torpid—she leaning off the mattress with two hands dangling and locked on his chest, both of them thinking that each had previously enjoyed easier, far less demanding sex than this, less awkward, far less ludicrous; and each determined to carry this secret to the grave.

Passion and intimacy, what a stew! Paul thought. But he said, "I do love you, Mad Lunatic, and I can call you that because I know you're not mad and you know I know it."

"*Now* you love me! Now that you beat out Dad and Steven!" But she laughed, thrust both hands into his ribs, and made him howl.

We must both be a little scared, Paul decided. When his wheeze had turned into ordinary breath he said, "It's not just women that need reassuring. Tell me you love me. Tell me you love me more than what's-his-name."

But from that position he could not see her lips, so the next silence made him tense; she might be murmuring anything—words of endearment, obscenity? The X chromosome: mystery. Her stillness stretched out, lengthened; when he rose to face her she had already finished answering him. Or had she said a word? He touched the awkward collar where it covered her larynx in case a vibration should linger there. Then his unbandaged fingers crept into her tangled hair; he lifted his face and drew hers until he could see her sweet mouth coming. This much at least was open, yielding. In the long wet heat that followed, he could no longer tell his tongue from hers. He began reaching under her clothes.

The telephone rang.

Just at that moment when their sharp physical edges had begun to liquefy and merge, the jangle from the bedside table stopped everything. Paul grunted. Each tried to pause, to wait, to hold the moment.

Luna answered, mouthed to Paul that it was her father, listened for a long, cooling time. "Yes I do know that's how you are. . . . No, with Paul . . . I don't know how soon . . . if you leave word on Mother's machine, she may call in for her messages? . . . Maybe you can get Corinne to grow up the way you want, then you get a daughter and wife rolled into one . . . all right. I'm sorry. I shouldn't have said that . . . I'll write her about the earrings. . . . Yes, I know you do . . . I said I know you love me. . . . Yes, me too. . . . All right. Yes. Yes."

She hung up and looked into her empty hand. "I told you he was always at his best by telephone."

"Come here." Paul was just getting some of the swollen warmth back into Luna's mouth when the telephone rang again. He grabbed for it, but she got there first and seemed to wait a long time, listening. He moved onto the bed beside her, lightly touched her alternate pale and sunburned skin, gnawed once at her vertebrae but from her every surface could feel desire waning. "I don't believe it!" she exclaimed into the telephone.

He didn't, either. "Tell him we'll send him a wedding announcement." He burrowed into her lap for another try, but Luna knew too well what to do; she flicked high the volume on his hearing aid and almost exploded his mastoid bone by bellowing right against it, *"Sam's been kidnapped again! Right out of the hospital!"*

"Never happen." He shook his ringing head. "Who says?"

Luna told an unseen policeman they'd be there right away.

They staggered into the bathroom to sponge their pink and puffy faces. Paul was aching both from the horse he'd ridden and the woman he hadn't. He said irritably, "Excuse me," and peed with discomfort while Luna, eyes averted, fluffed her hair and redid buttons. Perhaps what's-his-name's bladder had only functioned in private? Paul decided they still were at the bare edge of Intimacy, with great distances yet to go.

He muttered, adjusting his clothes, "This makes no sense."

"How could they track him down?"

"Newspapers. TV."

"Maybe Sam just ran away from all those do-gooders."

"They did say *kidnapped?*"

"Did you tell him he could come to Wisconsin with us? That he had to?"

Through the mirror they flashed grim expressions into each other's face while Paul said, "I wasn't even sure you were coming."

"Neither was I," she said sadly, looking so guilty that he wrapped one arm around her waist.

"You're sure now?"

"Too fast, everything's happening too fast."

Nothing was fast at the police station, where everybody seemed calm and unhurried and busy with other cases. They were sent to wait in a windowless room with three straight chairs tucked under a metal table. They sat across from each other, staring at the table as if food might eventually be set before them, but it would be cold and unappetizing.

Paul squeezed her hand. She said, "I should have stayed with him." Light fell in a circle around their hands but could not reach the room's dark corners.

"Maybe he felt abandoned," she said.

"Mother was going over there this morning. And you were—"

"Having a tantrum, don't remind me. Besides, Sam doesn't know her the way he knows us."

Paul agreed. "Not that she's hard to know."

"What if his real family saw him on the news and just showed up and took him?"

"That's possible." For resale? "It makes no sense that those same two men would take the risk. They're long gone."

She rubbed her forehead and said gloomily, "Who knows how many men there are like them?"

It made Paul think of Original Sin, how that outmoded concept persisted under other names, how harsh backgrounds and bad social conditions and weak genes and the sins of the fathers were still functioning in the modern world—renamed—and their consequences accumulated in certain places, had settled into the shadowed edges of this particular room. He shifted his muscle aches in this very chair where rapists and killers had offered their long excuses.

Somebody opened the door and closed it again. Luna said, "We never ate lunch—you must be hungry."

Paul, who had preferred eating her, only nodded. She complained that it was nearly three o'clock.

He went on thinking about sin. He decided that in the popular mind only serial killers might be guilty of it anymore. Everybody else made mistakes or committed errors of judgment.

In the uneasy silence, Luna took her hand from his and studied her fingers as if trying to imagine how much a wedding ring would weigh. "I like your mother, by the way."

"I'm afraid I don't like your father."

"That's all right." She rose, paced around the table, sat down in the light. "Just pick what percent you'll settle for—whether you can see him on holidays sometimes if you're able to like seventy-five percent of his personality. Or sixty." She leaned closer. "Forty-two?"

Like Lot, bargaining over Sodom.

"We'll telephone him on Christmas Eve," she said.

"I don't like the way he just walked in and took over and stirred up trouble, but I'll try to get over that."

"It's a habit. When he came home after two or three months away, he'd always think Mother and I had gotten slack and it was his duty to shape us up. Occupational hazard, I guess."

"No wonder you thought we'd had a meeting to arrange your future."

"Maybe you did—men can't seem to help it." She made a noise of exasperation. "I did lose my temper."

"You sure did," he said, wondering about the ultimate amount of total temper she had available to lose. He was more accustomed to people who swallowed their anger the way Popeye swallowed spinach, so it would pour into their biceps and become available for heavy lifting. He thought in Wisconsin she might view the Germanic temperament as sluggish.

She was touching her temples now, wishing for aspirin, and that made him tender toward her. "If Sam's really gone, you'll still marry me? You'll come without him?"

"Oh, I can't think about that now, how can you?"

The door opened and a man in a seersucker suit came in and sat across the table from them. Without preliminaries, he asked, "Mr. Cowan, where's your mother?"

"What?" Paul cocked forward his better ear. "Mother? Back at the hotel, I guess. She went to visit Sam this morning." He grabbed Luna's hand. "They didn't take her, too?"

"We don't think so. How about you, Miss Stone? You were discharged from the hospital early this morning. Have you seen the boy since? Seen Mrs. Cowan?"

Luna shook her head. "She came with us to the hotel, and Paul said she was going later to see Sam."

"Spoken by telephone?" Luna said no, just to her father, and he had called from the airport.

"Major Stone, yes, I met him," the man said, his face not moving. "I see your van is still parked in the hospital lot."

"It was more comfortable to come by taxi," she said. "Paul is going to get—"

Paul demanded, "Where is my mother?"

"I'm sure she's fine. Just a minute." He left and closed the door.

Paul had jumped up to follow when a uniformed policeman came in, opened a file in a pool of light in front of them, and stood leaning onto his knuckles as he spoke in a dry and summarizing voice. The glare on his thick eyeglasses made it hard to see his face.

"At about ten a.m., Mr. Steven Grier signed in to visit the boy known to us and on hospital records as Samuel Cristo." (Luna whispered, "Cristo?") "Mrs. Cowan was already on that floor, and they spoke briefly, according to one of the nurses, and went into the boy's room together. Then both of them left and Mr. Grier went to the airport, but your mother signed back in about eleven. She was in there with the boy maybe thirty minutes before an orderly took in his lunch tray. He says they were gone then, but he didn't think anything of it. He left the tray because some nurse told him Sam Cristo had gone riding off in a wheelchair with his grandmother, or somebody like his grandmother." The officer turned a page in a file but looked at the two of them instead of the next paragraph. "You know how hospitals are these days, do you? Family members often take the patients to X ray or some lab or other. They're understaffed."

He shrugged and went on. "Nobody thought anything about it. They never came back. Mrs. Cowan's not here in Reno in a vehicle? We've checked on your van, of course."

In unison they said, "She flew in."

"Round-trip ticket," Paul added. "She thought it was exorbitant."

The policeman turned another page, shaking his head as if the words there were unsatisfactory. "The ticket's still outstanding. There's no reason anybody would look twice at a gray-haired lady that was rolling a patient's wheelchair right out the front-door ramp, you see, because discharge papers don't get down to the reception desk for quite some time. Understaffed, you see. One volunteer thinks—only *thinks*, you understand—that she might have seen them because the woman was walking funny and she offered to help push the chair, but the woman said no, it was just that she'd been wearing her Sunday shoes too long."

"But the kidnappers?" Luna cried.

"Nobody at the hospital saw any kidnappers. Nobody's sure that was Mrs. Cowan in her Sunday shoes. There's more than one exit. They don't keep good count of the wheelchairs because they get left all over the building all the time."

Paul had begun to pace. "But then what? Where could they go?"

"Not on the grounds anywhere, we've—" On the policeman's belt a beeper went off, and he stepped into the hall.

As one, Luna and Paul bent to read the file. Today's page said little more than they had already heard except for the added news that Steven Grier's flight to Riverside was already in the air; that Major Stone was in the lounge at his departure gate and had no information and didn't expect to have any and needed to sleep off his jet lag as well as his irritation at local inefficiency; that Erika Cowan's ticket had not been reissued nor canceled nor was there a second ticket in her name or Sam's, and that her small suitcase remained in the room at Circus Circus.

"Did you see that?" Luna asked. "I really didn't notice."

Paul said slowly, "Mama's got him?"

"And gone where? Sam's still in a cast! He's on pain pills!"

Paul rolled his eyes, remembering that his mother believed in toughing things out.

The policeman brought in another sheet of paper, added it to the file, and closed the folder. "Your mother know how to rent a car?"

"Certainly not. This was her first plane ride."

"Credit cards? Driver's license?"

"She doesn't believe in credit cards. I guess she still drives the old pickup truck."

"Without a credit card," the cop said softly, thinking aloud, "she'd have to show good ID and put up a lot of cash."

Paul admitted that Erika Cowan could manage both.

The policeman tapped the file against the table. "Here's what I think right now. I think foster parents and juvenile homes some-times work and sometimes don't. I think if your mama's got the boy and he went of his own free will? I think if nobody files a com-plaint except the welfare people and they don't know which office owns the case?" He was shaking his head left and right. "I think if the hospital collection agency already knows that boy can't pay his bill? If there's no insurance, no family?" He sighed. "I also think we got bigger fish to fry, Mr. Cowan, Miss Stone, beg your pardon." He put up a hand and braced the air between them. "Not bigger like more important, just bigger like more urgent. Like that girl somebody shut up in a wood box and set afire and burned off half her feet, for instance." He grunted and snapped a look into one of those dark corners of the room before reaching overhead to stop the light fixture from swinging. He looked tired.

"But I want you to let me know," he said louder, "if the boy's *not* with your mama going across"—he took a breath—"state lines in a rented Ford Taurus, dark blue," and abruptly he rattled off a full Nevada license-plate number.

They stared at his bald head, shining with light, the glasses shiny, too.

"What'll happen," he said, and perhaps his mouth relaxed a bit, "is that in some few more days that car will be turned in to an airport rental office in, say, Illinois? Florida? Maybe even Wisconsin, though there's not an airport in Stockholm, right? And the bill will be settled. By then I expect to hear if either one of you has any reason to worry about the boy's whereabouts. Or his well-being." He handed a card to Paul and one to Luna. "If you're not worried at that time, then I won't be."

"OK." Paul put the card in his shirt pocket, but Luna stood still and read every word on hers before they all shook hands.

"You're OK on this, Miss Stone?" She nodded. "I wouldn't want your daddy to take any offense at how this was handled. He looked like a letter writer to me."

"Telephone."

He carried the file and opened the door. "Have a good trip," he said—his tone as mild, as meaningless, as a checkout clerk's routine murmur of have-a-good-day.

Left alone, they stared at each other. Paul could not read her face, was not sure whether she now felt trapped by a need to go after Sam and maybe get married as part of some package deal, whether Erika Cowan's act had left her glad or angry, whether everything was just—as she'd said—too fast, too uncontrolled, or too much controlled by him. Because of the neck brace, Luna had to twist her whole body to see him directly; he squinted at her unmoving lips before turning up his hearing aid so high that the earpiece suddenly shot a whistle through his skull.

While he was turning down the next-lower whistles he heard Luna say, "She's pretty enterprising, your mother. Pretty sure of herself. Reminds me of somebody else."

"It seems so impulsive, not like her at all. Maybe Sam asked her to?"

"Sure of herself, sure of you, and of me also."

"Why did she ever expect to get away with it?" said Paul as he took her hand. But his question was rhetorical. He was beginning to think that Erika Cowan had merely taken for granted that God would be on her side in removing any hurt boy from wicked Reno to pastoral Wisconsin, that she had moved with the serene confidence of some Old Testament prophet who happened to be passing through Babylon at the time God snapped His fingers.

PART 6

Wisconsin Life Trip

~

Reno to Stockholm

FOR THE FIRST FIFTY MILES, between anxious frowns into the rearview mirror, Erika stiffly twisted the wheel of the getaway car and occasionally wiped her palms on her skirt. The car seemed skittish to her, nervous, leaping left and right at the mere touch of the wheel and willing to stop dead if she merely flexed her toes. These needed flexing; she could not remember anytime in her life when she had worn Sunday shoes quite so long.

But near the end of their first hour on the road, abruptly, glee overcame her, and she began to shoot triumphant glances from Sam to passing motorists. In fact, she speeded up so much that few of them could pass. Nothing provides so much freedom as realizing that no one knows you here and, besides, you'll never come back to this place again. Her liberty first sprang to life when, braked at a traffic light, she read on one sign the neon message above a travel agency; *PLEASE GO AWAY!* it ordered in hot-pink italic. She giggled. "You see that?"

Sam shook his head. Not, she already knew, a boy much given to word-jokes. A tactile boy, maybe. A spatial boy.

What in the world was she going to do with him?

She shot a look sideways. He had drawn his face tight and kept sucking his lips as if the whole mouth cavity were puckered with alum. "Hurting, are you?" Again he shook his head. "There's aspirin and Tylenol in my purse," she said, driving. "Which one works best for you?"

"I don't know."

It made her sick to think they had cut his hand with no sedative, and that behind those days he had lived in a home that allowed fevers to run their course. Erika felt blindly among objects and gave him the first bottle that came to hand. He swallowed two of whatever was inside, paused, ate another.

"You sure she's coming?"

Erika said she was pretty sure.

Before leaving Reno they had tipped back his passenger seat and built up a platform in front for his extended leg, using hospital pillows and blanket pads. Everything had been hasty, on impulse. She had found Sam so eager to leave the hospital that it wasn't necessary to make much case for the future, but now that they were rolling northeast across Nevada with lawmen possibly in pursuit, she felt he was owed one. She herself was hoping that tardy rationalizations would surface soon and make what she had done seem plausible. At the time she had thought only that Jamie, if he had lived, would have been old enough to drive, drink, marry, go to war.

Sam pointed out his window. "The river's gone."

"Oh that's no river, not a real river!" she said with growing confidence. "The Truckee's a dry ditch mostly—wait till you see the Mississippi! The Chippewa!" She floundered. "The Kickapoo? If you can't fish in it, it's not a river!"

He was leaning back waiting, she saw, for his pain to ease. "Tell me again about Wisconsin."

How to describe your own room, or make an ordinary yesterday seem worth living twice? She thought about it while she swept around a truck and enjoyed the way this rented car accelerated underneath her almost independently. She had never driven a car so new, so speedy.

"You remember the map I showed you, that western border of

Wisconsin that looks like an Indian head? In the profile, we live down in his throat. Pepin County."

"But you still get snow," Sam insisted, shifting in search of a comfortable position.

That made her drive faster. "Oh, there's snow—not as much as the North Woods gets, but plenty of snow for a California boy. It's not all play, though; you'll have to help shovel it, you know, for the old folks or the sick ones. Strong boys do that."

He only grunted.

Of course: not used to helping others. *If he really acts up, he's too big to whip,* she thought. She slipped off her right shoe and felt the ridges in the gas pedal through her stocking. The car took a few short rabbit hops. "Laura Ingalls Wilder started out in Pepin, you know."

"Who?"

"On TV. *Little House on the Prairie?*"

To himself he muttered something ugly and contemptuous.

Well, he was hurting. Paul had already told her Sam would need a lot of time, a lot of love, and discipline besides.

Erika could not think of one single fact that would make her state interesting, and he seemed to have failed geography, so she shifted nearer home. "Behind my house I grow a garden. Beside that are six apple trees. The apples are wormy now since Bruce isn't there to spray." She changed the catch in her voice to a cough. "There's a barn with a milkhouse built on, though I don't use it much, and a corncrib and some empty outbuildings. I haven't kept chickens for several years. . . ." It sounded terrible, deserted. "There's a bantam rooster left. And I always seem to attract stray cats. They like goat's milk."

"They'll kill that rooster."

"He's too mean." She overlaid the road ahead of them with memory. "My TV antenna is on top of the old windmill. We'll need to oil the hooks on the porch swing, in fact the swing's still out in the garage this season—it's too heavy for me." She wasn't sure Sam knew what a porch swing was. "Paul's already said you need a dog."

"It'll kill the cats *and* the rooster."

"Oh no, cats are fast. And a puppy can be trained." She couldn't help wondering if Sam was too old to train. If she had misjudged Paul's plans, she might be out there alone on the farm with a teenage delinquent who had been warped by abuse.

They drove on while she strove for other things to tell him. "Where I live, out from Stockholm, most of the people have light hair and light-colored eyes." Sam had closed his. "Except for Indians. There's a good school and a bus that takes you there, but it won't start till nearly Labor Day. You'll have plenty of time to explore the countryside. Plenty of time for your leg to heal."

He might be sleeping. After she lost Jamie, she had been anxious about people asleep, their guards down so Death could get close. Had waked up Paul in the night, thinking a snore might be a death rattle getting up steam. Had waked up Bruce if he dreamed. Had wanted to dream that Jamie was alive but different on the other side, growing in wisdom and stature. Never did.

She couldn't help herself now but reached across and shook Sam's shoulder.

"What? What?"

"Nothing. I thought Wisconsin had put you to sleep."

He closed his eyes again. For some reason she thought of herself, maybe ten years old but already as tall as Sam, out hunting in that countryside for milkweed pods to help the war effort. The fluff would be sewn into life vests, didn't mildew, would keep navy pilots afloat in the Pacific until rescue came.

He asked suddenly, "Any ghosts in Wisconsin?"

"Ghosts? Oh, stories of ghosts, I'm sure. There must be; there always are wherever people have died in the mines or on the railroad." She drove a bit slower, frowning. "I think there might be a Ouija board up in the attic." She was thinking that Mexicans had crazy customs; wasn't there a story that sometimes they nailed up a neighbor to celebrate Easter?

"Luna Moon saw a ghost."

"Did she now?" Uneasy, Erika set her stocking foot harder on the gas pedal and by willpower had to slow down and say firmly, "I never did and you won't either."

"I want to," he said and fell asleep, leaving her to wonder if Luna had only told him some childhood fantasy or whether all artists had their thermostats turned up too high. Paul said he loved her. Start from there.

With Sam asleep, her driving became more relaxed, even more daring. She experimented with swoops and acceleration. She thought about trading in the pickup truck at home.

Then she wondered what painkillers Sam might have swallowed in the hospital and whether three Tylenol on top of that might prove fatal, so she tried to drive and take his pulse at the same time. It beat under his skin and her two finger pads like a tiny live fetus, the way Paul had throbbed in her womb, and Jamie. With Jamie and summer they'd had time to get to the hospital, but Paul had come out of her body into the same bed where Bruce had first pumped him into her. A red meaty chunk. She'd felt then as if her own heart had been born and could never get crammed back inside where it belonged—and she'd been right about that.

And Jamie? You never think children can die. Even when they fall off skyscrapers their mothers run screaming down the stairs praying they're still alive.

Sam's pulse seemed OK. Maybe now she could love this ready-made boy without so much risk and, besides, Sam might be the means by which Paul would come closer home and get her heart back within reach. *Oh, I'm selfish! Selfish!*

Some kind of police car showed up in her mirror. By reflex she hit the brake and, when the car jerked, let it up. The trooper or sheriff stayed behind her at matching speed. He seemed to be talking into his radio. Erika sat very straight and drove carefully, after a quick look to check whether Sam's dark head was visible over the seat back; no, it had drooped onto his shoulder as he slept.

The officer continued to follow, patiently, as if he meant to be in position when she crashed.

At exit 105 she veered sharply off to Lovelock, concentrated on every car on the ramp behind, but finally decided he had ceased to follow; so merged again onto I-80 without spotting anyone in ambush there. Sam did not wake.

Near Winnemucca another car rushed toward them from behind, passed so slowly she could read the phone number for Humboldt Law Enforcement painted on its door. Two uniformed men in the front seat studied her; the passenger was making notes on a clipboard. The word "escort" came into Erika's mind. She drove away from them into the sunny streets of Winnemucca as if she lived there. Rolling down the car window felt like opening a kiln. In this heated afternoon, people must be home taking siestas. She parked under skimpy shade trees in a city park and studied the map.

Sam mumbled, "What is it?"

"That's another thing—Wisconsin has some real trees. I'm not sure what's going on; remember the convoys in World War Two? No, of course you don't. Hold this end, please."

He fixed one map corner under his scarred hand. Every time some surface touched that corrugated skin it made her shiver.

"I'm going straight north on 95, that'll be a surprise," she announced. "If I can find the turnoff." She located the intersection on paper, then U-turned into harsh sunlight.

With a yawn Sam said he didn't care which road she took. He was getting hungry.

"I'll confuse the issue," Erika muttered, frowning at road signs. "See what's what," as she made the turn. "Because the first main thing is just to get out of Nevada." Then she laughed. "Maybe the law thinks this old lady is carrying an underage boy across the state line for illicit purposes!" At his frown she explained, "To se-duce you?" She saw with a pang that Sam had only been educated in acts, not in words that described them, and that seduction would be an act too mild for him to comprehend. Her throat ached. "I'm glad you were able to sleep. Your leg still hurt?"

He said it did. "Let's have the radio."

At his touch so much sound exploded into the car at once that it seemed all four doors would bulge. Above a booming bass that vibrated up through the floor mat and tingled Erika's foot soles, several banshees kept screaming. "Sam! Turn that down! More! Even more!" Such a roar was enough to loosen every filling in her teeth. She'd need to buy a TV with a bigger screen. This was all going to be expensive.

The pounding music was still too loud. When at last an ordi-nary human voice came on between songs, speaking English, she said, "Does it hurt so much you want to go back?"

"You want me to?" He sounded suspicious.

"No."

"No."

The radio talk-show host was editorializing about Waco, whether government forces should have waited, whether the pos-sible sexual mistreatment of children warranted desperate action. Sam changed the station.

"Then everything's all right." Erika felt her smile widening even before she began to mean it. More music came on, still loud, but he said, "I heard you the first time," and turned down the volume.

"And before school starts," she said, "we'll get you to a first-class dentist."

IN THEIR ROOM at Circus Circus, Paul and Luna waited into late afternoon for the telephone to ring. "I'm sure she'll call," he re-peated for maybe the tenth automatic time.

Luna, pacing, wasn't a bit sure. Besides, it was driving her crazy to watch Paul practice lip-reading TV soap operas with the sound turned off. Most of those actors turned their pained faces directly into the camera. Any sincerity led to a close-up. Occasionally a Vaseline tear would ease across reddened cheeks. She couldn't stand it. And once left alone on the set, every wanna-be Hamlet would mouth a soliloquy of thoughts too mundane to overhear, much less for Paul to strive for.

Even when she closed her eyes, the afterimage of one more anguished unwed mother was visible. Tamsen might be an after-image, an unhappily-ever-after image.

She said loudly, "I still think we ought to set off after them right away." Not so much to catch Erika Cowan and Sam as to close the gap, to draw alongside, to arrive in Stockholm, Wisconsin, at exactly the same moment. The next moment was blank.

"But where," recited Paul in a slow, hesitant monotone. "No; but *what* if it's really Link's baby? Then what will Aster do?" He frowned. "Aster?"

Luna shook his sleeve. "What do we gain by waiting?" she asked even louder. "Even if your mother does call, she says what? Sam is safe with me? We already know that."

"We'll know where they are and if Sam's all right. They could have a wreck. The car could break down." He fixed his eyes on television. "But Aster has been in a home? In a home? In a *coma!* Since Christmas."

This time Luna fixed her body between him and the actress on-screen. "I've got to call *my* mother before the major gets to her without tying up this telephone and, anyway, I just can't sit still another minute."

He nodded and embraced her, but she could feel his neck craning beyond. "Sorry." A pause. "The coma she got when the duck, the truck overturned."

"I'll walk on over to the hospital and get the van. And I've got library books still out—you think they're in the van?"

"The search people packed up everything for us."

She found her purse and keys. "And before we go, I've got to say good-bye to Tamsen."

This time he clicked off the remote control. "Not by yourself. Don't you go up there all by yourself."

"That's the only way she'll come."

"I'll go with you and wait in the car." When Luna shook her head he said, "Do you cross yourself when Tamsen comes?"

"No. I only cross myself on airplanes when they take off and land."

"Maybe you should and she'd go away. You never drew her picture, either."

"Someday I might." At the door she said, "I may have to wait for her. It's not like table-tipping, you know."

Paul shook his head. "If it's after dark I want to go with you. I'll stay out of sight."

"Your mother might call." She was trying to decide from his face whether or not he really believed one word about Tamsen Donner.

"Why are you trying to see her at all? Is this some kind of exorcism?"

Maybe so. Luna opened the door.

"After all, she never knew you were coming—why does she need to know you're going?" He forced a laugh. "Unless you promised to leave your forwarding address."

"That's not funny."

"All right. Take it back."

She made him read *her* lips as she mouthed the soundless explanation, "I've got to tell her what happened to Hastings." Watching him, she decided that Paul probably didn't believe in Tamsen's ghost, had only accepted as fact that Luna believed it. It made her feel lonely.

"Why?"

She saw that it pleased him to read her pantomimed sentence

so well. "It'll ease her mind," she added in a stage whisper. "Yes. I said mind." She hit the final *d* hard with her tongue. "Tamsen's mind."

"Call me from the library so I can let you know if Mother's been in touch. I ought to go with you."

"I will." From the hall she knew he had turned down the volume, since a singing commercial was coming on. Paul hated those. He said it gave him a case of existential despair to lip-read a lip-synch.

She walked through the heat to St. Mary's, letting her eye find the window that marked her former room. So many do-gooders had been on hand at the time that police had parked her brown van in the far back lot. Delivery trucks came to that loading dock as well as, Luna saw, a hearse to collect the doctors' failures. That made her remember an old belief that the human soul did not depart its corpse at once but slowly leaked out, so the dead limbs had to be straightened lest anything obstruct the exit.

In the van Luna located books about the Donner Party, Gold Rush, Lost Dutchman, Mark Twain, California history, and apparitions. She now knew more about the history of apparitions than was good for her. She knew that Saint Augustine had hoped his dead mother would visit him after she died, but she never came. She knew that Homer said that on the Trojan battlefield the spirits left dead Aegeans, darting and squeaking like bats. And that sometimes a murderer's ghost could be identified because the wicked spirits smelled of sulfur. No help at all.

Driving through the crowded lot and along busy streets, she saw no Ford Taurus, but could not help watching for it all the way to the Sparks library, where she returned the books. There was a poster at the check-in desk, an upcoming lecture on Rudolf Steiner. AN EARLY KORESH, it said. STEINER SAW AURAS AND DE-SCRIBED THE CHILDHOOD OF CHRIST.

In a street-side phone booth she took out the note from the hotel clerk that said Priscilla Stone had called from Florence,

Italy, left this number, requested a callback, stated the time difference, left also a telephone credit-card number to use for that callback. The moment Luna had first read this message she instantly dropped about twenty years and sixty pounds. *I want my mother! I want her to meet Paul Cowan!*

She felt she was being microwaved in the hot booth. She dialed the hotel room and identified with a half smile the click made when the receiver touched Paul's hearing aid. She understood now that any defining mark could make her feel tender, his mutilated beard or the way his hand seemed always to be coming toward her as if she gave off a good aura herself. "Paul? Did she call?"

"Not yet. Where are you?"

"I'm on my way to Donner Park. I may be late."

"Let me come with you, Luna."

"You stay by the phone in case your mother calls. Or even the police. If you're worried about a wreck or something, they'll hear it before you."

He admitted that thought had crossed his mind; his mother had never done long-distance driving. "Maybe at least Sam will call."

"This is not some latchkey boy who had to let Mama know where he was at all times. You know they just expect us to figure it out and come right behind them." Talking, Luna had begun to fiddle with the telephone cord as if it were a rosary: fifty-nine beads, one medal, a crucifix; *Hail Mary, Lord's Prayer, Salve Regina.* "What?"

"... midnight the last time."

"Maybe this time Tamsen knows I've got an early wake-up call."

He asked her again to take him with her; the hotel clerk could write down Erika's message. "By the way, did you reach your mother?"

"I'll call her from Truckee. See you tonight, Paul, and don't worry if it's late." She was remembering how she had left Steven in another hotel when she first went up in the mountains. "Bye."

"Wait!"

She got the phone back to her ear. "Hurry up, it's hot in here."

"How late do you plan to wait for Tamsen before you, well, decide that maybe she's quit coming? Or you've quit seeing her." He waited, but she said nothing. "I want some estimate of when you'll be back so I'll know when to start worrying."

Getting stiff in the booth, Luna grew an inch taller. "Are you saying that now that you, Paul Cowan, have come into my life and now that I'm so much better adjusted, there'll be no ghost at all? That I don't need my hallucinations anymore? Is that what you're saying?"

He also sounded irritated. "All I want to know is if you're going to hang around all night on the mountain giving C.P.R. to the late Tamsen Donner!"

"No," she said, "I'm not." And hung up.

To Luna's surprise, a number of men and women were climbing out of cars beside the still-open, well-lit Emigrant Trail Museum though it was dusk, and several had to be reminded to go back and turn off their lights. From their loud greetings and conversations in the parking lot, all were members of the Truckee-Donner Historical Society, arriving at their monthly meeting place. She moved among them, smiling; through them, smiling; then finally beyond them at increasing speed with her face set, hurrying toward the campsite where Tamsen had first appeared to her.

As soon as their voices faded so did all her doubts and disbeliefs as well. There was something about being on Tamsen's home territory that made her previous appearances real and convincing. Luna understood why pilgrims chose to leave home and be refreshed in Mecca, in Bethlehem.

She moved quietly down the trail, through light and dark. Sam and Erika at this moment were probably driving headlong under the low sun and then beyond it into earlier time zones. If Luna could imagine a passage that reversed time, surely she could accept the possibility that a woman's dark shadow, peeling loose from the body that had originally cast it, could turn inside out and pale, visible in darkness, bleached out by daylight, and go drifting forward across wider calendar time. It was a question of speed and persistence. Hadn't Aquinas believed that the soul exists in a greatly diminished state until it can be reunited with the body?

Then the strangest thing happened. Frowning, Luna stood in the center of what must certainly have been her first campsite here, the spot on which both Sam and the late Mrs. Donner had intruded. Here she pivoted slowly, shaking her head as much as the neck brace would allow. It didn't look right. This table, this spigot? In the wrong places? Was not the tree much taller? She trotted up the path to the next cleared area. Though this one seemed more familiar, already an empty yellow tent had been set up with a backpack alongside. The same tree, the same boulder, stood in their usual places. Or did they?

How was such uncertainty possible? Luna rushed back to the first location, then tried the empty sites left, right, and below, trying to summon déjà vu on purpose. It was like being a pawn on a checkerboard, testing each adjoining square. In the growing dark, all of them seemed much the same.

Feeling a fool, she called softly, "Tamsen? Where are you?" Nothing happened, of course. Still, there was no certainty of a specific threshold Tamsen had to step across—she had come to two other places. "Tamsen? Oh, Tamsen!"

Luna planted herself facing the path down which (she thought) Tamsen Donner had first drifted into view. She remembered that the hem of the ghostly skirt had been torn, uneven, the fabric oddly colorless, and on her first visit the apparition had not spoken, merely spread her pallid hands above the fire.

Fire. It might help to build one.

Luna rounded up wood and, after a few false starts, got it alight and held her own hands so smoke and light rose between her fingers. Its light shone through that thin, tender web between each finger just as Leonardo had said. Perhaps to God's eye light glowed through the fattest torsos. She could not remember if firelight had shone through Tamsen's skinny hands, inedible as Jezebel's. She could not remember shoes nor feet. Paul had asked her: *Does Tamsen breathe?* She didn't know.

Into the thickening dark she whispered, "It's me, Tamsen. Luna Stone." Silence. She had never offered her name before, perhaps a breach of etiquette? "I'll be leaving soon. Probably tomorrow." She paused, listened. "I have something to tell you. Before I go." There came a rustling but not near. "Tell you about Hastings?" Again it rustled, then stopped. A cooler breeze lifted a dried leaf or two to boost her hopes, but these turned in air and resettled themselves.

As she waited, it occurred to Luna that every member of the Truckee-Donner Historical Society must know the story of what eventually befell Hastings, that perhaps Mrs. Donner's ghost was now eavesdropping at one of their windows downhill, waiting for the minutes and treasurer's report to end. However, it had taken Luna some time to trace the life of Lansford Warren Hastings from his birth (Mt. Vernon, Ohio, 1819) to his death while leading new emigrants, this time a second shipload of unreconstructed Confederates to build new plantations "way down upon the Amazon River." He had meant to walk them five hundred miles into Brazil to land where they would reestablish Southern gentility among monkeys, jaguars, snakes, and man-eating fish.

She thought that if Tamsen had ever regretted giving up that Donner farm back in Illinois—240 acres, orchard, house with two brick chimneys—she might have been ready to scoff at the irony of Hastings's advertisements about Santarém: "a world of external verdure and perennial spring" for only twenty-two cents an acre,

"640 acres per family, 320 to single men," in a part of the world that had never yet known plow, harrow, rake, or spade.

The fire was burning brightly now, and Luna walked once around it to be certain she was visible. If this was to be her last word with Tamsen, maybe she ought to cross herself, to exorcise the ghost. Maybe to get her to come and then go she needed to pray. *This is my body broken for you.* Absolutely not.

Luna decided to speak aloud to the tree and boulder. "Hastings wanted to be governor of California, you know, and with wagon trains like yours he thought he was importing his own constituency." She stood very still, but nothing answered her. "He became a lawyer in San Francisco," Luna went on. "You'd been dead two years when he was a member of the California Constitutional Convention, but maybe you Donners cost him high office at least. Are you listening, Tamsen?" She cocked her head. Silence. "There must have been plenty of fallout for him because of Cannibal Camp." Fallout. A word Tamsen could not possibly understand nor Luna explain. "I don't suppose you've met an artist named Dalí over there? He used to dream about being eaten alive. You might be able to straighten him out."

Pointless, such sarcasm. Luna sat down again to wait.

But if Tamsen can see me, *can she see that a train goes west of here now through the very pass they meant to cross? Does she know that winter storms now ground planes at Reno and Sacramento airports? Does she ever wander around Truckee where people eat at the Donner Lake Kitchen, or does she visit the children's hospital near the Donner Pass Road? Has she asked John Wesley if that was a real poltergeist in the rectory?*

Against the boulder Luna leaned back, closed her eyes, tried to slow her own pulse and breathing rate. The surface felt gritty on each shoulder blade.

After a while Luna whispered into the dark, "Isabel Breen lived to be ninety. You ever see her?"

But of course phantoms needed silence in order to come through; only fake mediums had used spells and tunes. Luna made herself still and then stiller. She lifted her chin where the brace had chafed it.

Waiting, yawning, she listened to her heart, its tick making her drowsy. The heart "moves of itself and does not stop unless forever." Leonardo again. Her mind was wavering. She visualized those children in the Truckee hospital looking at medical picture books of hearts that needed repair. No, at TV pictures, of the Waco compound on fire with children for fuel.

I won't think about Tamsen, and she'll come when she's ready.

Luna let her thoughts flow into other books, other pictures; maybe she and Paul could somehow combine their interests; he'd teach religion at some Lutheran seminary; she'd illustrate a series of children's books. Handicapped-children's books. A rabbit character wearing an elongated hearing aid. Mr. Owl in unbelievably thick eyeglasses. A rooster with one crutch under his scarlet wing and a fish that swam crooked from amputated fins.

Animal characters began to walk around in her head, chirping. Here was an eagle with shiny bald head but broad winged and thoroughly majestic, for those child-readers who were outliving chemotherapy. But could anything be written about a blind bat that would not be cruel? It had radar, OK, but vampires and guano left little room for—

In the midst of this day-dreaming, night-dreaming, Tamsen's very soft voice broke in. "We saw mirages in the Salt Lake Desert."

Luna, who had flinched, was now afraid to open her eyes. "Fata morgana. I thought you weren't coming."

"I won't."

Anymore? Won't see more mirages?

Still with her eyes squeezed shut, Luna said firmly and rapidly, "Hastings died on a ship in 1870 of yellow fever. The mosquitoes got him down in South America where he was taking Confederates to start over."

She whispered, "Son of a bitch."

"No! No, no, I don't believe that's you talking, Tamsen. That's *me;* that's what I might say! Gotcha!" Luna opened her eyes and started to rise, but the woman was standing uphill on the path. Her shimmering dress appeared to be blue again—as did the Virgin's whenever she appeared to European children.

Perhaps as a result of this association but also because she was half kneeling on her bandaged knee, Luna let out a groan and said, "You might as well forgive him."

"Never."

"I just don't—I'll never understand why you people don't ever see each other over there, why you don't catch up on things. If the spiritualists are right, you ought to be some kind of control bringing *me* a message from beyond; you've got it all backwards. Do you know any history at all? Have any sense of time?" She got off the knee, stood slowly erect, adjusted her neck brace, but all Tamsen did was wait.

So Luna, growing irritable, said, "Hastings was a major in the Confederate Army and there must have been thousands and thousands of dead Civil War boys to come your way in the 1860s, and nobody—nobody, not a *soul,* heh heh—had any news of him? You all don't talk?" She floundered. "Have no memories? No, because *you* have a memory. Are you earthbound down here all by yourself?"

Tamsen, her eyes downcast if those dark hollows still held eyes, said, "Hastings was still misleading people right up to the end."

"End? Well, that's a funny word for you to use, I must say." Determined to touch at least the blue fabric that looked so real, Luna eased a few feet forward from the rock, but her movement made Tamsen slide back exactly the same distance.

Luna made her voice more soothing. "He was a serious secessionist, you see. He wanted to add Arizona and New Mexico to the Confederacy and gain an outlet to the Pacific, and Jefferson Davis even liked the idea. But his army people didn't. And Hastings married a Southern girl with family ties to Venezuela. So right after Appomatox—" Tamsen lifted her head, but Luna decided not to explain Appomatox; let Tamsen make some of the effort here! "In 1865 he was already trying to move Southerners down to South America where they still had slavery. And he wasn't the only one. In the next five years over ten thousand Confederates left the country." Tamsen twitched her skirt—this hem was smooth and even, but her feet were still covered—impatiently. "Most of them came back home eventually. And they never did keep slaves down there."

"All Hastings wanted was money and power."

"Maybe so." Luna took a step forward; Tamsen eased back. "Maybe so, but there were even preachers leading that kind of expedition, Methodists, Presbyterians, Episcopalians. Robert E. Lee was offered the chance to go to Mexico but didn't." She was trying to decide if a ghost's vaporous face could look bored. "In *Gone with the Wind* Scarlett O'Hara considers a flight to Latin America at least twice? Well. Never mind her. The South Carolinians went to São Paulo. Santarém is a big city now. They say bartenders still fly the Stars and Bars."

"The what?"

"If you ever get out of here, Tamsen, you can ask at least a million dead people about that flag. And I don't want you to think the Donners laid any kind of a curse that later killed Lansford Hastings. They didn't have modern medicine then. Even Teddy Roosevelt got sick down there."

Again came a quick snap of her sky-blue skirt. There could have been no sky-blue skirts at Alder Creek. "I can't figure out how you manage to change clothes. They called one of the cities Americana. You've got to quit dwelling on Hastings and on what happened to you and—"

"And to all of us."

"It ought to be Keseburg you're mad at. I mean, his protein was made of—" Luna despaired of finishing the sentence. She was feeling a little crazy. "I know Eve was made out of somebody else's flesh but after all—"

"I hate Lansford Hastings," said Tamsen through her teeth.

Yes, definitely teeth. Teeth were durable. Some Hispanic children ate spun-sugar skulls at religious feasts.

Luna let out a long breath, a sigh, fearing her sanity might be expelling itself, but no; she still felt like a body-mind unit, like a person who was going to outlast this moment and be able to tell it to Paul.

At thought of his name she was able to say, slowly, "I've been thinking how much is luck and the time and place you get born plus your genes. Well, leave out the genes; that would take too long to explain. But you, for instance, didn't you get born on the Feast of All Saints? Some of the books say the first and some the third of November. But maybe that's why you can come back? Who knows? As to Hastings, what if he'd been—say—an officer in the British navy? A different story then, I'll bet. But he was affected by his time. After that war there were thousands like him trying to survive, trying to think up their own futures." Tamsen seemed to be listening. "One book said times got so hard in the South, then, that a crow couldn't fly over Virginia without carrying his rations with him."

Luna tried to laugh but stopped when Tamsen said, "Don't you mention rations to me!"

"All right, OK." She was glad she had not mentioned candy in the shape of bone. "Oh!" said Luna suddenly. "I've just realized! When you camped up here, when the snow started falling—you'd just had your birthday! It was two days after your birthday!"

"We were in the wagons, we were hurrying, it didn't matter."

Luna doubted that George Donner had been the birthday-cake type. "I'm not handling this very well," she said. "This isn't what I meant us to talk about." What Luna wanted was a dispossession, some amateur *Ritual Romanum* that would enable her to go off to Wisconsin with no fear that Tamsen would come through those snows to haunt her new house.

She stepped once; Tamsen slid. Change of tactics. Reason and science. "I'm told that when you die, Mrs. Donner—that's a generic *you;* when *anybody* dies—that the white blood cells can live on for thirteen days." Luna hesitated; she was fairly sure this meant by themselves and not inside an actual corpse but decided not to be specific. "Red cells last one hundred and twenty days. But nerve cells can go on living for one hundred years! I guess that's in laboratory conditions, in a petri dish or something, and I don't know that they started any in a laboratory in 1893, but you see what I mean? So it's one hundred and forty-seven years later for you, and a fluke, but I think maybe hatred of Hastings set up a special circumstance?"

Tamsen shook her gleaming head.

"Hatred of Keseburg, then. Of what he did."

Silence.

"Love of George Donner?"

Tamsen drifted toward the fire and seemed to see something in the coals.

Luna also decided not to mention the sole photograph she had seen of Lansford Hastings, bald halfway across his head, with the remaining hair earlobe length. The description said he had possessed "high color," a ruddy face in which the eyes were deep set and intense. Probably high blood pressure, high cholesterol. Keseburg had somewhat resembled him, though all daguerreotypes resembled one another? And Keseburg also resembled Alferd Packer, himself half bald. And those eyes, sunk in those heads? They were like Major Stone's.

She stopped thinking about this row of male faces and said to Tamsen, "Maybe the reason you can't rest easy isn't from hatred at all. Maybe it's because you know you could have gotten out with Frances and Eliza when that rescue party came. You were certain George Donner would beg you to go, to save yourself; he must have known nothing could save him anymore, not with a rotten arm like that? Then you'd have had ten years at least to live on in California. It might even have been the promised land Hastings promised. At least you might have lived long enough to hear about Hastings's death!"

Tamsen shook her head.

"Admit it, you'd have liked Hastings to die first."

Another wavery headshake, like something seen through smoke.

Luna persisted. "George Donner had already buried two wives and fathered ten children when he met you. He'd lived his life. Why didn't he make you get out when you could? He was selfish. He's the one kept you up here in the snow, not Hastings."

"No! A good man!"

"Selfish! I bet you don't see him over in the Great Beyond, either. You thought George was older and wiser. You thought it was your duty to stay!" Now Luna waited, drew a step closer. She could almost see Tamsen's feet. They looked bare and very thin, and twigs and stones showed through them both. "When you got to the boiling springs, wasn't it George's decision to leave behind your cases of books? There went your girls' school."

In the silence, a coal rolled out of the fire with a small thunk and landed near Tamsen's skirt. Nothing ignited; she bent with fluid grace and took it up in one icy hand and smothered it. Smoke rose through the gaps in her small closed fist.

Then Tamsen moved off the path, tossing the black lump aside, moved almost out of sight under the trees, and the folds of her skirt fell so gracefully that she might have moved on wheels. But her voice could still be heard, quiet, contemplative.

"The wagon train formed in Springfield, and everybody met to make plans for the trip."

Yes, she had memory. Luna waited, tense. Her knee had stopped hurting; her body was eclipsed; she had gathered herself whole behind the forehead. She wanted to ask if Tamsen had met

Abe Lincoln, said to be a friend of some in the emigrant party. In fact, she wanted to know about Lincoln as much as Tamsen wanted to know about Hastings!

Before she could ask, Tamsen said, still softly, "We women didn't vote on anything of course. We had thirty children to look after. *Then* we had thirty children."

Luna had heard sister-bitterness before, its milder feminist counterpart in some airport or beauty shop, but Tamsen's tone did not tell her what she most ardently wanted to know. Did you love George Donner more than Tully Dozier? Both gave you children. How was the sex? Even in your heart, you compared?

Before these hot thoughts, there scattered the high-flown ones about Hamlet's father or Odysseus seeing Tiresias or Samuel blowing upward, full bearded, from Sheol when the Witch of Endor called.

"Don't go, Tamsen," she breathed. "Not yet. I'm not ready yet."

Under the trees, the dress was growing dimmer, like bluing diluted in the wash. "Tamsen?"

Less clear came the voice. "Before all that," Tamsen said, as if in confidence, "my first husband, my first children—they all died within three weeks. It was Christmas."

Luna, much too well read, whispered, "Eighteen thirty-one."

"Hush up. Numbers tell nothing. Be quiet."

"You were only thirty."

The phantasm lifted her head. Her features were sharper, as if all had been recently honed.

"I'm not thirty yet," Luna said. Her years seemed paltry.

"Be quiet," said Tamsen. "Go away."

"Yes. All right. I will." A wind blew between them. Perhaps it had blown Tamsen's flimsy replica downhill?

Luna took a few more steps and Tamsen held still, almost close enough to touch. *We all eat the dead*, Luna wanted to say.

This close, she felt cold. Some auras were cold.

Not moving, Tamsen asked quietly, "Is it May? Hastings said in California every Christmas would be like May."

Luna decided both to answer and to put out her hand. "Things are very different now." She didn't know whether she meant heat or air-conditioning or life in general. Her fingers went forth into cool air, then chilliness, and at last frost. Barely audible was the rustle of Tamsen's dress passing over forest duff, bottle caps, and papers—too blue to be real!—as she slid farther away, going out of hearing first, and at last out of sight. There settled on Luna's face a distilled dew, a coldness that seemed at the source to be one or two feet wide. "Tamsen?" She stepped aside, into the current climate. "Tamsen Donner?"

This time only the light Sierra Nevada wind came back, down the young trees, over the old rock, grazing Luna's body with a breeze that was only cool as it sheared past and blew on.

IN THEIR SUITE in the Pension Annalena, Priscilla Stone walked back and forth and talked to the ceiling. "You say Madeline was calling from some truck stop? I don't understand that at all."

"Truckee. I wrote it down. Don't pace, honey." Aunt Evelyn, who was stretched out on a chaise longue, turned another page in her Florence guidebook. "It's a wonder your feet aren't worn out already. She said she'd call back."

That afternoon they had walked for hours through the nearby Boboli Gardens, taking many side trips off the main tree-lined Viottolone. "She had an appointment up the mountain and would be back, she said. She got your message."

"I could kill Martin Stone."

Aunt Evelyn inserted, "So you've said."

But Priscilla would not be stopped. "For leaving such a cryptic message on the machine. One wedding canceled, one replacement. This one deaf as a post. Madeline's Zulu brain in the ascendant. He'd been to Reno and was glad to get out. Over and out to the Female and Catholic Principle. What does that mean?"

"You'll have to ask him."

"Their phone doesn't answer."

"So how can I?" Patiently, for the third time, Aunt Evelyn said, "Open that glass door, will you?"

"This room is Hee-oh-H-T-Hot," said Priscilla as she snapped the brass latch. "I wonder if she needs money. I hope she's not skipping meals."

"The room is just fine, but you're hot. Ah, feel that breeze. And you worry too much about that girl, who takes after me—I've always thought. What Martin calls Zulu, I call eccentric. Have you seen my throat lozenges?"

During their trip, Priscilla had performed much like a nineteenth-century "companion," one of those spinsters of diminished means who fetched scarves and spectacles and penned by dictation long travelogue letters home. She answered now, "In your pocketbook," but then moved to find and carry the packet to where Evelyn sat with her stocking feet high on a brocade cushion.

During this trip through England and onto the Continent, such personal chores had seemed well worth the reward of travel in style, and especially here in Florence—where Priscilla had kept storing up images of the Renaissance that she would later share with her daughter, her soon-to-be-married daughter, her soon-to-be-safe-at-last daughter, her soon-to-be-visited-in-sunny-California daughter. Out of the cloister and into the surf. And she had been buying for Madeline reproductions of her own favorites (Botticelli's *Annunciation*, Fra Angelico's *Naming of John the Baptist*, Raphael's *Madonna del Graviduca*), hoping all three paintings, while speaking in somber tones of Art, might whisper playfully about babies. Grandchildren.

On this tour with Aunt Evelyn, Priscilla Stone had decided that once she was home, she would seek out the biggest art supply store in Richmond and outfit the girl with oils and tempera. Was it true that Andrew Wyeth had favored tempera and, after using the egg yellows, fed the whites to his hound? Yes, she would buy Luna easels, canvas, sable brushes, whatever it took to make mere painted colors fold like cloth and shine like halos.

On the balcony, Priscilla fanned her warm, slightly sunburned face with the memo pad on which strange things were written. Circus. Paul. Mountains. A vision.

Into that circumscribed hot breeze she said, "Oh, Aunt Evelyn, you don't know, you'll never know. You never had children."

"No, and that's why I've got money. But Madeline's how old? Twenty-six?"

"Twenty-eight."

"Well, *there* then. Twenty-eight!" Aunt Evelyn massaged her own toes while waiting. "Are you just bored with the Grand Tour? I admit I got to that point in Venice. All that talk of Pellegrini when I knew his painting had been moved whole cloth—is that the phrase? Moved in toto to the Biltmore House in North Carolina. Money does count."

"You're getting me down, Aunt Evelyn." Priscilla looked off the balcony at the tops of people's heads. They had never told Aunt Evelyn about Madeline's nervous breakdown during college, knowing it would make her thereafter alert to signs of craziness and the need to adjust her will.

"If money didn't count, Martin Stone wouldn't send me such lovely birthday greetings," Aunt Evelyn said. "As if I would ever underwrite an earring business! Leave him to one side. What's this about Madeline?"

"She's sensitive. Things bother her too much."

"Who isn't sensitive? I'm sensitive myself!" From growling, Aunt Evelyn's words sounded garbled around the melting cough drop—and a lie if Priscilla had ever heard one. "I can't follow all this. Is the bridegroom a problem?"

Priscilla shook her head, though she had only met Steven Grier once and hadn't liked him much. And he wasn't Catholic—though neither was Aunt Evelyn. Steven was something theologically serious and obscure. "It's just that he looks . . . looks stingy."

Aunt Evelyn asked exactly how did stingy look.

Priscilla leaned over the marble rail again, thinking of childhood, of spitting off heights, shooting raisins, dropping flour-filled balloons, and thinking—too—of how short childhood had to be. Had Madeline's been happy? There swarmed through her all the Christmas trees, Halloween costumes, visits to grandparents while they were still cognizant, reunions with Daddy in this international capital and that.

Aunt Evelyn muttered something, so she had to step back into the room to ask, "What?"

"I said it surprises me how strongly you've encouraged young Madeline to marry. Your own experience with my nephew wasn't all that good."

"You never get lonely, Aunt Evelyn?"

"Well, I *read!*" she said in a loud voice, and waited. By way of revision she added, "Nothing that can't be cured by a glass of Scotch and a murder mystery."

Sleeping alone. Priscilla was learning to do it, but without alcohol. She dropped into a chair and tried not, by touching, to beg the nearby telephone to ring. It was so gold and ivory and gilt as to mock her mundane wishes. She said firmly, "Even though things didn't work out for Martin and me, I still do believe in marriage."

"Maybe your next beau will show up on a cruise, then; I hear the cruise lines hire old-age gigolos!" said Aunt Evelyn with a crunch as she popped open her lozenge so its liquid and medicated center could flow past her palate. "Uh," she grunted briefly with satisfaction. She kicked off her open-toed, back-strapped high heels, for which she was far too short and heavy. "These ankles go down so fast you'd think I would fart," she said with a coarse laugh. Priscilla said nothing. "So marry Madeline off—that's your religious upbringing!" she said through her teeth. "Bride of Christ, bride of somebody."

Priscilla got her mouth shaped like a prune. "I know you're Unitarian, Aunt Evelyn. But I've never regretted my religious upbringing."

"Up? Never got free of it, either. Ought to read Emerson."

Priscilla said she had *read* Emerson, that Catholics were not reared in intellectual eggs.

"Oh, they taught you to argue, all right; they taught you to believe that every single stupid soul was going to be saved; that's why I like your company."

They sat in dissatisfied silence, Aunt Evelyn sucking the candied shell, Priscilla keeping her fingers so still they dared not drum on the telephone table. She felt chastened. *Maybe I did push Madeline to marry that bookish boy precisely because he was a bookish boy and that neutralized him, not a man's man; I knew that type; maybe what I believe in is not marriage as such but just the hardscrabble hope that any two are better than one. Two paychecks. Two bodies keeping the mattress warm. Two to play Santa Claus.*

Priscilla sighed. *All I wanted was to see Luna settled. I thought any man, any child, would anchor her to the earth. She kept me centered, so why not? I thought if she had to cook meals for other people, she'd take in her own vitamins.*

She stole a glance at lazy, fat, and semiconscious Aunt Evelyn. *How does anyone ever sort out true motives from false?*

Maybe I even believed Steven Grier would leave Madeline someday for a young graduate student who spoke the latest academic jargon, and then at last she would understand me, sympathize with me, blame all the men who get led around by their dicks.

"Priscilla? You're not going to sleep, are you?"

"I'm thinking," Priscilla said.

Pages in Aunt Evelyn's guidebook went flipping. "Tomorrow the Cathedral of Santa Maria del Fiore. I see there's a bus."

"You're so inconsistent!" Priscilla waved at the handsome furniture, the gilt frames, the tapestry. "Why bother to save money by using a bus?"

"The more to leave to you, my dear!" She gave a cackle that choked itself off. "You do expect me to leave the stocks and bonds to you, don't you?"

Relaxing into it, Priscilla said, "Well, I should hope so!" and they both smiled, smiled wider, snickered, and at last were laughing helplessly.

"Oh!" Aunt Evelyn gave a wheeze. "You're a comfort, Priscilla. Martin would lie."

Priscilla could not get her laughter stopped, from fatigue and sunburn and worry more than amusement. Through the spasms she took a moist inventory of Aunt Evelyn, whose waved white hair rose in a tower held by combs that should have been tortoiseshell but were only plastic. Aunt Evelyn ate imported chocolate but saved on lightbulbs. In her house, the maid was instructed to save the wrappers from margarine sticks and use these to grease the skillet.

Priscilla had long memories of Evelyn coming for Christmas, slumming at army bases, flocking their cedar tree with some snowy flour-and-water recipe she mixed in the bathtub, plus sparkles, adding the biggest presents under that fake-snow tree. When Martin was overseas, she had sometimes sent plane tickets so Priscilla and Madeline could come to Boston. Once she had given Priscilla a fox-fur stole complete with mummified eyes, nose, and tail, long after such wraps had been driven out of style by animal rights activists. When Madeline enrolled in grade school in West Berlin, the mail had brought audiotaped German-language courses.

It was hard to look at Aunt Evelyn without counting a history of presents all the way back to mohair nursery blankets, the monogrammed sterling spoon, the napkin rings nobody put linen napkins in anymore, the rocking horse with its genuine horsehair surface that gave Madeline a rash.

Remembering that sometimes she and Martin had mocked Aunt Evelyn behind her back, Priscilla crossed the room, bent low, gave her a hug. "Mind my glasses," warned Aunt Evelyn, shaking loose.

They survived another half hour before she stopped Priscilla's pacing and announced she'd read in bed awhile.

"You need anything? I'm sorry to be so jumpy. Waiting makes me so tense. I'm about to Pee-oh-pee-Bang-POP!"

"I can see that, honey. You want a tranquilizer? Well, I do. One and a Scotch—that's permissible, isn't it? Good." She got herself upright on those tiny feet, balanced lopsided, then straight, and moved at a slow limp. "You tell Madeline if I'd gotten to check out this cactus boy I could maybe have saved her a lot of trouble." At the door to the bedroom she said, "Don't wake me up unless it's something serious."

Behind that closed door, Priscilla knew, she would also be indulging in her daily smoke. She bought cheroots by the boxful and transferred them to a humidor whose insides she regularly sprayed with brandy she stored in a Windex bottle. Priscilla was not sure what effect this treatment would have, but it must be lethal. Afterward she lit her cigars with matchbooks she had taken from hotels and restaurants.

When she had gone, Priscilla sank into a soft chair, feet up (big, solid feet), guidebook open, and tried to imagine Dante crossing the Arno or thinking divine thoughts while he lived in that reconstructed building at the end of Piazza Alighieri. The effort made her feel feverish, as if she were attempting to resurrect a famous hero from his death mask alone.

Why didn't Madeline call? It was hard to make sense of Martin's bluster. Deaf as a post, he'd said. But Martin always raised his voice anyway.

She thought about Madeline bursting into tears when she got to the part in *Little Women* where Jo March chose Professor Bhaer and not the handsome Laurie.

After a while she dozed, still hot from effort and red cheeks, having turned and returned the cushions behind her head.

So the ringing phone broke into her doze with terror. She had been dreaming that Madeline was high on a swinging bridge, like the ones in old Tarzan movies, and its fibers were fraying and snapping, but Priscilla could not reach her.

Out of the chair, crouched, she had to wait for her heart to slow. The noise struck through her head another time.

"Priscilla?" came from the other room.

She called, "I've got it, OK," as she groped on the table and picked up the ornate phone. "Hello? Thank God. Madeline? What's wrong? I just can't tell you all the thoughts that—what?" She waited, listened, interrupted. "Slow down, Madeline. Start over. Who got lost?" Sinking into the chair, waiting, she finally said, "Well, I'm altogether lost."

Their connection was bad, broken by a recurrent buzz. "Let me call you back, Madeline. Where? What are you doing *there*? I've already got your hotel number but when will you be there? OK, I'll wait fifteen minutes till you can get there."

By now certain that something had gone badly wrong, Priscilla could not endure the agreed-upon delay but soon had the operator ring straight through. A man answered on the first ring.

"Steven?"

"No, this is Paul."

Frowning, Priscilla pulled the phone away from her ear and checked her notes. He seemed to hear perfectly well. "May I speak to Madeline Stone?"

"Luna should be back soon. Who is this?" He said louder, "Is this about my mother?"

"I'll call again, thank you." Hanging up, she shouted to Aunt Evelyn, *"No, not yet!"* Pungent cigar smoke was leaking around the bedroom door, so she stood on the balcony again. She wondered if Madeline was eating enough, an anxiety from which she'd never be entirely free. During the eighties she had tried hard to understand anorexia, which seemed a direct rejection of mother-nourishment. Secretly, that had hurt her feelings. *I thought we were very close when Madeline was growing up; we were like sisters.*

Priscilla checked her watch, looked into the lighted sky above Florence, waited impatiently. Good people fasted in the Bible, she thought, but toward some purpose and with a specific duration. The fasts of modern Trappists had no similarity to Jane Fonda's vomiting her meals at Vassar or singer Karen Carpenter's heaving her food out an upstairs window until she finally died of hunger.

After Madeline's terrifying college episode, Priscilla had been able to recall other, younger times when the child's appetite had waned, times when she and Martin had reacted with either bribes or punishments and gradually prevailed, managed to impose the normal routine of eating properly, three times a day, and cleaning one's plate. *We talked too much about food,* she thought now. *Madeline was the one thing we could both agree on. We ganged up on her.* Priscilla also suspected that Madeline might have been a slightly hyperactive child, a word she had not known then, and that anorexia was some form of low-key tantrum.

But when I saw her all skin and bones?

She closed her eyes, remembering, and patted her own expanding waist, still distended from today's opulent lunch and wine at Ottorino, then supper and wine here at the *pensione. I wanted her to love food, to love life. I never got over the tables where we nuns were granted such rare and tiny amounts of mustard, pepper, vinegar, and spices—inflammatory foods that might cause lonely women to masturbate.*

Any weight gain, in the novitiate, had signified lack of self-control.

I wonder if Steven Grier makes love to her sweetly. Maybe they don't make love at all. Maybe that's the trouble. Who is Paul?

Priscilla tried the Reno telephone number again, and this time her daughter answered.

Right away Madeline's greeting went rushing ahead into long, confusing paragraphs, too fast for any response. It was like losing a tug-of-war, hanging on, but still being dragged ahead. Instead of Steven there seemed to be Paul and Sam; instead of Riverside, Madeline had been lost on some mountain; yes, Martin had flown in and out again, but she was no longer furious about it; and policemen were looking for Paul's mother and two kidnappers.

Touching her forehead, Priscilla felt physically dizzied by this whiplash of words that seemed to have gotten warped in zipping so fast across the sphere of the world. Crack-the-whip, that was the game they had played in the back field, not tug-of-war. She was being cracked.

"Stop!" she cried. "Stop." There was silence. In the hospital, Madeline had been almost entirely silent. Was this mania or just a return to the extroverted girl she once had been? "Let me get this straight. You're still getting married but to a different man?" Yes. "And you're still moving a long way off, but it's not California anymore. Wisconsin, did you say? Pabst and Schlitz?" Near Stockholm. No, not Sweden. "And instead of a botany teacher this Paul is some kind of"—Priscilla grabbed a shallow breath—"professional Protestant?"

Then Madeline was off again. She loved him, yes, and she loved Sam, too; and no, it wasn't necessary to choose between.

Priscilla began to get the cast of characters straight. She could not resist saying, "It's just like Martin Stone to butt in, he's such an A-double-ess-ess-Fool!"

"Now you stop," Madeline said. "I've got some kind of truce with him. It's time you did."

"How many calories have you had today?" There was some acetone reaction when people didn't eat. Maybe digesting their own muscles made them high. "Madeline, try some of those supplemental milk drinks I wrote you about with all the vitamins. Sustacal, Ensure, Nutrament—all the supermarkets carry them."

"Mother, I promise I'm eating. This is not about lunch, this is about the rest of my life. Will you come to the wedding in Wisconsin?"

"Certainly and Aunt Evelyn, too, but don't let's hurry so much here. You sound like you're trying on men like clothes. First you had no boyfriends at all, and now you're promiscuous. Aunt Evelyn's right; your father and I set a poor example. This is our fault."

"I haven't been thinking of either one of you *at all.*"

"Thanks a whole lot." Priscilla glanced aside at the closed door. "We did love each other once, your father and I; we just didn't keep love in very good repair. Listen, Madeline, Aunt Evelyn has said in so many words that I'm her heir, so you could just move on back to Richmond and draw and paint in those rooms over the garage without having to earn a living or having to depend on a man to earn a living."

"It's not about economics, either. I think I can keep on loving Paul."

"Think? You think? That's what everybody says. Are you sure or do you just *think?*"

Madeline replied calmly that lately thinking had become very important to her, very. "And here's something else I think, Mother. I think now that love isn't something that happens to you. It's something you decide to do."

Priscilla felt frantic. "Maybe so after you've cooled off, maybe then; maybe on your fifth anniversary you're down to decisions; maybe then that's true; but a marriage ought to start off—well—hot. Passionate. That gives you a running start."

"You and Dad had a running start?"

Yes. They had. Running and leaping. They were young.

The bedroom door opened, and Aunt Evelyn, wearing a pale green robe, came in and set a hotel glass with straight Scotch in it by the telephone. Priscilla took a sharp swallow in her mouth, closed her teeth, let it run down. She shook her head to the small white pill in the extended palm of Aunt Evelyn's hand. "That was Paul who answered the phone? And is he right there in the room with you, listening to you say you *think?* Maybe you just think you love him and you think wrong?"

"Paul's here." There was a silence. *She's touching him or he's touching her.* Madeline said, "We're not without passion."

"Well, whoop-te-damn-do!" She drank more Scotch.

"He's going to divinity school," said Madeline, causing Priscilla to think of that white meringue candy. "And I'm going to draw and paint."

"And in what church will you raise any children?"

"Sam's already Catholic. We haven't talked about the others."

Of course, Sam. The boy-victim. "Everything's settled then? You didn't call to ask me. You called to tell me."

"That's right."

Priscilla took a deep and calming inhalation, cool on the alcohol scalding her mouth. "So I've been notified." She waited. "We've seen some wonderful museums. I'm going to buy you oil paints and tempera. It's time you moved on beyond drawings."

"That would be a wonderful wedding present—tell Aunt Evelyn, because she can afford the best. I've got this idea about doing children's books. We'll be fine, Mother. And Sam is going to need a lot of attention from us both."

Her ready-made grandson. Attention. Love?

Aunt Evelyn stood in front of her, plucked eyebrows high, but Priscilla shook her head as fast as she could to keep from crying.

"I'll let you both know the wedding date if you and Dad promise to be polite."

"I can be polite to him, but you get me close to that Corinne and one lighted candle and you won't be able to tell her from Joan of Arc," said Priscilla, blinking hard. Aunt Evelyn applauded soundlessly.

"Paul's Lutheran. I'm not sure they use candles."

She heard a bass monosyllable near the phone but could not tell if the new and unknown bridegroom had said yes or no. When Aunt Evelyn tapped a pink fingernail on the glass, she drank once more. "You've got our itinerary? You won't get married without sending for us?"

"We'll wait. We want you there."

They were making the usual good-bye murmurs, and Priscilla had even started to lower the phone when she suddenly snatched it back to her ear and heard her own sharp, high voice say, "Oh, Madeline Lunatsky Stone, it's cold in Wisconsin! It's so cold!"

"It gets cold everywhere."

Priscilla was left with the singing empty wire and an expression on her face that made Aunt Evelyn ask softly, "What is it, honey?"

"I wish I was sure." Priscilla cradled the phone, lifted it in case some delayed word or two had been left behind in the earpiece. She drank more Scotch. "Madeline has certainly learned something since I saw her last—that's obvious—but I wish I were sure? Maybe she's matured, Aunt Evelyn. Maybe. Or maybe she's just become resigned or even defeated. I can't tell which over the telephone."

"I doubt there's much difference," Aunt Evelyn said.

NOT UNTIL THE NEXT MORNING did Paul finally hit on the idea of phoning their family doctor back in Stockholm, the aging one who had not only attended Erika Cowan in childbirth but signed Bruce Cowan's death certificate. He had to make several calls, and the struggle to hear final consonants from soft-voiced nurses made Paul think of Alexander Graham Bell, whose wife had been deaf, and whose main invention had been auditory. In the movie, Don Ameche had loved her very much. Perhaps it had been true in life, also.

It took a while to locate Dr. Erlander, even through his beeper, but finally he returned the call about ten.

Paul went through a web of connections and slightly modified recent history before getting to the point. "So the first thing Mother will probably do is bring Sam by to see you, have him checked over."

"We've already spoken," Dr. Erlander said.

"She's there already? No, she must have phoned you—"

"From—" he called aside to somebody. "Was it Pocatello? Idaho, I think. I faxed a prescription to a pharmacy. It's in the file."

"Oh. I see." Paul felt torn between admiration and resentment that Erika Cowan was managing so nicely by herself.

As if accused, Dr. Erlander said in a defensive tone, "I've known your mother over thirty years. If she says Tylenol isn't doing the job, then it isn't."

"Oh, she's reliable, all right. And you expect to see them?" Paul let his voice trail.

"The next few days, depending on their stops. Your mother's not what I'd call a fast driver. Now it's good to hear from you, Paul, and Erika says you're coming back home yourself. To stay, she says. Getting married, she says. We ought to look into a cochlear transplant, don't you think so? I keep up, you know."

Later when Paul reported this conversation, Luna said, "So both our mothers have been notified. But Sam's in pain."

"Not for long with the stuff he sent, Dr. Erlander said, and he didn't seem to take it seriously. He said there was no fever. He called it a normal pain."

"You never mentioned a transplant."

But Paul said he was probably not a good candidate for ear surgery. "We'll see, though. Lately I've begun to think that anything can happen." They sat together on the bed thinking over the doctor's news while the television picture flickered, its audio turned down to nothing. Absently he began to lip-read the commercials.

With one finger Luna traced Paul's hairline, thought she would do his portrait first when the new paints came. She ran her touch onto the soft lobe of one ear. *If we have children and they scream with bad dreams in the dark, he'll never hear,* she thought.

Just as aimlessly he reached out to feel the shape of her own face, as if blind. *I can wake him up when they cry,* Luna thought.

Suddenly she swooped down on him, tickling, scuffling, and they wrestled across the wide bed with gasps and giggles until their breathing changed and clothes got snatched loose and slung aside and they almost slammed into each other. Luna came early to Paul's hand well ahead of his penis, but being synchronized didn't matter. Being together, that mattered. They fell back in a tangle of bedclothes, deflated as balloons, their breathing conscious and hurried, then slower, automatic, at last so normal as to be beyond their notice.

Oh yes, Mother, we're not without passion.

"We're getting so good at this that we'll turn sex into an art," Paul said huskily. "But next time, slower. I promise, slower."

"Fast is OK," she said. "With you. But slow is good, too."

In such lazy times, Luna would have liked to whisper, but Paul could not hear whispers. He rarely whispered himself. Nor would she ever be able to stand in the backyard and call toward wherever he was located—upstairs, unseen. She was trying to work through the changes that were coming into her life. Most marriages—90 percent—between the deaf and hearing, Paul had warned her, ended in divorce. Prevention. Prevention.

She lay very still, hearing his breath slow down, knowing he could not hear hers. It could be a serious asset to have to verbalize everything face-to-face, all the way from devotion to quarreling; and she'd never be able to yawn and mumble, could never allow a word like "baby" to be lip-read as "paper." *The paper is crying, Paul. Put the baby in the trash.*

Her throat hurt, perhaps from having left off the neck collar. She kissed him where she thought the mastoid bone must lie.

"You went to sleep and missed the Hollywood late show," she said against his ear. "This fellow said that Errol Flynn used to put cocaine on the tip of his penis."

"If you get it, I'll try it."

"I don't think we need it."

Using both hands, Paul moved her shoulders until he could

read the motions of her mouth. By lip and tongue alone, with no sound, he said, "I love you," and she used her softening mouth to mirror his. "I love you. I told my mother."

"Then that *is* serious." Paul propped himself on an elbow, looked into her face. "If you don't like Wisconsin, I promise we'll move to wherever you say."

Luna wondered if brides on their wagons west had been told the same. "I plan to like it. And surely Sam will."

"It won't be easy for Sam, for us and Sam together. He might never get over the things that were done to him. Maybe he'll run away or steal things or beat people up, who can tell?" With one finger he traced her eyebrow, cheekbone. "If I had your talent, I'd draw your own face when it gets excited, or worried, or sad. Your face shows everything you think. Or maybe you've lately been teaching it to do that, for my sake." He drew a warm line to her ear, then repeatedly pressed and released the flap of flesh there so it made a seashell roar inside her head. "I'm very hard of hearing now, but in the future I may go altogether deaf."

"Edison was deaf. Look at Beethoven." He had left her ear canal blocked so she could hear her life-blood rush by at speed. "You hear me better than anybody else ever has."

"I have no right to ask you to—"

"I'm volunteering," she interrupted. "Open my ear."

Paul laughed and fell back on the pillow. "You can tell, though, that hearing is primary. You see how you'd miss it? When Jesus healed the deaf mute, he took care of hearing first and speech second."

She half lifted herself to be sure he could lip-read. "If you go altogether deaf, I'll draw you pictures."

They drowsed in each other's arms, her head tucked between his neck and shoulder. She could look down the slope of his naked body. Her curly genital hairs were darker than his and thicker. She wondered how their genes would mix, in coloring, in temperament. She felt for the spot where Adam had forfeited a rib, then goosed him.

"Let's go right now!"

"What?"

"Wake up, get up, we're just burning money staying here. She's not going to call, and we know they're all right. She might call when she gets home, but we can be halfway there by then! Come on! Wake up!" She lifted his damp penis in one hand and shook it; he muttered that if Flynn had known Luna, he'd have dipped his in sedative.

"Without even a nap? You want to go right now?"

"I'll pack my stuff, you do yours."

While they were gathering clothes and shoes, each moving contagiously faster and faster, Paul said, "I'm not sure that van of yours will make the trip."

"Ours. If it doesn't, we'll push it off a cliff and hitchhike."

Another time, frowning, he said, "I wanted to buy you a ring."

"With what?"

"Steal you one, then."

She handed him one of the loose charcoal sticks she had been wrapping and, after a puzzled stare, he slowly smiled, took up her left hand, drew a black line around her ring finger, and kissed the knuckle.

"Good," she said. "And your mother's suitcase is here, still packed, and her photo album? Start carrying down stuff?"

While he was gone she found her old diary, the late pages now full of telephone numbers, local newspaper names, doctors, and policemen they had met. Paul had used one page when he was tracking down Dr. Erlander. She had doodled tulips and hearts at the top of one page and then deteriorated into very small livers, kidneys, and lungs.

Paul came for the second load but said they ought to count money first, so they poured a puddle of coins and wadded bills on the bed and figured the total. Luna said the gas tank was full. "I'll cash a check."

"It's Sunday, surely you can't?"

She had forgotten Sundays, but Paul never did. The way some people got hungry three times a day, his worship-appetite flared every seven days. *We'll face some adjustments,* she thought, but said over her shoulder, "The hotel will cash it. You want to go to church before we leave?"

"It's past eleven."

In one more trip they carried down the rest of everything they owned, even Paul's books and some current magazines with cover photos of Mount Carmel at Waco on fire and congressmen discussing blame. They arranged bags and boxes in the van so its driver would still have tunnel rearview vision.

Paul said, "With all my worldly goods I thee endow," sounding more chagrined than he probably intended.

Luna could not at first understand why the van was more crowded than before, and then she remembered Sam's possessions, including the new tennis shoes she had not given him yet, because of his plaster cast. After doing subtraction in her checkbook and finding she could pay the bill and to spare, she went into Circus Circus and checked out. Nothing inside the hotel, except for the dateline on the newspaper she bought, suggested it was Sunday. The clerk, bored, cashed her check promptly.

"You drive so I can read the news," she said.

Paul started the car, waved in the sunlight at all the bright buildings. "You don't want to gamble once before we go?"

"Honey," she said, "we *are* gambling!"

She flapped open the paper while Paul, craning his neck because even with the hearing aid turned high he distrusted his ability to hear and pinpoint car horns, got them slowly out of the hot parking lot, out of Reno, onto the interstate. He adjusted the air-conditioning.

"You don't think your mother's making Sam go to some church this morning, do you?"

He didn't know.

"I just can't picture Sam in either your church or mine. If I'd lived Sam's life, Jesus would owe me a lot of explanations."

Paul's mouth turned down and almost opened, but his face muscles showed him making the decision not to argue. *At this rate, we'll soon be able to read each other with no words at all,* Luna thought, and turned past the page that had display ads for various churches. She was thinking that the Cistercians, bound to silence, used hand signals—didn't they think that was cheating?

Driving northeast through Truckee Canyon and then into the Great Basin, they were soon into land speckled with sagebrush and creosote bush, where it took miles of desert to feed two cows, or miles of distant mountain to yield one nugget. The straight stretch of I-80 along which they drove was much the same route Hastings had touted in his western guidebook: the Humboldt Trail, the Emigrant Trail, crossing this high sandy plateau on the edge of its forty-mile desert that would eat wagon wheels to the hub, drink up rainfall, swallow whole rivers. Surely the very sight of this alkali stretch had shriveled poor Tamsen's heart like a prune.

But no, Luna was leaving all that behind and Tamsen, too. Quickly she said, "I guess we'll get married in your home church? Could we do a Catholic ceremony, too?"

Paul smiled, took one hand off the wheel to grasp hers with the ring drawn around her finger. "And walk under West Point swords if it'll keep your father off our backs."

"My mother wondered if Lutherans light candles. And do you take the Eucharist from the priest?"

"From the pastor. There are parallels."

She fixed the picture in her mind: she, Paul, and Sam at the altar rail, kneeling—she in a lace scarf, maybe a mantilla in honor of Sam's heritage; then Erika kneeling next, and then Priscilla Stone beside her but slightly turned away from Martin and mouse-brain Corinne and above them with the sacrament the pastor in . . . in what kind of vestment? Luna made his suit satin and blue, with gold embroidery. *Take, eat. This is my body.*

She shivered once. Paul lowered the air-conditioning and pulled her close with one arm around her shoulders. "Are you cold?"

"Sometimes," she said.

They rode on. She said, "I've made a decision to read all of George Eliot. That'll keep me busy this winter." Paul nodded. "George Eliot was ugly. Maybe I'll get fat."

"That's not required," he said. "Oh. Reach me that magazine, no. Not the one with Waco. That's it. About three or four pages from the back. The cartoon. I think it's funny. If you don't laugh, I'm in trouble."

She leafed backward through the slick and colorful pages until she came to the drawing he meant. A clown in full costume was immersed in a boiling pot. One cannibal with a bone stuck through his hairdo was dipping a ladle while another looked on. "Listen," said the first, "does he taste funny to you?"

Luna laughed.